Lord and Slave—Their Destinies
Were Bound to an Exquisite Gold Statue

LIONELLO ANDREAS—Soldier and shipbuilder, as honorable as he is strong, obligated by vows to protect the Wind Dancer—even when he yearns to be free from the bonds that hold him, even when seized by a true passion as sudden and ferocious as the fires that threaten to engulf all he holds dear.

SANCHIA—With a rare brand of remarkable beauty, and her wits her only armor against an angry world, she can withstand abuse and even torture, but her will crumbles in the face of the unexpected cruelty of kindness.

CATERINA ANDREAS—The magnificent and strong-willed matriarch who would dare anything to protect Mandara, the Andreas domain—she is a fierce warrior whenever fate hurls its arrows . . . yet only the tender nurturing of her splendid rose garden betrays the warm heart within her regal breast.

LORENZO VASARO—Cold, calculating, an assassin by trade, his only weakness is his passionate attachment to the Andreas family—an attachment so deep, so obsessive it brings him to the brink of destruction.

MARCO ANDREAS—Gentle, sensitive, a painter who is the opposite of Lion, his impetuous brother—Marco burns with chaste but forbidden love for the one woman he can never have.

FRANCISCO DAMARI—Rising from the house of an Andreas mistress, he became a hateful force whose appetites for power and women were as twisted as the mazes he delighted in building to "entertain" his "guests." Determined to destroy Mandara and its greatest treasure, the Wind Dancer, he plots with the rapacious, cunning Cesare Borgia and Cesare's ruthless father, the Pope.

GUIDO CAPRINO—Procurer of prostitutes and thieves, he leads Lion to Sanchia. But his soul and his information belong to the highest bidder. When his greed couples with the jealousy of a vengeful whore, the lives of Sanchia and Lion are catapulted into a terrifying realm—where death might provide the only tolerable escape.

THE
WIND
DANCER

Iris Johansen

BANTAM BOOKS

NEW YORK · TORONTO · LONDON · SYDNEY · AUCKLAND

THE WIND DANCER

A Bantam Fanfare Book / February 1991

FANFARE and the portrayal of a boxed "ff" are trademarks of Bantam Books, a division of Bantam Doubleday Dell Publishing Group, Inc.

ISBN 0-553-28855-5

Published simultaneously in the United States and Canada

Bantam Books are published by Bantam Books, a division of Bantam Doubleday Dell Publishing Group, Inc. Its trademark, consisting of the words "Bantam Books" and the portrayal of a rooster, is Registered in U.S. Patent and Trademark Office and in other countries. Marca Registrada. Bantam Books, 666 Fifth Avenue, New York, New York 10103.

PRINTED IN THE UNITED STATES OF AMERICA

OPM   0 9 8 7 6 5 4 3 2 1

The Wind Dancer was born of a
      white-hot bolt of lightning.
So legend has it.

The Wind Dancer's worth was beyond price;
      its beauty beyond belief.
So legend has it.

The Wind Dancer could punish the evil,
      could reward the good.
So legend has it.

The Wind Dancer wielded the power
      to alter the destinies of men and nations.
So legend has it.

But legend, like history, can be distorted by time,
      robbed of truth by cynicism—
            yet be gifted with splendor by imagination.

THE
WIND
DANCER

One

Stop, thief! Stop her! I've been robbed!"

Sanchia tore across the Mercato Vecchio, raced past the church and on down the street, jumping over an emaciated brown-and-white mongrel that devoured garbage scattered over the flagstones. She ducked under the outstretched arm of a leather-aproned cobbler, but his large hand caught the coarse woolen shawl covering her head. She jerked it from his grasp and kept running.

The merchant chasing her was plump, but still he was closing the distance between them, and Sanchia's heart slammed against her ribcage in a delirium of panic.

She was going to be caught.

Her hands would be chopped off at the wrists.

She would be thrown in the Stinche to be eaten by the rats.

Hot, agonizing pain shot through her left side. A stitch. She had to keep running.

What would Piero do? she wondered wildly. The others were older; they would find a way to survive. But Piero was only six. So many things could happen to so young a child. . . .

"Grab her, you fools. The slut stole my purse!"

Dio, Sanchia thought, he sounded close. How could he run so fast with all those rolls of fat hanging around his middle? She dodged around a wheelbarrow filled with fish, turned the corner of the Canto di Vaccereccia, then bolted down an alley yawning between a goldsmith's shop and an apothecary.

Darkness. Twilight lay over the city but full darkness reined in the alley.

Bright eyes glittered in the deep shadows at the base of the small buildings.

Rats. Dozens of them!

She stopped short, involuntarily recoiling.

The stones beneath the thin soles of her shoes were greasy from the garbage thrown out there by shopkeepers. She need have no fear of the rats, though, while they were feasting on the garbage.

The smell of rotting food in the closeness of the alley was overpowering. She swallowed, trying to fight down the nausea caused as much from terror as the stench.

"Which way did she go?"

The merchant's voice was wheezing and sounded a little farther away. Had she lost him when she darted into the alley? She shrank back into the densely clotted shadows of the goldsmith's shop, her palms pressed flat against the stone wall. Her breath was coming in harsh, painful gasps. Could he hear her? She tried to hold her breath, but there was no breath to hold. *Cristo,* what if he had heard her?

The cold, wet slime-covered wall chilled her back as it penetrated the wool of her gown. Her muscles felt leaden, the blood frozen in her veins. She was suddenly acutely conscious of the sharp, rough texture of the stone wall against her palms, but the sensation was almost pleasurable. Touch. What would she do without her hands? How could she live? How would all of them live?

"This way, you stupid blunderer."

She stiffened. The voice was not that of the fat merchant but one with which she was bitterly familiar. Her heart gave a wild leap of hope. The alley door of the apothecary shop had opened, and even in the darkness she recognized Caprino's slight, foppishly dressed silhouette.

She darted the few yards separating them and almost fell through the doorway into the shop. Her gaze flew to the front of the store, but the apprentice behind the small counter was scrupulously avoiding looking in her direction.

"He's safe," Caprino said. "He does work for me."

Poison, Sanchia thought with a shiver, or perhaps the strange white powders Caprino gave his whores.

Caprino slammed the door and held out his hand. "The purse."

She fumbled beneath her shawl for the soft leather pouch and then dropped it into his palm. She leaned back against the door, her knees shaking so badly she could barely stand upright.

"You were clumsy," Caprino said harshly. "I should have let that fat fool catch you. Next time I will."

She had to wait until she could speak without panting. "There won't be a next time. I'm never going to do it again."

"You will," Caprino said coolly. "You're frightened now, but it will pass. You'll forget the fear and remember only the money that buys bread. You're not usually this clumsy. You may not come this close to being caught for the next ten lifts."

"I'll find another way." Sanchia's hands clenched at her sides. "There has to be another way."

"You didn't think so when you came to me." Caprino opened the door. "I have no more time for you. I have important business at Giulia's. Stay here for another few minutes before you go back to Giovanni's." The door swung shut behind him.

He hadn't given Sanchia her share of the purse, she realized dully. Trust Caprino to try to steal even the smallest purse, if given the opportunity. She would have to seek him out tomorrow and demand her portion. She had mouths to feed and Caprino was right about hunger being a sharp dagger that might goad even a saint into thieving.

But was hunger worth the risk of having her hands chopped off?

Fresh panic clutched at her as a chilling memory returned. Two months before she had seen a thief thrown out of Stinche Prison into the streets, his arms ending in bleeding stumps. Since then the fear of that punishment had lived with her during the day and invaded her dreams at night, She had tried and tried to think of another way to earn money to feed them, all the while fearing her frantic scheming would come to nought. There was no other way.

As there would be no other way the next time or the time after that. She would have to steal again just as Caprino had predicted. But he was wrong about the terror holding her in helpless thrall; it wasn't a thing of the moment.

She knew the fear would never go away again.

"Good evening, noble messeres, I have the honor to present to you my greetings. I am Guido Caprino." Caprino stood in the doorway and smiled ingratiatingly at the two men sitting at the polished table across the chamber. "The enchanting Madonna Giulia assured me I could be of some slight service to you."

He carefully kept a bland expression on his face as he appraised the two men. The older had to be Lorenzo Vasaro, he decided. His high cheekbones and deepset eyes matched the description Giulia had given him of the man—and besides, Caprino's own instincts responded to the shadowy aura of menace surrounding him. The man was lean, faultlessly elegant in his fashionably slashed black doublet, and clearly more dangerous than his companion. He gazed at the other man and felt a ripple of distaste. He was so *male*. Lionello Andreas might stand well over six feet, Caprino surmised, and he was too big-boned to lay claim to elegance no matter how richly he was garbed. Now, dressed only in gray hose and a loose white shirt, he appeared to be exactly what Caprino had expected: a barbarian warrior with more brawn than brains, he was not wearing a weapon, not even a dagger. Andreas might be the lord of Mandara, but Caprino would wager it was Vasaro who was the shrewd power behind the scenes there.

"Come in, Messer Caprino." Andreas picked up the silver goblet on the table in front of him and waved it at a cushioned chair beside the window before raising it to his lips. "Be seated."

The arrogant bastard hadn't bothered to stand up to greet him properly, Caprino thought as he smiled politely and crossed the room to take the seat indicated. No doubt Andreas did not think him worthy of respect. He would soon learn differently.

Lorenzo Vasaro rose and moved with silent grace to lean against the wall to the left of the window. He folded his arms across his chest and gazed blandly at Caprino.

A good move. Caprino's respect for Vasaro rose even higher. His action had placed Caprino between Vasaro and Andreas. Caprino was tempted to address Vasaro as the worthier of the two but turned instead to Andreas. "I am always overjoyed to accommodate any friends of Madonna Giulia. What is your pleasure?"

"I need a thief." Andreas leaned back in his chair and studied Caprino with narrowed eyes.

Caprino met his eyes and continued to smile politely. "It will be my pleasure to provide you with the finest thief in all of Florence, Your Magnificence. Only a thief, or must he possess other talents? An assassin, perhaps? I have a few associates who have talents in that direction, but no one with the extraordinary skills of Messer Vasaro."

Andreas stiffened. "You know of Vasaro?"

"How could I not?" Caprino remained sitting forward in his chair, one graceful hand resting with seeming casualness on the jeweled hilt of his dagger. "He shines in the firmament like a bright star, dazzling all who see him. Is it any wonder I should recognize him?"

"Not at all." Andreas cast an amused glance at Vasaro, who was still gazing at Caprino with no expression. "Do you hear that, Lorenzo? A star, by all that's holy. Aren't you going to thank the kind gentleman?"

Lorenzo inclined his head in acknowledgment.

"No thanks are needed," Caprino said quickly. "I merely gave homage where homage was due. It was foolish of me to suggest you might need an assassin when Messer Vasaro is in your service. Why should you need any—"

"As you say, I need no assassin," Andreas interrupted with sudden impatience. "I need a thief with hands as swift and sure as an arrow drawn by a master bowman and a touch as delicate as the kiss of a butterfly."

"There are many thieves in Florence," Caprino said thoughtfully. "I myself have trained an honored few."

"So I've been informed." Andreas's lips twisted in a cynical smile. "No doubt you've also tutored many individuals in my friend Lorenzo's former profession."

Caprino shrugged. "One or two. But to be an assassin requires a certain fortitude not found in every man. A thief is different. Easier. Not as profitable but . . ." He trailed off. "How long would you need this thief, my lord Andreas?"

Andreas went still. "You know me also?" His voice was dangerously soft. "Does my name, too, shine in the firmament?"

Caprino's hand tightened on the hilt of his dagger. He could feel a bead of moisture dampen his temple as he realized his mistake. He had judged Vasaro to be the threat. A stupid error. In his experience most soldiers, even condottieri, had none of the skill and subtlety Caprino admired. But he shouldn't have let his contempt for the profession overshadow his judgment of the man. No, that was not entirely true, Caprino admitted reluctantly. His instinctive revulsion at Andreas's overpowering virility had also contributed to the blunder by keeping him from a serious study of the man.

Now he discerned the intelligence, as well as cynicism, in Andreas's brilliant dark eyes which were fully as merciless as those of Vasaro. Caprino moistened his lower lip with his tongue. "Your fame has spread over all Italy, my lord. An illustrious condottiere such as yourself must expect to be recognized and—" Caprino broke off. "I had no idea your visit to our city was in secret. If you wish to go unrecognized, then it goes without saying that I never have seen your face, never heard the sound of your voice, never even heard your name pronounced."

"And who did pronounce my name to you?" Andreas asked silkily. "And on what subject? I asked Giulia to tell no one I was in Florence."

"You know how careless women can be, *Magnifico*. When Madonna Giulia summoned me here, she mentioned your name but nothing else. I swear this, my lord Andreas. Would the Madonna have sent for me if I wasn't a man of discretion and honor?"

"Lorenzo?" Andreas's gaze never left Caprino's face.

Vasaro's voice was hoarse and scratchy as a wooden coffin pulled over flagstones. "He will betray you for a price high enough. Shall I dispose of him?" Lorenzo asked as casually as if he'd inquired about throwing out the dregs of the wine in Andreas's cup.

Caprino leaned forward in his chair, prepared to spring, his dagger at the ready for a—

"I think not," Andreas said. "He doesn't know enough to hurt me, and I'd find it inconvenient to search out another procurer."

"A wise decision." Caprino's grasp on his dagger relaxed. "A man should always keep the long view in mind. Now about this thief?"

"Just this moment I have thought of a quality he must possess," Andreas said, looking down at his heavy leather gauntlets on the table. "I must own him."

"Own?"

Andreas's long, broad index finger rubbed at the brass riveting of the gauntlet. "He must be mine body and soul. I'll not have him running back to you with tales you can sell to the highest bidder." Andreas smiled. "Of course, I could have him removed after he finishes his task, but I dislike rewarding good work in that fashion. Not an intelligent way to proceed."

"I can see that." Caprino's uneasy gaze darted to Vasaro. Rumor had it that Vasaro had accepted service with Andreas when the condottiere was a boy of seventeen. How had Andreas managed to hold such a skilled assassin all these years? Did he own *him* body and soul as he wished to own the thief? It was something to ponder, for who but Satan was capable of possessing a demon? "Such men aren't easy to find. How could I—"

"You must know ways." Andreas pulled a purse from his belt and tossed it on the table to Caprino. "Greed, revenge, a woman. We both know the weapons to bind a man. Use them."

Caprino opened the pouch and counted the ducats. "A fair price."

"A princely sum for one insignificant thief, as well you know, but a small price for the soul of a human being."

Caprino smiled. "I'm sure you'll discover shortly whether or not that is so." He paused. "I'm to keep this?" he asked as he tucked the purse inside his belt. "I'm honored by your trust."

"I can afford to trust you, Caprino. I know where to find you, if you disappoint me. When can I expect you to send me the thief I've paid for?"

"I'm not sure." Caprino stood up and edged toward the door. "I must consider and de—"

"Tomorrow." Andreas's tone had not changed, but his smile held the gleam of a feral creature. "No later than three. I'm an impatient man." His gaze searched Caprino's face. "You already have someone in mind. Bring him to me."

Caprino was startled. "But, Your Magnificence, I must study and think upon . . ." He stopped. How had that whoreson Andreas managed to read him so easily? "I do have someone in mind who might meet your requirements, but there are difficulties."

"Overcome them."

"I may need many more ducats than this pouch holds in order to do so."

Andreas's lips tightened. "I have an aversion to being preyed upon by the greedy. It would be wise to remember that."

Caprino lowered his lids to veil his eyes. "I'll not be beggared to obtain what you want. I'm worthy of my hire."

"If I slip a dagger between his ribs tonight, tomorrow there will be another Caprino in the streets of Florence," Vasaro said with little inflection. "Perhaps a man less greedy to deal with, Lion."

Caprino felt a chill quiver through him but carefully kept himself under control. He nodded. "Tomorrow or the next day or the day after that. I'm not so foolish as to think I'm irreplaceable. But Your Magnificence is impatient, and I'm the man who can help you today."

Andreas was silent for a moment during which Caprino tasted the sourness of fear.

Then Andreas made an impatient gesture. "I must see the skill of your light-fingered villian." He paused. "Tomorrow."

"But it's too soon. I can't—" Caprino stopped. He had gained a valuable concession, and it would be best not to push too hard at this juncture. "As Your Excellency bids me. I will move heaven and earth to do as you wish."

"I'll be at the Piazza of San Michele tomorrow at two with another purse containing an equal number of ducats," Andreas said. "If your thief can claim it from my person, the purse is yours. If not . . ." He shrugged. "Then I will be most unhappy with you. So unhappy they may end up fishing you out of the Arno." He waved a hand of dismissal. "Good night, Caprino. Why don't you see the gentleman to his home, Lorenzo?"

"It isn't far. I have a house near the piazza." Caprino moved quickly toward the door. "Good evening, my lords. Until tomorrow."

Andreas smiled mockingly. "Do accompany him, Lorenzo. The streets are so dangerous for a man with a purse full of ducats."

Andreas was toying with him, Caprino realized with a surge of rage. He turned at the door and smiled through clenched teeth. "You test whether I'm afraid of Messer Lorenzo? Well, I do fear him. I'm not a brave man, but it's not courage that's made me what I am. You might consider who has called the tune this night." His index finger tapped his left temple. "Up here. That's what counts." He bowed. "As you shall see tomorrow. "

The door swung shut behind him, and the breath immediately rushed from Caprino's lungs in a soft explosion of sound as the tension eased from him. He straightened his short scarlet cape, meticulously adjusted his velvet cap at the angle he preferred, and started down the stairs. He gazed appraisingly at the painting of Venus in all her naked glory on the wall beside the stairs. The painting was new and exceptionally well executed, but the Venus was not overly beautiful, a circumstance which did not surprise him. Giulia would never permit anything or anyone to overshadow her own charms in her own *casa*.

"Buona sera, Caprino." Giulia Marzo met him at the bottom of the stairs. She smiled sweetly. "All is well?"

Caprino shifted his cloak to reveal the purse.

She held out her hand palm upward. "A joy to work with you, Caprino."

"Tomorrow," he said as he tried to edge past her.

"Now." Her smile never wavered. "Or I'll tell my lord Andreas you have no intention of fulfilling your promise to find his thief and even now are hurrying toward the city gates. I doubt you would ever reach that splendid house paid for by the ducats stolen from your whores and thieves."

He stopped short and turned to look at her. He should have known Giulia would have been listening to everything taking place in Andreas's chamber. It was not only the slut's golden beauty that had caused her to rise from one of his own brothels to own this fine *casa*. He reluctantly opened the pouch and pressed five ducats into her palm. "Someday, when I lose patience with you, I'll have you brought back to me," he said softly. "And I'll strip you naked and stake you out in an alley and sell that sweet-smelling flesh to every man who walks by.

How do you think your fine lords will like you after a few weeks of such use?"

"You don't frighten me." She shrugged. "You cannot hurt me, Caprino. I have the protection of many powerful men here in Florence."

"Like that bastard up there?" Caprino jerked his head in the direction of the door at the top of the stairs. "Andreas has no power here in Florence. He rules only in Mandara."

"At present." Giulia's gaze lifted to look at the door he'd indicated. "Lion could rule anywhere. Men such as he are rare."

Caprino's gaze narrowed on her face. "Do I detect a trace of lust, *madonna mia*? Be careful, or you'll lose your one weapon in Cupid's battle. A whore must never lust; she must only be lusted after."

"He *does* lust after me," she said fiercely. "For two years he has come to my *casa*. Never has he asked for any of the other women, only me." Then as she met Caprino's satisfied gaze she tried to shrug unconcernedly. "Not that it matters."

"I think it does matter to you." He studied her. "I wonder why? You have the most peculiar tastes. I find him quite ugly."

"How would you know? I've provided you with too many pretty young boys and wretched-looking men not to know how peculiar are *your* tastes, Caprino."

He tucked the purse into his belt and said mockingly, "He's far too rough for my refined taste. Soldiers can be so crude. But there's another five ducats for you if you find out why our brave condottiere wishes the services of a thief."

Giulia's gaze returned to the door at the top of the stairs. "I'll consider it. But he's not a man who babbles to a woman."

"Not even to *la bella* Giulia?" He turned away. "Seven ducats."

He opened the door and strode out into the street.

It had been a good evening's work, he thought contentedly. The stakes Andreas was hoping to win must be very high to make him yield to Caprino's demands with so little argument. If he was clever he might be able to milk this situation until it rained even more gold into his coffers.

He turned at the next corner and instead of proceeding to his own house off the piazza, he started in the direction of the Via Calimala and the print shop of Giovanni Ballano.

"You gave in too easily," Lorenzo said as the door closed behind Caprino. "I could have persuaded him to take less."

Lion lifted the goblet to his lips. "If Caprino brings me what I want, it will be worth the price."

Lorenzo shrugged. "If you believe it to be so."

"I do." Lion propped his feet on the table, crossing his legs at the ankles. "We leave the day after tomorrow for Solinari."

"If Caprino's thief succeeds in your little test."

"He'd better, or I'll let you have Caprino to persuade as you deem fitting."

The faintest smile lifted Lorenzo's lips. "No, you won't."

Lion lifted a black brow. "You think I'm too kind to condemn Caprino to your tender care?"

"I think you would take pleasure in punishing Caprino yourself, but you'd not give him to me." His gaze met Lion's. "Why do you persist in trying to save my soul when I lost it long ago? When I was a child of eleven, to be precise. That was when I killed my first man. What were you doing when you were eleven, Lion?"

"Following my father's banner, watching his men pillage and rape cities. I killed my first man when I was thirteen." He paused. "And I don't consider my soul lost."

"Ah, but your killing was bathed in glory and honor," Lorenzo said softly. "There's no glory in the world of an assassin."

"Killing is killing."

"If you thought that was true, you'd let me go after Caprino."

Lion smiled. "Perhaps I will."

"No, you won't. To do it, you'd have to live in Caprino's world. My world."

"It's not your world. Your world is Mandara now."

"Because you say it is?"

"Because you earned a place there thirteen years ago."

"With an assassin's knife."

"Which saved my life and avenged my father."

"Glory and honor." Lorenzo's gravelly voice was mocking. "You see how your mind works? I fear you have a grievous fault, Lion. Somehow you've managed to acquire the instincts of a bygone age. Chivalry will never prevail in a land where men like me can grow rich."

"Chivalry? My God, you're demented, Lorenzo. No one is more of a realist than I. If you want chivalry, I'm afraid you'll have to apply to Marco."

"I agree your brother is sickeningly pure and honorable, but I suspect you're infected with a less virulent form of the same disease." As Lion started to speak, Lorenzo held up his hand. "Perhaps you don't adhere to the philosophy, my friend, but the instinct is certainly there. Look how you've insisted on trying to keep me by your side so I wouldn't return to cutting the throats of the illustrious noblemen of Naples."

"Most of them needed killing."

"But I never inquired whether they did or not." Lorenzo smiled faintly. "Killing is killing."

"By all that's holy, Lorenzo, will you stop turning my words against me? Why will you not admit that you're no longer what you were?"

"Because I am what I am and what I was and what I will be."

"*Cristo!*" Lion drew an exasperated breath. "And what are you then, damn your cryptic soul?"

A sudden smile lit Lorenzo's narrow face. "I told you I had no soul. I am many things but I can think of only one that has merit."

"And what is that?"

"I'm the friend of Lionello Andreas," Lorenzo said softly.

Lion gazed at him suspiciously. "I have the uneasy feeling you're making mock of me again."

Lorenzo raised his brows. "But of course," he said blandly. "How can a man who has no soul know friendship? I'm glad you're so perceptive. It shows I've trained you well in these last thirteen years."

Lion swore softly beneath his breath. "Lorenzo, someday I'll—"

"My lord, the hour grows late." Giulia Marzo was standing in the doorway smiling at them. "If you please, I'll show Messer Vasaro to his chamber. Does he wish a companion? I have a sweet little Sicilian girl who could show him much pleasure."

"Lorenzo?" Lion glanced at Vasaro.

Lorenzo shook his head. "Not tonight."

"Nor any night of late." Lion gazed at him speculatively. "I fear you're beginning to have the tastes of a monk. It was not always so."

"I'm an old man of forty-four. Perhaps I've lost my virility," Lorenzo said lightly as he turned and moved toward the door. "I find my books more stimulating than these fair flowers at present. But pray don't let me stop you from frolicking in Venus's garden."

"I won't." Lion's lingering gaze ran over Giulia's bare shoulders and then down to the fullness of her breasts. "I promise you."

When Giulia returned minutes later, Lion was still sitting in the same position, his feet propped on the table, his gaze fixed thoughtfully on his wine goblet.

"Vasaro is a strange man." Giulia closed the door and leaned back against it. "Are you not afraid to call him your friend? Caprino says Vasaro is—"

"No worse than any of us," Lion interrupted. "We live in violent times, and a man must be violent to survive and hold what is his."

"Or take what is another's?" Giulia asked, amused. "Is that why you need a thief?"

His gaze narrowed on her face. "I have no liking for questions, Giulia." He smiled. "In fact, I consider the forming of words a sinful waste from lips that are so accomplished at other occupations. Take off your clothes, *cara*."

Giulia felt the muscles of her stomach clench as she looked at him. She was breathless and trembling—but not surprised for it had been this way with Lion, since his first visit over two years before. Caprino was right in judging Lion as not handsome. Some might even call him ugly as Caprino had done. His features looked as though they'd been carved from stone by the bold stroke of an ax instead of the delicate chisel of an artist. His cheekbones were too broad, his black brows straight slashes over eyes that were night dark and seldom held any emotion save wariness and cynicism. His lips were well shaped but they, too, held a hint of both sensuality and cruelty. His dark hair was still as closely barbered as the days when he had worn a soldier's helmet, and his body, though lithe, held none of the slim grace of the courtier. Even as he reclined in an indolent position now, his loose white shirt gave hint of the power of his massive shoulders, and the gray hose revealed the might of trunklike thighs and muscular calves.

Power, Giulia realized with a start of surprise. Not only did Lion Andreas possess physical strength and power, but also an inner strength and power far beyond those of other men . . . certainly beyond those of any man she had ever met. His curiosity about life, about what was going on around him was more intense, his potential for good or evil more extreme, his appetites stronger, than in anyone of her experience.

"I'm growing impatient, *cara*. Must I beg?"

"You never beg." She started across the room toward him, unfastening the rope of pearls binding her fair hair. "You take." She dropped the pearls onto a table beside him. "And take." Her palm caressed his thigh and she felt the muscles harden beneath her touch. "Until I cannot even lift one little finger."

"How cruel." He lifted her hand from his thigh and pressed the palm to his lips. "I wonder that you still receive me when I so misuse you." His tongue stroked the sensitive flesh of her palm. "You always smell of roses. When I'm away from you I always remember the scent . . ."

"When you're between the thighs of one of your other whores? You come to Florence only two or three times a year. Who pleasures you when you leave me?"

He glanced up, his dark eyes twinkling. "Perhaps, like Lorenzo, I find solace in Plutarch and Aristotle."

She smiled reluctantly. "Not you. There's too much hunger in you. I doubt you could last a week without a woman. Do you keep a strumpet at Mandara to service you? I know that—" She broke off as she felt the sharp edge of his teeth on her palm exerting just enough pressure to send a thrill of lust, not pain, through her.

Lion's large hand reached up to caress her throat. "Does it matter that there are other women?" His fingers gently stroked the hollow where her heart was pounding wildly. "Why? I never ask you how many men you service when I'm not here." He pulled down the square neckline of her gown to bare her breasts, one callused palm moving to the left. He spread his fingers over her breast and watched the nipple tauten in response. "It's what we are together that concerns me." He leaned forward and his lips closed on her now distended nipple, and she felt his warm tongue tease and caress the distended tip.

"Lion . . ." She swayed toward him, her fingers tangling in his hair. "I could come with you to Mandara."

His head quickly lifted and his eyes became shuttered. "No."

How stupid to make such an offer. It had tumbled out before she'd thought it through, and, she knew, it was generated by sheer jealousy of those other women in his life. Lion would never take her to Mandara. He would not even talk to her about his life away from her. "I was only joking," she said quickly, rubbing her swollen breast teasingly against his lips. "Why should I give up my fine life here in Florence? I have everything I want.

Money, beautiful jewels, and one man is much like another."

"True." Lion's tension eased. "But there's only one Giulia," he said lightly. "Giulia, the divine." He stood up and pulled her toward the bed across the room. "Giulia, the generous."

She could see the hunger growing in him, his manhood pressing hard and bold against the material of his hose. Lust speared through her. "Generous?"

"I'm in the mood to test your kindness tonight." He smiled as he sat down on the bed, spread his legs, and pulled her down on her knees before him. He took her palm and brought it to his lips before lowering it to cover his rigid manhood. "And you are going to be generous to me tonight, aren't you, *cara*?"

Tonight, tomorrow, for a few days. It would never be more than that with Lion. But what did it matter? Her hand moved slowly, teasingly on his body as she gazed up at him through her long lashes. He was aroused, hurting, feeling with an intensity that made her heady with power. She was filled with breathless excitement. Lion would be wild, strong and lustful as a satyr, insatiable as he always was when aroused. *More.* "Yes," she whispered. "I'm going to be very generous, *amo mio*."

"You don't seem to understand, my enchanting Sanchia," Caprino said mildly. "You have no choice. You will go to the piazza and relieve the gentleman of his purse. Then you'll bring the purse to me and I'll see that you're suitably rewarded. You will do this or you will never lift another purse in Florence ever again."

"Why me?" Sanchia asked fiercely. "I told you earlier today that I didn't want—"

"This is a special task."

"It's too soon. I can't—" She broke off as she realized her voice was rising. She cast an anxious glance at the door of the shop set in the alcove behind her. Giovanni mustn't know she was out here with Caprino. It was only because Giovanni had started on his third jug of wine of the evening and was unlikely to notice her absence that she had dared to slip out when Caprino had appeared a few minutes before. "You know I can't leave the shop in the middle of the day. Giovanni will ask questions."

"And you will lie." Caprino shrugged. "It's not as if you haven't lied to him before."

"Not often." Lies were sometimes necessary to survive, but Sanchia had found that an occasional lie surrounded by the truth was much more likely to be believed. "And not unless it was important."

"But this is important. It was you who came to me three years ago and asked to be trained. Out of the goodness of my heart I made you one of the finest thieves in all of Florence and what did I ask in return? Nothing."

"Two thirds of every purse I stole is far from nothing."

"I could have asked for all but a few ducats."

And gotten it, Sanchia thought wearily. She would have had no choice but to give in to his demands. Caprino got his share or there were no thefts, whoring, or killings in Florence. "I've never tried to cheat you of your share, Caprino."

"I know. Such a virtuous child. It warms my heart." He took a step closer. "How are your three little friends? I hear Bartolomeo is becoming quite as skilled as you as Giovanni's helper in the shop. How old is he now?"

"Ten," she said warily.

"And Elizabet? I saw her a few days ago. Such a lovely maid, all golden hair and soft pale skin. She must be fifteen by now."

Sanchia stiffened. "Fourteen."

"Old enough," Caprino said. "When are you going to send her to me? There are easier ways for a pretty pullet to make her way in the world than the one you've chosen for her."

Sanchia's initial surge of panic was quickly washed away by anger. "Stay away from her, Caprino."

"Ah, now that's what I like to see. A little fire." He studied Sanchia objectively. "You're really not bad-looking. A little color in your cheeks and a few pounds on those skinny bones, and I might be able to use you too." He brought his lace-trimmed kerchief to his nose with a moue of distaste. "After a dozen scented baths and a thorough perfuming."

"You do use me." Her lashes lowered to veil her eyes. "I steal for you."

"Only enough to feed that brood you hold so dear."

"It will have to satisfy you."

"But I'm never satisfied. I'm a very greedy man. Haven't you realized that yet, Sanchia?" He smiled faintly. "Give me Elizabet and I'll share the ducats I get for her. I might even be able to persuade Giulia Marzo to take her. Your Elizabet could become the courtesan of a rich and powerful lord. Fine food, pretty gowns—"

"No!" Sanchia saw the frown forming on Caprino's face and instantly began to placate him. "Not yet. Perhaps in another year."

"Why not now?" Caprino's voice lowered to a silky threat. "I'm desolate you're not returning the kindness I've shown to you. Ingratitude make me very unhappy. First you refuse to do me a small favor in the piazza tomorrow, and now you're hoarding that sweet child from me and telling me—"

"I'll steal the purse," Sanchia interrupted. Then, as she saw the flicker of satisfaction on Caprino's face, she realized with frustration that he'd gotten exactly what he wanted from her. He had used the threat to Elizabet to force Sanchia to steal again. Why had she expected anything else? Caprino always got what he wanted through guile or cunning or force. Still, it had been only a threat this time, she thought with relief. "Why do you want that particular purse? If I see an easier—" She stopped.

Caprino was shaking his head. "It has to be the man I point out to you. And why I want it is no concern of yours." He turned to go. "The piazza at two. Don't be late." He glanced back over his shoulder. "If I don't get that purse, I'll have to seek . . . compensation. You understand, Sanchia?"

"I understand." A shiver ran through her as she met his gaze. "You'll have your purse."

"Good. Such a sweet child." A moment later he had

faded into the darkness, and the breath Sanchia had not realized she had been holding came out in a rush.

Dio, she had been frightened. She had known it was only a matter of time until Caprino realized Elizabet's potential value to him. Nothing and no one escaped Caprino's notice for long if it meant money flowing into his purse, but perhaps she had staved him off for a little while.

She stood gazing at the darkness into which Caprino had disappeared. Something would have to be done soon about Elizabet, who was becoming too comely for Sanchia to protect. She had caught Giovanni gazing often at Elizabet of late. His eyes held the same lust he had had for Sanchia's mother. Soon he would attempt Elizabet, if Caprino hadn't already forced the girl into one of his brothels. One solution to Elizabet's problem had occurred to Sanchia, but it would take more ducats than she could manage to salvage from her share of the purses she snatched for Caprino. Perhaps if she could find a way to get away from the shop more often—

She jumped as a crash of splintering pottery sounded in the shop behind her. The sound was immediately followed by Giovanni's loud cursing. "Sanchia! Where the devil are you?"

She consciously braced herself and turned to open the door. "I was just getting some air. It's so—" She gazed in horror at the disaster across the room. A pottery jug lay broken on the scribe table, and Giovanni was making futile dabs with a cloth at the rich red wine spreading on the two leaves of parchment in front of him.

"No!" Sanchia hurried across the room to stand looking down at the first leaf. It was ruined, the ink running over the parchment. She carefully lifted it away from the one beneath. The second leaf was still legible, but the liquid had soaked through and it would also have to be recopied. "You've ruined it."

"You can fix it," Giovanni mumbled, shaking his shaggy graying head. "I don't have to deliver the work until noon tomorrow." He turned and walked unsteadily toward the room at the back of the shop. "Sleepy . . . You can fix it."

Yes, she could fix it, Sanchia thought in weary exasperation, but it would take all night and most of tomorrow. Thank the saints Bartolomeo had put the rest of the folio neatly away in the cabinet as soon as he had finished setting the type for each leaf, or this accident could have been a true catastrophe. He had only left these last two leaves out to have them in readiness to set the type early tomorrow morning. Though this disaster was certainly bad enough. Messer Rudolfo was a scholar as well as a merchant, and he would have been furious to have his original *Convivio* destroyed. He might have yielded to the current fashion of having copies of books in his library printed on the modern marvel of a printing press, but he still had a fondness for the beauty of the originals as well as a merchant's appreciation for their intrinsic worth. She would have not only to replace Rudolfo's original leaves with two of equally fine script but to start setting the type herself tonight. She and Bartolomeo had judged it would take both of them working at high speed from the first light of dawn tomorrow to print those last two leaves and finish on time. Now that Bartolomeo would be forced to do the printing alone while she did the hand copying, some of the typesetting must be done tonight.

"I'll clean off the table."

Sanchia turned to see Piero at the door leading to the small storage room. He was rubbing his eyes with the backs of his hands and looked endearingly tousled and warm, even younger than his six years. She felt a rush of affection and suddenly the world didn't seem such a grim place. Life had its ugly patches but it wasn't all ugly. There were children like Piero and beautiful words on parchment and probably hundreds of other wonderful things she couldn't recall or still had to learn about. "Go back to your pallet," she said gently. "I can do this myself."

He shook his head as he came over to the table and began to clean up the shards of pottery. His small, sturdy body was swaying a little and he was almost asleep on his feet, she thought tenderly. Yet she knew he would stubbornly continue to try to help her. Yes, there were many wonderful things that men like Caprino and Giovanni couldn't besmirch, and companionship and love were two of them.

"I'll get Bartolomeo up." Piero carried the pottery shards to the big straw basket across the room. "He can set the type."

Sanchia shook her head. "Bartolomeo went to sleep only an hour ago."

"You haven't slept at all," Piero answered. "I'll get Bartolomeo up." He disappeared into the room where the four of them slept.

A moment later Sanchia heard the grumbling protests of a very sleepy Bartolomeo and then Piero's determined voice. "No, I won't let you go back to sleep. Sanchia needs us."

Sanchia smiled. Young as he was, Piero could never be deterred once he had decided something must be done. Her smile faded when she remembered it was only his stubbornness that had kept him alive when his mother had abandoned him to the streets and gone into one of Caprino's brothels. Piero had been like a fierce young animal for weeks after Sanchia had found him in an alley off the Piazza della Signoria two years before.

Bartolomeo was yawning as he appeared in the doorway. "Sanchia, I don't—" He stopped, suddenly awake, and shouted, "*Dio!* Can you save anything?"

Sanchia shook her head. "They'll both have to be recopied."

Bartolomeo glowered at the door leading to the room where Giovanni lay snoring. "It's the third time this month. Soon no one will come to him. Messer Arcolo does much better work and doesn't drink like a swilling pig." His gaze went with possessive pride to the printing press crouching like a giant wooden grasshopper across the room. "Giovanni doesn't deserve such a fine instrument. It's wasted on him."

"But not on you," Sanchia said affectionately. "I don't know if you are mother to that press or it is mother to you."

Piero was tugging at Bartolomeo's wool shirt. "Set the type."

"*Dio*, give me a minute." Bartolomeo frowned down at Piero. "Will you at least let me wash the sleep from my eyes?"

Piero shook his head. "Sanchia needs you. She's tired and wants to go to bed."

Sanchia made a face. "There'll be no sleep for me tonight." She handed Bartolomeo the leaf that could still be read. "If you can get this now, I'll try to have the other leaf recopied by morning."

Bartolomeo nodded briskly as he glanced down at the page. His drowsiness had completely vanished, and Sanchia could see the familiar eagerness light his face as he imagined changing the elegant script to his beloved block print. "I can do it." His tone was already abstracted as he crossed the room. "It will only take . . ." He trailed off as his fingers began sorting through the letter blocks.

Piero finished cleaning off the table and then began moving about the room putting things in order.

Sanchia went to the cabinet, drew out a leaf of Giovanni's finest parchment, crossed back to the scribe table, and seated herself. She glanced at the ruined document and quickly set it aside. No help there; the letters had run together until they were completely indistinguishable. Thank the saints she had read the entire work earlier in the week, as she almost always did when Giovanni received a new commission. It was the third *Convivio* the print shop had copied this year, but there were several tiny differences she had noted in this version. Rudolfo's folio had been obtained from the monks of a Franciscan monastery, and the holy man who had copied Dante's work had arrogantly deleted a number of sentences and added others. It would be futile to hope that a scholar like Messer Rudolfo had not pored over these leaves until he had memorized them to the last stroke of the pen.

Piero dropped onto the floor beside her chair and leaned his head against her knee. She absently stroked his fair hair as she tried to clear her mind of weariness.

She felt a sudden rush of panic. What if she couldn't do it this time? What if she couldn't remember? She took a deep breath and tried to steady herself. There was no reason why she shouldn't remember. Since she was a small child she had been able to remember everything she had seen down to the tiniest detail. Surely she hadn't lost the ability now that she needed it so desperately. God was not always kind, but he couldn't be so cruel as to take away this gift.

She closed her eyes and tried to relax, willing memory to return to her.

And it did!

The leaf was suddenly before her with all its willful inaccuracies. Sweet Mary be praised, Sanchia thought with relief.

Her lids flicked open and she quickly reached for the quill.

TWO

"You're late," Caprino jerked Sanchia into the shadows of the arcade surrounding the piazza. "I told you two o'clock."

"It couldn't be helped," Sanchia said breathlessly. "There was an accident . . . and we didn't get finished until an hour ago . . . and then I had to wait until Giovanni left to take the—"

Caprino silenced the flow of words with an impatient motion of his hand. "There he is." He nodded across the crowded piazza. "The big man in the wine-colored velvet cape listening to the storyteller."

Sanchia's gaze followed Caprino's to the man standing in front of the platform. He was more than big, he was a giant, she thought gloomily. The careless arrogance in the man's stance bespoke perfect confidence in his ability to deal with any circumstances and, if he caught her, he'd probably use his strong hands to crush her head like a walnut. Well, she was too tired to worry about that right now. It had been over thirty hours since she had slept. Perhaps it was just as well she was almost too exhausted to care what happened to her. Fear must not make her as clumsy as she had been yesterday. She was at least glad the giant appeared able to afford to lose a few ducats. The richness of his clothing indicated he must either be a great lord or a prosperous merchant.

"Go." Caprino gave her a little push out onto the piazza. "Now."

She pulled her shawl over her head to shadow her face and hurried toward the platform where Luca Brezal was telling his story, accompanying himself on the lyre. She had heard Luca many times before and didn't consider him overly talented. She wished the storyteller were Pico Fallone. Pico could hold an audience spellbound and would have made it much easier for her to ease close enough to snatch the giant's purse.

A drop of rain struck her face, and she glanced up at the suddenly dark skies. Not yet, she thought with exasperation. If it started to rain in earnest the people crowding the piazza would run for shelter and she would have to follow the velvet-clad giant until he put himself into a situation that allowed her to make the snatch.

Another drop splashed her hand, and her anxious gaze flew to the giant. His attention was still fixed on the storyteller, but only the saints knew how long he would remain. Her pace quickened as she flowed like a shadow into the crowd surrounding the platform.

Garlic, Lion thought, as the odor assaulted his nostrils. Garlic, spoiled fish, and some other stench that smelled even fouler. He glanced around the crowd trying to identify the source of the smell. The people surrounding the platform were the same ones he had studied moments before, trying to search out Caprino's thief. The only new arrival was a thin woman dressed in a shabby gray gown, an equally ragged woolen shawl covering her head. She moved away from the edge of the crowd and started to hurry across the piazza. The stench faded with her departure and Lion drew a deep breath. *Dio*, luck was with him in this, at least. He was not at all pleased at being forced to stand in the rain waiting for Caprino to produce his master thief.

"It's done," Lorenzo muttered, suddenly at Lion's side. He had been watching from the far side of the crowd. Now he said more loudly, "As sweet a snatch as I've ever seen."

"What?" Frowning, Lion gazed at him. "There was no—" He broke off as he glanced down at his belt. The pouch was gone; only the severed cords remained in his belt. "Sweet Jesus." His gaze flew around the piazza. "Who?"

"The sweet madonna who looked like a beggarmaid and smelled like a decaying corpse." Lorenzo nodded toward the arched arcade. "She disappeared behind that column, and I'll wager you'll find Caprino lurking there with her, counting your ducats."

Lion started toward the column. "A woman," he murmured. "I didn't expect a woman. How good is she?"

Lorenzo fell into step with him. "Very good."

"A woman . . . offers interesting possibilities. The guards at the Palazzo wouldn't be expecting a female."

"Especially not when the woman smells like spoiled trout. I doubt if even a fishmonger would find her alluring."

"That problem seems easy enough to sol—" Lion broke off as Caprino stepped from behind the column and started toward them.

A smug smile on his lips, Caprino held up Lion's purse. "You are satisfied? A lift as graceful as the steps of a pavane."

"Where's the woman?" Lion squinted into the shadowed arcade.

"Gone. I let Sanchia go back to the shop until I learned your decision. There was no point to involving her further, if you found a woman unsuitable for your purpose."

"She may be adequate," Lion said slowly. "If she proves pliable."

Caprino's lids lowered to veil the sudden glitter in his eyes. "A woman you can own is always pliable. Did you think I'd forgotten your second requirement? Sanchia is a slave as her mother was before her. You can buy her and command her to do whatever you wish her to do." He smiled faintly. "And she would never dare betray you by running back to tell me or anyone else of your concerns."

"A slave," Lion repeated. Slavery was not allowed in his own city-state of Mandara, but there were many slaves in other parts of Italy brought from Turkey, Spain, and the Balkans. "In your service?"

Caprino shook his head. "She belongs to Giovanni Ballano who owns a print shop on the Via Calimala."

"Who sends her out to steal for him?"

Caprino shook his head. "He doesn't know about it. Giovanni is a drunkard and a fool who will soon lose his shop and everything he owns. He needs Sanchia's help, but hand him a jug of good wine and a few ducats and he'll be persuaded to give her up to you."

"More gold?" Lion asked dryly. "This thief is costing me dearly."

"I found what you wanted," Caprino protested. "You can't expect me to impoverish myself by buying her for you." A thoughtful frown suddenly wrinkled his brow. "However, out of the goodness of my heart, I'll return half of this purse to you if you decide to buy Sanchia."

Lion's gaze narrowed. "Indeed? Now why is it you're so eager for me to accept your little slave girl?"

"It suits me to have her removed from Florence. I have my secrets also, my lord. Is it agreed?"

Lion gazed at him for a long moment before nodding slowly. "If Ballano can be persuaded to sell her, I'll accept your lady thief." He took the pouch from Caprino's hand. "Come to Giulia's tomorrow morning, and I'll return half the gold in the purse."

"You do not trust me?"

Lion's lips twisted in a mirthless smile. "Trust?" He turned and strode across the piazza.

Lorenzo strolled beside him. "You're going to see Ballano now?"

Lion nodded. "We've wasted too much time. I want to be at Solinari by Thursday."

"You think Camari may move the statue?"

"Who knows what that whoreson will do? He seldom does anything without a reason."

"He hates you," Lorenzo observed. "To keep you from getting something you want may be reason enough."

"Well, he won't succeed." Lion's lips tightened. "The Wind Dancer is mine, and I'll not let anyone take what belongs to me."

Lorenzo stopped as they reached a table near the door of a *trattoria* beneath the arcade on the south side of the piazza. "I'll wait for you here." He dropped onto a chair at the table and drew a slim volume from beneath his cloak. "You're being depressingly grim about this matter, and I have no interest in your petty haggling."

"By all means," Lion agreed ironically. "Heaven forbid you should be bored."

"My thought exactly." Lorenzo opened the book. "Though heaven gave up any interest in me a long time ago. Run along and conduct your business."

Lion shook his head, a faint smile on his lips. "As you command." He turned and strode away in the direction of the Via Calimala.

The rain was falling hard when Sanchia arrived at the print shop; a worried frown marred the serene beauty of Elizabet's face as she met Sanchia at the door. "Giovanni isn't back yet." She pulled Sanchia into the shop. "You're soaked. You're sure to catch a chill. Come and have some wine to warm you."

Sanchia shook her head. "Not now. I have to sleep." She moved heavily across the shop to the storage room and sank to her knees on her pallet. Sighing with weariness, she stretched out and pulled the worn quilt up to cover her chin. "Wake me when Giovanni comes back. Where are Piero and Bartolomeo?"

"Giovanni sent them to the wine shop to get a fresh jug for him." Elizabet leaned down to tuck the quilt more closely around Sanchia's thin body. "Sleep. I'll try to keep Giovanni from waking you."

Sanchia's lids felt as if they were weighted, and she could hold them open no longer. She had to sleep, if only for a little while. It probably would be for a mere few precious moments. She knew Elizabet would try to protect her, but the girl was too gentle-natured and free from guile to keep Giovanni from doing anything he wanted to do. If Messer Rudolfo was pleased with their work, Giovanni would quite likely bring back another commission and want them to start on it at once.

And Messer Rudolfo would be pleased, she thought with a glimmer of pride. She and Bartolomeo had done excellent work on the *Convivio*. Really excellent work . . .

"No, you can't wake her! What do you want with Sanchia?" The note of panic in Elizabet's voice pierced the heavy clouds of sleep beginning to surround Sanchia. Something was wrong, she thought drowsily. She had to force her eyes open. No, it was too difficult. Finally, she managed to awaken herself enough to stare sleepily at the man standing in the doorway.

Brilliant dark eyes looked at her from a face as stone hard as the statue of Lorenzo de'Medici in the piazza. Piazza! Shock cleared the last vestiges of sleep from her mind. This was the man in the piazza!

She sat bolt upright, her heart pounding wildly as she gazed up at him. The giant's massive body completely filled the doorway, and the tiny storeroom seemed to grow smaller by the second as if he were draining it of dimension in some magical way. Like Zeus drawing power from the heavens to loose his thunderbolts, she thought dazedly.

He smiled grimly. "I see you recognize me. It seems the theft of my purse didn't weigh on your conscience. You were sleeping as soundly as an infant in its mother's arms. Do you always nap after your thefts?"

Elizabet, somewhere beyond the giant's broad shoulders, gasped. Sanchia was too frightened to gasp, too frightened to speak, to frightened to do anything but stare at him.

He frowned. "Answer me."

"I don't . . ." She stopped and swallowed hard. "Are you going to imprison me?"

"Isn't that what should happen to thieves?"

Elizabet sobbed brokenly. "Sanchia, I told him not to come in. I told him . . ."

The man was ignoring Elizabet, his gaze fixed intently on Sanchia's face. "Isn't the Stinche where you belong?" he repeated.

"Yes, that's where thieves belong." She forced herself to meet his gaze. "But I no longer have your purse, and if you imprison me, you'll never get your gold back. They'll just cut off my hands and—" She had to stop as terror dried her throat. The bloody vision danced before her eyes and it was a moment before she could continue, "If you let me go free, I'll find a way to pay you back. I promise, my lord."

"The promise of a thief."

"I keep my word."

"A thief but not a liar?"

"I do lie," she said honestly. "Well . . . only when I must. Sometimes it's better to lie than have bad things happen to people. But I don't break my promises."

"Don't hurt her," Elizabet sobbed. "Please don't hurt her."

"Stop weeping," he said impatiently over his shoulder. "She's the one who should be crying."

"Sanchia never cries," Elizabet said.

"Sanchia what?" He turned back to Sanchia. "What's your full name?"

"Just Sanchia." She moistened her lips with her tongue. "I have no other."

He bowed mockingly. "Lionello Andreas, my illustrious lady thief. I think we're destined to become very well acquainted. Stand up and let me look at you."

She scrambled to her feet, hugging her shawl close

to her body to try to stop the shivering that attacked every limb.

"Come here."

She took one hesitant step toward him, then another.

"Stop." He held up his hand and grimaced distastefully. "Do you never bathe?"

"I bathe, my lord." Her eyes were enormous in her thin face as she gazed up at him. "Please, my lord, trust me. I'll return the money."

"I trust only a very few people in this world and none of them is a thief." His gaze ran over her. He scowled. "*Dio*, you're scrawny as a starved cat. Does Ballano never feed you?"

She stiffened. "You know Giovanni?"

"I haven't as yet had that pleasure. Where is he?"

"He'll be back soon," Elizabet wailed. "Couldn't you go before he returns?"

"Elizabet . . ." Sanchia drew a deep breath and tried to subdue her impatience. "Why don't you stand by the door and watch for Giovanni while I talk to his excellency?"

"Yes, Sanchia." Elizabet gave Andreas an uncertain glance and hurried from the room.

"She has the brain of a chicken," Lion said bluntly. "God, how I hate a whining woman."

"She's only fourteen," Sanchia said defensively. "And she's not stupid. You frighten her."

Lion's gaze narrowed on her face. "But not you?"

She nodded. "Me, too." She swallowed. "But being afraid won't save me. As you indicated, weeping and wailing only make men angry."

"Has that been your experience?" he asked, his expression intent.

"Men don't like tears. It makes them impatient, just as it did you, my lord." She stood very straight, gazing at him. "What can I do to keep you from taking me to prison?"

"What would you do?" he asked curiously.

"Anything," she whispered. "I can't leave them. They have no one but me."

"Who are 'they'?" His words were abstracted as his gaze ran over her. By the saints, the woman truly looked the scrawny feline he had named her, he thought with a flash of unreasonable irritation. Sanchia appeared to be little older than the sobbing child across the room; she was as tiny and fine-boned as a kitten. Her triangular face was oddly catlike, too, with its high cheekbones, olive skin, and slightly slanted eyes. Those eyes were strange—gold-amber in color and utterly appealing, even filled with terror as they were now. Her chestnut-colored hair looked as if it had been carelessly chopped and hacked until it was even shorter than his page Nicolo's. Now it was so rain dampened it clung in sodden curls about her thin face. "Who are you so concerned about?"

"Piero and Bartolomeo and Eliza—"

"He's coming," Elizabet cried frantically. "Sanchia, do something."

Sanchia paled. "Please go away. I beg you, my lord."

"You're afraid of this Giovanni?"

"Not for myself. He needs me, so he'll probably only beat me. But if he becomes very angry, he may decide to send them all away and he mustn't do that. I couldn't—"

"A thousand apologies for keeping you waiting, my lord." It was Giovanni's voice booming from the doorway. "How may I serve you?"

Sanchia held her breath, her gaze clinging to Lion's in desperation. She could detect no softening of his expression, only that strange, searching appraisal.

Then Andreas abruptly turned away from her to face Giovanni. "Signor Ballano, I am Lionello Andreas, and I've come to make you an offer."

"A commission?" Giovanni brushed by Elizabet and entered the shop. "I copy by hand or print. My work is known throughout Florence." Giovanni waved a hand at the printing press across the room. "It's the best machine in all Italy and I—"

"I want nothing copied," Lion interrupted. "I need a servant, and I heard you have a slave that may meet my requirements." He stepped aside and indicated

Sanchia standing in shocked immobility behind him. "I'll give you twenty-five ducats for her."

"Sanchia?" Giovanni's bloodshot eyes widened in surprise. "You want to buy Sanchia?"

"Why not? She's young and appears strong and healthy. She has many years of service left in her. That's why I'm willing to make so generous an offer. You should be able to replace her with no trouble."

"Twenty-five ducats," Giovanni repeated. He shook his head, trying to comprehend. "For Sanchia?"

"Is it a bargain?" Lion asked. "Do you have her papers?"

"In my chest in the other room. A bill of sale for the mother and her." Suddenly Giovanni's bewildered expression was replaced by craftiness. "It's not enough. How would I conduct my business? I've spent many years teaching her the skills of copying and running the press. Now you think to take her away from me for a mere twenty-five ducats?"

Cristo, the man was as greedy as Caprino, Lion thought in disgust. "Twenty-five ducats is more than fair."

"For an ordinary slave, perhaps, but Sanchia is not only skilled, she has a talent." Giovanni paused impressively. "She remembers everything. She has only to look at a leaf of script and she can recite it back to you."

"A pretty trick but of no value to me," Lion said impatiently. "Will you sell her or not?"

Giovanni was thinking quickly. "She's young enough to bear you children. That should be worth something."

"I'm not buying her to occupy my bed. She's hardly appetizing enough to interest me in that fashion."

Giovanni looked at Sanchia and reluctantly agreed. "True, but a woman is a woman when a man's blood runs hot. Perhaps you could—"

"I'm weary of this haggling." Lion reached in his belt and drew out his purse. "Fifty ducats. No more. Agreed?"

Giovanni's gaze fastened hungrily on the purse. "It's still too little. She works hard and . . ." He stopped as his glance met Lion's and took an involuntary step back. "Agreed, my lord."

"No!" Sanchia had been enveloped in a nightmare of shock and bewilderment, unable to believe this was happening until Giovanni's final words of assent jarred her from her stupor. She rushed toward Giovanni. "You can't do this. I can't go—"

"Quiet! Do you know how long it would take me to earn fifty ducats?"

"I won't leave them." She clutched at his arm. "You can't do this. How will they—"

She broke off as Giovanni's hand cracked against her cheek and sent her reeling away from him.

"Sanchia." Elizabet started toward her, tears running down her cheeks. "Oh, Sanchia."

Giovanni turned swiftly back to Lion. "She's not usually so unruly. A good beating now and then keeps her in order."

Lion's face hardened as he gazed at the livid mark appearing on Sanchia's cheek. "Don't touch her again. She's mine now and I'll discipline her as I see fit."

"I *won't* go with him." Sanchia's eyes were suddenly blazing. "This is wrong. I've served you well, you stupid fool."

Giovanni took three steps toward her. "Be silent or I'll—"

"Don't touch her." Lion's voice held steely menace. "Or by the saints, you'll regret it, Ballano."

Giovanni stopped and took a deep breath. "She'll be more obedient when she's away from those three strays. I should never have let her persuade me to take them in."

"They cost you nothing." Sanchia's voice was fierce. "I saw that they were fed. I took care of them."

"Sanchia, don't," Elizabet whispered.

"Why not?" Sanchia's eyes glittered with a recklessness born of desperation. "What can he do to me that he hasn't already done? He's a greedy fool who cares for nothing but his *vino*."

"Her papers and a bill of sale," Lion said quickly. The terrified kitten had suddenly grown claws, he noticed with exasperation. In another minute she would have Ballano so enraged he would refuse to sell her just to have the pleasure of beating her senseless. "I have no more time."

Giovanni cast a furious glance at Sanchia, then strode over to the scribe table and scrawled a few lines on the parchment lying on it. "There's your bill of sale. She's yours now." He turned and strode to the door leading to his quarters. "I'll get her papers from my chest."

Elizabet was weeping softly, and Sanchia instinctively turned to comfort her. "It will be all right. I'll find a way to take care of you."

"But Sanchia, what can you do?"

Lion studied Sanchia. The fury illuminating Sanchia's face was suddenly gone, and it gave him food for thought. If he had allowed her defiance of Ballano to continue, the sale might well have fallen through. Had the girl's anger only been a pretense directed toward that aim? "Yes, Sanchia, what can you do?" he ask silkily. "I'm beginning to wonder who was the slave all these years you've been with Ballano."

She turned to look at him. "There was no question who was the slave," she said bitterly.

"But you don't deny you were pretending anger just now to get what you wanted."

She shook her head. "No pretense. I was angry, but I wouldn't have let it run free if I hadn't thought it might keep Giovanni from selling me."

"A dangerous device. He might have hurt you badly."

"I would have healed. He wouldn't have killed me while I still have value to him. He's a fool, not a madman."

"You appear to know him well. But you don't know me at all. I'm not a fool, Sanchia."

Sanchia shivered. "I did not think you a fool. I wouldn't make that mistake."

"Here it is." Giovanni hurried toward them, a frayed leather folder in his hands. He handed the folder to Lion and received the purse of ducats in return. "I bought them both from a Spaniard who assured me they came of good strong stock. You've made a fine purchase."

"An interesting one at any rate." Lion was abruptly filled with disgust and an overwhelming urgency to be done with the man. "Go get your things, Sanchia. We're leaving this place."

Giovanni said quickly, "There's nothing for her to get. Slaves don't have possessions, my lord."

Sanchia lifted shaking fingers to her throbbing temple, trying to think. "I can't leave yet. There's Elizabet."

Giovanni's gaze shifted to Elizabet. "Elizabet is no longer your concern. However, I may be able to use her. She keeps the shop clean and I'll need someone to—"

"No," Sanchia said flatly. "She isn't going to stay here."

"And where else would she go?" Giovanni asked. "I'll give her a roof over her head and food for her belly. She can't expect more. I may take Bartolomeo, too, but Piero will have to go. He's too young to be of any help."

"You'll not keep any of them." Sanchia turned to Elizabet. "Go find Bartolomeo and Piero and meet me in the piazza."

Elizabet gazed at her in confusion.

"Hurry!" Sanchia gave her a little push. "All will be well."

"Stay," Giovanni ordered. "Obey me, Elizabet."

Elizabet gave him a frightened glance and fled from the shop.

Giovanni began to curse vehemently and obscenely as he turned to Sanchia. "They'll starve in the streets. You'll see, you arrogant bitch."

"No, they won't. I'll not let them starve." She gave him a level look over her shoulder as she moved toward the door. "And I'll not let them be used by you either. I know what you'd do to them if I weren't here. Bartolomeo would soon be as much a slave to you as I was and Elizabet would become your whore. I'll see you burn in hell before I let that happen." She turned to Lion. "We can go now."

"Thank you." Heavy irony laced Lion's tone. "May I remind you that it's you who belongs to me and not I to you?" He followed her from the shop into the street.

"No reminder is necessary." She drew her shawl closer to ward off the chill that came as much from the emotions storming through her as the coolness following the rain. She had to plan, she thought dully, but she was so exhausted and dazed it was difficult to think. "Why did you buy me?"

"Because it suited me, a whim perhaps."

She shook her head. "You're not an impulsive man. I don't think you'd do anything without a reason."

"You find me so easy to read?" Lion asked softly. "You'd be more clever to hide that ability."

"I *have* to understand you." She turned to look at him, desperation threading her voice. "I have to try to see what you are and what you want so that I can give it to you. So that I can find a way . . ." She stopped and drew a shaky breath. "Are you angry with me for stealing from you? Did you buy me so that you could torture me at your leisure?"

His lips tightened. "It doesn't amuse me to torture children."

"I'm not a child. I've reached my sixteenth year."

A sudden glint of humor appeared in his eyes. "In that case, perhaps I'll change my mind. I'll have to see if I can't rummage up a few instruments in the dungeon with which to torment you when we arrive at Mandara."

"We're leaving Florence?" She frowned. "That may present a problem."

"My profound apologies. You must be sure to inform me if my plans further inconvenience you." His sarcastic expression was quickly replaced by a grim look of warning. "We're leaving Florence tomorrow, and I'd advise you not to defy me as you did your former master."

"You're not like Giovanni." Her answer was as abstracted as her gaze. "But I have to know what you want from me."

"It's very simple. I want a slave who'll obey my every

demand without question. Why else would I have bought you?"

"I won't kill for you."

He lifted a brow. "If that's your only reservation, I believe I can accept it."

She braced herself and then said in a little rush, "I'll make a bargain with you."

"Everyone in Florence appears to want to bargain with me," he said dryly. "I can see why it's known as a city of merchants. But I feel bound to draw attention to the fact that I've no need to bargain with you. I've just paid fifty ducats for the doubtful privilege of owning you."

"And you wouldn't want to lose your money, would you?" She moistened her lips with her tongue. "If you'll let me have seventy-five ducats, I'll promise I won't run away from you and I'll serve you in any way you choose with complete loyalty. No matter what you ask of me."

Lion went still. "A threat? Do you know the punishment for a runaway slave?"

"Yes." Her voice was uneven. "But I'd still have to do it. I couldn't leave Elizabet and the others here unprotected. They belong to me."

He gazed at her a long moment and she could feel the perspiration bead on the back of her neck. *Dio*, she was taking a chance. She had known from the moment she had seen him in the piazza he was a dangerous man.

"What do you want to do with the money?" he asked.

"Ten ducats for Bartolomeo so he can apprentice for Messer Arcolo in his print shop. Arcolo is fair, and he has no sons to carry on the business. He'll give Bartolomeo a chance to be more than an apprentice once he realizes what a hard worker he is. Fifty ducats for Elizabet. Alessandro Benedetto, the baker's son, would take her to wife, but his father won't permit it unless she has at least a token dowry."

"She has a fondness for the boy?"

Sanchia shrugged. "Elizabet has a very gentle nature. She likes Alessandro well enough and would grow to love him in time. At least, she'd be safe from Giovanni and Caprino."

Lion's gaze became intent. "Caprino?"

"Caprino wants to use her in one of his brothels. I won't let that happen, but Caprino will have her if I'm not here to prevent it."

"I see." Lion's lips tightened. "A very cunning man, Caprino."

"You know him?"

"I'm beginning to know him better as time goes on."

"He mustn't get Elizabet. She wouldn't live more than a year in a brothel. She's too—" She stopped and then went on. "Fifteen ducats for Piero. Elizabet would take care of him, but I couldn't expect Alessandro's family to accept him without compensation."

"A dowry for Piero, too?" Lion murmured. "I'm beginning to feel like a matchmaker."

"It is not much money for a rich man," she said urgently. "And it would mean they'd all be safe and cared for."

"And give you no reason to run back here."

She nodded earnestly. "I told you I keep my promises. I'll be whatever you want me to be, if you'll only help them."

His gaze searched her face. "Complete obedience without question?"

She nodded.

"Absolute loyalty to me for as long as I own you?"

"Yes."

A crooked smile touched his lips. "Seventy-five ducats. So that's the price for the purchase of a soul these days."

She was bewildered. "What?"

"Never mind." He shifted his gaze from her face to the piazza a short distance away. "You shall have your seventy-five ducats."

Sanchia felt dizzy with relief. "Now?"

"Why not?" He nodded at a slim, elegant man seated at table beneath the arcade. "I'm sure my friend Lorenzo will be overjoyed to go with you to settle your flock in their new havens. He has such a sweet nature."

Sanchia's eyes widened. "You're jesting." She was sure there was nothing sweet about the man sitting at the table gazing down at the open book on the table in front of him. Neither a sweet temperament nor good looks, she thought as she stared at him. His dark brown hair was frosted with silver at the temples, his nose was too long and his complexion swarthy. The hollowed planes of his face and his deepset eyes reminded her vaguely of Fra Savonarola, who had been burned in the Piazza della Signoria when she was a child. Then he suddenly glanced up and Sanchia tensed. The man's gray eyes did not burn with a fanatical fervor as had the monk's but were as remote from human emotion as the stars on a winter night.

He closed the book and, as they approached, his gaze ran over Sanchia in cool appraisal. "She's younger than I thought. Will she be adequate?"

"She'd better be." Lion grimaced. "She's becoming a very expensive acquisition. If we don't get out of Florence soon, I may have to sell Mandara to pay for her."

Lorenzo stood up and bowed mockingly. "Lorenzo Vasaro, at your service, Madonna Sanchia."

A hint of mischief crossed Lion's face. "As a matter of fact, there is a service you can do her. How kind of you to offer."

"There they are." Sanchia had spied Elizabet, Bartolomeo, and Piero across the piazza. "I'll go get them and explain . . ." Her words trailed away as she started off at a run toward the children.

Lorenzo's gaze followed Sanchia across the wide piazza. She reached the children and began speaking quickly and with great urgency. "You haven't, by any chance, bought those other waifs, too?"

"Not exactly. But it appears our Sanchia has a very motherly nature and wishes to get her brood settled before she leaves the city. Go with her and spend what you need to make sure the children are safe." He frowned. "And get her something to eat. She looks half starved."

"*Our* Sanchia?"

Lion shrugged. "My Sanchia, then. It seems reasonable to set her mind at rest before taking her to Solinari."

"Very reasonable," Lorenzo said solemnly. "I can see

that you'd never want your slave to suffer the distresses of worry."

"You find it amusing?" Lion asked. "Gold doesn't always buy what we want, and I need her loyalty."

"And you think settling these three children will purchase what you want from her?"

Lion's gaze flew to Sanchia. She was kneeling on the flagstones beside the smallest child, speaking persuasively, her features illuminated with such a loving radiance that Lion found himself unable to look away from her. "Yes," he said slowly. "This will buy me what I want."

Three

"Where are you taking me?" Sanchia asked as she hurried to keep up with Lorenzo's long strides.

"The *casa* of Giulia Marzo," Lorenzo answered. "We're staying there while we're in Florence."

"I've heard of her. She's a famous courtesan and has many rich lovers. Is my lord Andreas rich? I guess he must be or he wouldn't have been able to pay so much for me. He mentioned a place called Mandara. Is that where we're going when we leave Florence? I've never been away from Florence since we came here when I was three. That's when I was sold to Giovanni and—"

"Enough!" Lorenzo sighed. "Don't you ever stop talking? You've chattered unceasingly since we left the baker's house."

"I always talk when I'm frightened."

Sanchia smiled tremulously. "And I'm very frightened right now. I feel . . . strange."

"You didn't appear frightened when you were arguing with that baker about your pretty Elizabet's dowry."

"That was different. Messer Benedetto had to be made to realize what a bargain he was getting in Elizabet. He has a very prosperous shop and could make a much better match for Alessandro. I was worried that if he wasn't totally satisfied with Elizabet he wouldn't accept Piero." She turned to look at him. "Thank the saints you were there. You helped to settle it far more quickly than I'd hoped."

"Me?" He lifted a brow. "I said nothing."

"I know, but that didn't matter. You made him feel uneasy and he wanted you gone. I think you must make most people uneasy."

"I don't appear to intimidate you," he said dryly. "Did no one ever tell you that it's not wise to be so frank? Many men wouldn't like to be told their presence makes one uneasy."

She looked at him in surprise. "But you don't mind. You've lived with it so long it's become a part of you."

"You're very perceptive." He studied her face. "You read people well. I noticed that with Messer Arcolo and then again with Benedetto. You sought out their desires and motives and then used them to suit yourself."

"It was necessary," she said simply. "Sometimes our wits are the only weapons we have. Haven't you found that to be true, Messer Lorenzo?"

"Yes." He was silent a moment. "But I wouldn't attempt to manipulate Lion as you did the good baker. It might prove dangerous."

"I wouldn't do that. I've given him my pledge." She tried to smile. "But it would make me feel better if you'd tell me something about Lord Andreas. I've never belonged to anyone but Giovanni and that wasn't like being a slave at all."

"Indeed? Because he was so kind to you?"

She shook her head. "Oh no, Giovanni is too selfish to be kind to anyone. It's too much trouble for him.

When I was a child I resented him, but when I came to realize what a stupid man he is it was easier." She shrugged. "All I had to do was give him what made him comfortable and he would leave me alone."

"Manipulation again," Vasaro murmured. "Taking in three children off the street doesn't seem the act of a selfish man."

"I had to convince him that it would be a purely selfish thing to do," Sanchia said. "Bartolomeo and Elizabet are brother and sister and lived next door to Giovanni. When their parents died of the fever three years ago they had no relations to help them and I couldn't let them be tossed into the streets. So I told Giovanni how clever everyone would think him if he took them into the shop. It would be as if he had three slaves instead of one—and without having to pay an extra ducat for them. I promised I'd see to it they were no trouble and that I'd share my food with them."

"Evidently you kept your word. You're skin and bones."

She made a face. "It didn't work. There was never enough food to go around. Then when Piero came to live with us, I knew something would have to be done. I was a slave, so I could work for no one but Giovanni, and every time I asked him for extra money he would threaten to throw the children out."

"So you began to steal." Vasaro's tone was expressionless. "That particular bit of charity could have cost you your hands."

She winced. "I know, but it wasn't charity." They started across the Ponte Vecchio, which was lined almost exclusively with the shops of prosperous silk merchants and goldsmiths. Sanchia saw none of them as she gazed into the cloudy waters of the Arno. "They were my family. I was afraid but I'd still do it again. I was so alone before they came."

"And now you're alone again."

"Nothing lasts forever." She added philosophically, "I would have had to do something to protect Elizabet soon anyway. She's too pretty and that's a danger for a woman. And Giovanni was drinking more and more and the business was failing and that meant Bartolomeo would have had to take a position elsewhere."

"And Piero?"

"Piero . . ." Her expression became wistful. "I hoped I could keep Piero for a while." She shook her head and blinked back the tears stinging her eyes. How stupid to cry now when she had managed to stay dry-eyed all through their farewells. Elizabet wept when confronted with any change, and Sanchia had seen tears in Bartolomeo's eyes when they had left him with Messer Arcolo. But Piero hadn't cried. He had only gazed at her with those fierce blue eyes and grasped her hand so tightly it had hurt for several minutes after Sanchia and Lorenzo had left the baker's shop. "But Piero will be safe with Elizabet. She's very loving and—" Her voice broke and she drew a deep breath. "They'll all be much better off than they were with Giovanni."

"And what of you?" Lorenzo's gaze searched her face. "Do you think you're better off too?"

"I don't know." She looked directly at him. "Am I?"

"I, too, do not know the answer." A faint smile touched his lips. "Lion has never had a slave before. It's going to be interesting to watch his reaction to the situation."

"And you'll like that, won't you? I think you must always stand back and watch as if we're all players for your entertainment." She was silent a moment and then asked, "If he doesn't have any other slaves, why did he buy me?"

"I think I'll let him tell you his plans for you."

She grinned coaxingly. "Don't you want to watch my reaction, too? If you tell me, I'll promise you that my response will be very satisfying."

Lorenzo smiled in genuine amusement. "Are you also trying to manipulate me? You must enjoy walking along the edge of a precipice."

"I'm sorry." The vitality in her face faded and she suddenly looked like a weary child. "I suppose it's become second nature. It's not that I mean to . . ." She stopped and then continued haltingly, "I'm afraid. *He* frightens me."

"Lion? You certainly didn't act frightened when you persuaded him to provide a handsome dowry for your little friends. On the contrary, you were exceptionally bold."

"Only because it was something I had to do." She moistened her lips. "He makes me feel . . ." She paused, searching for words. "I feel like I do in that last minute before I steal a fat purse. Scared and trembling but excited too."

"Hmmm. Interesting."

"Help me." Her hand clutching the wool shawl at her breast tightened. "I didn't feel helpless with Giovanni, but I do with Lord Andreas."

"Why should I help you? Lion is my friend and you're nothing to me." He spoke with complete detachment.

Sanchia's hopes plummeted. "I can't think of any reason why you should help me." She paused, considering. "Unless it's because you'd find it more amusing to make things a little easier for me. A scared mouse scurrying around Lord Andreas wouldn't be nearly as entertaining for you."

He suddenly chuckled. "You are anything but a scared mouse." He paused. "Lion's fair. Serve him well and he'll not misuse you."

Sanchia felt a surge of relief as she thought she recognized the slightest break in the wall that Lorenzo Vasaro used to distance himself from everyone around him. "He has the manner of a great lord. Is he very rich?"

He was silent a moment, and she began to think he wasn't going to answer. "He's lord of the city-state of Mandara. He has great wealth but only the one fief. His father was a condottiere and raised Lion to follow after him. Lorenzo de' Medici gave Lion's father Mandara in payment for waging war against one of his less friendly neighbors."

"Where is Mandara?"

"To the south. Between Florence and Pisa."

"And now Lord Andreas is the lord of the city?"

Vasaro nodded. "Since his father died some thirteen years ago. Lion continued as condottiere and maintained his father's armies until he decided to disband them two years ago and return to Mandara." Vasaro gazed at her inquiringly. "Well, have you gouged enough from me to abate your fears?"

"No." She sighed. "I suppose you wouldn't reconsider and tell me why Lord Andreas bought me?"

Vasaro didn't answer.

"I didn't think so."

"Then you shouldn't have wasted—" he broke off and stopped short. "*Santa Maria*, what is that?"

They were crossing the Mercato Nuovo where bankers with ledgers and fat purses sat at their green-covered tables. However, it was not the bankers at whom Vasaro was staring but a plump man surrounded by a crowd of snickering onlookers. "Am I mistaken or is that obese personage peeling down his hose?"

"Oh, that's only a bankrupt," Sanchia said indifferently. "In order to be discharged he has to strike his naked buttocks three times on that black-and-white marble circle that marks the site of the symbolic Chariot of Florence."

"How undignified." Vasaro's lips suddenly began to twitch with amusement as he resumed walking across the *mercato*. "Lion was worried that you might beggar him. I must warn him if he does becomes bankrupt, it most certainly must not happen in this illustrious city."

"I did not ask for so much. It was necessary to—"

"Peace." Lorenzo held up his hand. "I'm not interested in your protests and explanations. Let me have a little blessed silence for a time."

They walked in silence for a short while until Lorenzo finally said, "Giulia's house is around the next corner." He cast a glance at her. "I wonder if she'll let you through her front door. I found Madonna Giulia very particular about all the appointments of her establishment."

She frowned. "I won't steal anything."

"Your larcenous nature wasn't what I was referring to." He wrinkled his nose. "You have a great and profound need for a bath."

"I'm clean. I bathed only this morning. It's the—" She stopped as they turned the corner, her eyes widening in pleasure as she caught sight of the impressive two-story house. "What a truly splendid *casa*. It looks as grand as a palazzo. You wouldn't think a whore could do this well for herself, would you? It seems strange that men would be foolish enough to pay so much to fornicate with a woman when the pleasure lasts for such a short time."

His lips twitched. "It doesn't seem strange to me. But then I, too, am one of those foolish men."

She turned and looked at him speculatively. His manner was so icy, so remote it was difficult for her to imagine him rutting with one of the strumpets in this splendid house. "Do you really fornic—"

"I think you've asked quite enough questions for the moment," he interrupted as he took her elbow and nudged her toward the elaborately carved door of the front entrance. He didn't look at Sanchia as he opened the door and murmured, "And yes, on occasion, I most certainly do."

"If you want your little slave girl to be permitted to spend the night here, I think you'd better come along and intercede with Giulia." Lorenzo stood leaning on the jamb of the doorway of Lion's chamber. He covered a delicate yawn with his long, slender hand. "I settled Sanchia's flock in their new nests but I refuse to involve myself between two quarreling women."

"Where is she?" Lion stood up and moved quickly toward the door. The glimmer of malicious mischief underlying Lorenzo's pretense of boredom always boded trouble. *Cristo*, what was wrong now? Nothing had gone as he had planned since he had caught sight of Sanchia on the piazza this afternoon.

"In Giulia's chamber." Lorenzo followed him down the hall. "We'd no sooner crossed the threshold than Giulia appeared in the hall and took offense at your little Sanchia's . . ." He paused before continuing euphemistically, "unusual fragrance. She insisted on calling her servants and dragging the child up to her chamber for a bath."

"Which Sanchia clearly needs."

"But which Sanchia clearly doesn't want. When I last saw her she was being forcibly restrained by two of Giulia's maidservants while Giulia herself was undressing her." Lorenzo opened the door of Giulia's chamber. "Ah, I see they have her in the tub. What wonderful progress."

"Why won't you *listen* to me, you stupid woman? I don't need a bath." It was Sanchia's voice, the tone almost as fierce as when she had spoken to Giovanni.

Lion strode into the chamber and then stopped short. "My God, what's happened here?"

Clothing was tossed all over the chamber as if blown by a gale wind, Giulia Marzo's golden hair was hanging loose about her shoulders, the rope of pearls usually binding it had broken and pearls were scattered over the floor. The bodice of her sea blue gown bore a three-cornered rip and torrents of water were splashed on the floor, on Giulia, and on the two servants holding the struggling Sanchia in the hip bath while Giulia attempted to scrub her.

Sanchia's gaze flew to Lion and she suddenly stopped fighting. "They wouldn't listen to me. I tried to tell them that it wouldn't do any good."

"She stinks," Giulia said between her teeth. "Lorenzo tells me this she-devil belongs to you, but I won't have her in my house until I've purged her of this vile odor." Giulia dipped a cloth into the water and then scrubbed vigorously at Sanchia's neck.

"You're hurting me." Sanchia's amber eyes blazed up at Giulia. "And it will do no good. I'm clean!"

She certainly appeared clean, Lion noticed bemusedly. The golden skin on Sanchia's shoulders gleamed above the cloudy water, and she wasn't nearly as thin as he had believed when she had worn that loose gown.

"Tell her to listen to—" Sanchia broke off as she met Lion's gaze. Her eyes widened, and she stared at him as if mesmerized while a delicate pink tinted the gold of her cheeks. Then she swallowed and drew a shaky breath. "Please, my lord, tell her to stop."

Lion gazed at her without speaking.

"*Please*, my lord." Sanchia's amber eyes were enormous in her triangular face.

"I do like a woman who says please."

There was an intensity in his soft voice that caused Giulia to look at him sharply over her shoulder. "Lion, don't interfere. This is necessary."

"Her body looks clean enough to me." He dropped down on the cushioned chair a few yards away from the tub and stretched his legs out before him. His intent gaze returned to Sanchia's pink-tipped breasts which could be glimpsed just below the surface of the water. The god Eros couldn't have created nipples more arousingly pointed and amazingly sensual. "There's no use scraping and reddening that exquisite skin if there's no need, Giulia."

"But the stench is—"

"It's my *hair*," Sanchia broke in with exasperation. "If you'd listened to me, I would have told you. Every morning after my bath I rub a mixture into it. It's my hair that stinks and needs cleansing."

Giulia sat back on her heels and gazed blankly at Sanchia. "You rub something this foul-smelling into your hair?"

Sanchia nodded. "Since I was twelve. Garlic, fish oil, and—"

Giulia quickly held up her hand. "Don't go on. I don't want to know."

"I do," Lorenzo said from the doorway. "Fascinating."

Lion's gaze narrowed on her face. "I'm not as interested in the mixture itself as in her reason for concocting it."

"Giovanni has a very keen sense of smell," Sanchia said simply. "When my mother was alive, every morning he would make her bathe and perfume herself. Then he'd have her kneel naked on the floor of the shop and take her as a dog takes a bitch in the street. After my

mother died I knew that soon I'd be old enough for
Giovanni to try to use me in the same way."

Lorenzo chuckled. "You chose an exceptionally
powerful deterrent."

Lion didn't feel the same amusement. He found he
was experiencing a multitude of wild emotions that took
him completely off guard. Anger and pity battled with
an odd sense of guilt at the mental image that persisted
in coming before his eyes. The image of Sanchia kneeling naked on the floor, looking back over her shoulder
with those huge amber eyes, her pink tongue moistening
her lips with nervousness.

Lust seared him, twisting through his groin in a
scalding tide as he realized that the man in his imagination, the man at whom she was gazing, the man she was
ready to receive into her body, was not Giovanni Ballano.

It was himself.

He abruptly rose to his feet. "Wash her hair," he
muttered as he turned away. "And then bring her to my
chamber."

Lorenzo followed Lion from Giulia's room, down
the hall, and into Lion's chamber. He strolled to the
table across the room and poured a stream of red wine
from a silver pitcher into two goblets. "Have a little
wine." He turned to hand one of the goblets to Lion, his
gaze flicking mockingly to Lion's lower body. "I think
you need cooling."

"Is that why you took me to 'intercede'?" Lion sat
down in the large chair by the window. "What game are
you playing at now, Lorenzo?"

"I don't know what you mean." Lorenzo gazed at
him with limpid innocence. "Your little street urchin
seemed very concerned about learning what and who
you are, and I thought it would be a kindness to throw
you both into a situation where revelations would naturally occur." He smiled. "Which they did. I had no idea
Sanchia would be so alluring. She has truly exquisite
breasts."

"Yes." Lion's hand tightened on the stem of his goblet as the memory of Sanchia clad only in wisps of steam and cloudy water returned to him. "But I didn't buy her to occupy my bed."

"I know. Which makes the possibilities all the more intriguing." Lorenzo dropped onto the embroidered cushions of the chair by the table and raised his goblet to his lips. "I look forward with great anticipation to watching developments between the two of you."

"You mean you look forward to watching us writhe on the stake you're trying to skewer us with," Lion said dryly. "I doubt if we'll furnish you with as much pleasure as you hope. I don't know why you foresee my bedding Sanchia to be in any way unusual when I've had more women than I can count in these last years."

"Ah, but there's one difference. You own Sanchia. She belongs to you." Lorenzo's gaze narrowed with satisfaction on Lion's face. "And no one in this world is more possessive than you, Lion. You can't bear to let anything you own be taken away from you. Look how you're moving heaven and earth to get the Wind Dancer back, and it's only a statue."

Lion's fingers tightened on the stem of the goblet. "It's more than a statue."

"To your family perhaps." Lorenzo shrugged. "To you it's some kind of holy relic you guard and protect. To me it seems more like a beautiful siren luring men to destruction."

"Sanchia isn't the Wind Dancer."

"No, but as your property she's bound to arouse the same instincts." Lorenzo sipped his wine, smiling at Lion over the rim of the goblet. "What do you think will happen when you take her to Mandara?"

"I'm not taking her to Mandara."

Lorenzo lifted a brow. "She said you told her you were taking her there."

"That was before I . . ." Lion trailed off, his dark brows knotting in a fierce frown as he took a long swallow of wine.

"Before you decided to take her to your bed?"

Lion met his gaze. "Yes." The intention that had

been forming since the moment he had seen Sanchia in the hip bath was suddenly made. "Why not? As you say, she belongs to me."

"There's no reason at all why you shouldn't take her." Lorenzo looked down into the ruby depths of his wine. "I thoroughly approve."

"Which should immediately make me wary. Why do you want Sanchia to become my mistress?"

"I admire her."

Lion gazed at him in astonishment. He couldn't remember the last time Lorenzo had indicated he felt anything positive for a stranger. True, admiration wasn't liking, but the confession was still out of the ordinary.

Lorenzo noticed his surprise. "No, it's true. She reminds me of myself when I was growing up in the streets of Naples. She fights with every weapon she has to survive and invents new ones when the old ones don't win the day." He shrugged. "It's a pity she has such a soft heart. It's a weakness that will probably destroy her."

"And because you admire her, you want to put her in my bed."

"It will give her a weapon. She has none against you now. The child has the ridiculous belief that promises must be kept. You'd think she would have learned better leading the life she has."

"She has no need for weapons," Lion said impatiently. "I have no intention of being cruel to her."

"Oh yes, she'll need weapons." Lorenzo's index finger circled the rim of his goblet. "When you take her to Mandara."

Lion stiffened. "I don't take my mistresses to Mandara."

"You'll take Sanchia. Because she belongs to you."

"No, *per Dio*, you know I never—"

"You will this time." Lorenzo cut in, lifting his gaze from the goblet. "I look forward to seeing what will result."

"Because you enjoy watching all our lives thrown into a turmoil for you to savor."

For the first time the mockery faded from Lorenzo's

face. "No, because that foolishness at Mandara has gone on too long. It's time someone changed the course of events."

"Stay out of it, Lorenzo. It's my choice."

The mockery instantly returned to Lorenzo's face. "I don't think I could bear to do that. Our last stay at Mandara offered me no amusement whatsoever. All that sweetness and knightly restraint . . . It made me quite ill."

"How regrettable. I fear you must resign yourself to it. I take no bedmates to Mandara."

"We shall see." Lorenzo drained the last of his wine, set the goblet on the table and stood up. "Now I bid you good night. Do tell me in the morning how you enjoyed your little Sanchia." He moved toward the door. "Do you suppose she's a virgin? The possibility never occurred to me until she told us of her ingenious perfume." His gray eyes gleamed silver in the candlelight as he glanced back over his shoulder. "How splendid for you if she is. Think how tight she'll be around you and how sweet to hear the little cries of wonder and newfound delight." He added softly as he opened the door, "And that would make her all the more yours, wouldn't it?" He started to close the door and then paused. "Ah, Sanchia, how charming you look . . ." He sniffed experimentally. "And smell. Go right in, Lion's expecting you." He threw open the door and stepped aside. "*Buona sera*, ladies."

Sanchia and Giulia entered the room, stopped just inside the door. With a jerky motion of her head Giulia indicated Sanchia. "Well, does she please you?"

Lion's gaze traveled slowly over Sanchia's small form. It was clear to Lion that Giulia was not pleased with the intruder and less with Lion's response to her and had probably given her the most humble garment in all the wardrobes in this house. The simple velvet gown Sanchia wore was of a rich brown shade, but had no elaborate trim or embroidery. The tight sleeves came to her wrists, and the line of the gown was straight and graceful falling from the low square neckline of the bodice. Yet the darkness of the gown made the olive of Sanchia's skin glow golden, and the low square neckline revealed the lovely line of her throat and the swell of her small breasts against the velvet of the bodice.

Lion's gaze lingered on the bare golden flesh of her upper breasts and felt a stirring in his loins so intense it approached pain. "Yes, she pleases me."

"It took three scrubbings to get that stench out of her hair." Giulia's lips tightened as she noticed Lion's gaze was still on Sanchia. "I suppose you'll not want me tonight?"

"No."

Giulia whirled, her blue velvet skirt flying. "You're mad. If you wish a change, I can supply you with ten women who are more beautiful than this . . . this . . . child!"

The door slammed behind her.

"I don't like her," Sanchia said flatly.

"Then I'm sure it won't bother you to know that she has the same feelings toward you." Lion's gaze lifted from the delicate line of Sanchia's throat. "Your hair is still damp."

"I don't know why it should be. She and those two women nearly smothered me toweling it dry."

The color of her hair was not the brownish red he had first thought, Lion realized. The mixture she had put on it must have dulled its color along with its luster. Now, though it was still water-darkened, the candlelight revealed the fiery shimmer of auburn. "Come here and let me look at you."

She hesitated and then walked slowly toward him. She moved with grace, her shoulders back, her spine straight. There was a militance about her stance reminiscent of a soldier marching into battle, he thought suddenly.

She stopped before him. "She's right, you know." Her voice was breathless. "I'm not comely. I'm too skinny, and I don't have that lovely pale skin that Elizabet and Giulia Marzo have. You won't be pleased with me."

Lion leaned back in his chair. "You're wrong. As I told Giulia, I'm very pleased with you." His gaze went again to the smooth flesh of her shoulders. "And I like

the shade of your skin. It reminds me of the gold of—"
He stopped. He had been going to compare her to the
Wind Dancer, he realized with a sense of shock. It must
have been Lorenzo's remark that had brought the
connection to mind. Possession. The Wind Dancer.
Sanchia.

He lifted his goblet to his lips. "You know why
you're here?"

"Yes." She moistened her lips with her tongue. "I
knew when I saw you looking at me when I was in the
bath. It's the same way Giovanni looked at my mother.
You want to use my body."

The comparison irritated him. "I'm not Ballano,"
Lion said harshly.

"You had me bathed. You had me perfumed." She
drew a quivering breath. "Do you want me to take off
this gown and kneel on the floor now?"

"No!" The explosive rejection surprised him as
much as it did her. "There are more pleasurable ways of
taking a woman than if she were a bitch in heat."

"Yet the idea excited you," Sanchia said. "I saw that
you were—"

"You see too much." A sudden thought struck him.
"Are you trying to change my mind by comparing me to
Ballano? Lorenzo said you use every weapon you
possess."

"But I have no weapons here," she said simply. "I
gave you my promise that I'd obey you."

No weapons. Lorenzo had said that, too, Lion
recalled with frustration. She belonged to him. It was his
right to use her body as he chose, with either tenderness
or brutality. She knew this and accepted it. Why, then,
was he feeling as if he had to make excuses for bedding
her? "It doesn't have to be as it was with Ballano. I'll give
you pleasure and—"

"No." Her eyes widened with bewilderment. "Why
do you lie to me? It's always the man who has the
pleasure. Women are merely vessels who accept them
into their bodies and take their seed. Never once did my
mother have pleasure."

"Because she was treated like an animal." Lion set

the goblet down on the windowsill with a force that splashed the remaining wine on the polished wood. "I'll show you ways . . ." He stopped as he saw she was looking at him with complete disbelief.

He smiled with sudden recklessness. "Ah, a challenge. Shall I make you a promise, my doubting Sanchia? Suppose I tell you that I'll not use you as my 'vessel' until you beg me to do it. Until you're willing to kneel and let me use you as Giovanni did your mother because you yearn to have me inside you."

She looked at him in wonder. "Why should you make me a promise? You need not consider my feelings. I belong to you. It doesn't matter if I feel nothing when—"

"It matters to me." His tone held exasperation as well as barely concealed violence. "God knows why, but it does." He took her hand and pulled her to her knees before his chair. "And I'll probably regret that promise a thousand times before this is over. Now lift your head and look at me."

She obediently tilted back her head and she caught her breath at what she saw in his face. His eyes held dark, exotic mysteries and the curve of his lips was blatantly sensual.

"What do you see?"

"You want me."

"Yes." His big hands fell heavily on her slender shoulders. "And whenever I look at you from now on I'll be thinking of what I'd like to do to you." One calloused hand released her shoulder and began to stroke her throat. Her skin was as velvet-soft as it looked and warm, so warm. . . . He felt hot lust tear through him, adding dimension to his manhood. "I'm going to touch you whenever I like." He slipped the material of the gown off her shoulders. "When it pleases me, I'll bare this pretty flesh and fondle you. No matter where we are. No matter who is watching."

She was gazing at him as if mesmerized, the pulse fluttering wildly in the hollow of her throat.

"Are you a virgin?"

She moistened her lips with her tongue. "Yes."

"Good." He felt a primitive jolt of satisfaction so deep it almost obliterated the memory of Lorenzo's words. "Thank the saints for that obnoxious mixture, whatever it was."

"It was fish oil and garlic and chicken dro—" She broke off as his hand slipped beneath the bodice of the gown and one hard palm touched the nipple of her breast. He could feel the hard pounding of her heart beneath his fingertips. She closed her eyes. "I remember now. You didn't want to know."

"I'd rather know why your breast is swelling so sweetly under my hand."

"Is it? I don't know why. Maybe I'm falling ill. I feel quite peculiar."

"You're not ill." His palm moved back and forth on her breast, stroking it as if it were a favorite kitten. "You'll always respond like this when I touch you." He squeezed her breast gently.

Sanchia's eyes flew open and wild color stained her cheeks. She looked down at his big hand covering her breast. "This gives you pleasure?"

"Oh yes, as much pleasure as it gives you."

"It doesn't give me pleasure. It makes me feel hot and I ache . . ."

Lion squeezed her breast again, running his thumbnail over the rosy tip. "So do I. That's how pleasure starts." His thumb and forefinger began to pull teasingly at her pointed nipple. How would it feel in his mouth when he sucked and teethed it? he wondered. The thought caused his fingers to tighten with unconscious cruelty.

A shudder trembled through her and her gaze flew to his face.

His fingers instantly released her. "That was a mistake. I didn't mean to hurt you."

"You didn't. It just felt . . . odd."

Lion looked down at her. He knew he had gone far enough for now. Not nearly far enough for him, he thought ruefully, but if he didn't leave her at this moment, he wouldn't leave her for the night.

Cristo, why was he leaving her when he was rock

hard and burning to be inside her sweet tightness? So she wasn't ready for him, he would be gentle and— His lips tightened as he realized he was lying to himself. He was too hungry for her and he could never control a hunger such as this if he were between her thighs. He would go wild and drive and plunge in a frenzy of lust until she would think him the same rutting dog as Ballano.

The comparison to Ballano caused him to reluctantly release her breast and draw his hand from the velvet bodice. "Stand up," he said hoarsely.

Bright flags of color burned in her cheeks as she gazed at him in confusion.

"Stand up. It's done." His lips twisted in a smile. "For now."

She scrambled to her feet and took a step back. "You're not going to touch me anymore?"

He stood up and started for the door. "Undress and go to bed."

"Where?"

He gestured to the bed across the room. "Did you think I meant for you to sleep on a blanket on the floor as Ballano did?"

"But that's your bed," she stammered.

"All the more reason for you to occupy it. My bed, my slave. Lorenzo says I have a very possessive nature. If that's true, then I should enjoy seeing you in my bed when I return."

"Where are you going?"

"To Giulia's chamber." Lion's smile held a hint of cruelty. "I need a woman, and Giulia is always accommodating. Unlike you, she knows how to take pleasure as well as give it. She doesn't care what arouses me as long as I pleasure her enough. She'll even be grateful to you."

"I don't think so." Sanchia frowned. "And perhaps she only pretends pleasure. I've heard whores do that."

He looked at her blankly. He had never even considered that possibility. Could Giulia really be . . .

Sanchia started to laugh.

Cristo, the little devil was needling him, he realized

with astonishment. First she had shown the most abject compliance, and now her face was alight with mischievous laughter. A laughter so infectious that a reluctant smile appeared on his own lips. "I'll ask her." His gaze met hers. "If you'll ask yourself if you were pretending."

Her laughter vanished as her long lashes quickly lowered to veil her eyes. "I told you—"

"That it wasn't pleasure," he finished for her. "Think about it when you're lying in bed while I'm gone. I believe you'll discover it was pleasure you felt tonight." His voice lowered to sensual softness. "And as you lie there know that I'm giving Giulia even more pleasure, the pleasure you could have had." He turned to leave. "Sleep well, Sanchia." The door closed with a firm click behind him.

Sanchia gazed wonderingly at the panels of the door. What a strange man he was. He had wanted to take her in the same animal way Giovanni had used her mother. Nothing had been clearer to her as he had sat there watching her while she was in the bath. Why had he not done it? Women were always fair prey to a man whether they were slaves or free women. Sometimes she had thought being a slave was even a little better. At least slaves, as property, were usually provided food and a blanket to cover them. A free woman, if she was comely, as often as not ended up in one of Caprino's brothels. If she was ugly, she might starve in the streets.

When she had awakened to see Lord Andreas standing in the doorway of the storage room, she had been filled with the greatest terror she had ever known. Not only because of her fear of retribution, but because she could not read him. She sensed enormous power and could not guess in which way it might be directed. His motives and actions were an enigma, and that frightened her. She had always believed that to understand was to conquer or at least survive, but without knowledge she was helpless.

She slowly began to unfasten the gown she had so recently donned, her gaze still fixed on the panels of the door. What would he do when he returned? she wondered. His words had been so queer. She had not meant to challenge him, but he appeared to think she had. Was it because she was a virgin? How strange, when remaining untouched had always meant very little to her.

She had known it was inevitable she would lose her virginity, either to Giovanni or to some other man who might catch her unaware on the street. It had almost happened a few months ago when she had been jerked into the alley by a seaman who'd been too wild for a woman to notice the scent of her. She had known better than to waste her breath screaming. Rape happened so often in those back alleys that it provoked no more than a raised eyebrow and a quickening of pace away from the scene. Only luck and a kick in the bastard's private parts had enabled her to get away from him.

Losing her virginity wouldn't have been as important to her as the unfairness of having it taken without her consent. It had always seemed to her that a woman's virginity was greatly overrated. She could see it would be important to ascertain whether a man's son was his own through a wife's purity, but where marriage was not involved it was surely stupid for men to obtain such pleasure from being first with a woman.

Yet Lionello Andreas was not stupid, and his face when he had learned she was a virgin had expressed such intense primitive satisfaction it had given her a queer hot feeling in the pit of her stomach. His hands on her body had evoked the same aching sensation that fell somewhere between pain and hunger.

Hunger? She shook her head as she took off the gown and undershift and laid them carefully on the chair by the table. Why had that word occurred to her? Hunger was for food and rest and for the lovely words in books, not for a man's hands on her body. It must be exhaustion that was making her so sluggish and dimwitted.

She pulled back the velvet spread and slipped beneath it. It was a pity she was too tired to fully appreciate the softness of the mattress and the clean fragrance of pine resin and laurel leaves that clung to the linens. She had never slept in a real bed before and wished she could savor the luxury of the moment. She had always believed moments of pleasure must always be lived to the hilt because the next might never come. During the bad times, she could bring out the memory of a moment of beauty and suddenly the situation would not seem so terrible that she could not get through it.

Sleep beckoned with an irresistible allure. She should really get up and blow out the candle so Lord Andreas would not think she was careless and wasteful. . . .

Four

Cristo, what the hell was the matter with him?

Lion gazed down at Sanchia seething with a frustration that almost exceeded the lust hardening every muscle of his body.

Candlelight flickered over the rich auburn of Sanchia's hair and stroked the silky smoothness of her bare shoulders above the coverlet. She was curled on her side, her cheek buried in the pillow, her pink lips slightly parted. Why did he not wake her and tell her she must take him into her body and let him use her to rid himself of his terrible need? She was his property. She had given him her promise that she would obey him in all things. She would yield her body to him without complaint.

Yield. He wished the word had not come to him, for it evoked memories of the many cities that had yielded to his sword. Rape and pillage invariably followed those surrenders.

Looting and raping were the rewards a victorious army expected, his father had taught, and Lion had grown accustomed to both over the years. In spite of Lorenzo's mocking charge he knew well that chivalry was only for fools.

Yet he did not want Sanchia to yield to him because he owned her and she had no choice.

Santa Maria, what was the matter with him? He had been unable to muster any desire for Giulia after he had left Sanchia, and the failure had shocked and outraged him. He had stormed out of her chamber with every intention of satisfying the hunger that Giulia had been unable to appease. A man was a fool to worry about challenges when he needed a woman's body to put out the fires. Since his body was issuing this peculiar demand for Sanchia alone, it was only sensible he should give it what it wanted.

He reached out and drew the coverlet down so he could see Sanchia from the top of her shining hair to her small feet. She was a brilliant butterfly against the stark white linen sheet, all velvet golden flesh and silky wine colored hair. Why did he find her slender loveliness a thousand times more arousing than Giulia's more voluptuous beauty? He had always preferred full-figured women. . . .

Ah, this was better. The blood was pounding in his veins and the quickening in his loins was gaining in intensity until it was almost unbearable. In another moment there would be no question of stopping himself from mounting Sanchia.

He bent closer, his gaze on the pinkness of her distended nipples. Her breasts were truly magnificent. The mere thought of touching them sent his heart slamming against his rib cage. He would have to have gowns made for her that would reveal the beauty of her bosom and—

Sanchia stirred, sighed, and rolled over on her back.

Dio, she was small. She looked like a child except for those erotic breasts and the soft thatch of hair protecting her womanhood.

But she was no child, he quickly reminded himself.

She had said she was sixteen; most women had been wedded and bedded for at least two years by the time they had reached her age. His mother had given birth to him when she was fifteen. He should feel no guilt about Sanchia's age, and not a single compunction because of her helplessness to resist him.

Sanchia murmured in the inarticulateness of sleep.

Lion's gaze flew to her face. Her long lashes cast dark shadows on the curves of her cheeks. But there was another shadow high on her right cheek, he noticed suddenly. Then he realized it was not a shadow but a faint bruise where Giovanni had struck her. He remembered Sanchia's head snapping back with the force of the blow and the fierceness of the anger that had torn through him. He had wanted to kill the whoreson. How dare that bastard touch his property? Couldn't he see how tiny and helpless Sanchia was, how easily she could be bruised and hurt? If that blow had been a little harder, it could have killed her or at least—

No, by God, he wouldn't think how vulnerable she was, but only how much he desired her. He deliberately summoned the image and feelings that had assaulted him when he'd first drawn down the coverlet to reveal her naked body.

A brilliant butterfly. All color and soft velvety textures.

But butterflies were the most fragile of creatures.

Butterflies could be broken and destroyed with only the careless brush of a man's hand.

And he was not Giovanni.

He could wait until she recovered from this exhaustion and felt more secure under his rule.

After all, the woman was vital to him as a thief. She would bring him what he needed and any additional pleasure he took in her would be only secondary.

He straightened and then reluctantly drew the coverlet up to Sanchia's chin. Yes, he could wait.

Perhaps.

He turned away and blew out the flame of the candle.

But he could not stay away from her if he remained

in this bed . . . or even in this room. He moved silently toward the door while considering his options. He couldn't return to Giulia's chamber. She had been most irate when he had left her. Only one solution occurred to him given the lateness of the hour.

He grimaced as he realized he would have to go to Lorenzo's chamber and face his raised brows and faintly malicious amusement.

Oh yes, Lorenzo would take an unholy joy in Lion's predicament.

"Wake up." Giulia's hand on Sanchia's shoulders was less than gentle as she shook her. "Get up. They're waiting for you downstairs."

Sanchia opened drowsy eyes to see Giulia Marzo's flushed face above her. Giulia was angry again, she realized hazily, almost as angry as she had been last night when she had left Sanchia with Lion. "I'm awake." She sat up in bed, and blinked as the early morning sunlight streaming through the window assaulted her with its brilliance. "What time is it?"

"Nearly eight o'clock."

Eight o'clock! Sanchia couldn't remember when she had slept past dawn. She scrambled out of bed, reaching frantically for the clothes she'd laid on the chair the night before. "I didn't mean to sleep this late. Is Lord Andreas displeased with me?"

"You'll have to ask him." Giulia moved toward the door. "He's not a man who likes to be kept waiting." She glanced back over her shoulder as she opened the door. "There's wine and fruit on the table. Eat quickly and join Lord Andreas downstairs in ten minutes."

"Five." Sanchia was dressing hurriedly. "I don't need to eat. Messer Lorenzo bought me bread and fruit yesterday at the baker's. I can—"

"Eat." Giulia's beautiful features were set with a less than attractive hardness. "Lion told me to make sure you broke your fast before you started the journey. He won't be any more displeased with you now than he will be five minutes from now." Giulia smiled with a hint of malice.

"Or perhaps you feel you need to curry favor after last night? I told Lion he'd find no pleasure with you."

Sanchia stared at Giulia in bewilderment. The woman was a wasp trying to sting her with hurtful words, but how could they wound when they made no sense? After all, Lion had spent the night in Giulia's bed. "That's what I told him too. He didn't appear to believe me."

Giulia's hand tightened on the knob of the door. "Insolence."

"No, I didn't mean—"

"You may please him for a few weeks, but he'll grow tired of bedding a child with no more meat on her bones than a scrawny foul." Giulia's blue eyes blazed. "And then he'll come back to Florence and to me. You'll never be able to hold him."

"The question will never arise," Sanchia said quietly. "You forget, I belong to him. *He* holds *me*."

For some reason her answer only seemed to make Giulia more angry. She muttered an obscenity and slammed the door.

Sanchia flinched, then thrust her feet into slippers and finished fastening her gown. She cast a wistful glance at the apple quarters and cup of wine on the silver tray on the table. A real apple. She'd had a taste of one a few years before, but this one certainly looked riper and more juicy. Perhaps she could have just one bite. . . .

She sighed and started for the door. Lion was too much the unknown quantity for her to risk angering him. She could put no store in Giulia's assurance that he would not be irritated if she kept him waiting longer since the woman obviously wished her ill.

Sanchia hesitated at the top of the stairs when she heard voices. Caprino was standing in the hall below talking to Lion. Her hand tightened on the marble bannister. However, her astonishment and wariness were quickly submerged in fierce satisfaction. She had no reason to be afraid of Caprino. He could not touch her; he could not hurt Elizabet. Serenely she now started down the stairs.

Caprino glanced up as she reached the third step from the bottom. "Ah, Sanchia, how charming you look." His gaze traveled appraisingly over her. "I had no idea you'd clean up so well or I might have hesitated about making you a present to the *magnifico*." He held up a leather purse and smiled smugly. "I fear I'll just have to be satisfied with young Elizabet. I believe I'll pay a visit to Giovanni after I bid you good journey."

Sanchia smiled back at him. "I'm sure Giovanni will be happy to see you. I've always thought you had many qualities in common. However, Elizabet is no longer with Giovanni."

Caprino stiffened, his gaze narrowing on her face. "And where is she?"

"With Messer Benedetto and his good wife. As I was forced to leave Elizabet, I thought it wise to have her future settled." Her smile deepened with mockery. "I'm sure you can sympathize with such a decision. I remember you were quite eager to have her settled yourself. She's to marry Alessandro within the month."

"Marriage! But she can't—" Caprino whirled to Lion. "I've been cheated. The money you paid for Sanchia is not enough."

"It was enough two minutes ago." Lion's tone was icy. "The arrangement stands, Caprino."

"But that was when I thought—" Caprino broke off as he met Lion's gaze. He was silent, struggling to subdue his anger. Finally he turned back to Sanchia. "You think you've bested me."

"I didn't try to best you. I intended only to protect Elizabet."

"From me," he snarled.

"From everything and everyone." She gazed at him directly. "But yes, from you most of all."

"You need not worry. Your Elizabet is no longer important to me." Caprino's voice was so soft the underlying malevolence was only barely discernible. "But you and your future are going to be of great interest to me, Sanchia. I don't like to be cheated of something I want."

A chilly finger of fear touched her spine. He couldn't hurt her or Elizabet, she reassured herself, but still she felt his menace. "You won't know my future. I'm leaving Florence."

"I can wait. I'm good at waiting."

"Leave, Caprino." Lion gestured toward the door. "Our business is finished."

"Good day, *Magnifico*." His voice sounded of nothing but politeness now. "I wish you joy in your purchase. May Sanchia bring you what you seek." He opened the door and slanted them a faint smile over his shoulder. "But you'd best hasten in your use of her. Young girls such as she are fragile blossoms that sometimes wither and perish overnight." He gave them no chance to answer as he closed the door behind him.

The tension eased from Sanchia's rigid muscles and she forced herself to release her grip on the bannister. "I'm sorry I overslept, my lord. I'm ready to leave."

Lion's glance shifted from the door to her face. "You do realize he just threatened your life?"

She nodded jerkily as she descended the last steps. "He's an evil man."

"Yet you're paying no more attention to his threat than if he'd just told you he was going to make you a present."

"What can I do about it? He'll try to hurt me and perhaps he'll succeed." She gazed at Lion gravely. "But he'd hurt me much more if I let him poison all my hours and days with worry and fear."

"An interesting philosophy." He gazed at her with an odd intentness. "You advocate living for the present and not the future?"

"All I have is the present. A slave has only the future her master determines."

The intensity of his gaze was making her uneasy and causing a tight stricture in her chest. He was so *big*. He towered above her and his simple apparel of black leather hose and boots and russet suede jerkin served only to emphasize the strength of his massive body.

"Then I agree we must make the most of every single minute," Lion said softly as he drew on his heavy leather gauntlets. "Tell me, did you miss me in your bed last night?"

The tightness in her chest increased until she had trouble drawing breath. "How could I miss you when I've never slept with you? I fell asleep right away and didn't stir until Giulia woke me."

"Remind me to teach you the virtue of flattery. A man has need of pretty lies on occasion." Humor glinted in his dark eyes. "It's an art required of all my slaves."

"But Messer Lorenzo said I'm your only slave."

He airily waved a gloved hand. "Not important. One is enough to set a standard."

He was joking with her, Sanchia realized with amazement. She had seen him in many moods since yesterday afternoon, but they had all been heavy—anger, suspicion, appraisal, lust. Now he appeared light-hearted, charged with energy and good humor. "You're happy today."

"I admit I'm very glad we're on our way. I detest waiting for anything." He touched her cheek. "Remember that, Sanchia."

The hard leather of the gauntlet was rough against the soft flesh of her cheek. She imagined the warmth of his finger beneath the leather and it caused a tingle of heat to spread from her cheek to her throat. She took an involuntary step back. "I'll remember." She moistened her lips with her tongue. "What kept you here in Florence? What were you waiting for?"

"Why, you, Sanchia." He turned to the door. "We were waiting for you."

She gazed at him in bewilderment. "Me? But—" She stopped as the significance of Caprino's presence earlier sank home to her. "Caprino said he sold me to you. The piazza . . ."

"A test of your skill, which proved very impressive." Lion opened the door. "Come along. Lorenzo is waiting outside with the horses. I purchased a few items of clothing for you from one of the women here; they're tied on the back of your horse." He frowned. "I was able to obtain a very gentle mare for you. I assume you've never ridden."

"No." She came toward him, her gaze searching his face. "A thief. That's why you want me." At least she knew now why he'd bought her and felt she was no longer blundering in the dark with him.

"When I bought you from Giovanni, I certainly believed I was getting only a thief." He studied her face. "You seem pleased. I got the impression that taking purses was not to your liking."

"It's not; stealing frightens me. But now that I know what value I have for you I feel better."

"So that you can seek a way to bend me to your will as you did Giovanni?"

Her eyes widened and she gazed up at him helplessly.

"For God's sake, don't look at me like that. I'm not going to beat you." He shrugged wearily, "Sweet Jesus, why shouldn't you try to manage me? I'll do my best to use you in the way I see fit."

"But I promised I would obey you in all things."

No weapons, Lorenzo had said, and she looked poignantly defenseless at this moment, Lion thought. What must it be like to be as helpless as Sanchia, and have to struggle to maintain even a modicum of dignity and independence in an uncertain world? The thought filled him with astonishment. Where did his anger at her situation come from? Why this inexplicable need to comfort? "One theft," he said curtly. "That's all you'll have to do. Once we're finished at Solinari you'll never have to steal again. I'll find some other—"

"Lion, *caro mio*." Giulia was walking down the stairs, a dazzling smile on her face. "Were you not coming to bid me good-bye?"

"I thought we'd said our good-byes last night," Lion replied. "I seem to remember you wished me a swift journey to . . ." He paused and gave her a half mocking bow. "A place with an extremely warm but unpleasant climate."

Giulia shrugged. "I was angry. You know my bad temper is fleeting. Forgive me for attacking you as an apothecary would a barber. *Caro,* I am so sorry for my venomous words. Come, we must part friends." She cast

Sanchia a careless glance. "We had no problem before she came. Do not bring her back and all will be well."

"I don't care for ultimatums, Giulia." Lion's hand encircled Sanchia's wrist and he drew her toward the door. "Nor do I care for viragos. I don't believe I'll be returning to your *casa*."

"But Lion, I didn't mean—" Giulia stopped. The door had closed behind them.

Giulia's hands slowly clenched into fists. She should never have pushed him, she thought. She had known it was a mistake to show her anger the night before, but she hadn't been able to stem the vitrolic words. Jealousy. *Dio,* she was jealous of that bony child. It was just as well that this madness with Lion was at an end. Caprino was right; a woman in her profession had to maintain control. Money was important, not pleasure . . . not the pleasure she had received from Lion, certainly.

She turned away from the door, lifting her skirts as she started up the stairs. Still, she did owe Lion a small debt for giving her so many hours of servicing in the bedchamber. She would repay him by waiting until late this evening to summon Caprino and tell him what she had overheard as she came down to the front hall. Caprino might be delayed as much as a full day before starting whatever it might be he chose to do with the information she would sell him. He'd promised her seven ducats for finding out what Lion wanted Sanchia to steal for him. In this she'd failed, but the name of the place where the theft was to occur should be worth at least five, Giulia thought shrewdly.

Solinari. The name sounded vaguely familiar, she mused. Now in what connection had she heard it?

"Where is Solinari?" Sanchia asked as Lion lifted her onto the saddle of the chestnut mare. She clutched desperately at the reins trying not to think how far she was from the ground.

"It's a palazzo just outside of Pisa."

"What am I supposed to steal there?"

"A key."

"A key to unlock what?"

"A door." Lion mounted his own black stallion.

"Oh." Sanchia was silent a moment. "What's behind the door?"

She heard a low chuckle from Lorenzo, who was already mounted behind her.

"You're very inquisitive." There was an edge to Lion's tone.

"I'll have to know sometime, won't I?" She asked anxiously, "Do questions displease you?"

"*Cristo,* what do I care? Question away as you please."

Lorenzo chuckled again. "I'm sure she will."

Lion scowled at him over his shoulder. "I never have to worry about you saying what you like, Lorenzo."

"That must be a great comfort to you."

"You'll have to tell me how to please you," Sanchia said quickly. "This is all new to me. I've had no master but Giovanni and he—"

"I don't want to hear any more about that man," Lion said tersely as he turned his stallion, Tabron, toward the south. "I find any comparison between him and me less than flattering."

"And I'm sure Lion will let you know what pleases him," Lorenzo murmured, "when he gains the courage."

Lion's expression was lethal. "It may please me to take a mace to your head in the very near future."

Lorenzo clucked reprovingly. "Such violence. How can you set a fitting example for the young when you are clearly a barbarian?"

"Lorenzo, I'm going to—" Lion stopped abruptly. "Sanchia, you may ask your questions when we stop at the Inn of the Two Swords this evening. I'm in a hurry now." He kicked the stallion into a trot. "Bring her." A moment later he was halfway down the street.

Sanchia frowned. "I made him angry."

Lorenzo shook his head. "The situation makes him angry, but that will change shortly. I'm surprised he's lasted this long." He edged his horse closer and took the reins from Sanchia's hand. "However, perhaps I shouldn't have goaded him so. I believe we can expect to have an extremely hard and fast trip today. Lion grew up on a horse and forgets there are others who prefer traveling on two feet rather than four." He grimaced as he turned his horse and began leading Sanchia's mare in the direction Lion had taken. "*Dio,* how I hate riding these foul-smelling beasts."

The trip was as grueling as Lorenzo had predicted, and Sanchia was near exhaustion when they finally stopped at sunset at the Inn of the Two Swords. A hundred times she had wanted to ask Lion to stop and let them rest, and a hundred times she had bitten her lip and remained silent. It was not her place to complain, and she had little opportunity to speak to him anyway. For most of the journey he rode at least a quarter of a mile ahead of her and Lorenzo.

The interior of the small inn appeared clean and a cheerful fire burned in the stone fireplace in the common room. The delicious aroma of roasting hare drifted to Sanchia's nostrils from the spit that a buxom maid was turning over the fire.

The innkeeper bustled forward, a broad, toothy smile lighting his angular face. "Welcome, my lord, it's a pleasure to have you again under my roof. How long will you be with us?"

"We leave at dawn tomorrow, Antonio." Lion drew off his leather gauntlets and tucked them in his belt. "See that our horses are cared for and water heated for us for washing."

"At once, *Magnifico*. I'll call my son to take your horses to the stable and they'll receive the finest care." The innkeeper snapped his fingers and the maid left the spit and hurried toward them, an eager smile on her lips. "Heat water and bring it to Lord Andreas and his companions at once, Letitia." His gaze went to Sanchia and he frowned. "You remember, we have only the two rooms, my lord. Will the lady—"

"The lady will occupy my bed," Lion interrupted. "Send Letitia with wine at once and with our dinner after we've had an opportunity to wash."

Sanchia caught the flickering expression of disappointment on the servant girl's face before she hurried from the room, trailing the innkeeper.

Lorenzo was already climbing the short flight of stairs. "I'm going to stretch out and rest these aching bones. When the wench brings the food call me." He grimaced as he glanced down at them from the landing. "I don't know why I let you persuade me to mount one of those beasts from hell, Lion."

"Because you're too lazy to walk," Lion said dryly. "And you're afraid you'll miss something if you stay at Mandara."

"Things were much simpler and more comfortable before you decided to save me from my life of iniquity." Lorenzo opened the door at the top of the stairs. "I managed very well in Naples without running from place to place jarring my bones and doing grievous harm to my person." He glanced over his shoulder. "By the way, you'd best care for your urchin. If you weren't avoiding looking at her, you would notice that she may collapse at any moment."

Lion's gaze flew to Sanchia.

"I'm not tired," Sanchia said quickly. "Well, perhaps a little." She tried to keep from swaying. "I've never ridden a horse before and the sun—"

"*Cristo!*" Lion's hand was on her elbow propelling her up the steps. "Why didn't you tell me you needed to stop?"

"You said you were in a hurry."

"So you let me drive you until you were ready to fall off the damned horse? Have you no sense?" Lion threw open the door next to the one through which Lorenzo had disappeared and half pushed her into a small bedchamber. "Lie down until Letitia comes with the wine."

"I don't have to lie down. I'm not ill."

He picked her up and tossed her unceremoniously onto the bed. "And you're not going to be ill. I have no time to be your nursemaid."

A ghost of a smile touched her lips as she thought of Lionello Andreas in a sickroom. He was so big, his energy and vitality so great, she couldn't associate him with illness. "I'll endeavor to ward off all maladies so as not to inconvenience you."

"Are you laughing at me?"

Her lashes fell to veil the glint of mischief in her eyes. "I would not dare, my lord."

"You'd dare." He stood looking down at her for an instant before turning on his heel. "Rest. I'll go next door and let Lorenzo laugh at me awhile. I'm more accustomed to his barbs than yours."

Sanchia raised herself on one elbow. "Barbs, my lord? I merely jested a bit. If you'd rather I wouldn't laugh, you must tell me and I'll—"

He held his hand up. "Must you be so obliging? I'm not so puffed up that I can't laugh at myself." Suddenly a smile lit his harsh features with rare warmth. "And I always get my own back eventually."

The door shut behind him before she could answer.

She gazed at the door for a long time before she settled her cheek on the pillow and closed her eyes. He was difficult to understand, she thought wearily. So many hard, sharp edges and so much brutal driving force and yet his hands had held nothing but rough kindness when they touched her just now.

And his smile had been beautiful. . . .

Five

"Well, if I must face the horrors of mounting that repulsive monster at dawn, I suppose I must bid you good night." Lorenzo pushed back his chair and rose to his feet. A faintly mocking smile was on his lips as his gaze rested on Sanchia sitting on a stool by the hearth. "A *very* good night. Shall I tell Letitia to take away the remains of this sumptuous repast so as not to disturb you . . . later?"

"I'll clear it away." Sanchia jumped to her feet, eager to have something to do to relieve the tension that had been building steadily within her during the meal. "There's no use your troubling yourself, Messer Lorenzo. I'll be glad to—"

"Sit down, Sanchia." Lion's voice was as lazy as the position of his big body sprawled in the chair opposite Lorenzo. "Tell Letitia to come and take care of it, Lorenzo."

"But I can . . ." Sanchia trailed off as

she met Lion's gaze. The room was suddenly close, airless. She quickly sat back down on the stool and looked at the reflection of the firelight in the ruby red wine in her wooden goblet.

Lorenzo nodded as he moved toward the door. "I'll see you at dawn."

The silence in the room after the door closed behind him was broken only by the hiss and crackle of the olive logs burning in the fireplace. Sanchia could feel Lion's gaze on her face but avoided looking up to meet his eyes.

The tension was growing, the tightness in her chest robbing her of breath. Why didn't he speak? Then when he let the silence drag on she realized she must be the one to break it. "You should let me serve you. It is my place."

"I didn't buy you to serve me at the table. Your time will come."

Involuntarily her glance flew to the bed across the room.

He chuckled. "I didn't buy you for that either. It will only be an extra delight for us both."

"Not for—" She broke off. It would be foolish to anger him when he seemed to be more mellow than she had ever seen him. There were answers she must have if she was to understand him. "What lies behind the door, my lord? The one that I'm to steal the key to unlock?"

"Why does it matter to you?"

"It's important for me to try to know about things that have an effect on my life. You're a very rich man. Why should you steal more?"

Lion smiled cynically. "My dear Sanchia, haven't you found there's never enough wealth for some men?"

"Yes." A frown furrowed her brow. "I do not know you very well, but I don't think you're one of those men."

"No, but Francisco Damari is." The wooden chair creaked as Lion leaned back and stretched his legs out before him, his gaze on the fire. "Ruling all the city-states of Italy would only whet Damari's appetite. He thinks to reign over the world." Lion's lips tightened.

"But he'll not use the Wind Dancer to buy him more power."

"The Wind Dancer?"

"A statue belonging to my family." In the firelight Lion's rugged features were softened to real handsomeness in sharp contrast to the bitter tone of his voice. "While I was away in France negotiating the purchase of another shipyard, he bribed one of my servants at Mandara, a man called Giuseppe, to steal it and bring it to him. He's now keeping the statue at his palazzo at Solinari."

"How do you know?"

"Lorenzo and I chased down Giuseppe and asked him a number of pertinent questions. He was delighted to answer . . . eventually."

Sanchia shivered and looked away from the stark brutality of his expression. "If the statue is yours, why don't you just march in and take it? Lorenzo said you were a condottiere."

"It may come to that. However, I disbanded my armies two years ago and it would take a good deal of time to form another condotti. I do not wish to bring Damari, even Borgia perhaps, down on Mandara until I have a chance to refortify. Mandara is well guarded but not strong enough to withstand a thrust by Borgia."

"Borgia?" Her gaze flew back to his face.

"Oh, you've heard of the illustrious Duke Valentino?" Lion's lips twisted. "But of course. All of Italy knows of the great Cesare."

"Yes, I've heard of him." Who in Florence was not familiar with the name? Borgia had been eyeing Florence with greed and speculation for many years and, after his recently completed conquest of the Romagna, every week there had been a new rumor that the duke was on the march to lay siege to the city. "I've heard that he wishes to rule all Italy, but who is this Damari?"

"Damari is a condottiere who is now serving under Borgia's banner. They have similar goals and similar methods for obtaining them."

Sanchia didn't have to ask the nature of those methods. The ruthless slaughter of women and children, the maiming of innocents by the captains serving Borgia had become legend over the years. "Then why do you not let him have the statue? You can buy others."

"There is no other statue like it in the world. It's part of my family history." His voice vibrated with intensity. "We guard it." He paused. "And it guards us."

"I don't understand."

"You don't have to understand. All you have to do is go to the palazzo, steal the key from the officer on guard, and bring it to me."

"It sounds very simple."

Lion's hands closed on the arms of his chair. "We'll make it so. No harm will come to you, I promise."

"I take comfort from your promise. I fear I'd not look forward to facing your Messer Damari. Men such as he don't regard the life of a slave as having any more value than a cool drink of water." She lifted her shoulder and let it drop expressively. "Less, if they have no thirst."

"Just do what I say and you'll not even see Damari. We've laid a path of gold to get into the palazzo and buy the information as to the location of the store house where Damari keeps his treasures."

"And you're sure Damari will have your Wind Dancer there?"

He smiled crookedly. "Oh yes, it will be there. Damari regards the Wind Dancer as the ultimate treasure."

"Why?" Sanchia took a final sip of wine before setting the wooden goblet on the hearth. "You said it was important to your family, but why should it be important to him?"

"Because it belongs to me," Lion said grimly. "And he knows I want it back. He knows I *have* to get it back."

"But why would Borgia let himself be swayed by Damari into protecting it?"

"The pope is a greedy man and dazzled by all things ancient and classical. Pope Alexander's treasury grows daily with the loot Cesare brings to Rome from his conquests. As long as Cesare continues to send him such treasure Alexander will protect his clever son and give him access to the papal monies for his campaigns."

"And the Wind Dancer is ancient?"

Lion smiled curiously. "Oh yes, very ancient. Damari is hoping to dangle the Wind Dancer before Cesare and Alexander and possibly gain a dukedom from the pope."

Sanchia's eyes widened. "But they would surely not give so much?"

"They might. Alexander is superstitious and there are many legends about the Wind Dancer."

"What kind of legends?"

Lion shrugged. "Power. Legend says the Wind Dancer can give any victory to the one who possesses it."

"But you don't believe it."

He was silent a moment. "I don't know. The lives of my family have always been too intertwined with the Wind Dancer for us to look at it objectively. If the statue does possess power, we've never tried to use it."

"Why not?"

"Kinship," Lion said simply. "The Wind Dancer is of our family. We of the Andreas family may not be shy about manipulating others to suit us, but we stand together. We will not use each other."

She shook her head in disbelief. "But a dukedom for a statue . . ."

"What's a dukedom in Italy today? Cesare gathered a parcel of little states into his basket this year alone." His lips twisted. "For that matter, what is Italy today? Genoa and Milan are gone, Naples torn between the French and Spaniards. Florence is licking at the French boots and still out to pluck Pisa. All the rest of the signories are maneuvering to survive and not be swept by the pope and Rome into the empire Cesare is trying to create for himself. While France, Spain, and England have finally become unified and have strong national armies, we still hire mercenaries who have loyalty only to the highest bidder. I don't wonder Borgia considers all of Italy ripe for conquest."

There was an indifference in his tone that surprised her after the passionate intensity with which he'd spoken of his family and the Wind Dancer. "You don't care? It's your country, after all. Is it not important to you?"

He shook his head. "Mandara is my country. I have no interest in what the rest of Italy becomes as long as they leave me and my people out of their petty bickering." He tilted his head to look at her curiously. "Is it important to you?"

She thought about it. "A slave has no country, I suppose." She paused. "But I think I'd like to feel as if I belonged somewhere. It would make me . . . warm."

His gaze narrowed on her face. "You accept being a slave so meekly?"

"I don't remember ever being anything else."

"And yet you have courage. I would have thought . . ."

She looked at him inquiringly.

"I couldn't *stand* it," he said with sudden violence. "I'd want to kill someone or run away to a land where I could be free. Haven't you ever wanted to do that?"

"I've never thought about it. From the time I was a tiny child my mother kept telling me I must accept my station in life and make the best of it." She smiled tremulously. "And I'm not really very brave. Sometimes it was hard just to live from day to day. I have had little time to think about what it might be like to be free."

"But you should have thought about it," he said fiercely. "Giovanni had no right to—*Gran Dio*, what am I saying? In another moment I'll be talking you into running away from *me*." He stood up. "Don't try it. I warn you that I'd find you and be most annoyed. And don't mistake a temporary madness brought on by the warmth of the fire and those huge eyes gazing at me for anything enduring. Your mother was right. Accept that you're mine and will stay mine."

She was bewildered. "But I have accepted— Where are you going?"

"To look to the horses." He was already at the door. "Antonio's son is a cowardly lout. The last time I was here he was too afraid of Tabron to unsaddle him."

"So you're going yourself to see if he's been taken care of?"

"A horse can be the difference between life and death to a man. It doesn't denote softness to see that an animal is well cared for." He scowled. "What are you smiling about?"

She quickly wiped any trace of amusement from her face. "Nothing, my lord."

"No? I'm getting very weary of being thought a weakling," he said with menacing softness. "First Lorenzo and now you. I think I must put an end to it." He paused. "I was stupid not to take what I wanted in the beginning and I'll wait no longer. When I come back I want to see you sitting on that stool wearing nothing but firelight. You understand?"

"Yes." The air in the room was suddenly charged with the same stormy intensity as earlier. She moistened her lips. "I understand, my lord."

"Good." He slammed the door shut behind him.

Sanchia started to speak quickly as soon as Lion entered the room. "Letitia came and took the trenchers and left fresh wine. Was Tabron well?" Her hands were locked together on her lap and she flexed her fingers nervously, her gaze fixed on the fire. "Will we go straight to Solinari tomorrow or must we stop at another—"

"Stand up. I want to look at you."

Sanchia tensed and then rose slowly to her feet. She turned to face Lion, but still would not meet his gaze. "You've seen me before. In the bath. There's nothing more to see."

"I disagree." His gaze ran over her naked body, lingering on the soft thatch guarding her womanhood. "There's always something more to see and . . . appreciate."

A wave of heat tingled through Sanchia that had nothing to do with the fire burning in the hearth. Her nails bit into the flesh of her palms as her hands clenched into fists at her sides. She welcomed the sharp pain; it pierced the rigidity attacking her every muscle. "Shall I kneel on the floor now?"

"No!" The sharpness of his voice caused her gaze to move to his face. Her breath caught in her throat and she felt as if she were suffocating. Lion's dark eyes were fierce, and the flesh drawn tight over the broad planes of his jaws hollowed his cheeks as if he were being consumed by a terrible hunger. "When will you learn I'm not Giovanni?" He took a step forward and she caught the clean scent of hay, soap, and crisp spring night clinging to him. "My name is Lion. Say it."

She could feel the heat his body was emitting though he hadn't touched her yet. The muscles of her limbs felt suddenly heavy, weak, unable to support her weight. "Lion." The name trembled uncertainly from her lips. "My lord."

"Just Lion." He reached out a gloved hand to caress her slender throat.

She inhaled sharply and a shiver ran through her.

He stopped with his hand still encircling her throat to gaze at her searchingly.

"The leather is cold," she said quickly, seizing wildly at the first excuse that came to mind for her moment of revealing weakness.

"Is it?" His smile was purely sensual. "Then we must do something to warm it, for I cannot trust myself to touch you without them right now." He turned to the fire and held out his gloved hands to the flames. "Do you know what I thought when I came through the doorway and saw you sitting naked on your stool?"

Her gaze was fastened in helpless fascination on the heavy, scarred gauntlets he held before the warmth of the fire. They came almost to his elbows, the brass rivets shining in the firelight, each finger now limned in blue-orange flame. "No, my lo-Lion."

"I thought what a stroke of fortune it was that brought me to Giovanni's shop."

"It wasn't fortune; it was Caprino."

"And that I want you to be like this always. I want to think of the fire shimmering on your flesh and shining on your hair while you wait for me to come to you." His gaze remained on the burning logs. "Come into you."

Her heart gave a jerk and then began to pound wildly. Her thoughts were an incoherent jumble and she was only conscious of the raw vulnerability of her own nudity, the dominance of Lion's fully clothed body, the violence she sensed beneath those garments.

And, most of all, the power of his leather-gauntleted hands held out before the flames . . .

"You're very small." His gaze was still on the fire. "It will hurt you the first time."

She didn't answer. She almost wished he would touch her and end the maddening tension between them. She felt as if the next breath she drew would shatter her composure.

"I'll try to proceed slowly but—" He stopped and was silent a moment before continuing haltingly, "My appetites are great. Sometimes it's like a frenzy, a madness. You must not fight me or I might injure you. I don't want that to happen."

"I will not fight you."

Lion's hands closed slowly into fists. "I know. You will yield because I own you." He smiled recklessly as he turned to face her. "And why not? It's the way of the world." His gloved hands reached out to encompass her breasts. "Why do you gasp? The leather is no longer cold. I made sure of that, Sanchia."

The leather *was* warm, almost hot, she thought hazily. The hard, seamed leather was strangely seductive against the smoothness of her flesh.

His hands were cupping her, squeezing her gently while his gaze studied her face. "My hands are even warmer," he said softly. "But I dare not take off these gloves yet. The texture of your skin excites me and if I touch your flesh I will need you at once . . . and I will take you at once. It will go easier for you if I do not." His left hand slid down her abdomen to the thatch of curls surrounding her womanhood and began slowly to rub back and forth. "Such a pretty nest." His voice was hoarser, his nostrils flaring as he looked at her. "I want to move into you and feel those curls brushing against me. Part your limbs now, Sanchia."

She was trembling so badly she wasn't sure she could move. His hand stroking her was igniting a strange burning sensation between her thighs.

"Sanchia." The softness of his tone failed to veil the underlying command.

She obeyed him, her gaze fastened blindly on the lacings of his leather jerkin.

"Wider." Her gaze moved up to his strong brown throat, and she watched in fascination as the pulse in the hollow abruptly accelerated. "Ah, that's right. Now stand very still."

His hand moved down between her thighs and she felt the warmth of his hand through the gauntlet as his palm moved against her, caressing, stroking. Everywhere he touched left a trail of that same moist burning sensation that was close to pain. She closed her eyes, swaying helplessly as sensation after bewildering sensation tore through her. "It . . . hurts."

"No." His palm cupped, squeezed, released. "It's not pain, Sanchia. Hunger." His voice was uneven. "It's hunger."

"I don't think so." She reached out to clutch desperately at his upper arms.

He stiffened. "Don't touch me."

She jerked her hands away. "I'm sorry, my lord, I didn't mean—"

"Lion," he cut in through clenched teeth. "It's too soon for you to touch me. I can't hold off, if you do." He lifted her in his arms and started across the room toward the bed. "There are many kinds of hunger." He laid her down. "This is the best." He parted her thighs, his index finger searching. "And the worst."

He found what he sought and began to gently press and rotate.

Her eyes widened with shock as she gave a little cry.

He was a huge, dark shadow bending over her, his expression intent, his lips parted to take in more air as his massive chest labored with the harshness of his breathing. His face was a devil's mask above her as the glow of the firelight lit only one side of his face leaving the other in darkness.

Darkness. Flame. Hunger.

She bit her lower lip to suppress a moan as the unbelievable ripples of feeling spread from his gloved finger to every part of her body. It *was* hunger, she realized dazedly, a hunger more terrible than any she had ever known. She couldn't bear it. She instinctively tried to close her thighs.

"No!" He stopped her, moving her thighs even farther apart until she felt totally vulnerable, totally exposed. His finger continued to press gently as he gazed down at her. "I want to look at you." His tone was almost guttural. "Beautiful . . ." His other hand moved down and he inserted one finger carefully within her. "*Dio*, you're tight." A second finger joined the first with some difficulty and he paused, his gaze lifting to her face. "Tell me what you're feeling."

The seams of the leather gloves pressing against her, his fingers invading her, the burning hunger increasing every second. She shook her head helplessly. "I . . . can't." She gasped and instinctively arched up against him as he plunged deeper, withdrew and plunged again. "Please, my lord—"

"What do you feel?" he demanded.

Her head thrashed back and forth on the pillow. "Heat." Her nails dug into the coverlet. "Hardness. The leather is . . ." The muscles of her stomach clenched as a third finger slipped into her. "Fullness."

"And hunger?" He moved slowly, then faster, then slowly again. "You want this?"

"Yes." The affirmative was a whisper. She was surprised she could speak.

"It's pleasure?"

"Yes, I think so."

"Good." His fingers left her and he straightened and stepped back away from the bed. "Let's hope you'll soon know so, for I can't wait any longer." He drew off the leather gauntlets and threw them aside. "*Santa Maria*, I want to *feel* you." He touched her breasts, his long fingers light and gentle on her flesh. A shudder ran through him. "I told you," he whispered. "I knew it would be like this." His callused palm cupping her breasts was nearly as hard as the leather of the glove, but it was infinitely different. His flesh was warmer, vibrant with life. "Your skin is like nothing I've ever touched before. It makes me—" He threw back his head, drawing in a great breath as if starved for air. "I'll show you how it makes me." He pulled her to a sitting position on the bed and began to strip off his clothing.

She crouched on her knees on the bed, her arms crossing her breasts in an attempt to still her trembling. "You're undressing too?"

He didn't look at her as he pulled off his boots. "As quickly as possible."

"Giovanni never undressed when he took my moth—" She broke off as he cast her a stormy glance. "I can't help comparing you. He was my master. Now you're my master. My acquaintance is not so large that—" She stopped, her eyes widening as his rampant arousal sprang free when he pulled off his black hose. She swallowed and moistened her lips. He was not like Giovanni at all. Naked now, Lion was all iron muscles and brawny power. The triangle of springy dark hair thatching his chest ended in a V before it reached the flatness of his stomach, but another thatch surrounded his manhood. Where Giovanni was soft and flabby, Lion was taut and muscular. Where Giovanni was small, Lion was—

"You see?" Lion asked softly as his gaze followed her own. "This is what you do to me. Looking at you, touching you . . ."

"I see." She couldn't keep her gaze off him. She stated positively, "You won't fit, you know."

He chuckled. "I'll fit very well. A woman's body is marvelously accommodating. After the first time it won't even hurt."

She had grave doubts his assurances would prove true but, since there was clearly nothing she could do, it would be foolish to worry about possible pain until it happened. Besides, she was still feeling the tingling urgency between her thighs that tempered her fears with curiosity and excitement. "You look very . . . strong."

"I notice you don't call me handsome." He threw the hose aside and stepped forward. "I know well I'm an ugly bastard. But, as you say, I'm strong as a bull and that can be of use in such jousts as this."

"You're not ugly."

He smiled cynically. "You learn the arts of flattery quickly. However, sweet words are futile when I have a mirror to look into each morning."

He didn't believe her, Sanchia realized. "No, truly, I do not—" She broke off as he knelt on the bed facing her. He was so close her nipples brushed the thatch of hair on his chest.

He cupped her face in his hands as he gazed down at her with an expression that hinted at anger. "I don't want this. I have no liking for taking virgins."

"Then don't do it."

"Easy words." His hands moved down to her shoulders and began to knead her flesh with yearning tenderness. "I must do it. From the moment I saw you I knew I must have you like this."

"Not from the first moment. Only when you saw me in the bath and found I wasn't as ugly as you thought."

"*Cristo,* must you always argue with me?" His hands tightened on her shoulders. "I like you better when the only sounds you make are gasps and moans."

Obediently, she kept silent. What was he waiting for? she wondered. She could feel the unbearable tension gripping his body and yet she also sensed reluctance.

"And don't look at me like that." He shook her. "I don't want to hurt you, dammit. It will bring me no pleasure, but I must . . ." He pushed her back on the bed and moved between her thighs. His arousal nudged against the center of her womanhood as he muttered, "One stroke and it will be over." He covered her lips with his palm. "One stroke . . ."

He drew a deep breath and lunged forward.

Pain. White hot. Lightning swift. Her cry was smothered by his hand but her eyes widened with shock and agony as they gazed up at him.

"Close your eyes," he commanded roughly as he eased farther into her tight passage. "Don't look at me."

Her lids fell and she was in darkness. The pain was

fading, and she was conscious only of an exquisite fullness and a sense of something lost that had been found. She could feel the soft prickle of the hair dusting Lion's thighs brushing the smoothness of her own and heard the harsh sound of his breathing above her.

He was still, filling her completely but not moving. "It's done." His palm petted her, smoothing her around him. "*Dio,* you've taken all of me. I wasn't sure you'd be able to do it. You're so tiny . . ." His finger began to press and circle that bewitching place he'd fondled before. A hot shiver ran through her and she could feel the muscles of her stomach clench. A moment before she had felt pinned, staked to Lion's body and content only to accept, but suddenly now she felt the need for something more. "May I . . . move?"

He froze. "I cannot stop." His voice was savage with frustration. "I'll try to hurry but I cannot promise."

"That wasn't what I meant. I wished only—" She broke off as he drew out and then plunged forward. Pleasure streaked through her. This was what Lion had meant, she thought dazedly as he began a wild, pounding rhythm. This must be the pleasure men felt when they fornicated with a woman. She wished Lion hadn't condemned her to darkness. She would have liked to watch his face to see if he was feeling the same pleasure as she.

Yet he must be enjoying her body for he was shuddering, trembling as he moved, his breath coming in sharp gasps that resembled sobs. The intensity of his need filled her with a heady excitement and increased her own hunger tenfold. It was as if he were feeding her his frustrated desire for completion and somehow making it her own.

He was petting her again, his big hands trembling, urgent. "Take me," he muttered. "Help me. I want all of you."

He sounded like a man in agony, she thought with a rush of maternal tenderness. What must it be like to feel desire with such overwhelming intensity? She clenched around him and heard Lion give a low groan.

"Sweet . . . That's right. Hold me. Only a little longer."

She tried to hold him but he was too wild, out of control, almost lifting her from the bed with the force of his thrusts. She was suddenly conscious of something building within her, growing stronger with every movement. Something . . . strange, coiling toward fever heat.

Lion was moving her, shifting her, trying to take more of her. The hotness pouring through her was a clear stream of pure desire. Then the stream merged with Lion's until there was only one river, one entity striving to reach . . . to reach what?

Then she knew!

The knowledge broke over her in a release of rapture that left her gasping and shivering in the shimmering aftermath.

Lion cried out thickly as if strangling on a surfeit of pleasure.

The silence in the room was broken only by the crackle of burning logs in the fireplace and Lion's harsh breathing above her.

"May I open my eyes now?"

She heard his breathing become arrested and then he muttered a low curse beneath his breath. "*Gran Dio.*" Then he was moving off her. "Of course you can open your eyes. Why the hell shouldn't you?"

Her eyes opened to see him striding across the room, the muscles of his tight buttocks rippling as he moved toward the washstand. Slowly she sat up and gave a wistful sigh. He was angry again. She wished she'd been allowed a few moments more to enjoy this odd sweet languor before having to gather herself to try to understand what was troubling him. "Because you told me you didn't want me to look at you."

"That was because I didn't want to see your—" He broke off and kept his gaze averted as he dipped a cloth into the water in the basin and wrung it out. "I didn't mean you had to keep them closed. Have you no sense?"

"I don't know you well enough to always know what you want from me," she said simply. "I thought perhaps it made your pleasure greater if I didn't distract you by looking at you."

"No, it wasn't that." He averted his gaze as he turned and came back to the bed carrying the damp cloth. He sat down on the bed and moved the cool cloth between her legs. His gaze remained fixed on the cloth as he asked in a low voice, "Does it still hurt?"

"There's a little soreness." She shrugged. "I thought it would hurt much more. You're right; a woman's body is very accommodating."

"Yes." His hand moved caressingly and she could feel the warmth of his flesh through the coolness of the cloth. "I've never known a body as sweetly accommodating. You're so small it was like handling a child and yet you're a woman here." He abruptly threw the cloth aside, pushed her back on the bed and stood up. "Sleep. I won't want you again tonight."

She looked at him in surprise. "I didn't think you would. Giovanni never took my mother more than once a day."

"Then I fear your lot will not be as easy as that of your mother." He moved back to the hearth to stare into the depths of the fire. "I told you I was different."

And she was learning those differences, she thought drowsily. He gave pleasure as well as took it and, since she was to become his leman, she was glad it was so. Perhaps after she learned the way of it she could perform this duty as well as she had the tasks she had been given by Giovanni. It was important to have pride in your work.

Sleep persisted in closing in around her, but she forced her lids to remain open to ask, "I did not displease you?"

He was silent a moment, gazing into the fire. When he spoke his voice was muffled. "No, you didn't displease me."

"I'll get better at it." Her eyes closed and she turned and curled up on her side. "I learn quickly. Show me how and I'll find ways to please you. Show me . . ."

She had drifted off to sleep. Lion didn't have to turn his head to know she was no longer with him. His senses were still so acutely attuned to her physical responses that he believed he was aware of the actual second when she slid from the state of wakefulness to the depths of sleep. Why in Hades should this be so when he had never been similarly attuned to any other woman? Yet, in some mysterious fashion, he *had* experienced her pain when he had robbed her of her virginity, he had felt her yielding and then the first stirring of response. It was as if he had somehow absorbed her into himself. Sweet Mary, it was all madness.

Show me, she had said. His lips twisted in a mirthless smile as he remembered the plea. There would be no question he would show her all the ways a man could take a woman. Even now he was stone hard and yearning to be back in the tightness that had cradled him and made him never want to leave. He desperately wished to wake her now and move once more between her thighs. There was no reason he should not do it, he told himself. She wanted to please him. She would not complain if he used her a score of times this night.

She would not complain because she was not free to complain.

She wanted to please him because to please him was to survive.

He whirled and strode back to the bed. He lay down beside Sanchia, stretching out full length, careful not to touch her. He stared straight ahead, his muscles locked, his groin aching and heavy. Perhaps the soreness she was feeling would be gone in the morning.

He would lie beside her and think of all the ways he would take her tomorrow.

For he knew well that he would not sleep tonight.

"Solinari." Caprino's brow furrowed in a thoughtful frown. "You're sure he said Solinari?"

"I'm sure." Giulia turned and lifted the lid of the exquisitely carved ivory box on the table and dropped the five ducats into the velvet-lined interior. "I seldom make mistakes when it means ducats."

"You waited long enough to tell me. I may not even be able to use the information now."

She avoided his gaze as she seated herself beside the table. "I was busy."

"Or soft?" Caprino suggested silkily. "It couldn't be that you wanted your ducats and to give Andreas his chance too?"

"I was busy," she repeated. Her gaze lifted to his face. "You know who is lord of Solinari?"

"Yes, and so do you. Francisco Damari. You should remember the name. We did some business with him some nine months ago."

"Oh, yes, I remember Damari, it was the name of his palazzo I'd forgotten. You handled the negotiations and the transporting." She grimaced. "If I'd known it was Damari, I might not have summoned you at all. You promised me he'd send Laurette back in six weeks. It wasn't easy to replace her."

"Accidents happen." Caprino shrugged. "You knew there was a risk when you let him have her, but he paid enough for his pleasure to persuade you to take that chance."

"I notice you didn't send him one of *your* whores."

"Damari wanted only the best, as is common in these condottieri who raise themselves up from the peasantry. He would have been insulted if I'd sent him one of my women. Besides, I had none so uniquely qualified as your Laurette. Most women are regrettably squeamish about having pain inflicted on them."

"He had no right to kill her. As you say, she was unique." Giulia made an impatient movement with her hand. "But I suppose there's no way to force him to recompense me now. Solinari is where you sent her? I knew I'd heard the name before."

Caprino nodded. "Solinari is his palazzo, but he has lodgings in Pisa as well. The question is where to find him now." He was silent a moment, thinking. "I'll send Santini with a warning to the palazzo first, but if he isn't there, tell him to go to find Damari in Pisa."

She looked at him in surprise. "A warning? When have you ever given a warning that was not paid for?"

"Since you gave me no time to negotiate." A snarl edged Caprino's tone. "I'm not going to forgive you for that, Giulia."

"If you have nothing to gain, why bother to send a messenger?"

"Oh, but I do have something to gain. Damari will be in my debt, and it's always valuable to have a man who is on the rise in the world owe you favors."

Giulia laughed. "You trust Damari to honor a debt?"

"Perhaps." He smiled. "But if he doesn't, I'll still win if he captures little Sanchia. And you'll win, too, Giulia. Rumor has it that you weren't pleased about your hulking lover's acquisition of my little thief. What do you think Damari will do when he lays hands on her?"

Giulia knew very well what a man of Damari's perverse tastes would do to a woman who angered him. For a moment she felt a remote sympathy for Lion's slave. The anger Giulia had felt toward Sanchia had vanished when she had set aside her attachment for Lion. One emotion could not exist without the other, and she would allow neither to get in the way of what was important to her. "You hate her so much?"

"Hate?" He looked astonished. "She's not worthy of my hatred, but she must be made an example. If word got out that she'd bested me, it would cause endless trouble in the streets. I'm not like Damari, who loves punishment for punishment's sake. For me, revenge must have purpose or it's not worthwhile." He turned away. "I bid you a profitless night, Giulia, and may the man to whom you give your favors have the same tastes as Damari. I'm not at all pleased at your delay."

"I'm sorry to disappoint you, but the man who occupies my bed tonight is gentle as an untried boy and trembles at my every frown." She smiled sweetly as she stood up. "And in the morning he will gift me with a jewel that will make you drool like a street mongrel in front of the butcher's shop."

"Very different from Andreas." Caprino opened the door. "How fortunate for you."

He shut the door behind him, and she stood there a moment before moving her shoulders as if shrugging off a burden. Caprino was right—she was very fortunate to be free of Lion Andreas.

She strode briskly to the bellpull and gave it a sharp tug to alert her maid to send Messer Gondolfo to her chamber.

Six

"*No!*" Sanchia sat bolt upright in the bed, her arms flailing wildly. "*Cristo*! No, don't—"

"*Santa Maria*, what in Hades is wrong with you?" Lion raised himself on one elbow, a frown darkening his face. "Are you ill?"

Sanchia gazed hazily around the room. This chamber was firelit and clean, not dark and vermin-infested. She raised her arms, and dizzying relief soared through her. "I still have them."

"Have what?"

"My hands." She held her hands out before her, flexing the fingers. "I thought they were gone. I thought they'd caught me stealing and thrown me into the Stinche and chopped them off. But they didn't . . ."

"A dream." Lion's voice was gruff as he lay back down again. "Go back to sleep."

"A dream," she repeated. She obediently lay down, but she didn't want to release the warmth and safety of wakefulness and return to sleep where those hideous nightmares stalked. She lay there, conscious of Lion beside her. How strange to be in bed with a naked man. She supposed she would get accustomed to it in time. If she was given time. Who could know how long Lion would choose to fornicate with her? Nothing stayed the same in this world.

"Do you often dream of having your hands chopped off?" Lion asked in a low voice.

"Yes, I told you I wasn't very brave."

He was silent for such a long time, she thought he'd fallen asleep. "You cannot help your dreams, and it's not cowardly to be afraid of danger. It's intelligent."

She laughed shakily. "Then I must be as wise as a seer. I'm almost always afraid. Ever since I saw a thief thrown out of the Stinche, his poor, bleeding stumps of arms waving as if begging someone to—"

"It will not happen to you."

"I hope not," she whispered.

"It will not. I must have the key, but no harm will come to you."

He was angry. She should try to placate him, but she was suddenly too weary to make the effort. She turned on her side. "I'm sorry I woke you, my lord."

"Lion."

"I forgot." Oh dear, he did sound fiercely impatient. Perhaps it would be better to return to the uncertain threat that lay waiting for her in sleep than face his displeasure. "I'll try to remember. Forgive me . . . Lion."

His only answer was a low imprecation.

She didn't fall asleep for a long time, but as she finally drifted off, she realized Lion still lay rigid and wide awake beside her.

"What are you smiling about?" Lion snapped at Lorenzo as he lifted Sanchia onto her horse.

"Why should I not be smiling?" Lorenzo asked innocently. "It's a bright, clear spring morning and I've had a good night's sleep. You should not be churlish just because you can't say the same. I'm sure you had compensations I didn't enjoy."

Lion didn't answer as he swung onto the saddle and spurred the stallion into a gallop that left the stableyard of the inn behind him in seconds.

Lorenzo sighed. "I foresee a day like yesterday on the horizon. I had hoped for something better after Lion had appeased his lust for you." He kicked his horse into a trot. "Come along, Sanchia, or he'll be half way to Solinari before we catch up with him."

Sanchia nudged her mare into a trot. "How did you—" She stopped. "You must know him very well."

"Well enough to know he'd reached the end of his patience last night when I left you." Lorenzo gazed at her objectively. "Lust can be a strong tie to bind a man, and you'll need that bond to keep you safe at Mandara."

"Safe? Why should I not be safe?"

A faint smile touched his lips. "The situation there is complicated. Lady Caterina will not be amused at your arrival."

Sanchia tensed. "Caterina?"

"The Lady Caterina Andreas, Lion's mother. She's a virago when she's displeased."

"Oh." Sanchia thought about it. "Then I'll have to find a way to please her, won't I?"

He chuckled. "You'll find Lady Caterina a challenge. There are still stories told of the way she defended Mandara when Lion and his father were away fighting in Tuscany. Nicolino, a condottiere who decided Mandara was a rich plum ripe for the picking, laid siege to the city. Lady Caterina rallied her troops to repel the attacking army, then led a foray into the enemy camp, captured Nicolino, and brought him back to Mandara. She stood on the battlements and called down to Nicolino's second in command that if they didn't give up the siege she'd hang Nicolino. Unfortunately, the officer didn't believe she would do it and renewed the siege."

"What happened?"

"She hanged Nicolino. Then she lowered his body by a rope to dangle from the battlements in full view of his condotti. The army retreated at dawn the next morning."

A sinking feeling fluttered in the pit of Sanchia's stomach. It wasn't enough she had to please Lion; now she'd also have his warrior mother to worry about. "She sounds very strong."

"Yes." Lorenzo glanced at her. "But you have your own strength. She'll respect you, if you don't give in and let her ride over you." He smiled. "And if you do give in, you deserve to be trampled and Lion will be well rid of you."

"I won't be trampled." Her brow furrowed as she considered this new factor complicating her life. "For some reason you want me to fight her, don't you? Will you help me?"

"No. I merely position the chess pieces on the board; I don't interfere with the play itself."

"Never?"

He met her gaze. "Never."

Sanchia's hands tightened on the reins. She felt very much alone. "He may not even take me to Mandara. He's angry with me this morning."

"It's not anger. You'll have to learn to read him better." Lorenzo's gaze shifted to Lion's broad back several yards in front of them. "He suffers the same malady that afflicted him last night. It's not a horse he wants to be riding right now."

"You mean—"

"Exactly, my dear Sanchia." Lorenzo's tone was definitely more cheerful as he kicked his horse into a lope. "Which gives me hope that we may stop before we reach Solinari after all."

They halted at noon beside a tiny brook twisting through a forest glade.

One moment Lion was riding several hundred yards ahead of them on the trail, and the next he was wheeling Tabron and galloping back to them. "We'll stop here until the sun is less hot," he said curtly.

"I hadn't noticed that it was the sun that was hot," Lorenzo murmured. "But I'll accept any falsehood, if it will get me off this animal."

Lion ignored him as he dismounted and strode over to Sanchia. "Get down." He reached up, his big hands encircling her waist. "Hurry."

The urgency in his tone surprised her until she saw his face. Her eyes widened and she suddenly lost her breath. Lorenzo was right; it hadn't been anger driving him. The expression on Lion's face held the same intense hunger she'd seen last night.

He almost jerked her from the saddle before setting her down quickly. His hands on her waist kneaded her flesh through the soft fabric of her gown. The heat of his body reached out to her, claiming her. "You wish to—"

"Be quiet." His voice was hoarse as he backed her against the mare. "Don't talk. Just give me what I need." He jerked her gown from her shoulders, baring her breasts.

She gasped and then collapsed back against the mare as his mouth enveloped her left nipple. He sucked avidly, strongly, his teeth pressed against her while his hand cupped her other breast and began to squeeze rhythmically. The same liquid burning she had known last night tingled between her thighs. Her eyes closed as her throat arched back, her head resting against the mare's saddle. "Here? But Messer Lorenzo—"

"Is politely averting his eyes," Lion muttered as he lifted his head. Color flushed the tan of his cheeks, and his nostrils flared with every breath. "And is more than pleased." He grabbed Sanchia's wrist and pulled her away from the horses, striding from the trail and deeper into the forest.

"Where are we going?" She had to run to keep up with him.

"Not far."

He stopped a few yards farther into the forest and pushed her against the bole of a tree.

Rough bark pressing against the soft velvet of her gown, the pungent scent of earth and leaves and the leather of his jerkin . . .

His fingers worked frantically beneath his jerkin at the points of his hose until his aroused shaft sprang free.

"Don't fight me," he ordered as he lifted her skirts and undershift to her waist. "Do as I tell you." His palms were cupping her buttocks, raising her, adjusting her body against his manhood. "Put your legs around my waist."

Her thighs obediently encircled him. "I won't fight—" She broke off as he entered her with one wild, urgent plunge. Her head sank back against the rough bark of the tree as she felt every ridge, every inch of the wild, hot length of him.

He cried out and stopped, flexing within her. His face held a pleasure and relief that was nearly unbearable. "*Dio*! Yes . . . yes." Then he was driving, plunging with a force that rocked through her. Her shoulders were pushed back against the bole of the tree as he took and took and took . . .

She should have been frightened by the violence of his hunger, but she wasn't afraid. She was somehow aware that he didn't want to hurt her but was driven by that voracious appetite of which he had warned her.

"Give . . ." He muttered. "Hurry. Give."

He wanted her to give him not only her body but the response she had shown last night, she realized dimly.

He reached between them and pressed, his thumb and forefinger plucking at her. She cried out and arched up to him.

"Now," he groaned in a guttural tone. "Now." He plunged deep.

She gave him what he wanted, what she was helpless to deny him. She bit her lower lip to keep from screaming as wave after wave of pleasure radiated through her.

"That's right," he gasped, his hot cheek resting against her temple. "That's what I wanted."

She had pleased him, she realized hazily. How fortunate that in pleasing herself she could also please him.

His hand was awkwardly stroking her hair as his other arm held her bound to him, even now refusing to let her escape his possession.

After a moment he slowly stepped back and lifted her off him. "I didn't mean to be rough. I waited too long," he said haltingly. Then, as if regretting the half apology, he added, "But you must get used to my ways, and now is as good a time as later." He quickly tied the points of his hose before straightening her gown. "When I need you, then you must take me into you. There will be many occasions when I won't be able to wait until we find a bed."

"I understand."

"Good." He turned away. "Refresh yourself at the brook and then let's be on our way. I want to be at Solinari well before nightfall."

Lorenzo was reclining lazily beneath a tree beside the path and pulled a face as he saw them coming out of the woods. "Already? You were hotter than I thought, my friend. I was hoping for a longer respite." He rose to his feet, meticulously dusting off his gray velvet jerkin. "But perhaps we'll have another rest later." A ghost of a twinkle glinted in his light eyes. "It's such a very hot day."

"We won't stop. Not until we've reached Solinari." Lion swung onto the stallion and started down the trail.

"*Now* he's angry," Lorenzo said as he lifted Sanchia onto the mare. Then, as her gaze flew down to his face in alarm, he shook his head. "Not with you. With himself. He allowed you to distract him from his quest for the Wind Dancer. Not for long, but he still considers it a weakness in himself that he won't tolerate. Personally, I find it a very good sign for the future."

"Why?"

He gazed at her a moment, as if trying to decide whether to answer. "Because Lion's sense of responsibility has become a form of bondage. He regards himself not only as the guardian of the Wind Dancer but of everything in his particular world. I suppose it's not surprising. I understand his father instilled that belief in him from the time he was hardly more than a babe. In a way, the statue is a symbol of that bondage."

"Bondage? He's a great lord. Responsibility is not bondage."

"In some men it is." Lorenzo shrugged. "So keep

him so aroused he can't think of responsibilities, Sanchia. It's the best thing for both of you."

"I don't know how to keep him wanting me." Sanchia's cheeks felt hot. "And I don't know if I'd want to make him forget his responsibilities. Surely it is only honorable to—"

Lorenzo groaned as he mounted his horse. "*Santa Maria*, another acolyte burning incense at the temple of honor and glory. I thought you had more sense." He shook his head. "Oh well, perhaps that's what draws him to you. Like to like."

Sanchia stared at him incredulously. "We're not at all alike."

"Yes, you are. But you, Sanchia, are also like me. It will be interesting to see which aspect of your character triumphs in the end." He turned to look at her with cool appraisal. "Power can be very heady. It may occur to you that it would be to your advantage to use the passion Lion feels for you to rise in the world. I have nothing against ambition, but I won't have Lion used. If you show signs of doing so, I will have to remove you."

"I have no power over him."

"Continue in that belief and you'll remain in robust health."

"You care about him." The knowledge that a man as chillingly objective as Lorenzo could care for anyone filled her with wonder. "Why?"

"Who knows?" His smile was self-mocking. "Do you wish me to mouth some maudlin drivel about Lion being the man I would have been in other circumstances? Or even the son I might have sired?" He shook his head. "What makes any man feel anything? Life is filled with strange, exotic emotions, with great mysteries. Which is what makes it tolerable." His horse moved forward at a faster clip as he touched his spurs to the animal's sides.

It was late afternoon when they approached a small farmhouse on the edge of a clear blue lake.

"We go no farther," Lion said as he reined in Tabron. "The village is only a short distance from here, and Solinari lies just beyond it. I don't want word of our arrival to be carried to the palazzo, so we'll wait here for Marco to come to us. I'll talk to the owner of this farm and make arrangements for us to stay the night in his house."

"Who is Marco?" Sanchia asked.

"My brother." Lion dismounted and strode across the barnyard and into the small sod farmhouse.

Another surprise. She really knew nothing about Lionello Andreas, she thought. Was this brother as fierce as Lion and the mother who had borne them both? It was more than probable. She experienced a sudden longing for blessedly familiar Florence where every danger was at least known.

"Marco is not at all like Lion." Lorenzo's assurance came as if he had read her thoughts. He dismounted, then helped her to do so too. "You may find him charming. Most women do."

"It's not her place to find him charming." Lion had returned and was standing on the step. "I have no intention of sharing Sanchia with him."

"How ungenerous of you," Lorenzo said. "Not to mention surprising. Why are you so miserly with Sanchia when you're so willing to share—"

"The house looks clean enough," Lion interrupted. "I've paid the farmer for a night's lodging, and he and his wife will go to his father's farm a few miles from here to shelter tonight. The man will walk to the village to seek out word of Marco and give him a message that we're here while the woman heats water for bathing."

"Excellent," Lorenzo said. "And since you're so fond of these four-footed beasts, I know you won't mind taking care of the horses while I rest." He prudently didn't wait for a reply but strode into the farm house.

Lion smiled lopsidedly as he gazed after Lorenzo. "He'd be very disappointed to realize that I don't mind." He took the reins of the horses and led them toward the small barn. "The hut has only one room, and there's going to be little privacy until we leave Solinari." He glanced over his shoulder. "Why are you just standing there? Come with me to the barn."

She finally understood and hurried after him. "You wish me to lie with you again?"

"If we can find a pile of hay or a blanket free of vermin." He opened the door to the small barn, led the horses inside, and tied their reins to an empty stall. "Otherwise we'll have to be content with a post to lean against." He suddenly stopped and turned to face her in the shadowy barn. "It makes no difference. Nothing matters but this." His hands reached out, moving over her shoulders as a great shudder ran through him. His gaze raked the barn with frantic urgency until he saw a small heap of hay beside one of the stalls. "I wanted you again not ten minutes after we left the brook. I ached with it. I ache now." He led her quickly to the pile of hay and pushed her to her knees. "Make it stop." His voice was low, fierce with frustration and anger. "*Santa Maria*, make it stop!"

He pushed up her skirt and took her with even more wildness than he had shown earlier that afternoon and had scarcely reached the peak when he took her a second time, drawing her with him into a vortex of fiery pleasure.

Lion moved off her, lying beside her on the hay, his chest laboring as he tried to catch his breath. She was also panting, still trembling helplessly from the emotional storm through which Lion had swept her.

"I hate this." Lion thrust his arm over his eyes, speaking through clenched teeth. "It won't last, you know."

"I don't know. I don't know anything about this," Sanchia whispered. "But it seems to me that if you hate it, you wouldn't do it." He didn't answer and she continued uncertainly, "Is it any different with me than it is with Giulia Marzo?"

His arm fell away from his face to reveal dark eyes still glittering with resentment. He smiled cruelly. "Of course; she's much better at it. Do you think I'd bother with you if she were here?"

She felt a wrenching pain that took her off guard. "I'm sorry you don't find me adequate. Perhaps if you'd tell me what I'm doing wrong . . ."

"What are you doing wrong?" His voice was suddenly savage as he jumped to his feet and began unsaddling Tabron. "You're too tight around me, your nipples are too rosy and pointed, your skin is too soft." He jerked the saddle from the stallion's back and dropped it to the earthen floor. "And you stare at me as if I were going to devour you until I cannot stop myself from doing it." He stood with his back to her, his head averted. "Take off your clothes."

She gaped in amazement. He surely couldn't want her again already.

"Stand up and take off your clothes!"

She scrambled to her feet and hurriedly pulled off her gown, slippers, and undershift.

"Come here."

She walked toward him, her gaze fixed anxiously on his averted face.

He turned his head and his gaze went over her body searching out every curve and hollow, every secret place. "Mine," he said hoarsely, his nostrils flaring. "Every bit of you is mine for as long as I care to keep you. Do you understand?"

She nodded quickly.

His hands reached out and cupped her breasts. "Mine. No one is to touch you. You will not let anyone lay his hand on you." His hands moved to the tight curls protecting her womanhood. "Never. You will give no other man so much as a smile unless I bid it."

His voice was so fierce she could do nothing but stare up at him helplessly.

"Say it. You belong to me."

"I . . . belong to you."

"No man will ever touch you but me."

"No man will ever touch me but you."

He seemed curiously tormented as he stared down into her face. Then his hands dropped away from her body and he turned away. "Now you can stop looking at me with those big frightened eyes and get out of here. Put on your gown and go to the house."

She stumbled back away from him and swiftly started to dress. "I could help you with the horses."

"Go to the house."

She walked across the earthen floor and glanced back over her shoulder as she reached the door. Lion hadn't moved; his spine was taut with tension. "I'm not really frightened of you any longer. I was at first, but I don't think you mean me harm."

His hands clenched on the mane of the horse. "I must have the Wind Dancer."

"I know you must," she said, puzzled at the sudden change of subject. "I'll get the key. I promised you and I keep my word. When do I have to go to the palazzo?"

"Tonight, if Marco has the information we need."

Shock ran through her. "So soon?"

"Yes." He turned away and began to loosen the cinches of the mare's saddle. "Go and tell Lorenzo to see that you're bathed and freshly gowned before Marco arrives."

Not garbed for Lion's pleasure this time, she thought numbly, but to go to the palazzo.

"Hurry!"

Sanchia whirled and walked quickly across the barnyard toward the house.

Marco Andreas rode into the barnyard just as the last glorious scarlet rays of sunset were caught and mirrored on the still surface of the lake. He stopped a moment gazing at the beauty before him and a smile warmed the chiseled perfection of his features.

"Well, what do you think of him?" Lorenzo murmured to Sanchia as they watched Lion as he walked across the yard to greet his brother.

Sanchia gazed at the handsome man laughing down at Lion and an involuntary smile touched her own lips. "He's one of the shining people."

"The shining people?"

"You know, the ones you see walking along the streets who always seem to be so happy and full of life. They wear the gayest clothing, they play the mandolin and sing serenades to their ladies. They usually paint or have a passion for sculpting or writing poems . . ."

Lorenzo raised a brow. "And what do you think is Marco's particular passion?"

She tried to gaze objectively at Marco Andreas who was now in deep discussion with Lion. Objectivity proved difficult when faced with such comeliness. Marco bore little resemblance to his brother. He was perhaps a few years younger and his features were classically beautiful in the manner of Michaelangelo's statue of David. His shoulder-length hair was not the onyx black of Lion's but a shining acorn brown, and his eyes were not cold, glittering ebony but warm hazel. At last she said, "He paints."

"And how do you come to that conclusion?"

"He was gazing at the sunset and smiling as he rode into the barnyard. A sculptor is usually concerned with solid shapes and probably wouldn't have noticed the sunset. A poet would have been frowning as he tried to transform the beauty he saw into words. Messer Marco accepted what he saw with joy, knowing that he need only copy what was there."

Lorenzo burst into laughter, and Lion and Marco turned to look at him inquiringly.

Lorenzo nodded at Marco, his lips still twitching with amusement. "Good evening, Marco."

Marco smiled easily. "You seem very happy to see me. Have I done something deserving of mirth?"

"Would I dare laugh at one of the shining people?" Lorenzo turned to Sanchia. "He does paint and, though he does not play the mandolin, he has quite a pleasing tenor." He turned back to Marco. "Tell me, have you sung any serenades of late?"

Marco grimaced. "I won't rise to your jabs, Lorenzo. I take it I'm the butt of one of your less than kind jokes?"

"You malign me. I was just verifying Sanchia's estimate of your character. She finds you very pleasing to the eye."

"Does she indeed?" Lion asked softly, his gaze narrowing on Sanchia's face.

"I meant no offense," she said quickly. "Messer Lorenzo merely asked me to— It was like a game, a puzzle."

"A puzzle you wish to solve?" Lion asked, his tone silky. "In what manner, I wonder?"

Marco cast a quick glance at his brother before stepping forward and bowing gravely. "I'm honored you find me of interest, Madonna Sanchia. Knowing Lorenzo, I'm sure his words have no real weight. He takes pleasure in amusing himself by setting us all topsy turvy. Isn't that so, Lion?"

"At times."

"Most of the time." Marco went on quickly, "Lion tells me you're going to aid us in retrieving the Wind Dancer. It's very kind of you to offer your help. When you see how beautiful the statue is, you'll understand why a man like Damari should never be allowed to possess it."

"Kindness has nothing to do with it. She has no choice. Sanchia does as she's told." Lion took the reins of Marco's horse and abruptly turned away. "Go into the house. I'll join you as soon as I've stabled and watered your horse."

"I can do it," Marco protested.

Lion didn't answer as he led the horse across the barnyard.

Marco pursed his lips in a soundless whistle. "Lion appears to be in a less than felicitous temper. I suppose it's to be expected considering this night's work. He'd much rather go after the key himself than have to wait while you bring it to him, Madonna Sanchia."

"Sanchia," she corrected. It was pleasing to be addressed with such unusual respect but it also brought with it a sense of awkwardness. "Call me Sanchia."

Marco smiled gently. "It would be my delight. A lovely name for an exquisite lady. And you must call me Marco." He gestured for her to precede him into the house. "We must make sure nothing happens to you tonight."

The words were spoken with such warmth Sanchia felt as if she had been touched suddenly by sunlight. She smiled back, feeling a surge of optimism. "Lion said I would be safe."

The faintest frown marred Marco's brow. "I hope so. The task won't be easy."

"You have the information?" Lorenzo asked as he followed them into the house.

Marco nodded as he reached beneath his cloak and pulled out a folded parchment from his belt. "I was able to bribe old Vittorio to draw me this map. He was a gardener at the palazzo before Damari bought it, and he greatly dislikes the new master. He was glad to have sufficient ducats so he could retire to the home of his grandson in Genoa, and he very wisely left Solinari this morning while Damari was still in Pisa."

"Damari isn't here?" Lion asked from the doorway.

Marco unfolded the parchment and spread it on the roughhewn table in the center of the room. "He's been in Pisa for two days and isn't expected back until early next week." His gaze lifted from the parchment to meet Lion's. "According to Vittorio, the captain of the guard said he went there to meet with Duke Valentino."

"Borgia?" Lion tensed. "Then we have little time."

Marco shrugged. "Perhaps more than we think. Cesare may not be in a mood to listen to Damari's proposals. He's had his hands full to overflowing with his conquest of the Romagna and, as you know, it was only a few months ago he used his old friend De Lorqua's head to decorate a pike in the piazza at Cesena because of the unrest there."

"Borgia's always in the mood to further his ambitions." Lion strode forward to peer down at the parchment. "What is this?"

"A map of the grounds of the palazzo."

"It's getting too dark to see in here. Someone light a candle."

Sanchia hastened to obey and set a fat tallow candle on the table.

The flickering flame illuminated a crudely drawn map that seemed to consist of a complicated series of dashes. "This doesn't look like a map," she said, puzzled.

Marco made a face. "Vittorio is no mapmaker, but I hope he's accurate." His slim index finger tapped the longest dash at the top of the paper. "This is the palazzo." He traced a complex square of markings near the middle of the parchment. "And this is the maze in the garden." He pointed at a square in the exact center of the maze. "And this is the storehouse where Damari keeps his treasures. The maze has only two entrances, each guarded by two men."

"Very clever." Lorenzo stepped closer to the table. "Even if someone manages to overpower the guards at one entrance the chances are that, without a map, a thief would become lost in the maze either before he reached the storehouse or when he was trying to leave with his loot."

"And Damari would undoubtedly have the guard-posts checked at frequent intervals," Lion said.

"Every thirty minutes," Marco agreed. "Damari usu-ally keeps at least fifty men in the guardroom at the palazzo, but he took an escort of fifteen to Pisa with him."

"Thirty-five men against three," Lion remarked dryly. "Let's hope we can move through the maze fast enough to avoid them."

"Is that where I have to go?" Sanchia touched the square in the middle of the maze. "The storehouse?"

Marco smiled reassuringly. "No, you only have to go as far as the south entrance to the maze. Rodrigo Estaban, the officer guarding the entrance, has the key to the storehouse on a ring at his belt." He reached beneath his cloak and pulled out a large iron key and handed it to Sanchia. "It looks a good deal like this one. Your task is to steal the key to the storehouse and substitute this key in its place on the ring in such a way that Estaban won't realize it's been stolen."

"Are there other keys on the belt?" Sanchia asked.

"Two. One to the dungeon and one to the gates of the high iron fence that surrounds the palazzo and the grounds. There's dense shrubbery bordering the fence that will be useful for cover, and you don't have to worry about the gates. Vittorio gave me his key to unlock them and passed on a bribe to the soldiers who usually stand guard there."

Sanchia gazed blindly down at the iron key in her hand.

"What's wrong?" Lion asked sharply.

"The other keys. I'll not only have to steal the key and put this one on the ring but keep the other keys from clanging together. I'm not sure I can do it."

"You can do it," Lion said. "You have to do it."

"Lion, for God's sake, if she can't do it . . ." Marco frowned. "I didn't consider the noise."

"Ducats clink in a purse, but she lifted mine with not a whisper of noise in the piazza." Lion's expression was unrelenting. "She'll just have to be careful. You can do it, Sanchia."

She swallowed and then nodded jerkily. "I can do it."

A rare smile lit Lion's face. "In a few hours it will all be over and you'll be handing me the key. We've tried to make it as safe for you as possible. We've hired three whores from the village who will distract the guards at the entrance of the maze and try to prevent the watch from making rounds on time."

"Won't they wonder why the whores decided to come to the palazzo?"

"They may wonder, but it won't keep them from availing themselves of their services," Lorenzo said dryly. "Most men don't think with their brains when a pretty whore offers to spread her legs for them."

Lion nodded. "You go in with the women and pretend you're one of them until you manage to get the key."

"Very well," she said faintly.

He frowned. "It will be all right, I tell you."

She tried to smile. "Do you use the key to steal the statue tonight?"

"No, tomorrow night."

"I see." Her hand clenched so tightly around the key that it cut into her palm. "Could we go to the palazzo right away? I don't want to think about it. I just want to do it. Could we go now . . . please?"

A multitude of emotions flickered across Lion's face as he gazed at her. "Yes." He turned abruptly away. "We can leave this instant. Marco can go to the village and get the whores and meet us at the gates of the palazzo in one hour's time." He turned to Lorenzo. "Marco tells me there's a grove about a quarter of a mile from the gates of the palazzo. We'll need you to come with us and wait there with the horses."

"Splendid. I always prefer the passive role. Though I could think of more stimulating companions with whom to spend an evening."

Lion held out his hand to Sanchia, and again the smile that made his strong, brutal features appear almost beautiful lit his face. "Come along, *cara*."

Cara. The word of endearment echoed warmly in her ears. No one had ever used such a word to her before and she was suddenly filled with a glowing eagerness. She took two steps forward and shyly took his outstretched hand. "I'm coming."

His big hand closed tightly around her small one. She was safe. For this moment there was no fear, no threat. Lion had called her *cara*, had sworn she would be safe and was holding her hand as if there was affection between them.

She let him lead her from the house.

Seven

I didn't realize the Wind Dancer actually existed." Cesare Borgia lifted an ornate goblet to his lips. His gaze was fixed on the muted colors of the tapestry portraying Diana at the hunt on the wall beside the door of the loggia. "I've heard how the Wind Dancer was brought to Italy, but I thought it only an exaggerated tale. You wouldn't be trying to gammon me would you, friend?"

Borgia's tone was idle, almost playful, but Damari was not lulled into a false sense of security. Cesare's temperament was known to swing abruptly from laughter to violence. "It exists and I have it in my possession."

The faintest flicker of interest crossed Borgia's features. "Here in Pisa?"

Damari shook his head. "In a safe place. You do not hire fools to fight your battles, my lord."

"True." Borgia sipped his wine, his gaze

still on the tapestry. "How do you know the statue to be genuine?"

"There could be no other like it. You will realize when you see it that it's beyond compare." Damari leaned forward in his chair, speaking quickly, persuasively. "Think, my lord. Think of the power it would give you. You know the legend of the Wind Dancer. You've heard the tales—"

"Oh yes, I've heard the tales. That the Holy Grail for which the Knights of the Round Table sought was not a grail but a golden statue, that Alexander the Great kept a golden-winged Pegasus in his tent during his conquest of Persia." Cesare shifted his gaze from the tapestry to Damari's face. "There are a hundred tales about the Wind Dancer and I believe none of them." He smiled. "And neither do you. We don't rely on talismans to bring us what we want when a sword is more certain."

"But your father does believe in talismans," Damari reminded him. "And so does King Louis of France. You don't have to believe in a pawn to use it."

Borgia laughed and for a moment his raddled face held a remnant of its comeliness before he'd been afflicted with the pox. "As you intend to use me."

"No one uses you, my lord duke. Your mind is too quick not to perceive deception."

"Sweet words won't buy you what you want from me. We're too much alike." Borgia set his goblet down on the Venetian carved table next to his gloves. "If Andreas owned the Wind Dancer, why did no one know it? It would have increased his consequence to possess such a treasure."

Damari shrugged. "He is a fool. His family brought the Wind Dancer from Persia over a hundred years ago, and they regard themselves as guardians of the statue. The Wind Dancer was kept in a tower room at the castle in Mandara. Even persons who were very friendly with the family were never invited to see Wind Dancer."

"Then how did you come to know of it?"

"I was born in Mandara and I served as an officer under Lionello and his father before him. I listened, I watched, I planned to form my own condotta, and I

knew that when I left Mandara I would take the Wind
Dancer from them."

"I detect a lack of affection." Cesare smiled. "Your
service with Andreas's condotti was not to your liking?"

Damari swiftly hid the bitterness festering within
him. Borgia's eyes were too sharp and he would use any
knowledge with lethal skill. "Lionello did not like my
methods when I served under him after his father died.
He thought me fit to be only a common soldier for the
rest of my life. He was wrong. I have known from
childhood that I was destined for great things."

"Certainly a mistake in judgment. You are definitely
not common." Borgia added, "Though I understand
your birth is not of the highest."

Typical of Borgia, Damari thought: a pat and then
a sharp jab of the spurs. He quickly smothered the fury
surging through him and said, "A man is what he makes
himself, Your Magnificence. Look at what you've become since you shrugged off your cardinal's cape. With
the Wind Dancer in your hands nothing would be
beyond your reach. If His Holiness won't give you the
armies you need for conquest, then take the statue to
France. Louis likes you well enough. Use the statue to
turn his favor into armies to strike at Spain or Florence
or Rome."

"Rome?" Borgia's gaze narrowed on Damari's face.
"You speak treason. You cannot believe I would attack
the papal states and my own father?"

"Yes, if it meant ruling a kingdom as vast as Charle-
magne's."

A frown twisted Cesare's face. "You go too far,
Damari."

"Men like us can never go too far, my lord. It's
beyond the realm of possibility."

Borgia gazed at him a moment and then began to
laugh again. "You're right, Damari. There are no limits
for a man with the stomach to do anything he must to
seize what he wants." He stood up and adjusted the
chain bearing the bejeweled insignia of the Order of St.
Michael that hung low on his chest. The jewels were set

off to great advantage by the black velvet of his jerkin. "I
will consider your terms for the Wind Dancer."

Damari rose to his feet. "Do not consider too long."

"By God, you're bold." Borgia's smile faded. "Don't
make the mistake of taking the Wind Dancer to another
buyer, Damari. It would not be wise."

Damari bowed. "When may I expect to hear from
you?"

"Soon. I must write my father for his views on
acquiring the Wind Dancer. Who knows? He may not be
as mad to have it as you seem to think."

"Perhaps." Damari changed the subject. "Will you
sup with me and then try out a little Turkish servant girl
I acquired recently? She's very beautiful and has many
skills."

"I think not." Borgia started to don the black velvet
mask he was seldom seen without in public these days.
He paused, a smile twisting his lips as he looked down at
the mask in his hands. "Perhaps we're not as alike as I
thought, Damari. You are not as vain as I. Our faces are
both pitted and far from pretty, but you go uncovered
into the world."

"I'm accustomed to my scars, since I had the pox
when I was a small child."

"I have the pox still. The French pox." Borgia
suddenly threw back his head and laughed. "And I'd
wager the little Sicilian wench who gave it to me was far
more captivating than the Turkish girl you so kindly
offered. The bitch was almost worth it."

"You might say that there was a bitch connected
with my pox as well, my lord," Damari said. "So you can
see our afflictions make us truly brothers in adversity.
Are you sure you won't stay and try Zaria? She's only
fourteen and ripe as a plum fresh from the tree."

"Your little beauties have no spirit and often bear
marks that spoil their comeliness. I'll find a woman more
to my liking elsewhere." Borgia slipped the mask over
his face and started for the door, his form supple,
manly, and full of grace. "You should learn to practice
restraint."

"Why?" Damari smiled. "Have we not just agreed

that men such as we should not be bound by limits? Excess can be very exhilarating."

"You clearly find it so." Borgia paused at the door. "Remember, you will do nothing until you hear from me. *Buona sera*, Damari."

Politeness called for Damari to accompany Borgia to the front entrance, but he had already decided not to accord him that courtesy. Borgia must be made to regard him as an equal from this day forward, not just a lackey trailing at his heels. "*Buona sera*, my lord."

Borgia hesitated and then closed the door behind him with a sharp click.

Damari smiled with supreme satisfaction as he turned and walked across the loggia to gaze out at the night sky. All was going extraordinarily well. Borgia wanted the statue and would crave it even more when Pope Alexander fired him with his own enthusiasm. Perhaps it would be possible to gouge even more than a dukedom from the pope. What a triumvirate the three of them would make! No army or country would be able to withstand them. Of course, a triumvirate could not last forever, and one man always emerged the leader in such an arrangement. Why should it not be he? As he had told Borgia, he had known all his life he had a great destiny. How far he had come already! He possessed a fine palazzo, this small but elegant house in Pisa, and a storehouse of treasures he'd secreted from the pope's greedy hands.

And now he had the Wind Dancer.

"My lord, a messenger from Florence begs to see you."

Damari turned to frown at the lackey standing at the door of the loggia. "By what name?"

"Tommaso Santini."

"I know no Santini."

"He said to tell you the message was from Guido Caprino."

"Caprino," Damari murmured. A sudden memory of soft white skin and frightened blue eyes wavered before him. Laurette. The thought of the whore sent a surge of heat to harden his loins. Perhaps Caprino had another choice bit of merchandise to offer him.

"Send Santini in. I'll see what he has to say."

"I've sent the other whores on into the garden," Marco whispered as soon as Lion and Sanchia reached the gates. "This is Maria. She says Rodrigo has come to the village and used her before. I thought he might more easily be distracted by someone he knew."

The dark-haired woman leaning against the gates smiled confidently. "For enough gold I could distract Satan himself, and Rodrigo has always found me pleasing." She held up the jug of wine she was carrying. "And this will do no harm."

"Make sure he believes you to be Venus incarnate. Your task is to keep him from paying any attention to Sanchia, to keep him so busy she'll be able to leave with no suspicion." Lion turned to Sanchia. "You know where you're to go?"

"The south side of the maze." Sanchia moistened her lips with her tongue as she peered through the tall iron gates. She could clearly discern the tall holly hedge looming fortresslike in the distance. She hadn't expected the maze to be so large, stretching at least three hundred feet in length and ninety feet in width, the hedges themselves rising to a height of more than nine feet. "I suppose I should go now." She cast a glance at Lion but his expression was impassive in the moonlight. She opened the gate. "You'll be here? You won't leave me?"

"We'll be here." Lion's hand clenched on one of the iron bars of the gate.

She drew a deep breath and then turned and followed Maria in the direction of the maze.

Lion stood watching her until she disappeared beyond the corner of shrubbery.

"She has courage," Marco said, his gaze following Lion's.

"Yes."

Marco shifted restlessly. "I have no liking for this,

Lion. Sending a woman into danger while we merely stand by—"

"Do you think I do?" Lion's tone was savage. "But she's the only person now who can bring me the key that will give us the Wind Dancer."

Marco fell silent and the minutes stretched on. "It's a great service she does us. How will you reward her if she does bring you the key?"

"What do you mean?"

"You told me she was a slave. Will you free her? It seems a fair—"

"No!"

Surprised at the violence in Lion's response, Marco asked, "Why not? You have no liking for slavery. You refused to have slaves at Mandara. Surely it's—" He stopped as comprehension dawned on him. "You use her in your bed."

"Is that so surprising?"

"No." Marco studied his brother, anxiety growing within him. He was aware that Lion was never celibate when he was away from Mandara, and he had known many of the women Lion had bedded. Without exception they had been knowledgeable in the ways of carnal pleasure and as invulnerable and cynical as Lion himself. Courtesans, bored wives looking for distractions, widows ripe and willing to enjoy the bed sport of which they'd been deprived. Never had there been a woman as vulnerable and young as Sanchia, and never had Lion's response been violent at the idea of parting with a leman. "You're not—" He stopped. *Dio*, he had no right to ask this and yet he felt compelled. He began again, "You're not going to take her to Mandara?"

"No."

Relief poured through Marco, followed immediately by a twinge of guilt. "It's not that I don't wish you to have everything you want, Lion. It's simply—"

"I know." Lion's gaze wearily shifted from the maze to his brother's face. "Don't worry, nothing has changed, Marco."

Marco had an uneasy feeling that a good many things had changed since Lion had gone to Florence to find his thief, but he preferred to accept Lion's words as truth. "Perhaps you could place Sanchia in a fine house in Pisa. Since you've acquired this passion for shipbuilding, you spend more time in Pisa than Mandara anyway. It would be a solution to—"

"Suppose we worry about solutions to other problems after we have the Wind Dancer back," Lion cut in as his gaze returned to the maze. "The Wind Dancer is all that's important right at this moment."

The false key had been exchanged for the key to the storehouse. Now Sanchia had only to return the key ring to Rodrigo's belt.

Only? Panic swept through her at the thought of leaving the comparative safety of the haven in the bushes across from the maze and venturing out once again to complete her task. She had been unusually lucky to be able to quickly, quietly take the key ring and carry it away into the shrubbery to make the switch. Only the fact that Rodrigo had been occupied with pulling the teasing Maria into the maze had made it possible to whisk it from his belt, but it would be madness to believe it would be as easy to replace it.

A shout of laughter followed by a squeal interrupted her thoughts and she turned toward the labyrinth to see the other guard once again mounting the whore with the bronze-dyed hair.

It was senseless to linger in the bushes cowering with fear. Rodrigo was still in the maze. She had no choice but to go after him. She tucked the key ring in her belt and drew her cloak more closely around her shoulders as she stepped boldly from the protection of the shrubbery into the moonlight.

"Ho, there you are." Rodrigo Estaban strolled out of the maze, carrying the jug of wine Maria had given him.

She froze. Had he discovered the keys were gone?

He lifted the jug to his lips and drank deeply before lowering the jug. "You shouldn't have run away. I have enough for both of you. I'm from Spain, where they grow us men as strong as bulls." He gestured toward the maze. "I left your friend so tired she was barely able to swing her hips."

Sanchia quickly lowered her lashes to hide her relief. "I was waiting." She walked toward him. "I didn't want to get in your way."

"I want you in my way. I've always liked redheads." He took a step forward. "Show me your breasts. I want to see how you compare with Maria." He didn't wait for her to show him but grasped the neck of her gown and ripped it downward with one tug, baring her breasts. "Pretty. Not as big, but pretty . . ." His dark head lowered and his wet mouth enveloped her left breast.

Violation. He smelled of garlic and wine and his teeth were hurting her. She felt . . . dirty. Bile rose in Sanchia's throat as she clenched her fists to keep from pushing him away.

She blocked out all thought and feeling. The key ring. She had to return the key ring. Her hands moved with purely automatic skill transferring the key ring back to Rodrigo's belt. He didn't notice. He was grunting, making animallike sounds, whispering vile promises. She should be grateful he was so distracted, she told herself.

She wasn't grateful. She hated it.

The key ring back on his belt, she had to find a way to releasing herself and getting back to Lion with the key. Dear God, where was Maria?

The man's head was lifting, his mouth leaving her breasts. "Come." He grasped her wrist and pulled her toward the maze. "I want you to lie beside that other whore so that I can take turns dipping betw—"

"Rodrigo, where did you go?" Maria emerged from the maze, her bodice still unlaced, her large breasts pale and ripe in the moonlight. A sulky pout pursed her lips. "I close my eyes for a minute and you're off to mount another woman. Send her away."

Rodrigo grinned. "Two is better than one."

Maria flowed toward him, her breasts jiggling as she moved. She stopped before him. "You're wrong. I'm more than enough woman for you." She smiled as she deliberately reached a hand between his legs and squeezed.

He inhaled sharply, his hand releasing Sanchia's wrist.

"You keep telling me what a bull you are. Now show me your *coglios*." Maria backed away teasingly.

"Wait here." Rodrigo tossed over his shoulder as he quickly moved after Maria. "Later I'll have . . ." The rest of the sentence was lost as he followed Maria back into the maze.

Sanchia ran!

The cool wind whipped at her face as she fled across the grass, her lips forming prayers of thankfulness. Only a few yards more.

Lion was opening the gate, his gaze searching her face. Then she was outside the gates, thrusting the key into Lion's hand. "Here," she gasped. "Here is what you wanted."

"No trouble?" Marco asked.

Sanchia drew her cloak more closely around her to hide her torn gown. "No trouble."

Lion's gaze mercilessly raked her features until she felt he must see the imprint of the foul violation she still felt on her flesh. Then, to her relief, he turned away and strode toward the grove where Lorenzo was guarding the horses. "Let's get back to the farmhouse."

During the journey back to the farmhouse, Marco was jubilant and Lorenzo his usual mocking and remote self.

Only Lion was grimly silent.

He knew, Sanchia thought miserably. Somehow he knew she had broken her promise and let herself be touched by another man. She could see it in the way he looked at her, in the tension of his hand grasping the reins, in the tightness of his lips.

When they reached the barnyard Lion dismounted, came around and lifted Sanchia from her horse. His gaze held her own with compelling force. "Who?" he asked softly.

She felt the panic rise within her. "Rodrigo. I couldn't help—"

He was turning away, his hand grasping her wrist with bruising force as he pulled her toward the barn. "Leave the horses in the barnyard," he said in a fierce rasp over his shoulder to Lorenzo and Marco. "I'll tend to them later."

The interior of the barn was dark and frighteningly alive with strange, scurrying sounds. Her heart was pounding so hard she was sure he could hear it.

His powerful body was silhouetted for an instant against the paler darkness of the night sky before he shut the doors. Then there was only blackness.

"Rodrigo?" The harshness of his voice vibrated in the silence. "No other men?"

"No one else." She rushed on frantically, "I couldn't help it. I had to get the keys back and Maria wasn't there and there was no other way to—"

"So you spread your legs and took him into you." His hands fell heavily on her shoulders and he shook her hard. "You let him mount you and—"

"No, he only touched me with his mouth and his hands. He didn't—Maria came and he let me go."

Lion went still. "You're telling me the truth?"

Sanchia nodded frantically, then realized he couldn't see her in the darkness. "I swear, my lord."

"*Cristo!* Then why in hell did you look so guilty?"

"I *was* guilty. You told me I was never to be touched. And he touched me." She shuddered. "I felt befouled. Unclean."

He was silent, his hands still heavy on her shoulders. Abruptly he released her and she heard him moving away.

"My lord?"

"I'm lighting the lantern."

The candle suddenly flared, revealing the grim harshness of his features. He set the lantern on the earthen floor. "Where did he touch you?"

She gestured to her breasts.

He crossed back to her and pushed back her cloak

to reveal the ripped bodice of her gown. His face was hard. "Did he hurt you?"

"Only a little. I'm sorry, my lord."

"My God, why should you beg my pardon? It was by my will you went where that whoreson could get to you." He glanced up and smiled crookedly. "Why are you so surprised? I have my rare moments of fairness. Unfortunately, since I've made your acquaintance my sense of justice appears to have been obscured by my appetites." His palms gently cupped her breasts. "Poor Sanchia, you haven't had an easy time of it since you left Giovanni, have you?"

His voice was almost tender. She held her breath, waiting for more.

There was no more. His hands dropped away from her and he stepped back. "You're not unclean," he said quietly. "You're a clear, sweet river wandering through very muddy banks. But you've reached the sea now and that mud will never touch you again." He gazed gravely into her eyes. "Just as danger will never touch you again. You've done your part to help us and done it well. I'll not ask you to do more."

"You're not angry with me any longer?"

"No." He gazed at her a moment unsmilingly before turning away. "I'm not angry with you." He opened the doors of the barn. "I must get back to the house. Now that we have the key, plans must be made for tomorrow night." He frowned. "I'll have to study the map again. Vittorio's scrawling gave me no idea of the size of the maze. There may be problems." He stepped out into the barnyard. "Tidy yourself and then come to the house. I have no desire to have Marco and Lorenzo gasping at those pretty breasts."

"Lorenzo has seen me unclothed before."

"That's no reason he should do so again. He gets enough enjoyment from tormenting me without your giving him any additional rewards. Things are going to be different."

"Different?"

But he was gone, striding swiftly across the barnyard toward the house.

Sanchia made a futile attempt to adjust the torn
gown before finally giving up and drawing her cloak
over it. She could do nothing to mend the rip since
neither needle nor thread was at hand. Perhaps she
could find both when she returned to the farmhouse.
Her gaze fixed dreamily on the glowing windows of the
house. Different. What had he meant by saying things
would be different? Nothing could be more different
from her previous life than the hours and days since
Lion had purchased her. Yet he must mean there would
be still other changes on the horizon.

She had never been afraid of changes before, but
now she felt a queer stirring within her that could be
fear . . . or the first fragile beginnings of hope.

"Is all well with you?"

Sanchia turned to see Marco standing a few feet
away from the door of the barn. "Did Lord Andreas
send you to fetch me? There was no need. I was just
coming."

Marco shook his head. "Lion is studying the map of
the maze. I thought to seize this opportunity to—" He
broke off and then added, "I knew he was angry with
you."

"No more."

He looked relieved. "I wasn't sure. I cannot always
read Lion."

So Marco had come out to the barn to make sure
she had met with no harm, Sanchia thought with a rush
of warm gratitude. "Yet it's obvious there is a deep
affection between you."

"We are brothers." He smiled and shook his head.
"No, it's more than that. We don't think alike and seldom
act for the same reasons, but the bond is still there."

"It doesn't surprise me that he mystifies you at
times. I have no understanding of the way he thinks,"
Sanchia said. "He has so much. Why should he risk his
life for a statue? He says the Wind Dancer is of his family
but I cannot see how anyone can think of a piece of

metal as if it were flesh and blood." Her gaze lifted to meet his. "As if it were alive."

"But then you've never seen the Wind Dancer," Marco said softly. "The first time I saw it when I was a child I thought it *was* alive. It took away my breath and filled me with wonder." He bent and picked up the lantern from the earthen floor. "Come, we will go back to the house. Lion may need me."

"What does it look like?"

"The Wind Dancer?" Marco took Sanchia's elbow and steered her through the doorway of the barn. "It's not easy to describe it. Let's see, it's a bejeweled golden statue of Pegasus, the winged horse of the gods. It stands only eighteen inches high and is no more than fourteen inches in width. And the wings . . ." His slender left hand made a graceful motion as if caressing the statue. "The clouds on which the Pegasus is running are—"

"Running, not flying?"

Marco nodded. "The horse is running, his wings folded back against his body, the wind braiding his mane. His lips are slightly parted and his eyes are huge almond shaped emeralds. Only his left hind hoof is touching the cloud on the base of the statue so that, unless you look closely, it appears the Wind Dancer is truly sailing through the air."

"It sounds very beautiful."

"Too beautiful. It hurts to look at it."

That was a strange thing to say, and the sadness in his expression was even more strange. "Lion said the statue was very ancient and that there were many legends told of it. How old is it?"

Marco shrugged. "Who knows?"

"Well, how long has your family possessed it?"

The sadness was suddenly gone from Marco's expression and his hazel eyes twinkled with amusement. "You wouldn't believe me if I told you. We're a *very* old family."

Sanchia chuckled. "You go back to Adam and Eve in the garden?"

"Don't we all?"

"No, tell me. You must have some idea when—"

"Back to the ancients of Greece, near the beginning of time. Have you heard of Troy?"

She frowned. "Oh, yes. From a storyteller in the piazza . . . and once in a manuscript brought to Giov—" She stopped. He could have no interest in her former life. "Troy?"

Marco smiled down at her. "According to the stories passed down from generation to generation in my family, it was in Troy where Andros was first given the Wind Dancer."

"Andros." Sanchia repeated thoughtfully. "Andreas."

"Names change through the centuries. We're not sure whether Andros was our ancestor's true name. It is said he was of the Shardana and consequently very tight-lipped about himself."

"I've never heard of a people called the Shardana." She gazed at him uncertainly. "You're jesting with me, are you not? Is this a story you've concocted to punish me for being too curious?"

He shook his head. "I only tell you what I've been told."

"Troy never existed. I have heard of the *Iliad*, but thought it was a myth, a fiction."

"Alexander the Great thought Troy existed, and so did Julius Caesar. Many scholars believe Homer merely repeated what centuries of storytellers before him had handed down through the ages."

"You think the *Iliad* is true?"

"I have no idea. Stories, like names, become twisted through the centuries. The tale I was told certainly didn't agree with Homer's."

"What story were you told?"

"You won't believe that either." He turned to gaze out over the mirrored stillness of the lake. "But I'll tell you anyway, if you like. Andros was a Shardana, one of the sea people. They were great raiders and warriors and very secretive about where they came from. They had reason to be discreet. For centuries they had raided the cities of Greece, Persia, and Egypt, and there had sprung up tales of the splendid city which had been founded from the wealth of their raids. All the cities of that time raided and pillaged but the Shardana were the most successful."

"Corsairs."

Marco nodded. "Andros's ship was storm-wrecked on an island off the coast of Troy, and Andros and his crew were captured. His crew was sacrificed to the god Poseidon, but the Trojans saved Andros to be tortured to try to get him to reveal the location of his homeland." Marco grimaced. "Evidently Troy was quite a raiding power itself and wished to bring home even more treasure and slaves. Andros refused to reveal the location of his city and would have died under the lash if Agamemnon hadn't chosen that time to launch his attack on Troy. The Trojans became distracted."

She frowned. "But the Trojan war went on for years and years, didn't it?"

"That is Homer's story. Our version has it that less than a year passed until Troy fell. Andros was given to Paradignes, the king's brother, to recover his strength until they could once more direct their full attention toward getting the information they wanted from him. The two men became friends over the months of the siege and after Traynor opened the gates they—"

"Wait." Sanchia held up her hand. "Who's Traynor and why would he open the gates?"

"Traynor was a Trojan warrior, and he opened the gates for the oldest reason in the world. He was bribed. He was captured outside the gates in a foray and kept in the Greek encampment for over a week before he supposedly escaped and returned to Troy.

"One night, a few days after he returned, he opened the west gate and the Greeks rushed into the city. They were finally beaten back, but the Trojans lost many warriors and the Greeks managed to set fire to the gate as they left Troy. Traynor had been seen opening the gates and the king ordered that he be hacked to pieces, his remains burned in the square of the city." He paused. "In Traynor's lodgings the king's guards found the Wind Dancer."

"The bribe."

Marco nodded. "The king gave the statue to Paradignes and ordered him to burn it until there was nothing left of the Wind Dancer but molten rubble."

"But he didn't do it."

"He was a lover of beauty and couldn't bring himself to destroy the statue. He didn't want the Greeks to have it either and knew it was only a matter of time until they conquered the city." He smiled at Sanchia. "Can you guess what he did?"

"He gave the statue to Andros?"

"And showed him a way to get out of the city. It seems Troy had been destroyed and rebuilt many times and there was an underground passage that led to a hill far beyond the city. Paradignes showed Andros the entrance to the tunnel and wished both him and Jacinthe well before—"

"Jacinthe?"

"One of the conditions of Andros's release was that he take not only the Wind Dancer but a woman from Troy. Paradignes didn't want the Greeks to have her either."

"Was the woman Paradignes' wife?"

"He had no wife."

Sanchia's eyes widened. "Helen . . ." she whispered.

"There was no mention of a woman called Helen, only Jacinthe." Marco smiled faintly. "But I find it significant that the word *Jacinthe* means 'the beautiful one.'"

"And they both left Troy that night with the Wind Dancer. Where did they go?"

"South. Toward Egypt. The legend says the two of them stood on a hill some distance away from the city and watched it burn."

"So that was the night the Trojans brought in the Greeks' wooden horse?"

Marco chuckled and shook his head. "That's Homer's tale again. There was no great wooden horse. There was only the Wind Dancer."

Only the Wind Dancer. A statue so beautiful that a man would betray his home and his people to possess it. A work of art so exquisite it would inspire tales that would endure for over a thousand years. "Do you believe what you've been told is true?"

"Sometimes. Is it not more reasonable that the gates of Troy would fall because of bribery and betrayal than such a stupid ploy as a wooden horse?"

"I suppose it is," Sanchia said slowly. "Where do you suppose the Greeks got the Wind Dancer?"

"Before he died Traynor said the Greeks told him two shepherds found it in the hills above Mycenae during a great storm and brought it to Agamemnon. They claimed it appeared in a flash of lightning."

"Nonsense."

"Legend. And not nearly as unreasonable as some of the other legends connected with the Wind Dancer through the centuries."

Sanchia was tempted to ask him to tell her those other legends, but suddenly she knew she didn't want to know more about the statue. The Wind Dancer was now looming in her imagination with an odd sentience, taking on a dimension and life of its own. She could almost see the golden statue shimmering in the darkness of the storehouse, waiting patiently for Lion to come for it, uncaring what danger he ran to free it from its prison.

Foolishness. She had never even seen the statue. Her nerves were merely on edge and crying out from the terror and strain she had undergone this evening.

She forced a smile as she turned away from him. "A fantastic tale, but certainly an entertaining one. You're a far better storyteller than Pico Fallone, who entertains in the piazza in Florence." She glanced back over her shoulder. "But, of course, I don't believe any part of it."

A gentle smile lent fresh beauty to Marco's fine features. "Of course not. You're clearly a very sensible woman. Why would you believe such a preposterous legend? I only told you the story because you asked."

"I was merely curious." Sanchia quickly opened the door and stepped inside. "But naturally I realize none of it actually happened."

"It's going to take longer than thirty minutes to make our way through the maze to the storehouse, find the Wind Dancer, and then travel back to the maze entrance again." Lion scowled down at the map. "There's no question that the watch will discover we've entered the maze and have guards waiting for us at both ends."

Marco bent closer. "*Jesú*, you're right. We'll have to stop every few turns and study the map." He made a face. "What a puzzle. That labyrinth looks like a passage through hell."

"Then Damari must feel completely at ease there," Lion said.

"I could go with you and wait in the shrubbery across from the maze to dispose of the watch," Lorenzo offered.

Lion weighed the suggestion. "I don't like having no one to watch the horses, and it would probably give us only another five or ten minutes before someone else was sent to see why the watch hadn't returned. I doubt if that would be long enough."

Lorenzo shrugged. "What other choice do we have?"

She wouldn't answer, Sanchia thought, looking down at her hands clenched tightly together in her lap. They weren't talking to her. She could sit on the stool by the fire and not say a word. Lion had told her she need do no more to reclaim the Wind Dancer. She would be foolish to go back to the palazzo when Lion said she did not have to help them.

"No choice," Lion said.

She would remain silent. Lion had said she need not endanger herself again.

But she had promised him loyalty as well as obedience. Was it loyal not to speak now?

"Then you and Marco go inside the maze and I stay outside and take care of the watch," Lorenzo said. "Marco can carry the lantern and you can try to read the map."

"And hope we don't lose our way among all those damned dashes," Marco said ruefully, "or we'll find ourselves hacking our way through those hedges with a broadsword."

"Those hedges are almost four feet thick. At any

place but the last outer hedge that borders the perimeter it would take the better part of a day to cut our way through." Lion grimaced. "Providing we knew in which direction to cut. We'll just have to—"

"I can lead you through the maze."

The three men turned to look at Sanchia.

Sweet Jesus, why had she spoken? she wondered, slowly unclenching her clammy palms and rubbing them on the skirt of her gown. She stood up. "I can lead you to the storehouse and back to the entrance in less than thirty minutes."

Marco shook his head. "I know you want to help, Sanchia, but this maze is hellish. No one can—"

"I can." She came forward and looked down at the map. "I won't have to stop and check the map every few minutes and I won't lose my way. I'll know exactly where I'm going every minute."

"Astonishing," Lorenzo said. "And unbelievable."

"No, it's true." She closed her eyes and envisioned the map before her. "When you enter the maze you turn right, go past two passages and then turn left, go past another three passages and turn left again, then—"

"Enough," Lion said.

She opened her eyes to see him looking at her with a faint smile on his lips. "It seems Giovanni wasn't trying to raise your price as I suspected."

She shook her head. "I remember everything. From the time I was a small child I had only to see something once to keep it forever in mind."

"Surely a mixed blessing, but in this case a fortunate one for us." He paused. "If you choose to come with us."

"Choose? You do not command me?"

"I told you that you need not go back to the palazzo. I won't break my word."

Lorenzo cupped his hand to his left ear. "Hark, do I hear the glorious peal of trumpets? I don't think I can bear many more of these appallingly honorable moods to which you persist in subjecting me, Lion."

"Be quiet, Lorenzo." Lion's gaze did not leave Sanchia's face. "I won't force you to go back with us."

"But you have need of me."

"Oh yes, we have need of you, Sanchia." He smiled that rare, brilliant smile that always succeeded in touching some mysterious emotion within her that had never been tapped before. A smile was a mere expression, she thought, puzzled. It should not have the power to cause this warm flowering of hope. A smile should not be able to make her do something so foolish as to go back to the palazzo. She should ignore his smile and tell him she would never return to the palazzo again.

"I'll go," she whispered. "I'll lead you through the maze."

Eight

Sanchia shivered as she gazed through the iron bars of the gates at the maze. When she had first seen the tall hedges of the labyrinth last night she had thought they resembled the walls of a fortress, but she had never dreamed she'd actually have to breach them.

"I still don't think we should enter the maze through the south entrance," Marco whispered. "Why don't we try the north entrance where there's no officer in charge?"

"No." Lion didn't look at him as he opened the gate. "We go through the south entrance."

"But we should—"

"I want Rodrigo," Lion said savagely. "Give me five minutes and then bring Sanchia." He faded into the dense shrubbery bordering the gate.

Her body icy now with foreboding in addition to fear, Sanchia wrapped her cloak closer about her and continued to stare at the maze. Death. Rodrigo Estaban was going to die within minutes at Lion's hand.

"It's time to go." Marco took her elbow and propelled her gently forward. "Quickly, Sanchia."

There was no sign of Rodrigo or the other guard at the south entrance of the maze. Lion came out of the maze and knelt to wipe his sword on the grass before sheathing it. Blood edged his scabbard. Sanchia couldn't seem to tear her gaze from the wet, dark stain on the grass.

"I dragged them both just inside," Lion said tersely. "Be careful not to stumble over them." He turned back into the maze.

Marco lit the lantern as soon as they had joined Lion within the screening confines of the hedges.

Rodrigo Estaban and his fellow guard lay on their backs, their dead eyes staring sightlessly up at the black heavens.

Sanchia swallowed to ease the queasiness in her stomach. She wheeled sharply away from the bodies. "This way." She kept her eyes fastened straight ahead as she moved swiftly down the first passage and turned right.

After several minutes of convoluted, twisting turns, Marco asked doubtfully, "Are you sure you didn't take the wrong path, Sanchia? I think we may be going around in circles."

Sanchia shook her head. "Two more turns and we should reach the storehouse." She had a sudden terrifying thought. "If the map is right." What if Vittorio had drawn the map incorrectly? She took the last turn and felt weak with relief. A small, windowless wooden building lay before them. "There it is!"

"We don't have much time." Lion moved quickly forward and inserted the key in the lock of the door. "It must have taken us at least ten minutes to make our way here." The door swung open. "The lantern, Marco."

Sanchia waited outside as Marco and Lion disappeared within the storeroom. Now that she was alone she was beset with a fear so intense it almost suffocated her. The air seemed to vibrate with a sense of waiting menace.

Marco emerged from the storehouse a few minutes later. "We found it!" His hazel eyes were shining in the lantern light. "It was there, Sanchia."

Lion followed him, carrying a medium-sized wooden chest. "Considering the trouble we've suffered I would have been a little irritated if it wasn't," he said dryly. "Get us out of here, Sanchia."

She nodded eagerly, her gaze on the mahogany chest. The Wind Dancer was in that plain wooden container. How strange that such a small object, an object she had never set eyes upon was important enough to Lion and his family to cause all this effort and fear. But soon the terror would be over, soon they would all be safe.

She turned and began the complicated trek back to the south entrance. She had been foolish, she told herself, to let her own cowardly fear give way to an icy sense of doom. She took a right turn and then a left, her pace increasing. Everything was going well. Lion had his Wind Dancer. They would be back at the entrance before the watch passed.

She turned right, left, right again. The high walls of greenery were pressing in on her in a smothering blur. She was almost running now, the pulse in her temple pounding wildly. "The entrance is right ahead," she called back to Lion and Marco. "One more turn and we'll—"

Drawn swords glittered in the moonlight!

She skidded to a halt, her eyes widening in horror. "No!" The narrow passage ahead was crowded with men in armor dressed in the same yellow-and-white livery Rodrigo and his comrades wore.

Sanchia heard Lion's low voice cursing behind her. "Damari."

"Greetings, Lion." A man at the forefront of the soldiers took a step forward. "What a pleasure it is to see you at my palazzo under such intriguing circumstances. I don't suppose you'd be willing to put down the Wind Dancer and surrender to me?"

"No."

"I didn't think so." Damari took another step forward and the light cast by the lantern in Marco's raised hand fell full on him.

Sanchia was taken aback by the looks of Damari. Barely of medium height with a barrel chest and overdeveloped torso, his muscular legs were round as tree trunks and far too short. He seemed almost grotesquely malproportioned to Sanchia. And when her gaze rose to his tea-colored eyes glittering in the lantern light, she realized his soul was as misshapen as his body. She saw only malevolence in him.

"I hoped you wouldn't give up too easily," Damari said lightly. "Of course, that is why I permitted you to come into the maze and retrieve your property instead of cutting you down as you entered the gates. I knew you'd struggle harder once you had the Wind Dancer in your hands. It's always more difficult to give up once victory is in our grasp."

Lion's expression was impassive. "A trap. You knew we were coming."

Damari nodded. "What a wonderful surprise when I learned you were going to visit me. I hadn't even realized you'd returned from France and discovered my acquisition of your statue until I received a message last night in Pisa that you'd made plans to get it back."

"Then you didn't permit Sanchia to steal the key from Estaban?"

"Oh no. Either your thief is exceptionally skilled or Rodrigo was extraordinarily thick-headed. I wasn't happy with Rodrigo." He shrugged. "And so I assigned him to guard duty tonight."

"In order that I would kill him?"

"A fitting punishment for his stupidity, don't you think?" His gaze shifted to Sanchia. "And this must be your clever little thief. Present me to her, Lion."

"Who sent the message?"

"Guido Caprino." The smile lingered on Damari's lips. "He requested one thing only in return—that I use your little slave in the fashion which will give me the most pleasure."

Marco began to swear softly yet vehemently.

"That distresses you, Marco?" Damari asked. "But then you always did have a soft heart where the ladies were concerned. Lion and I are of a tougher breed. We don't balk at using any means at hand to get what we want." His gaze remained on Sanchia. "Do we, Lion?"

"But I protect what is my own." Lion's grip tightened on the wooden chest. "You should have known I'd never let you take the Wind Dancer."

"But I did take it, just as eventually I'll take everything from you, Lion. After I'm done toying with you, I may even let you live so that you can appreciate your loss."

"And are you toying with me now?"

"Of course." Damari's smile widened as his pale eyes returned to Lion. "Isn't that clear? When are you going to begin wriggling on my hook, so that I can enjoy myself? Perhaps I should detail your predicament. There are ten men blocking this passage and another ten outside the entrance. I've deployed another ten outside the north entrance of the maze." He lifted his gloved hand and slowly closed his fingers into a fist. "The trap is closed. Consequently, either you surrender or you run."

"Run where?" Lion asked warily. "You have a fancy to chase us through this damnable maze?"

"How clever of you to understand. Naturally, it will be to no avail. I know this maze and, even with the map I assume you've managed to bribe from one of my men, you'll soon become hopelessly lost. It's impossible to read a map while you're being pursued. How long do you think you'll be able to avoid capture, Lion? Fifteen minutes? An hour? And every minute you'll know we're right behind you or waiting around the next hedge."

Lion studied Damari's expression. "You've played this game before?"

"Only on a few special occasions. I make it a practice not to indulge myself too frequently or the pleasure loses its bite. Though I admit the maze was the reason I purchased this particular palazzo. I immediately saw its splendid possibilities." He drew his sword from its scabbard. "Now, which shall it be? Surrender or the maze? I do hope you choose the maze. I'll even give you a few minutes' head start as an incentive."

"Then I'd hate to disappoint you." Lion shifted the chest under his right arm and his left hand closed on Sanchia's elbow. "The maze."

He turned and ran down the passage from which they had come, dragging Sanchia behind him.

Marco was right behind them as they made the first turn. "*Cristo*, Lion, what's the use in letting him play with us when we—"

Lion's words cut through his question. "Damari's right; a map is useless in a chase through this maze, but he doesn't know about Sanchia's gift." He turned his head toward her. "Take us to the western perimeter and hurry!"

Sanchia wasted no time in questioning him. She turned and started at a dead run through the maze.

"Your head start is over." Damari's voice rang through the greenery. "Do you hear me, Lion? I'm coming after you!"

Sanchia's heart plunged and she began muttering frantic prayers beneath her breath. What if she became too frightened to remember the way? No, there was the long border hedge directly in front of her.

"This is it." She gasped. "But there's no entrance here. Why do—"

"The south and north entrances are blocked." Lion set the chest down, drew his sword and begun to hack at the hedge. "But Damari didn't say that the entire maze was surrounded. If we can hack our way through this hedge, we have a chance to slip away into the shrubbery that skirts the gate."

Marco drew his sword and joined Lion, slicing away at the branches. "The gate has to be guarded now."

"We'll worry about that when we get out of the maze. *Dio*, it's like cutting through stone."

Sanchia stood watching as the two men attempted to cleave their way through the living wall. It was taking so *long* and she could hear Damari's taunting voice. He was closer.

"Take the lantern and go to the end of the passage, Sanchia." Lion didn't look at her as he gave the hedge another mighty blow. "If you see or hear any sign of Damari run back to us and we'll forget about getting through this wall and try the east hedge."

"Yes, my lord." She snatched up the lantern and ran the several yards to the end of the passage, desperately glad to be able to do something to help.

The whacking of the swords against the hedge branches was ominously loud to her ears. Surely Damari would be able to hear if he drew closer.

And he was very close! Damari's voice carried faintly to her from a distance that could not be farther than two passages over. "Are you lost yet, Lion? Are you beginning to choke on your fear?"

Sanchia's throat tightened in response to the taunt. *She* was the one choking with fear. She cast a frantic glance over her shoulder at Lion and Marco. She was too far away to determine how near they were to penetrating the hedge.

"We're almost through," Lion called softly as if in answer to her unspoken question. "Damari?"

She realized he hadn't heard Damari's voice over the sound of the chopping. "He's drawing near."

Lion muttered a curse and assaulted the hedge with even more force.

"Your precious Wind Dancer must be a burden to you as you run from me," Damari called mockingly. "Soon you'll be glad to abandon it just to gain a little more strength for the chase."

He couldn't be more than one hedge away, Sancha decided. She would have to warn Lion and Marco.

But they were almost through the hedge and, if they abandoned the attempt, who was to say Damari would not discover the mutilated border and realize they would now be trying the same ploy on the opposite side of the maze. There had to be some other way.

If she could draw Damari and his men away through the maze and then double back . . . She closed her eyes and tried to visualize the passages leading away from the western border. Two right turns would put her on the same path they had traveled previously to reach the storehouse. Then she could circle the small building and come straight down the western border passage and rejoin Lion and Marco. She could give Damari only a glimpse of her skirt going around the corner, or a gleam of the lantern disappearing down the passage and he would think all three of them were still together.

She could hear the clank of armor in the passage diagonally across from the one in which she was standing. If she was going to do it, it must be done now. Her grasp tightened on the handle of the lantern and she drew a shaky breath. An instant later she was flying across the path intersecting the passage Damari's men were traveling.

She heard a shout as one of the guards caught sight of her and then Damari's low, pleased laugh.

The jagged opening in the hedge was scarcely three feet long and two feet wide, but it would have to suffice.

Lion sheathed his sword, picked up the chest containing the Wind Dancer and pushed it through the opening before calling softly over his shoulder, "Sanchia!" He started to crawl through the hedge as he said to Marco, "Watch over Sanchia. I'll go first and make sure the way is clear and get rid of any guards at the gate." He was already halfway through as he added, "be quick!"

He heard Marco's assent as he wriggled the last two feet, sharp broken twigs and thorny leaves tearing at his jerkin and flesh like daggers. Then he was through the hedge and on his feet. He paused, swiftly looking over the area. They were in luck. As he had hoped, Damari had concentrated his forces at the two entrances and, though he could hear the sound of voices issuing from the far side of the maze, this side of the labyrinth was deserted. He picked up the Wind Dancer's box and moved quickly into the cover of the bushes bordering the fence, then ran at full speed toward the gate. He slowed as he neared the end of the shrubbery, moving cautiously forward. If the gate had been refortified, then there should be signs of the guards soon.

"Do remind me to teach you the rudiments of stalking through a grove without sounding like a pregnant ass." Lorenzo emerged from the bushes beside Lion.

"The guards?" Lion whispered.

"Dead. Behind me in the bushes. I thought there might be something amiss when three of Damari's men appeared and started to search the woods. After I got rid of them I decided to come and see if I could be of assistance. Where are the others?"

"Following. I think I hear them now." Lion looked over his shoulder.

Lorenzo grimaced. "How could you not? They're making even more noise than you did. Still, I think we'll make sure it's not one of Damari's guards." He receded into the bushes.

Seconds later Marco pushed back the screen of branches and bolted into sight. He pulled up at the sight of Lion. "*Dio*, Lion, she wasn't there." He panted. "She was gone. I tried to—"

"What do you mean? Sanchia was only a few yards away from us." His hand closed on Marco's arm with bone crushing force. "What the hell do you mean?"

"They've got her."

"You don't know that." Lion whirled and started back toward the maze. "You *left* her, God damn you."

Lorenzo stepped in front of Lion. "Listen to him, Lion."

"He left her in that maze alone." Lion's voice was trembling with rage. "You whoreson coward, why didn't you look for her?"

"She screamed," Marco said simply. "I was going to try to search for her when I heard her scream. Damari has her, Lion. Should I have stayed and let Damari capture me too? It would have been of no help to her to have me in the same cage."

"And you won't help Sanchia if you let Damari get his hands on you, Lion," Lorenzo said. "You can't do anything at this moment to free her."

Lion glared at him, his eyes wild in his white face. "I promised nothing would happen to her. You're telling me to abandon her?"

"I'm telling you that you'll have to wait until later to help her," Lorenzo said. "Think, Lion. You're not reasoning clearly."

He wasn't reasoning at all, he was only feeling. *She screamed.* "I promised her."

"Then keep your promise," Lorenzo said. "But you won't keep it by letting Damari toss you into his dungeon."

Lion knew he was right. He couldn't help Sanchia, and he was endangering Marco and Lorenzo by lingering. But, Jesus, she needed him and he couldn't help her. The guilt was his, not Marco's.

"Damari won't kill her at once. We both know that's not his way," Lorenzo said. "We have time. You can ride to Mandara and get more men."

No, Lion thought in rage, Damari wouldn't deprive himself by killing her immediately. He would want to go slowly with her, very slowly, and wrench every vile pleasure for himself that he could from Sanchia's torture. Frustration—acid hot, bile bitter—tore through Lion. He whirled and strode toward the gates. "Mandara's too far away. We'll ride for Pisa. Let's go."

Sanchia screamed.

Damari's hand cracked against Sanchia's cheek with such force that she fell to the ground.

"You mustn't scream again. Were you trying to warn your master?" Damari smiled down at her in the moonlight. "But that's not how the game is played. Now, tell me where he is."

"I don't know." Sanchia struggled to raise her head. "We became separated."

"I don't think so," Damari said slowly. "Now that I think back on it, you were a little too slow in getting away from us. We caught far too many glimpses of you before I managed to intercept you. You were leading us away from him, weren't you?" His pitted cheeks creased as his smile widened. "Such inspiring loyalty. Did he tell you to distract us? How unkind of him when he must have known we'd catch you eventually."

Sanchia shook her head, trying to clear it of fear as well as the ringing pain of Damari's blow. "No, we were separated," she repeated hoarsely.

He bent down and effortlessly lifted her to her feet. "You mustn't lie to me." His voice was seductively gentle. "I'll find them anyway, you know. It's amazing that I haven't located them already. It's never taken me this long before." His smiled faded. "But fortune has always been on the side of that bastard. Tell me where you left him."

"I don't know. We were separated and I became lost—"

Agony rocked her when Damari struck her other cheek.

"Tell me." His voice was even more gentle, almost tender. "Was he going toward the north entrance?"

The maze was whirling, blurring around Sanchia. "I don't know."

He struck her again.

She swayed. "We became separated and I lost my way. I don't know where—"

Pain exploded again and she hurtled down into a welcome darkness.

"Come now, wake up. I'm becoming very impatient. You've been unconscious the better part of the night."

Sanchia slowly opened her eyes to see Damari gazing down at her.

"Very good. I was afraid I had done you some grievous physical damage." He waved a hand. "No matter. I had to send for Fra Luis anyway and would not have been able to start."

"Start?" Sanchia whispered. She tried to sit up before realizing with a surge of panic that she couldn't move. She was no longer in the maze but strapped at knees, waist, and shoulders to a hard surface. She glanced wildly around her but could see only the wooden table to which she was bound. The aureole of light cast by a torch in Damari's outstretched hand barely illuminated his face. "Where—"

"In the dungeon." Damari strolled a few yards from the table and thrust the torch into an iron bracket on the wall. "As is proper for a thief."

She became chillingly aware of the darkness surrounding her, the odor of the damp earth, the smell of pitch and decay.

"I'm very angry with you, you know." Damari returned to stand beside her. "I lost not only Andreas but the Wind Dancer. I sent my men riding after him in all directions but he appears to have vanished. All I have is a slave who will be of absolutely no use in getting either back. Lion obviously cares nothing about whether you live or die or he wouldn't have sent you to divert me from his escape." He frowned. "And my lovely hedge is quite ruined. It will take years to replace it with new growth."

He seemed more upset by the damage to his shrubbery than by the escape of Lion and Marco, she thought dazedly. "You lie. They wouldn't have left me."

"Still loyal? They most certainly did leave you. But what did you expect? You're property—far less valuable property than the Wind Dancer. You notice he didn't leave the statue behind. Surely you don't think he'll return for you?"

Lion had promised nothing would happen to her. He had vowed she wouldn't be hurt. She had to believe he'd come back for her or she would be overwhelmed by the terror and despair closing in all around her.

Damari carefully smoothed the hair at her temple. "Poor little slave girl. You're frightened, aren't you?"

He wanted her fear; she could see it in his expression. She didn't answer.

"And you should be." His fingertips drifted lightly over her cheek, leaving pain in their wake. Her bruised flesh was exquisitely sensitive. "I'll get the Wind Dancer back and I'll punish Andreas. It's only a question of time." His fingers had reached her hairline and he reversed the direction, retracing the painful caress. "But I must have some satisfaction to keep me patient."

Her gaze was fixed in helpless terror on his face. Lion had promised her she wouldn't be hurt. Lion had promised her. . . .

"I've always believed punishment should fit the crime. I kept one of Giulia Marzo's whores here at the palazzo for a number of months. She quite enjoyed the pain at first, but alas, it didn't last. She was a pretty little strumpet, though incapable of tolerating more than minor pricks of chastisement. You can understand how this annoyed me when I had paid such a handsome sum for her." His index finger followed the outline of her lower lip. "So I decided I had a right to compensation. Do you know what I did?"

Sanchia couldn't speak, her throat was locked with terror as she gazed up into his pale eyes.

"I stripped her naked and sent her into the maze. Then I sent twelve of my men in to find her. Naturally, they expected reward when they ran her down. A whore's reward." He shrugged. "She died."

He was a monster. Sanchia could imagine the horror of that poor, frightened woman running frantically while she was chased by a pack of taunting, savage animals seeking only to rape.

"A fitting death for a whore, don't you think? But you're not a whore, you're a thief." He lifted her left hand, playing with her fingers. "Tell me, what is the punishment for thieving, Sanchia?"

"*Santa Maria* . . ." She didn't realize she had spoken until she saw him smile again.

"We cut off their hands, don't we?" he asked softly. "I think we'll start with your fingers. One by one." He dropped her hand. "And I have a very skilled companion who will know just how to do it. I met Fra Luis when I was campaigning in Spain and persuaded him to come back to Italy with me. He was much favored by Queen Isabella as a torturer, but he realized there would be more opportunity for advancement in my employ."

Her hands gone. Her worst nightmare— No! This was real. Horribly, hideously real.

She heard the creak of a door beyond her line of vision, and Damari's gaze lifted. "Oh, there you are, Fra Luis, she's awake. We can begin."

Sanchia instinctively began to struggle against the bonds holding her to the table as Fra Luis came to stand beside Damari. He was dressed in a mud-colored monk's robe that only enhanced the unhealthy sallowness of his complexion. His face was full, his lips pouty, and his green eyes coolly objective.

"Greetings, my child." Fra Luis's deep voice resonated hollowly in the chamber. "My Lord Damari tells me you have sinned and must be chastised."

Sanchia shuddered and closed her eyes.

It was going to happen. She was alone and helpless to stop them from torturing her . . . and cutting off her hands.

Lion had abandoned her.

Nine

Her left hand throbbed, waking her. Was it bleeding again? She supposed she should do something to stop it. She rolled over, then slowly, sluggishly, inched herself until she was in an upright position.

Panting, she collapsed, back against the damp, slimy wall of the cell. What did it matter? They would be coming for her again soon and then it would start again. What did anything matter?

But it did matter.

It wasn't fair that she should be made to suffer like this. Fury burned away the despair numbing her emotions. What had she done? She had obeyed, as a slave must obey. She had been used, as a slave would be used.

She had been used.

A cockroach scampered over her throat and into her hair. She listlessly shook her head to rid herself of it.

Filth and pain and vermin . . . and betrayal.

Promises to slaves need not be kept. They were nothing, less than nothing.

She tensed, every muscle becoming rigid. She could hear the slap of Fra Luis's sandals on the flagstones of the corridor. He would take her to that room and strap her down on the table, place her hand on the block. He would look down at her with those cool, unfeeling eyes and the agony would begin again.

And Damari would stand there drinking in her pain watching her face, stroking her hair and whispering of pain to come. There was no justice in any of it, she thought fiercely. She did not deserve to be tortured. It was not right that she should submit herself to the will of others when it brought this agony.

The door swung open and Fra Luis's fleshy silhouette was outlined against the flickering amber glow of the torch lighting the corridor.

Sanchia braced herself for the command to rise and follow him. She should be frightened, but the fear had been seared out of her by the anger now possessing every portion of her heart and mind.

"Are you ready, child?"

She rose clumsily to her feet, using only her right hand to push herself from the wall, wanting to hurl herself at him and pound his white, pasty face with her fist. She had done that last night when they had come for her and they had made sure she had paid for it.

But someday she would find a way to escape them. Someday she would escape all the people who had brought her to this.

Until then she could only endure.

Fra Luis held out his hand. "Come, Lord Damari is waiting. He suggests we do the thumb this morning."

"My God!"

It was Lion's voice and yet not Lion's—hoarse, oddly broken . . .

But how could it be his voice when Lion had gone away and left her to Damari? Sanchia tried to fight her way out of the darkness she had purposely drawn about her to shut both madmen away, but the barrier was too solid, too strong. She mustn't lift her lids or move her body or the pain would start again. Pain was hiding everywhere, living in the darkness with the cockroaches and the rats. But she didn't have to open her eyes; she was only dreaming.

"*Jesú*," Lorenzo said. "Don't just kneel there staring at her. *Move*, Lion. We've got to get her out of here before Damari comes back with reinforcements."

"Look at her," Lion whispered.

"She's not dead, and you've seen worse," Lorenzo said impatiently. "Let's get her away from this hellish filth and we'll see what they've done to her."

Terrible things, she wanted to tell them. Cruel and senseless things that had somehow burned away what she had been and left someone else in her place. But it was no use talking to a dream. . . .

She was being gently lifted. Strange. None of her other dreams had seemed so real. Scent too. Leather and soap and that distinctive male fragrance she remembered as belonging to Lion. Perhaps it wasn't a dream after all.

She stirred and tried to lift her head.

"Don't move. You're safe now." Lion's voice was thick, his words muffled. "We're taking you away from here."

She would will the darkness away and see if it was really Lion. Lately she had discovered that her will could triumph when her body failed. She had only to concentrate all her energy and channel it into effort. Slowly her lids lifted and her eyes focused on the face above her.

Dark eyes glittering with a moist brilliance gazed down at her. Lion's eyes. "You . . . you broke your promise."

A muscle jerked in his jaw. "I know." Lion's arm tightened around her. "But I'm here now and I'll take care of you, Sanchia. I'll always take care of you."

She shook her head. "It's too late."

She heard him draw a harsh, strangled breath before her lids fluttered closed again.

The cell was moving, shuddering, falling.

Another nightmare. Sanchia moaned softly, and tried to crowd closer to the wall to keep from falling with the crazily shifting cell.

"Don't be afraid," Lorenzo said. "It's only a small squall, nothing to fear."

A squall was a storm, wasn't it? How could there be a storm in a cell?

Sanchia opened her eyes to see Lorenzo lounging in a chair across the room, one leg thrown over the arm, his booted foot swinging.

"Oh, you're awake. Excellent. I have a craving for conversation. You've been very dull of late, but Lion was most insistent I stay with you until you regained your senses. How do you feel?"

It wasn't a cell, and it wasn't a dream either. The room *was* dipping crazily! She tried to sit up. "What's happ—"

"Lie still." Lorenzo's tone was testy. "I have no desire to have to jump up and run over there to keep you from falling out of bed. When the sea is rough I make a practice of staying in one spot and not moving even if I grow barnacles. It saves a measureless amount of indignity and humiliation."

"Sea?" Sanchia's eyes widened.

"We're on Lion's ship *Dancer* enroute to Genoa."

"Genoa," she echoed. Perhaps she had been wrong about this being a dream. "But how—" She dazedly shook her head. She was immediately sorry as the room swung in sickening circles and she collapsed back against the pillows. "I was in the dungeon."

Lorenzo nodded. "For three days." He grimaced. "All of which time Lion was roaring like his namesake."

She had to have been in that dungeon for more than three days. Cockroaches, slime, the block . . . "No, it was longer than that."

"Stop shaking." Lorenzo frowned. "It's over. Lion managed to get you away from Damari."

It wasn't over. It could never be over now. "How?" she whispered.

"He rode to Pisa and hired a troop of men from Count Brelono and then rode back and attacked the palazzo. Damari realized he was outnumbered and fled with Fra Luis." He sighed. "Which was a pity. When Lion saw what he had done to you I'm sure he would have insisted on a spectacular death worthy of Damari's villainy, if the bastard had remained at hand. I was quite looking forward to it."

Sanchia closed her eyes, trying to understand what he was telling her through the throbbing ache at her temples. "You must have taken him by surprise. He didn't expect you to come back for me. He told me I'd be in the dungeon forever and I was helpless to do anything about it."

"What a sweet-natured bastard he is. Did you tell him he was a liar?"

"No." She opened her eyes. "Because he told the truth. I was there forever."

Lorenzo was silent, studying her face. "It must have seemed so, but truly it was only three days."

She lowered her gaze to the blanket. "Why are we on this ship?"

"Damari's condotti were quartered only twenty miles from the palazzo and Lion reasoned he would ride directly there and return with a sizeable force, far larger than the one we were able to hire so quickly from Brelono. Consequently, we couldn't linger at Solinari but rode to Pisa to get you to a physician. The physician said you were too frail to travel by land so Lion sent Marco home with the Wind Dancer to guard Mandara on the chance that Damari decided to march against it. Then we set sail for Genoa. He intends to settle you comfortably there, safely out of Damari's reach before returning to Mandara."

"Does he think Mandara is in danger?"

Lorenzo shrugged. "Not really. Damari is too crafty to attack a city as strong as Mandara with the condotti he commands. He would need reinforcements from Borgia, and Borgia has too many irons in the fire to release any men right now. Damari will probably wait until he has a good chance of victory before he attacks Mandara."

Condotti, attacks, Borgia. She was too hurt and weary to think about all this strife. She needed to go back to sleep and withdraw until she was healed and could contend with that world. She closed her eyes again.

"Aren't you going to ask how Lion is?"

"No."

"Or about your hand?"

Her eyes opened and she gazed at her bandaged left hand. During those last hours of torture she had tried to pretend it didn't belong to her, that both the pain and the hand itself were not her own. She found that a certain sense of being remote still lingered. "It doesn't hurt any longer."

"It will hurt if you try to move it. The physician splinted the fingers that were broken and snapped the others back into the sockets." He paused. "Would you like to tell me what Damari did to you?"

"You saw what he did to me."

"The thumb and three of the fingers will heal. The little finger was shattered in three pieces, the bones piercing the flesh, and the physician said it was doubtful you'd ever be able to bend or use it."

"The hammer," she said dully. "It bled . . ." She firmly closed her eyes. "I'm going to sleep now."

"Then I'd better try to make my way to the bridge and tell Lion you've awakened to a bright, new world. After your nap I'll help you bathe and dress. Lion purchased a few gowns and shawls from the wife of his shipwright at the yard before we left Pisa, but they're not as elegant as the ones Giulia supplied."

She heard the scrape of his chair as he rose to his feet and then his footsteps as he lurched with evident difficulty toward the door. "It *is* a bright, new world, you know," he said quietly. "Remember that, and be grateful, Sanchia."

She didn't answer and a moment later she heard the door close behind him.

"She's awake."

Lion turned quickly to see Lorenzo clinging desperately to the rail as he struggled toward the forecastle over the rain-slick deck.

"And I hope you appreciate the extreme discomfort I'm suffering to inform you of the fact."

Lion's hands tightened on the tiller. "She is . . . well?"

"If you mean, did Damari succeed in driving her mad while he tortured her, he did not." Lorenzo drew his short cape about him to protect his nape from the cold, driving rain. "I didn't think he'd be able to break her."

Lion's face was a savage mask. "*Cristo*, he tried hard enough. Did she talk about it?"

"No." Then, as Lion continued to look at him, he shrugged. "She said something about a hammer."

Lion felt as though he had been struck in the stomach with the same mallet. "Take the tiller," he said to the seaman standing behind him. He moved to the rail beside Lorenzo, gazing blindly out at the tempest swept sea. "I should have gotten there sooner."

"Three days to ride to Pisa, persuade Brelono to release his troop, and launch an attack on the palazzo smacks of miracles."

Lion reached out to grip the rail with white-knuckled force. "I shouldn't have waited. I should have thought of another way."

"You're becoming boringly repetitive. There was no other way."

Lion hadn't thought so at the time, but that didn't help him to forget the moment when he had found Sanchia curled up unconscious on the floor of the cell. She had looked . . . broken.

And then he had seen her hand.

"I'm going to kill Damari."

"I presumed as much. I suppose you wouldn't let me do it for you?"

"No." Lion released his grip on the rail and turned. "I'm going to the cabin to see Sanchia."

"She's probably asleep again."

"Then I'll wait until she wakes up." He had a hunger to see her, to know she was no longer the pale, shattered child he had carried aboard the *Dancer* two days before.

"Lion."

He glanced over his shoulder.

"She's not mad." Lorenzo hesitated before finally finishing, "But she's different."

"In what way?"

"I'm not certain."

"By all the saints, what do you mean?"

"I think she's . . ." Lorenzo paused again, thinking about it. "I think she's more than she was. There's a strength . . ." He shrugged. "I could be wrong. Judge for yourself."

"You leave me with no other choice." Lion strode down the steps of the bridge and across the deck toward the cabin.

A moment later he stood beside the bed looking down at Sanchia's pale, drawn face. Strength? It must be Lorenzo who had gone mad. Sanchia looked as delicate as the most fragile of blossoms. Rage seared through him as his gaze fell on her bandaged hand. Damari. Dear God, he wanted that son of a bitch.

Sanchia's lids twitched as if she had become aware that someone was watching her. She opened her eyes abruptly. Her gaze was totally alert and without fear.

Lion's muscles locked with tension as her compelling gaze fastened on his face. She stared at him without speaking and Lion suddenly found himself uneasy. He reached out awkwardly and touched her cheek. "Lorenzo tells me you're feeling better."

"Yes."

"Soon you'll be well."

She did not answer.

His hand dropped away from her face. "Is there anything I can get you? Are you thirsty?"

"No." Her gaze moved over him indifferently. "You're very wet."

"It's raining."

"Then you're foolish to be out in it."

"It was necessary. It's not a bad storm but there's always danger. It took me two years to build this ship, and I dislike the idea of its sinking to the bottom of the sea because I am not at the helm."

"I understand." She was silent a moment. "Why are you here?"

The bluntness of the question startled him as much as that first piercing glance had done. "Because I wanted to see for myself that you were on the mend."

"I don't want you here. Will you leave?"

Surprise held him wordless for a moment and then he smiled. "And what will you do if I won't?"

She failed to return his smile. "Nothing." She closed her eyes. "I'm too weak to fight you . . . now."

The last word held an odd quality of threat, Lion realized. Threats from Sanchia who had always been so frightened? So eager to please? "And later?"

"Later I will deal with you." Her eyes remained closed. "Lion."

She had not addressed him as my lord, as was her custom, but Lion. It was the address he had requested from her, but now his name came with no hesitation or prompting. She could not have shown more confidence and authority if she had been raised to be the lady of a great house.

He deliberately turned and sat down in the chair against the wall. "I will stay. You may need me."

"I don't need you. I'll never need you." She deliberately turned on her side. "But stay if you like. Your presence or absence mean nothing to me."

She had closed him out. She had stepped away from him to a place he couldn't follow, Lion realized with a queer twisting sensation in his belly. Nothing could be more clear from the crystalline coldness of her manner toward him. Why should he be surprised that she blamed him for all that happened to her? He knew the fault rested squarely on his shoulders and she was right in her anger. She had suffered and she deserved his patience. "It means something to me," he said gently. "I'll stay by your side, Sanchia."

She didn't answer, and he realized she had stepped even farther away from him into the realm of sleep.

"I brought Sanchia up on deck to get some air. Really, Lion, I'm not the woman's nursemaid." Lorenzo added plaintively, "Though anyone would draw that conclusion from the way I've bathed, dressed, and tended her these last days. If you wanted her cosseted and cared for, you should have brought a servant on board before we left Pisa." He paused. "Or done it yourself. You haven't set foot in her cabin since the first day she woke."

"You know I had no time to find a maid for her with Damari on our heels."

"I notice you don't address my second suggestion."

"She had no desire for my presence." Lion's grip tightened on the tiller. "She made that clear."

"So you meekly run and hide away from her lest your offensive self distress her."

"She's ill, damn you."

"Not any longer." Lorenzo's gaze went to Sanchia, who stood at the rail several yards away. The strong afternoon sunlight stroked her auburn hair with flame as gusts tossed it about. Her face was raised as if she were drinking in both the warmth of the sun and the vigor of the wind. "She has her strength back and she's come alive. Damari did no real damage, except to her hand, and it's healing nicely. She's in a far from delicate state." He nodded toward Sanchia. "Go see for yourself."

Lion looked quickly at her, then away. "For God's sake, quit prodding me. Do you want her in my bed so badly you'd yank her into it when she's still not well?"

"Did I mention bedding?" Lorenzo asked innocently. "Could it be your thoughts aren't as pure as you'd have me believe? She's changed, you know. We both noticed it. Tell me, Lion, has it not occurred to you that it would be like bedding someone else entirely now? The same sweet body but there would be certain differences. You've always had such a curious mind. Would you not like to explore those differences?"

Lion averted his face. "No, it hasn't occurred to me."

"Lies." Lorenzo chuckled. "You'll have to go to confession when you get back to Mandara and be absolved of that sin. Do you think Sanchia will like Mandara?"

"She won't get the opportunity to like or dislike it. She's staying in Genoa, as you well know."

"And we arrive in Genoa the day after tomorrow?"

Lion's lips twisted. "Not enough time for you, Lorenzo?"

"I would prefer more, but it should prove sufficient. However, since you're displaying an unusual amount of resistance, I shall stop being subtle."

"Subtle?"

Lorenzo ignored the sarcasm in Lion's tone. "I will have nothing more to do with Sanchia while we're on board the ship. She's your property and you must care for her as you see fit." He frowned thoughtfully. "Except to change her bandage. I'm having enough trouble contending with these idiotic feelings of responsibility you're experiencing without having you go squeamish. I might never get you to see sense." He turned away. "You notice the wind has come up and Sanchia does not have her shawl. She could take a chill."

"But she's not at all delicate," Lion ironically repeated Lorenzo's words.

Lorenzo shrugged as he walked over to the rail and leaned his elbows on it. "Perhaps she's more fragile than I thought. Who am I to say? I'm no physician."

And he proceeded to gaze placidly out to sea, ignoring both Lion on the forecastle and Sanchia on the deck.

Lion stayed on the forecastle for another fifteen minutes before he said sharply to the seaman behind him, "Take the tiller." He strode past a grinning Lorenzo, down the steps, then across the deck to where Sanchia stood at the rail.

"The wind is sharpening. Go back to your cabin," he said tersely.

"Soon." She didn't look at him. "I like it here. I feel as if I can see forever. What's beyond the horizon?"

His gaze followed hers to the point where the sea met the sky. "It depends on how far you travel. Until recently most men believed that there were only dragons waiting to devour you as you fell off the edge of the earth."

"Tales to frighten children," she said impatiently. "I've heard stories of great explorers who have sailed vast distances and discovered wondrous treasures."

"Lands overflowing with gold and silver, boundless forests, fierce savages." He paused. "And dragons."

"Christopher Columbus found no dragons." She glanced up at him with a frown. "You surely don't believe in such monsters?"

"I believe there are dangers for the unwary whenever you travel the unknown and that you must be prepared for them." He smiled faintly. "And that there are many kinds of dragons."

"But the possibility of dragons wouldn't stop you from seeing what is beyond that horizon?"

"No."

"It wouldn't stop me either. There is so much out there. . . ." The passionate intensity vibrating in Sanchia's voice was reflected in her luminous expression and eyes glowing with eagerness. Bemused, Lion gazed at her. She had come alive, as Lorenzo had said. It was as if she had been asleep before and now had come fully awake.

"Don't you see? There is so much promise in that horizon."

A pang of tenderness stirred within him. He had felt that same sense of revelation on a day over two years ago when he had stood on the dock in Venice and realized a lifetime of dissatisfaction had led him there. "Yes, I do see. Endless promise."

"I want to see all the lands that Columbus saw and more."

He smiled indulgently. "Perhaps someday I'll take

you on a voyage of discovery and we'll find—" He stopped as he watched her expression become shuttered. A poignant sense of loss that withdrawal brought kindled him to sudden anger. "What am I thinking? Voyages of discovery are not for women." He paused before adding with deliberate provocation, "but, if you're very good and obedient, I may bring you back a gift to solace you for what you've missed."

She didn't answer. Her gaze remained fixed on the horizon.

"Why do you not speak?" His tone was taunting. "You know I'm right. Women have no place on great journeys. They must stay at home and weave tapestries and—"

"And where do they have a place?" Sanchia whirled to face him. "In a man's bed, waiting to take his seed? In a dungeon, waiting to take his punishment?"

He felt as if she had struck him and his anger abruptly dissipated. "Sanchia, I would not have left the maze had I known you were in danger. I had no idea Damari was so close."

"Because I chose not to let you know. Because I was foolish enough to try to lead them away to give us all a chance."

Lion gazed at her incredulously. "You led him—" He reached out and grasped her shoulders. "Were you mad? Why didn't you let me know? I could have—"

"You could have done nothing." Sanchia broke free of him and stepped back. "And I knew there was nothing you could do so I led Damari away. I was going to double back and join you, but Damari caught me." She stared into his eyes. "And you left me."

"Sanchia . . ." Lion didn't know what to reply. What could he say to defend himself when the charge was true? "At the time I could see no other way. If they had caught the rest of us, we all could have gone to our deaths."

"Do you think I'm a fool who cannot reason? For a while I was stupid enough to hold on to the blind belief that you'd be coming for me any moment, simply because you had promised me." She drew a deep breath and made an impatient gesture with her bandaged left hand. "But then I forced myself to weigh what was true and what was not true. I had to do so or I would have been destroyed by anger. At times I thought I'd choke and be consumed by rage."

Lion felt a wrenching pity as he looked down at her bandaged hand. "I would have felt the same."

"Yes, you would have known anger, but you have no true idea how I felt in that dungeon." She turned away and gazed out to sea, the line of her spine straight and unyielding. "Because you were never as helpless as I was in that cell, as helpless as I've been all my life. You abandoned me, but I knew it was my fault in part for choosing to lead Damari away without telling you. You're not a man to give a promise lightly, and you probably would have tried to keep it." Her smile was bittersweet. "Even though your promise was given to a slave."

"I had every intention of keeping it."

"So, in a way, it was my choice. It wasn't the broken promise that made me so angry."

His gaze was intent on her face. "Then what?"

"That I was in the maze with you at all."

He stiffened. "You chose to go. I didn't force you."

"Do you know the reason I went?" She laughed incredulously. "It was because you smiled at me. Because I was so grateful you were treating me with kindness and a sort of camaraderie that I would have gone anywhere, done anything to have you continue to treat me so." Her gaze shifted to his face. "And I think you knew that if you were kind to me, I would go with you and you need not feel accountable."

His lips tightened. "You believe me to be so ruthless?"

"Yes." She held his gaze steadily. "I think you would have done anything to get the Wind Dancer back from Damari. In comparison, I had no real value to you. I was only your slave to be used." She shrugged. "Perhaps you didn't even know you were doing it."

Could she be right? He had wanted the Wind Dancer desperately and he had needed her help to retrieve it. Had he tried to woo her with kindness when his promise had kept him from commanding her to come with him? If that were true, then his guilt was even greater than he had thought. "You do have value for me."

"Do I? Now that you have the Wind Dancer back you have no need for a thief. Do you intend to use my body and make me into a whore for your pleasure?"

Her words stung him. "A whore is paid and I have no intention of paying for your services. Both you and Giovanni have already received quite enough from me." He smiled caustically. "And why should I not use you? You didn't seem averse once I showed you the way of it. I found you extremely eager to please. My pleasure was also your pleasure."

The color rose to her cheeks. "You did give me pleasure but . . ." She stopped, searching for words. "It was a false pleasure, a forced pleasure, because I did not choose it. You took my body because you thought you owned it." Her eyes suddenly glittered with cold rage. "You do *not* own it. You do not own me."

Shock ran through him, whatever he had expected it wasn't this complete rejection. "I have a bill of sale that states otherwise."

"I don't care what your bill of sale says. It's wrong for a person to be able to own another person. It should not happen. All my life I accepted being a slave because my mother said I must. She told me I would always be a slave. She said Giovanni had a right to do anything he wanted with us because he had bought us. Well, she was wrong, Giovanni was wrong, and you're wrong. When I was in Damari's filthy dungeon I realized no one has a right to make me do what I don't want to do because of a piece of paper." She drew a deep breath and went on with a rush, "I'm no longer your slave and I won't obey you."

He went still. "The hell you won't," Lion said softly. "You may think of me as the devil himself, but you belong to this particular devil and I'll tolerate no defiance."

"I have to defy you."

"Your memory is short. You gave me your promise of loyalty."

"Not because you bought me but because you helped Elizabet and the others. I paid that debt in Damari's dungeon." She held up her bandaged hand. "You took your Wind Dancer but I was the one who paid its ransom. We're even now, Lion."

He glanced away from her hand and out to sea. "Perhaps in your eyes but not the eyes of the law."

"And in your eyes too," she said fiercely. "You know my debt is paid to you. Why do you not admit it?"

"I do admit it. Your debt is paid," he said quietly. "But the bill of sale remains."

"Then tear it up. Free me."

He shook his head. "Why should I free you?"

"Because it's just," she said. "Dear God, there has to be some justice in the world or nothing makes sense."

"You believe you want to be free now. But think about it. As my slave you're under my protection. Life isn't easy for a woman alone."

"I know. I used to believe a slave was sometimes luckier than a free woman. But I was wrong." She took a step closer. "A free woman has choices. I had none. What I suffered in Damari's dungeon was only because I was your slave—doing what you willed. If I ever have to suffer like that again, it will be because I believe what I'm suffering for is worth the price of my pain." She shook her head. "You would give me no choices. I don't want to be under your protection."

"How very unfortunate, since you most certainly are under my protection and will remain with me."

"You will not free me, even though you know it's right to do so?"

He smiled at her mockingly. "How do I know what is right? What is wrong? Is it right to deprive myself of my own property? Would it not be wrong to take away my protection when Damari would like nothing better than to lay hands on you again?" His mockery faded to be replaced by grimness. "Don't seek to tutor me on what is right, Sanchia. Rightness lies with the holder of power."

"Then I must find a way to obtain power, for I will not let you own me." She gazed at him unflinchingly. "And I will not permit you to use either my body or my mind again. You might as well release me, for I will give you neither pleasure nor service."

"You do not have to give. As your master I'm entitled to take." He paused. "If I so desire. However, there is no hurry. I'll give you opportunity to grow accustomed to me again before I summon you to my bed."

She stared at him in disbelief. "Did you not hear me? I will no longer serve you."

"I heard you." He turned away and strode toward the bridge. "But I've decided not to let you anger me. You've suffered much for my sake and are entitled to a few harsh words."

"I'm entitled to my freedom."

"Then you will be disappointed, for you will not receive it. Go to your cabin. I won't have you catching a chill and falling ill."

"You won't have—"

"No, I won't have it," he repeated deliberately over his shoulder as he started up the steps of the forecastle. "Though you choose to think me as much a monster as Damari, I suffered because Damari captured and hurt you. And you do have value for me."

"As property?" she asked scornfully.

"As . . . Sanchia."

Her eyes widened. She was startled by his revelation. As he motioned the seaman away and took his place at the tiller, she quickly turned her back and gazed out to sea.

"She doesn't appear to be pleased with you," Lorenzo observed as he leaned on the rail to look at Lion. "What did you say to her?"

"She wants her freedom. She says she's no longer a slave and wants me to tear up her paper."

"Hmm, I'm not surprised." Lorenzo frowned. "Though I must admit I'm disappointed she decided to strike her blow for freedom at this particular time. It would have suited me better if she had continued to prove herself willing to render whatever you demanded of her. I take it you didn't give her what she asked?"

Lion's grip tightened on the tiller. "No, I did not."

"Ah, there's hope for you yet. You're not totally lost to the dark joys of corruption."

"She's mine," Lion said harshly. "She has no right to leave me. She—" Sanchia's words came back to him. She had said he had no right to hold her, but she was wrong. Even if the papers didn't exist, a man had the right to win whatever prizes were within his power and then hold on to them. So it had always been and so it would continue forever. Besides, she'd be better off with him than without him. Too many hazards threatened a woman alone in a world populated by men like Caprino, Damari, and Borgia.

And Lionello Andreas.

No, he was no threat to Sanchia. He quickly rejected the ridiculous thought. He would care for her. He would give her gifts of great beauty and fill her life with pleasure.

And fill her body with himself, sate himself in that tight silken sheath until he was rid of the obsession for only Sanchia.

And what was wrong with that? She had been learning all the ways of pleasure and he could not mistake the response she had given him.

False pleasure she had called it.

"Then do you bed her tonight?" Lorenzo asked. "She's well enough. Look at her, there's a bloom about her."

He didn't have to look at Sanchia to remember her clear, glowing beauty as defiance reddened her cheeks. His loins ached as he recalled the sight of her standing naked in the barn gazing up at him with frightened, wondering eyes. He could see her that way again, enter her again, hear her cry out . . .

But she would fight him this time. She would not be too frightened or hesitant to strike out at him, if he tried to force her. No matter what it cost, she would not give him what he wanted from her.

And if he compelled her, he might hurt her.

"Well, she did give you pleasure, didn't she? You were wild enough for her before this experience with Damari."

He was still wild for her. He should be feeling remorse and pity, not lust. Somewhere within him he did feel both those emotions, but the lust was greater. He could not let her go, so he had to find a way to convince her that remaining his slave was best for her. "Yes, she gave me pleasure."

Forced pleasure.

The memory of Sanchia's words knifed through him.

Force meant pain and he could not inflict more pain when she had already suffered so much for his sake.

"I'll not bed her tonight. Though I know it will disappoint you, it will do no harm to show a little patience."

Lorenzo started to say something, but thought better of it, and merely commented, "You're right, of course. It will do no harm and it might do a great deal of good. By all means, take as long as you like. I'm sure the practice of self-restraint will be wonderfully beneficial to the development of your character—and we both know how abstinence affects you, don't we, Lion?"

He didn't wait for an answer but strolled down the steps of the forecastle, a smile of satisfaction returning to his lips.

Ten

The dream came again that night.

Sanchia lay in the darkness, willing her heart to steady its wild cadence. It was only a dream, she told herself over and over. She wasn't in the dungeon, she was on Lion's ship, hundreds of miles away from Solinari. It was only a dream.

It did no good. The walls of the cabin were too close and seemed to be drawing closer with each breath she drew. She had to get *out*.

She got up and began to dress with frantic speed. She would go out on deck and look at the sea and breathe the sharp, clean air and think about what lay beyond the horizon. Freedom and adventure . . .

And perhaps the blessed absence of dreams.

A few minutes later she was standing at the rail looking out at the moonlight-dappled sea. Yes, this was what she had needed. She could feel the peace flow into her, banishing the tumult, blurring the memories she could not forget.

"What are you doing out here? Do you realize it's the middle of the night? You persist in trying to make yourself ill."

Her feelings of serenity were splintered as she recognized Lion's voice. *Dio*, she didn't want him here. Tonight she desired peace and he brought only turbulence. "I'm wearing my shawl." She drew the wrap closer about her. "I'll go in shortly."

He moved to stand beside her at the rail. "Now."

"No!" Then she tried to temper the sharpness of her voice. There must be no conflict now. Peace. Serenity. "I cannot sleep. Leave me and I promise to go in within the next hour."

"Bargains?" A note of surprise colored his tone. "You must already be ill. You were considerably more defiant this afternoon." He suddenly frowned. "Why can't you sleep? Does your hand hurt? Lorenzo said it was healing well."

"My hand doesn't hurt. It grows better every day. I'm just restless."

She could feel his gaze on her face. "Dreams?"

"What difference does it make? Go away. You disturb me."

"You disturb me too." His tone was abstracted. "The same dream? About the thief thrown out of the Stinche?"

"Not the same dream."

"Then what do—"

"Why do you not leave me alone?" She whirled to face him. "I dream of Damari's dungeon, not the Stinche. I dream that the hammer is a sword and Fra Luis is cutting off my fingers one by one. That's what he was going to do, you know. But first they wanted to let me think about it, so they played with me. They brought out the wooden block and put my hand on it and—"

"Hush." She was suddenly in Lion's arms, her cheek pressed against the leather of his jerkin, his fierce voice vibrating low beneath her ear. "Don't talk about it. Don't think about it."

"And after they had finished with me for the time they would take me back to the cell for a few hours so that I could recover and think of the next time they would—"

"I said no!" Lion's palm was suddenly covering her lips. "I don't want to hear any more. I want you to forget it."

She shook her head to rid herself of his hand. "I can't forget. I don't have that capability. I remember everything and, when I refuse to think of it during the day, I dream of it at night." She smiled bitterly. "But I will cease talking about it, if it troubles you."

"It does trouble me. I . . . feel it." Lion gazed down at her, his dark eyes glittering in the moonlight. "Tell me," he demanded suddenly. "Everything. From the first moment you were captured until I came for you. Everything they did to you. Everything you felt."

"Why? You said you didn't want to hear it."

"*Gran Dio*, I don't, but I have to share it. It was my responsibility you were there and I'll not leave you alone with it."

"It will do no good to—"

"Tell me."

And she told him, haltingly at first and then with a feverish rush, releasing all the memories, giving them to him.

And he listened, his expression impassive, his gaze locked to hers. Accepting.

Her words finally dwindled, slowed and then ceased altogether.

"Is it over?" His voice was harsh, strained.

She nodded jerkily. "That's all." She turned her face away from him. She felt lighter, she realized in surprise. As if in some mysterious fashion Lion had managed actually to lift a portion of those hideous memories from her own mind and into his.

"Thank God!" He jerked her back into his arms and held her crushed against him, his fingers buried in her hair. His chest was moving in and out as if he were running, but there was no passion in his embrace. "I did *not* like this. It hurt me."

She found herself laughing shakily. "It hurt me, too." The laughter brought its own easing and diminished Damari's importance in her memory as nothing else would have done.

"I know," he said thickly, then he was pushing her away, his gaze on her face. "Can't you see that it must not happen again? You belong to me and I must protect—"

"I don't belong to you." Yet even as she spoke she realized she felt more bound to him in this moment than when she had held him within her body. She took a panicky step backward. "I belong to no one but myself. I will—"

His hand quickly covered her mouth. "We will not talk about it now. Can you not be still?"

She took another step back and turned her face to elude his hand. "I have no choice, if you persist in covering my mouth with that huge paw," she said tartly. "If you do not wish to hear me speak, then leave me."

He stood looking at her with a scowl. "I don't want to leave you."

Sanchia felt an irrational rush of relief. She found she no longer wanted to be alone and Lion's presence was bringing its own rough comfort. "Then you must let me speak when I wish to speak."

Humor banished the frown from Lion's face. "I've done little else but listen since the moment I came on deck." He took her elbow and propelled her across the deck. "Come."

She tried to pull away from him. "Where are you taking me?"

"Here." He had stopped at the steps leading to the forecastle and now pushed her down on the second step. "Sit." His smile held a hint of little boy mischief. "Did you think I was dragging you to my bed? I'm trying to prove what a patient man I can be. You're safe from me for now." He jerked his head toward the seaman at the tiller a few yards away. "And, since I have no intention of sharing you, it would be cruel to him to take you here in front of him."

She glanced at him curiously. "Have you ever shared a woman with other men?"

He shrugged. "Many times. There are never quite enough camp followers to go around."

He saw the distaste on her face and his own expression hardened as he dropped down on the step beside her. "Yes, I've whored, and killed, and even taken women against their will." He saw her go rigid and continued, "What did you expect? I'm no gentle courtier like Marco. I'm only a rough soldier. When a town is taken, the women are part of the prize."

"It still doesn't make it right," she said clearly. "How did you feel when you were doing it?"

"You get used to it." He paused. "Most of it." He was silent for a moment, remembering, before admitting, "Though only once did I take a woman when she wasn't willing. I was fourteen and drunk with power and victory and hurting for a woman. She was a merchant's wife I found hiding in a shop. I thought, why not? No one else hesitated to take what was theirs by right. I had even seen my father ease himself with comely women, apparently uncaring whether they were willing or unwilling." He hesitated for an instant and then burst out, "But I had no liking for it. Her eyes were empty and she wept. . . . I could not please her. I kept her with me until the condotti left the city and gave her money when we parted. I let no one else touch her but—" He broke off and said again, "I had no liking for it."

Sanchia said nothing.

He turned on her as fiercely as if she had attacked him. "I make no excuses. I am what I am and I do what I have to do. I have little gentleness but I'm honest and return what I'm given, be it good or evil. You must accept me as I am."

She was startled by his sudden intensity. "Why are you telling me this?"

Conflicting emotions darkened his face. "I don't know." He smiled crookedly. "You have a strange effect on me. Lorenzo says I have a great need to go to confession. Perhaps I want you to absolve what cannot be absolved."

Her gaze dropped from his face and silence fell between them again.

"You didn't like being a soldier?" she asked finally.

He shrugged. "I knew nothing else from the time I was a boy. I did it well. My father was pleased with me."

"But you didn't like it?" she insisted. "Is that why you gave up your condotti and began to build ships?"

"The sea has always been in our blood. It was not until my family came from Persia to Italy over a hundred years ago that we moved inland away from the coast." He made a face. "We are not farmers by nature and did not prosper. So my great-grandfather took up the sword. War suited us much better than tilling the land, and we grew rich on it."

"But you gave it up."

"We were rich enough, and I was tired of noblemen who paid me to do battle for them one day and then hired someone to steal my fee the next." He leaned back against the step, his gaze on the sails billowing in the wind. "Then one day I was on the docks in Venice watching a ship from Madagascar sail into port. I had spent the morning squeezing the last half of my fee from the signory coffers and I was sickened to death of the *Serenissima*." He smiled reminiscently. "The wind was lifting the sails, and I could smell the scent of the sea and the cargo of cinnamon being unloaded and suddenly I knew—" He broke off and turned to face her. "Do you think you can sleep now?"

"It's unlikely." She paused, her eyes never leaving his. "Knew what?"

He stood up and reached down to pull her to her feet. "I knew it was time that we returned to the sea where we belonged."

"But why shipbuilding? Why not exploring or trading?"

He shook his head. "We've talked enough. Go to bed."

Sanchia felt a sharp thrust of disappointment. For the first time since she had met him, Lion was becoming more human and less the powerful enigma to her. She was reluctant to let that fleeting glimpse of him out of her sight for fear it would fade away. "I'm not sleepy."

"Neither am I." He added bluntly, "But my body is readying and if you don't want to take me, then leave me now." He smiled faintly as he saw her eyes widen. "Did you think I no longer lusted for you? It's always with me when you are near. You must accept that too."

"I must accept only what I wish to accept."

"What you choose to accept," he amended with soft emphasis. "I can make you 'wish' to accept me."

She gazed up at him, feeling a familiar stirring between her thighs. No, she would not feel like this. She was no longer his leman and must not yield him any response or he would seize on it. "Then I choose not to accept you. I don't want—" She broke off as she met his knowing gaze. "Release me, Lion."

"Come to my bed, Sanchia."

"I cannot."

"And I will not."

She felt a surge of desperation as she looked at him. His expression was without mercy, completely implacable. She wished she had gone to her cabin as he had bade her when he had first come on deck. Before he had shown her comfort, before he had let her glimpse the raw brutality of the life that had carved those jagged edges and helped to make him what he was. Now, though she could not condone, she could understand and, through that understanding, she was drawn to him. "I won't stay in Genoa, you know. I'll run away from you."

He stiffened. "Don't be foolish. You'll be safe in Genoa. Damari won't trouble himself to go so far to seek you out, and I'll make sure you're settled in comfortable lodgings before I leave."

"And when you return?" Sanchia shook her head. "If you want a strumpet, go back to Giulia Marzo and free me."

"I won't free you."

"Then you'll have to send someone to hunt me down. I won't be here when you return." She gazed at him beseechingly. "Why will you not free me? You said you wouldn't be able to bear slavery yourself, that you would run away."

He stiffened. "You know the punishment I could mete out for such a crime?"

"You think I'm afraid of punishment?" She smiled bitterly. "I've learned to deal with pain; Damari was an excellent tutor." She shook her head. "And you would not hurt me."

"You're very sure."

"Yes, so do not threaten what you won't execute, Lion. I do not fear you any longer."

Lion's expression reflected both anger and frustration. "Perhaps I'll have to change my ways. I've obviously become too predictable." He turned on his heel and strode across the deck. "You're a very troublesome woman." He yelled to the seaman at the tiller, "Turn the ship around, dammit. We're returning to Pisa."

"Pisa." Sanchia gazed at him with the same astonishment shown by the sailor at the helm, who was hurrying to do Lion's bidding. "We're only a day away from Genoa."

"And you've just told me you'll run away from Genoa as soon as I sail out of the harbor." His lips tightened. "So I'm keeping you with me."

"In Pisa?"

"I'm going to Pisa only to dock. I can't stay there. I have to make sure Damari hasn't launched an attack on Mandara."

"But Lorenzo said that was extremely unlikely."

"Mandara belongs to me. I have to be sure."

"Then you're taking me to Mandara?"

"You've given me no choice."

The moonlight was strong and full on his face, and Sanchia had never seen a more grim expression on it.

"Yes," he said, "I'm taking you to Mandara."

"There's Mandara, Sanchia." Lorenzo reined in his horse and leaned forward in the saddle, his gaze intent on the walled city in the distance. An odd eagerness warmed the usual remoteness of his features. "It's not as far as it looks. We should be there within thirty minutes."

Lion cast him a less than pleased glance over his shoulder. "Which should make you exceedingly happy."

"Yes, as a matter of fact, it does bring me a good deal of satisfaction." For once there was no mockery in Lorenzo's voice. "Though I'm not at all sure there is any such emotion as happiness." He shrugged. "But there are many words that have no meaning for me."

"It's beautiful." From this slight rise in the foothills Sanchia could see both the walled city of Mandara and, to the north, a large vineyard in the valley. Her gaze shifted to the castle that dominated the city. Her grip unconsciously tightened on the reins and the mare tossed her head in protest. Sanchia deliberately forced herself to relax. She should not be intimidated at the thought of meeting Lion's mother. The woman posed no threat to her. Lion had told Sanchia that she was not even to go to the castle but to occupy a small house in the town itself. It would be obvious to the Lady Caterina that Sanchia's place in Lion's life was too minuscule to be of any importance to her, and she would doubtless ignore her.

She would find a way to leave Mandara. A surge of dismay accompanied the thought as she looked at the high stone walls of the city. Escaping from Lion had proved impossible since they had landed in Pisa and might prove equally difficult now that she was to enter his own domain.

"Give it up, Sanchia."

She turned to see Lion's gazed fixed on her face. "You'll not leave Mandara."

"You're wrong. I'll find a way." Sanchia's gaze shifted back to the castle. "You forget that I'm a very good thief. You'll have difficulty keeping me locked up."

"I don't have to keep you locked up. No keys are needed here. You'll notice the moat and drawbridge and the city gates are guarded by my own men." He smiled pleasantly. "And I'll be careful to tell those guards that I'll be forced to emasculate them if they allow you to step outside the gates of Mandara."

"I think that should prove more than persuasive," Lorenzo said mildly. "Lion's right. Give it up, Sanchia."

She didn't answer as she spurred her horse down the incline toward the distant city.

The gates of Mandara were flung open when they were still some distance away, and two riders rode out of the city. One rider on a huge gray horse immediately spurred ahead of the other and approached them at a hard gallop.

"It seems we're to be honored by a personal escort," Lorenzo murmured. "The Lady Caterina."

Sanchia tensed, her gaze on the rider galloping toward them. She could not distinguish the woman's features from this distance, but there was no doubt this was an *illustrissima*, a great lady. She rode with her spine straight, her carriage indomitable and with the same driving force and skill as her son, Lion. Since the lady was on horseback it was difficult to determine her size, but she appeared tall and slim, her shoulders broad beneath a crimson velvet cloak.

"Courage, Sanchia." Lorenzo's gaze never left the approaching rider. "At least, she's left her mace at home."

"Sanchia won't need courage," Lion said as he urged Tabron forward a few paces. "My mother will do her no harm."

Lorenzo snorted derisively but said no more.

Caterina Andreas reined in her gray stallion a few yards from where Lion sat waiting and Sanchia unconsciously braced herself. Lion's mother needed no weapons to impress and intimidate.

The lady Caterina's features were too strong to be considered beautiful, her jaw too long, her chin too firm, her brows a feminine version of Lion's black slashing ones. She had the bold, authoritative manner of a man, yet there was nothing masculine about the sculptured beauty of her high cheekbones nor the dauntless spirit in her fine dark eyes. Her glossy black hair was threaded with silver but her face was firm and virtually unlined.

Her keen gaze raked Lion's face. "You are well?"

Lion nodded. "Damari?"

"He did not march on Mandara." She shrugged. "The cur would not dare. He prefers to bribe others to do his villainy. Marco sent inquiries to Pisa and we received word that after Damari learned you had set sail for Genoa he left to seek out Borgia." A sudden glint of humor appeared in her eyes. "No doubt to make excuses as to why he cannot produce what he promised. I'd like to have been there when he attempted to explain to his lord how he could not hold on to the Wind Dancer against only three men."

"And one woman," Lorenzo added softly.

Caterina's gaze moved to Lorenzo's face and she nodded formally. "Lorenzo."

He inclined his head in a mocking bow. "My lady."

Then Caterina turned to Sanchia. "You are the slave Sanchia?"

Sanchia drew herself up. "I am Sanchia. I am no longer a slave."

Caterina glanced at Lion. "You freed her? Marco said you had no intention of freeing her."

"I didn't free her." Lion added dryly, "She appears to think saying the words makes it true."

"The debt is paid," Sanchia said. "I am free."

"What does she do here?" Caterina asked Lion. "You were to leave her in Genoa. Marco said—"

"She's here and that's the end of it," Lion cut in harshly. "It will make no difference."

Caterina's gaze narrowed on his face. "You do not bring her to the castle?"

Lion shook his head. "She stays in the town."

"Unless you want to honor her with an invitation as your guest," Lorenzo said. "I'm sure Lion would give in to your urging. He's such a dutiful son."

"No!" Lion said. "Stay out of this, Lorenzo. This isn't your concern."

"Our Messer Vasaro seldom lets that consideration stop him." Caterina asked with dangerous softness, "Is this your doing, Lorenzo?"

Lorenzo merely smiled at her.

"Why?" Caterina turned back to Lion. "If you're

grateful to her for her service to you, then free her, give her money, and let her be on her way. She has no place in Mandara."

"She has a place wherever I choose to give it to her," Lion said. "Let be, Mother."

"I shall not—" She broke off as she heard the clatter of approaching hooves. "I will deal with this later. It is not ended."

"We didn't think it would be," Lorenzo said.

Caterina shot him a lethal glance before wheeling her horse to greet the woman riding toward them. "You were slow, Bianca. You must show more eagerness or Lion will think you're not happy to see him."

"I'm always happy to see Lion, as he very well knows," the woman addressed as Bianca answered serenely. "Do you forget I am not so good a horsewoman that I would dare to ride at breakneck speed as you do?" She smiled warmly at Lion, her deep blue eyes glowing with affection. "Welcome back to Mandara, my lord. We have missed you."

She was possibly the most beautiful woman Sanchia had ever seen. Sunlight shone on the streaks of blond weaving through the ash brown braids wrapped around her small head and revealed the perfection of features that might have graced a statue of Aphrodite. No, not Aphrodite, Sanchia amended her thought with sudden certainty. This woman's face was too innocent to be likened to the worldly goddess of love. She glowed with a childlike purity that was more reminiscent of Psyche.

"I missed you as well, Bianca." Lion smiled gently. "You appear to be flourishing. You have more color than the last time I saw you."

"Oh yes, I'm very well. Marco makes me spend hours in the garden posing for his paintings. I was quite reddened from the last week."

"Marco should take better care of you."

"But she won't have to worry about Marco taking care of her now that you're home, Lion," Caterina said briskly. "You can—"

"Aren't you going to introduce Sanchia to Bianca, Lion?" Lorenzo interrupted. "Where is your courtesy?"

"This is Sanchia?" An eager smile lit Bianca's face. "Marco told me how brave you were in helping to get the Wind Dancer back. How proud I am to meet you. I know we're going to become fast friends."

Sanchia was warmed by Bianca's sincerity; her smile held the same gentle, loving quality Sanchia was accustomed to seeing on Elizabet's face. "I'm most pleased to meet you, my lady."

"But you haven't been introduced," Lorenzo said. "I suppose I must be the one to perform the happy duty. Sanchia, may I present the Lady Bianca?" He paused. "Lion's wife."

Why did she feel so stunned? Sanchia wondered wildly. Just because no one had mentioned that Lion was wed did not mean a marriage did not exist. She quickly forced a smile to hide the shock she knew must be revealed on her face and nodded her head. "My lady."

"Bianca." Lion's wife urged with another smile. "You must call me Bianca."

"Bianca . . ." Sanchia repeated numbly. She would not look at Lion. She would not let him see the pain twisting through her now that the first shock had passed. She felt betrayed . . . more so than she had in the dungeon when she had believed Lion had abandoned her. How stupid and unreasonable she was to feel this way. She should not mind that he had a wife.

"And I will call you Sanchia." Bianca turned to Caterina. "Could we put her in the chamber close to mine? I would dearly like to—"

"She's a slave, Bianca," Caterina cut in harshly.

"Still?" A frown marred the smooth perfection of Bianca's brow. "But I'm certain Lion has only overlooked the formality of freeing her. He has no liking for slavery." She turned to Lion. "Is that not so?"

Lion's face was expressionless. "As you say, there are formalities. But the question of her status is irrelevant at the moment. Sanchia will not stay at the castle."

As Bianca started to protest Lion raised a hand to silence her. "Perhaps later. Sanchia has suffered greatly and needs solitude. I've made arrangements for her to occupy a house off the piazza where she can rest and recover her strength."

Bianca's frown vanished as her gaze went to Sanchia's bandaged hand. "I can understand," she said softly. "You are right, my lord. She must have solitude so that she may commune with God and pray that he return her to full health." She nodded. "I will pray too, Sanchia, and we'll soon have you at the castle."

"Thank you," Sanchia said faintly.

"And I will bring cushions and coverlets from the castle," Bianca went on. "Perhaps a servant. What think you, Lion?"

"I'll arrange for the servant," Lion said. "And you must not trouble yourself, Bianca. Sanchia is my responsibility and I will see to her comfort."

"But I'm sure Bianca doesn't consider it a hardship," Lorenzo said. "Charity is God's will, isn't it, Bianca?"

"Lion is quite right, Bianca," Caterina said with an annoyed look at Lorenzo. "It's not your place to defy him in this."

"Defy him?" Bianca's eyes widened in distress. "I would never defy him. You understand, do you not, my lord? I only thought to—"

"I know, I know," Lion said with sudden impatience. "My mother's words were too harsh. Just accept my will in this."

"Certainly, my lord. Whatever you wish," Bianca said, relieved. "May I send her strengthening food from the kitchens?"

"Send what you like," Lion said between his teeth as he urged Tabron into a trot. "And now, may we end this chatter and continue to the city? I need to question Marco about Damari and speak to the guards at the gate."

The whitewashed house to which Lion led them was small but charming, with window boxes overflowing with coral-red geraniums on the balcony overlooking the piazza.

"I know this house," Caterina said slowly, her gaze

lifting to the curtained doors leading to the balcony. She turned to Lion.

Lion met her gaze and his face softened. "I had no time to find another place. It's this house or the castle."

"I'm not quarreling with your choice. I find it very fitting."

"Mother, it's not my choice. I would—"

"I have no time to linger here. I presume you have the key?"

"Since the house has been empty the key has been held by the shopkeeper next door."

"Then you will have no trouble. Come, Bianca, we must hurry and make sure there is sufficient for supper." Caterina wheeled her stallion and trotted away with Bianca following close behind her.

Lion cursed softly beneath his breath before turning to Lorenzo. "Will you get the key and settle Sanchia before you come to the castle? I must talk to my mother."

Lorenzo nodded, his gaze on Caterina, her back rigidly straight. "I gather the house belonged to your father and was used for the usual purpose?"

Lion nodded. "*Cristo*, why did she have to come to meet me? She wouldn't have had to know Sanchia was occupying the house."

"You thought to hide me?" Sanchia asked clearly. "If I'm proving inconvenient, you have the solution."

Lion gave her a fierce glance. "Don't anger me, Sanchia. I'm having trouble enough without you pricking at me."

Lorenzo's gaze was still on Caterina. "Yes, go after her and give her kind words. I think she has need of them." He turned to smile at Sanchia. "We will deal very well together without you."

"Very well," Sanchia repeated emphatically.

Lion cast her a black look, wheeled his horse, and set out after Lady Caterina and Bianca.

Lorenzo dismounted and came around to lift Sanchia from her mare and tie the horses to the gate post of the iron fence that surrounded the house. "Wait here and I'll get the key."

He was back in a few minutes, not only with the key but with a plump, homely young woman whose sunny smile was only slightly quenched by Lorenzo's chilling presence. "This is Rosa Lanzio. She's the youngest daughter of the owner of the silk shop next door. She will serve you."

Rosa murmured something inaudible and gave Sanchia a quick curtsy.

Sanchia gazed at her, stunned. It was incomprehensible to her that she, who had been a slave for her entire life, was now offered someone to serve her. "I need no servant."

"Lion evidently thinks differently." Lorenzo unlocked the door and wrinkled his nose distastefully as he swung it open. "Come along, Rosa, the entire place needs airing out and a thorough cleaning."

Rosa gave him a frightened glance and then fled wordlessly into the house.

"At least she doesn't chatter," Lorenzo said blandly. "I detest a jabbering woman." He glanced at Sanchia. "Though I should have no complaints about you. You've scarcely uttered a word since I introduced you to Bianca."

"I was . . . surprised."

"I gathered that." Lorenzo smiled. "A lovely child, Bianca, and as good as she is lovely."

"Yes."

"You notice how kind and patient Lion is toward her?"

Sanchia felt a queer jolt of pain. "It's not out of the ordinary for a man to be kind to his wife. He must love her very much."

"Oh yes, everyone loves Bianca."

Sanchia turned to face him. "You didn't want me to know about her until I arrived here."

"I certainly thought it better that you remain in ignorance as long as possible."

"Better for whom?"

"All concerned. You'll understand once you're acquainted with the situation." He looked intently at her.

"But I think you've had quite enough to absorb for the time being."

"I won't be here to come to understand very much about Lord Andreas and his family."

"Oh, I believe you will. Lion will take all the necessary precautions to assure your stay. He's not gone through all this turmoil to see you flit away from him now." He smiled. "So why not enjoy yourself? A pretty house, someone to wait on you, nothing to do but rest. Tomorrow we will look at fabric, and I'll order you gowns so exquisite that Giulia Marzo would gnash her teeth with envy. Are you not tempted?"

"No."

Lorenzo frowned, then his face brightened. "I forgot for a moment you weren't brought up to appreciate the usual female pleasures. Books. I'll bring you several books from the castle to amuse you until I can order your own. There's a skilled young scribe here in Mandara who does both swift and beautiful work and you may choose whatever works please you for him to execute."

"Books?" Sanchia could not keep the eagerness from her tone. A book of her very own! What a delight it would be to possess the magic of words, not only in her mind but on fine parchment, to touch lovingly and keep forever.

"Bound in fine crimson leather," he said persuasively. "With gilt edges."

Sanchia suddenly smiled. "You're surely an emissary from Satan, Lorenzo."

He nodded. "That's what I continually tell Lion, but he prefers not to believe it. So you will take the books and—"

"If I accept the books, it will not keep me from trying to run away," she said quickly. "I must be honest with you."

"Then I am fair warned." Lorenzo shrugged. "Now come with me to the *trattoria* across the piazza and we will have wine and cheese while we wait for Rosa to clean your house. I cannot abide this smell."

"It's not my house," Sanchia said as she fell into step with him.

"It could be, if you'd stop worrying about being free and start worrying about how to please Lion."

Sanchia's lips tightened. "He has a wife to please him."

"True. Sweet, gentle Bianca."

Sanchia walked in silence for a moment before asking abruptly, "Have they been wed long?"

Lorenzo nodded. "Since before I met Lion. I believe he was sixteen and Bianca fourteen. She was Bianca Garlondo, a connection of the Baglioni, and the merging of the families was considered very beneficial to Mandara. The marriage was arranged by Lion's father and, as is the custom, they never saw each other before the contract was signed."

"Are there children?"

"No." Lorenzo smiled. "What a pity. No heir for Mandara. But then Bianca appears almost too beautiful to be subjected to the desecration of childbirth, doesn't she?" His gaze suddenly narrowed on Sanchia's face. "Tell me, what was your first impression when you saw her?"

"Psyche," she answered without thinking.

He looked at her blankly and then chuckled. "You never cease to amaze me. What an interesting comparison."

They had reached the *trattoria*, and he pulled out a chair for her to sit and snapped his fingers for service. "The *vino* is excellent here, much better than in Florence. Mandara is growing famous for its vineyard." He dropped into the chair opposite her. "Now let us speak on a subject that brings us mutual delight. Which books do you most wish to acquire?"

Eleven

The flames of the smoking torches affixed to
the stone walls on either side of the tall front
doors of Mandara cast an eerie orange-red
light on Lion's dark hair. He strode out of the
pools of light, hurrying across the courtyard
to Lorenzo.

"*Cristo*, you took long enough." Lion motioned for the lackey to take the reins of
Lorenzo's horse as he dismounted. "She's
settled?"

"As much as she'll let herself be settled.
Did you talk to Marco?"

"Yes, Damari is definitely with Borgia.
He rode for Cesena directly from Pisa."

"Which means you can't touch him yet
without pulling Cesare down on Mandara.
You'll have to be patient."

"I don't feel like being patient. I may not
be able to touch Damari, but I can drag down

Caprino. I leave for Florence tomorrow at dawn."

"Then do you go to Sanchia tonight?"

"No." Lion turned abruptly and started up the stone steps. "Not tonight."

"Ah, I understand. You wish to spend the evening in the arms of your sweet wife."

"Lorenzo, someday I'll—" Lion stopped. "You have what you wanted, but I'll not give you total victory."

Lorenzo followed him into the great hall. "But the victory will be yours. That will be the beauty of it." He started up the wide oak stairs. "But I admit I'm weary of all this destiny shaping. Even God rested on the seventh day. Do what you wish tonight. I intend to spend the hours before sleep wandering with Dante in his inferno. He doesn't truly understand the nature of hell, but it comforts me to know that someone believes there's a Hades other than the one we make for ourselves. It strikes a certain balance in the universe."

"Sleep well, Lorenzo."

Lorenzo looked down at him from the landing and a rare smile lit his face. "Thank you, my friend, and may your own sleep bring you counsel. It's all so simple, if you would but see it." He continued up the stairs to the chamber he had made his own for the thirteen years he had been with Lion.

It was more than two hours later when the door of Lorenzo's bed chamber was thrown open and Caterina Andreas marched into the room. She wore a splendid midnight blue velvet gown with a low round neckline bordered in sapphires set in filigree silver. Combs ornamented with sapphires held her dark hair smoothly in its bun on her nape and she looked very much the grand lady of the castle. Which had probably been her intention, Lorenzo thought in amusement as he closed his book and leaned back in his chair.

"It was your doing, wasn't it?" She slammed the door behind her. "Lion has never brought a woman to Mandara before. I won't have it. Do you hear me? I won't have it, Lorenzo."

"Good evening, my lady. I trust you had a pleasant evening? I was sorry to miss the joyous homecoming repast." Lorenzo pushed his chair away from the desk. "Sanchia and I had to make do with bread and cheese at the *trattoria*. Sanchia was content, but then she's not accustomed to anything else." He gazed at her in reproach. "Do you not feel guilty in depriving the poor child of a better life here at the castle?"

"I do not. Let her make a better life away from Mandara. Lion spends little enough time here as it is. I won't have him distracted from his duty."

"Duty? Ah, the impregnation of the lovely Bianca. You'd think, considering Lion's appetite for that sport, he would have a dozen offspring by now, wouldn't you?"

"Stop playing, Lorenzo. I *will* have a grandson and Mandara will have an heir. This foolishness has gone on too long."

"My exact words to Lion. It's gone on far too long." He shook his head. "And you know he won't touch Bianca. He regards her as a little sister now."

"That could change." Caterina drew two steps closer, glaring at him. "She's very beautiful."

"She's dull."

"She's gentle and obedient."

"She's a child."

"She's almost as old as Lion, far older than that redhaired urchin you persuaded Lion to bring here."

"In years, perhaps, but Sanchia's upbringing has given her a maturity Bianca will never have. You know that as well as I do." He met her gaze. "And I did not persuade Lion to bring Sanchia here. You should know your son well enough to realize words would not sway him. Circumstances conspired to bring Sanchia here."

"With your help?"

"I certainly offered every encouragement. Sanchia may be the answer to Lion's quandary. She has courage and intelligence and I think they suit very—"

"Sweet Mary, you're surely not telling me he could love her?" Caterina gazed at him in astonishment. "Good God, have you lost your senses? Passion, perhaps, but he's no fool to mistake lust for those mawkish emotions mouthed by troubadours."

"No, he's no fool." Lorenzo smiled. "And we both

know love is a word for fools and children. Still, it could do no harm for him to have a woman who could offer him a mind as well as a body to enjoy."

"Let him have her then," Caterina said. "But not here. I must have an heir for Mandara."

"You could marry again. You're young enough to bear another child."

She suddenly averted her face. "I like my life well enough as it is without bringing in a man to call lord, and perhaps, covet what is Lion's."

"Lion does not want Mandara. He guards it because duty is his nature, but he cares only for that precious shipyard of his in Pisa."

"That's only a whim. He'll tire of it and return to Mandara."

"No, you're wrong. He's found something there he was lacking and from now on he'll return to Mandara only when he must. Mandara is what you want, not what Lion wants. He has no wish to continue your dynasty."

"I desire no dynasty. I want only to keep what I've built here." Her dark eyes blazed at him. "Who do you think protected and nurtured Mandara while my husband and Lion were away fighting their battles? Carlo took Lion from me when he was little more than a baby, and Marco was always absorbed in his painting and music. I have no—" She broke off and then continued with steely determination, "Mandara is my child. It must go on."

"Then you must look elsewhere for the means."

"You will not help me?"

"Are you asking me for help?"

She lifted her chin proudly. "No."

"That is good. I'd hate to refuse such a grand and noble lady. By the way, that gown is truly superb. Was it meant to overwhelm me with your consequence?"

"Yes."

"You've succeeded. I stand abased and chastened."

"You lie." She gazed at him silently for a minute. "Well, aren't you going to ask me to take it off and come to bed?"

"No."

"Do you want me in your bed?"

"Oh, yes." A brilliant smile warmed the coldness of his face as his gaze moved over her caressingly. "Yes, my dear Caterina, it's my most earnest desire."

"Why do you never come to me?" Caterina rubbed her cheek against Lorenzo's naked shoulder with catlike contentment. "Why must I always come to your chamber and ask to be taken to your bed?"

Lorenzo gently stroked her silky hair. "You're a great lady. I would not have your name bandied about by your servants." His index finger moved to lazily trace the straight line of her brow. "And then, too, my self-love is very fragile. What if I should ask and you refuse? I should be devastated."

"I should have known I'd get no satisfaction from that twisted tongue of yours." She raised herself to gaze down at him with a smile. "It's just as well you give me such satisfaction with another part of your anatomy or I would not bother sinking my pride to come to you."

"Such bawdiness." He lifted his head and kissed her lips. "Should the lady of the castle conduct herself so?"

She stiffened and then rolled away from him. "I'm not a bawd. Just because I come to you like this does not mean that I fornicate with all who ask me."

"I did not say it did," Lorenzo murmured. "I jest. You are overly sensitive tonight."

"Yes." She was silent a moment, gazing into the darkness. "It was the house."

"I thought it might be."

"It was the house Carlo kept for his mistresses. I wasn't supposed to know about it." Her voice harshened. "How could I help but know about it? There were always those ready to taunt me with the knowledge of Carlo's latest woman." She paused before continuing fiercely, "There was never affection between us, but I was his wife and he should have spared my pride."

And she had such great pride, Lorenzo thought, as great as the splendid spirit that matched her equally splendid body. "You had no affection for him?"

She shook her head. "There was lust at first. But after the children were born and he had his heirs, he no longer came to my bed. He easily grew tired of a woman and wanted variety."

"A most foolish man."

"I didn't care. I was never so stupid as to think he would be faithful to me. Men are not constant by nature."

"How wise of you to realize and accept our faults." He could feel the rigidity of her muscles against him and sensed the painful tumult the memories had resurrected within her. "Would you turn over? There's a lovely hollow between your shoulder blades that intrigues me."

She turned over on her side with a chuckle. "My shoulder blades?"

"You have magnificent shoulders." He pressed his lips to her right shoulder. "And I could write an ode to your shoulder blades." He brushed his lips against her left shoulder. "And a sonnet to this cunning hollow between them." His lips nuzzled the hollow affectionately. He could feel the tautness ebbing from her stiff muscles and deliberately kept his tone careless. "Go on, you were telling me of this idiot, Carlo. Though why we're bothering to discuss the boring fellow I don't know. I'm almost sorry I helped Lion dispose of his murderers. He obviously deserved that knife between his ribs." His lips moved down the hollow of her spine. "I suppose you were equally foolish and remained faithful to him?"

She frowned. "Why do you say that? Why should I have remained faithful to him when he was not so to me?"

"You shouldn't, but you probably were. You're the rare creature who finds it impossible to break a vow."

She was silent a moment and then said truculently, "I would have taken a lover, if it had pleased me. I just happened to find no one who roused my lust."

"Until after your husband died and there was no vow to break?"

She suddenly began to laugh helplessly and turned to face him again. "Yes, you villain, but don't gammon yourself that you're the only man who has come to my bed since Carlo died."

His expression was suddenly grave. "You were only generous enough to take me to your bed three years ago and your husband has been dead for many years. I'm glad if you had lovers who could please you in the time before. I hope they brought you joy." His long fingers gently caressed the line of her jaw. "You deserve joy, Caterina."

She went still, gazing at him uncertainly. "Lorenzo?"

For an instant the gravity remained on his face and then he smiled. "And so do I." His hand moved from her face to her throat, his fingertips teasing skillfully. "And I've just thought of yet another way we can both enjoy what we deserve."

She shivered in anticipation. "Indeed?"

His caressing fingers trailed down her shoulders. "I was just pondering your charge that my twisted tongue gave you no satisfaction." His fingertips grazed the very tips of her breast. "I think we must definitely remedy that, Caterina."

"It's time for you to go," Lorenzo said softly. "It's almost morning and the servants will soon be stirring."

"What of it?" Caterina gazed sleepily up at him. "I don't care what people say about me."

"I do. Go now."

She made a face as she slowly sat up, got out of bed and began to dress. "You know I'm still angered by your interference?"

"I know."

"And that I will have my way in this?"

"I know you will try."

Caterina quickly pushed her hair back and fastened it with the sapphire combs. "Why can you not admit that I'm right? Bianca and Lion will deal very well together. They'll have mutual interests, children, and companionship. Nothing else is important in a marriage. It's far more than most marriages offer." She smoothed the velvet skirt of her gown. "We both know you're being stubborn only to annoy me."

"Am I?"

Caterina moved across the room and opened the door. "Do not cross me, Lorenzo." She glanced back over her shoulder. "Why are you smiling?"

"Because it gives me pleasure to look at such a beautiful lady. Are you going to visit me again tomorrow night?"

Her gaze narrowed on his face. "Do you ask me to come?"

"No."

"Then I will not come." She glared at him belligerently. "Well?"

He was silent.

"I *may* come," she said. "If I decide it suits me."

She slammed the door behind her.

Lorenzo immediately closed his eyes tightly, striving to retain that last vision of her. Strong, fiery Caterina. Less fierce and more vulnerable than she would ever admit.

But he must not think of Caterina.

He was always careful not to think of Caterina when she was not with him, for then the loneliness always within him became unbearably intense. He opened his eyes and gazed thoughtfully at the flame of the candle in the copper stand on the table. He could not sleep now, but he had no desire to immerse himself in Dante's journey into the inferno either.

He abruptly sat up, threw back the coverlet and got out of bed. He would dress and go for a walk on the battlements and look out over Caterina's kingdom of Mandara. He would walk until he grew tired enough to return to his chamber and sleep.

But he would not think of Caterina.

"Sanchia."

Sanchia jerked upright in bed with a low cry, her gaze wildly searching the chamber.

"*Dio*, it's only me. I didn't mean to frighten you."

Lion's voice. Lion's big frame silhouetted against the pearl-gray light streaming through the door leading to the balcony. Her relief was suddenly followed by tension. "What do you do here?"

"I'm going to Florence. I just wanted to make sure you were well." His hesitancy in speaking, his awkwardness of movement puzzled her. "I'll return within the week. Lorenzo will care for you while I'm gone and see to your needs."

"I need no one to care for me and you may be sure I'll make every attempt not to be here when you return." She clutched the coverlet to her chin, her tone hostile. "Why shouldn't I be well? You've put me in this fine house, filled with fine tapestries and silver ornaments. You've given me a servant to see to my needs. In payment all I have to do is kneel on the floor and let you thrust into me as Giovanni did my mother. How truly fortunate I am."

"At the moment the thought of you on your knees brings me a good deal of pleasure," Lion said harshly.

"I will not kneel to you. Go home to that poor woman you call wife. She seems eager to do your bidding."

He stiffened. "Bianca has nothing to do with what is between us. It's foolish even to speak of her."

Sanchia felt a sharp pang knife through her. "Why not? She seems a sweet, kind lady. Do you not feel shame at bringing me here to hold her up to humiliation?"

"I had no choice."

"You had a choice. You have it now." The words tumbled from her lips in a wild, fierce stream. "Let me go. Do you think I don't know what the men of your family use this house for? I'm not an ignorant child like your Bianca. I understood what Lorenzo meant. Your father used this place to house his whores and now you use it to house yours. Well, I'm not a whore and I won't be—"

"Hush." He was suddenly kneeling beside the bed. "Cease, I tell you." His hands gripped her bare shoulders and the sudden hard warmth of his palms sent a shiver through her. "You are not my whore." His voice was hoarse, tormented, "You are my . . ." He stopped.

"What? Your slave?"

"*Cristo*, I don't know," he whispered. "I don't know anymore. But I must have you near. I don't think I would have left you in Genoa even if you hadn't threatened to run away." His hands kneaded her bare shoulders yearningly. "Let me look at you. God, it seems a long time since I looked at you."

She caught her breath as a wave of heat tingled through her. "No."

"Yes." One hand left her shoulders to jerk the coverlet down and away from her body and then returned to her shoulders to hold her immobile while his gaze ran lingeringly over her. "Do you remember in the barn when I came into you and—"

"I'll fight you." She could feel her breasts swelling beneath his gaze, ripening, the nipples hardening. No, she must not feel this. In that direction lay a captivity more certain than the bill of sale he held in his possession. "Loose me, Lion."

"In a minute." His head bent slowly to her breasts. "Look how hard and sweet these buds are now. They want attention." His lips enveloped her left breast and he drew on it gently and then more strongly. She gave a low cry, swayed, held upright only by the hands on her shoulders. His lips moved to the right breast and he gave it the same attention. His head lifted, his lips releasing her. "Mine."

"No."

He rubbed his broad cheek back and forth across her breasts with a yearning movement. "Yes." His left hand moved down her body to cup between her thighs as he had in the barn at the farm. "Always."

She closed her eyes as the warmth exuding from his callused hand caused the muscles of her stomach to clench and spasm. He began to rub slowly, teasingly. "Do not do this. It is not my will." She added haltingly, "You . . . shame me."

His hand stilled. She heard the harsh sound of his breathing in the silence of the room. Then his hand was no longer between her thighs and he was releasing her.

Her eyes opened to see him rise to his feet, a massive shadow in the predawn gloom. He moved swiftly across the room to the door and tossed harshly over his shoulder, "Cover yourself."

She drew the coverlet over her, her gaze fixed in bewilderment on his broad back. He had wanted her. She had been sure he would ignore her words and take her. Why had he not done it?

"My mother may come here and try to drive you away." He opened the door. "She does not want you here for reasons of her own. You must not let her words hurt you. I will deal with her when I return."

"It's natural that she wishes to protect Bianca."

His lips twisted cynically. "It's Mandara she wishes to protect." He turned at the door. "I cannot blame her for fighting for what she wants. Life has not been easy for her. We all must . . ." He trailed off, looking at her. "Will you wish me a good journey?"

"You don't need my good wishes."

He flinched, and then shrugged. "You're right. I have done very well without them until now." He started to turn. "Goodbye, Sanchia."

A thread of pain ran beneath the carelessness of his words, waking a strange echoing ache within Sanchia. Her hands gripped the coverlet hard to keep back the words he'd asked of her. They came anyway. "Good journey, Lion."

He stopped and stayed framed in the doorway for an instant. Then he quickly shut the door behind him.

Sanchia sank back against the pillows and turned on her side, gazing at the door leading to the balcony. Her breasts were swollen, the aureoles of her nipples still distended and aching. Santa Maria, she didn't want to feel lust burning through her. It was as unwelcome as the tenderness she felt for him. As unwelcome as the impulse she'd had to call him back.

Sweet Jesus, how she had wanted to call him back.

The winds of dawn blew crisp and cold on Lion's face as he rode out of the gates of the city.

He needed that cold, Lion thought grimly, as he put Tabron to a gallop. He gazed blindly at the sky now turning from pearl to palest pink. Why had he stopped? Unwilling or not, her response had been as strong as his own and he would soon have been able to quench her resistance.

Why had he not done it?

This inner conflict had to end. The emotions Sanchia aroused in him were like nothing he had ever felt before, alternating between lust and a strange, wistful tenderness. It was all madness.

He must think. He must find a way to resolve his dilemma and put an end to this lunacy with Sanchia.

"You no longer have the Wind Dancer?" Borgia asked softly. "I believe I cautioned you about offering it to anyone else, Damari. My father has written expressing interest in it . . . such interest he informs me of his plan to travel to Cesena to inspect it. I don't intend to disappoint him."

"You will not disappoint him, Your Magnificence," Damari said quickly. "If you'll but write him to delay his trip for a few short weeks, I'm sure we will be able to retrieve the Wind Dancer."

"We?" Borgia smiled. "You expect my help? If my help is given, then no further payment is required. Is that what you wish?"

Damari felt the frustration and rage rising in him and sought desperately to control his temper. "Andreas managed to get the statue back through no fault of my own. My information is that it has been returned to Mandara. My condotti is small and the city well guarded. If you could just let me have the service of the forces you've quartered in Cesena, I could—"

"My God, are you mad? I'm surrounded by rebellion and discord here in the Romagna. You wish me to lend you an army when it might mean putting down an insurrection here when you deign to return it?" Borgia shook his head. "You offered me a bargain and I hold you to the terms of it. You supply the Wind Dancer and my father supplies a dukedom."

Damari's eyes widened in excitement. "The holy father agreed to my terms?"

"I told you he had expressed interest." Borgia smiled. "But if you cannot furnish me with the Wind Dancer, perhaps I'll go after it myself. After the Romagna is completely secure, I could launch an attack on Mandara."

"No!" Damari said sharply. "The statue is mine."

"Then bring it to me."

"I must have time to make plans."

"I'll write my father that there's been a slight delay," Borgia told him. "Only a *slight* delay. In five weeks' time I go to Rome with either the Wind Dancer in my hands or you by my side to explain to him why I don't have it in my possession. Tell me, Damari, have you ever been to Rome?"

Damari shook his head. "I have not had that pleasure."

"A magnificent city with a lovely river winding through it. Perhaps you've heard that my own dear brother was found floating in the river Tiber with many knife wounds in his body. No one has ever determined who tossed him into the water since little attention is paid to such an act. So common an occurrence in Rome." He paused. "Do I make myself clear?"

"You always make yourself clear, my lord."

Borgia turned away contemptuously. "Then you may go, Damari."

He was being dismissed like the lowliest lackey. Damari smothered the venom rising within him and forced himself to bow courteously. "Be assured I'll find a way of obtaining the Wind Dancer with no trouble or expense to you. My apologies for suggesting you aid me, my lord duke. I was only concerned for the disappointment of His Holiness."

"You'll gain my forgiveness when I have the Wind Dancer. I expect you here in five weeks' time."

"I'll be here." Damari, bowing obsequiously, backed from the room.

He abruptly straightened after he had closed the door, standing quite still while he fought the bitterness boiling through him. Only a short time ago it had been he who had controlled both Borgia and the pope. Now he was no longer the duke's equal but subservient once more.

And he had come so close!

No matter. He would regain his power and status as soon as he reclaimed the Wind Dancer. There would be no more bowing and scraping once he had what Borgia wanted.

But how to get it?

Bribery had succeeded once, but it was doubtful that Andreas would allow even the most trusted servant close enough to steal the statue again. Damari would be foolish to launch his small condotti against Mandara in the vain hope that luck would carry the day. Andreas was too able a commander and Mandara too strong a fortress to fall without overwhelming numbers launched against it in the field.

Not bribery. Not force. The elimination of both weapons meant he would have to wait and study the situation to find a way to overcome the disadvantages he was facing. In the meantime, a spy could be insinuated into the town, if not into the castle itself, and surely he would be able to think of something before the five weeks Borgia had given him expired. He had not raised himself to his present status by lacking in imagination.

Damari descended the stone steps to the courtyard where a lackey was holding the reins of his horse. Swinging up into the saddle he noted the sky was leaden, clouds roiling, scudding with the wind preceding a storm. He was going to get a wetting before he reached shelter but he refused to go back to Borgia and beg to stay.

He lifted his head and smiled as a gust of moist wind touched his cheeks. Besides, he would not mind riding through the rain. The fact that the storm was heading north was a good portent. Mandara lay due north, safe and snug and arrogant in its small world.

And a storm was coming to Mandara also, as soon as

he thought of a way to send it thundering over Lion Andreas and his bitch of a mother.

. And the little slave, Sanchia.

He'd been startled when Andreas had launched an attack on Solinari to get her back. Clearly she was important to his foe.

Yes, he'd have to be sure his plans for the future held a prominent place for the slave girl.

Twelve

I do not wish to look at one more piece of goods," Sanchia said firmly as she turned away from the shop of a leather craftsman.

Lorenzo halted as he saw the determination on Sanchia's face. "Oh, very well. We've bought many lengths of fine fabric, the dressmaker has your measurements now, and she can work 'round the clock without you. Still, I do not understand you in this. You are not behaving with the enthusiasm I thought you'd show considering your former deprivation."

"I must be careful not to take too much," she said soberly. "It would be foolish to become accustomed to riches that can never be mine."

"How depressingly sensible. They could be yours if you'd be amenable."

She shook her head, beginning to walk

across the square toward her house. "I won't stay here longer than I have to do so."

"Why not? Mandara is a very pleasant place to live. Ask anyone. Lion has built many things of beauty, while he levies few taxes, and his laws are strict but fair. Lady Caterina makes sure the poor are fed and the sick are cared for." He smiled. "Why should you want to go back to Florence when Mandara can give you so much?"

"I may not go back to Florence. I don't know where I'll go, but I won't stay here." She met his gaze. "And you know why, Lorenzo."

"None of us is really free, Sanchia."

"I'd like to see if I could prove you wrong. I don't know anything but servitude and I'll have to learn the way of freedom. When I first awoke on the ship I thought everything was so clear and that I was strong enough to shift the world." She shook her head ruefully. "But now I realize it's as if I have just been born and have to learn everything from the beginning."

"I would wait until Lion freed me before venturing into these realms of knowledge."

"You know he won't do so. I must free myself . . . when the opportunity arises." She paused. "Why did Lion go to Florence?"

"Can't you guess?"

"Caprino?"

Lorenzo nodded. "He can't get his hands on Damari at present, so he's settling for Caprino."

She shivered. "Caprino is a dangerous man."

"But so is Lion," Lorenzo said calmly. "And Caprino will pose no problem for him. Don't worry; if I'd thought otherwise I would have gone with him."

Sanchia quickly averted her eyes. "Why should I worry?"

"You might ask yourself that question. The answer could—" He stopped and then smiled. "I believe you have visitors, Sanchia."

Sanchia's gaze followed Lorenzo's to the two horses tied at the iron garden gate. "Lady Caterina?"

"I'm sure you can expect a call from her shortly, but

that's not her horse. If I'm not mistaken, your visitors are Marco and Bianca."

Sanchia winced. Sweet Mary, she didn't want to see Lion's wife again. The very thought of Bianca brought a surge of unreasoning guilt mixed with an emotion even more incomprehensible and infinitely more base in nature. "What is she doing here?"

"Her charitable duty, no doubt." Lorenzo took Sanchia's elbow and propelled her forward through the shallow garden. "But I'm glad they decided to come. I believe you'll find their visit very illuminating."

"Illuminating?" Sanchia asked, puzzled.

Lorenzo opened the front door and stepped aside for her to precede him. "You have keen eyes, use them."

"Sanchia!" Bianca rushed forward, a smile lighting her face. "I hope you don't mind our visiting so soon. I wanted to go to the cathedral this morning and took the opportunity to bring you a strengthening herbal remedy."

"No, of course I don't mind." Sanchia smiled tentatively. "But it really wasn't necessary. I'm quite well now except for my hand."

"Don't tell her that, Sanchia." Marco strolled into the hall from the direction of the salon. "She delights in concocting foul-tasting remedies for all who will condescend to swallow them."

"It's not foul-tasting," Bianca protested. "I added honey to sweeten it. You aren't kind, Marco."

Marco smiled at her. "You're kind enough for both of us." He turned to Sanchia. "You look well, Sanchia. I think you'll soon have no need for remedies."

Marco's beauty struck her anew as he came forward and bowed. Dressed in a bright blue velvet jerkin and blue-and-white partihose he lit up the small hall with elegance and grace. "Undoubtedly you don't remember our last meeting in that cell at Solinari," he said soberly. "However, it's one I'll never forget. You were very brave, Sanchia. I regret you were forced to suffer for our sake."

She shook her head. "I wasn't brave. It's not brave to endure what must be endured." She smiled with an effort. "But I don't like to think of that time. Did Rosa give you wine? I know nothing about fine wines, but Lorenzo brought a jug last evening and he says it is full of the very best."

Marco shook his head. "We just arrived and cannot stay. Bianca spent hours at the cathedral in the confessional." He shot Bianca a mischievous glance. "She was weighed down by her mountain of sins and required much absolution."

Bianca made a face at him. "You would do well to go to confession yourself. You are puffed up with the sin of pride. Wasn't it only yesterday you were boasting about the beauty of the painting you're working on?"

"It wasn't pride in my skill but in my subject," he said softly. "Bianca, the beautiful."

Bianca smiled radiantly at him. "You tease me. It is the painting that's beautiful." She tore her gaze away from him and turned to Sanchia. "You must see Marco's work. He's a splendid artist."

"I look forward to it," Sanchia said absently, as she looked from Bianca to Marco. They were like two radiant children, filled with the joy of life and with each other. "Are you sure you won't stay and have a goblet of wine?"

Bianca shook her head. "I must return to the castle. It's our day for visiting the sick." She smiled gently. "Good day, Sanchia. Drink my remedy and you'll soon be able to come to the castle and see Marco's beautiful painting."

Marco hesitated. "Will you assist Bianca onto her mount, Lorenzo? I'd like a word with Sanchia."

"It would be my pleasure." Lorenzo opened the door and bowed to Bianca. "If I give her service, perhaps she'll be grateful enough to pray for the forgiveness of my sins."

"God forgives all," Bianca said. "Go to the priest and have him intercede for you."

"I think God would listen more readily to the prayers of the beautiful Bianca. He is, after all, the originator of good taste." Lorenzo's fingers closed on Bianca's elbow and urged her forward. "I'll return shortly, Sanchia."

Marco turned to Sanchia as soon as the door closed behind them. "You're not planning on staying at Mandara?"

"No, I'll leave as soon as possible."

Marco nodded, relieved. "That would be best. If I can help in any way, please call on me."

"I may ask for your help if it becomes necessary."

"You understand I wouldn't want to deprive you of safety or contentment, but Bianca is very innocent."

"I understand." She smiled warmly at him. "And I wouldn't want to hurt her in any way. Believe me, Marco."

"I do believe you." He bowed and crossed the few feet to the door. "Thank you, Sanchia."

A few minutes later Lorenzo entered the hall, closed the door and leaned back against it. "He asked you to go?"

"No, only if I planned to do so." She met his gaze. "He wants to protect her from hurt or shame." She paused. "He loves her?"

"Yes."

"They're quite beautiful together."

"As exquisite as two dancing sunbeams." He smiled. "And with a relationship just as substantial."

Sanchia glanced away. "Does she love him, too?"

"Oh, yes, as much as she can love any man. She won't admit it to herself, of course, for that would be a sin. She's loved Marco since she was brought here to Mandara to marry Lion. They were drawn to each other at once and thrown together constantly as Lion was always away with his father fighting with their condotti."

"Lion knows?"

"Since the first time he came home from battle and saw them together. They were then as they are now."

"Was he very angry?"

"No. Saddened. He loves Marco."

She had seen the affection between the two brothers, but she couldn't believe Lion would react without anger toward anyone who encroached on his property. "But Bianca is his wife. He would not—"

"Psyche," Lorenzo interrupted. "You saw it that first

moment. Pure, childlike. How do you think Psyche would respond to Lion? Bianca is as unsuited to Lion as a woman can be unsuited to a man. If she hadn't been the daughter of a great house she would have gone into a convent. Marco's adoration suits her very well; he is her Cupid for his love is divine, pure."

"I don't want to hear any more." She moistened her lips with her tongue. "This isn't my concern."

"You will hear more because Lion is not one of Bianca's saints; he's my friend and I've grown tired of seeing him give all and get nothing in return." He went on bluntly, "Bianca is not only a Psyche; she's a child who will never grow up. There's something wrong . . . She was only fourteen when she was wed and at first Lion thought her childishness natural, but she's never changed. She's a child in a dream world playing at being a grown woman. He gave Marco endless opportunities to cuckold him during those first years and would have happily accepted Marco's child as his heir." He paused. "But then he realized that Bianca would never accept Marco as her lover. She doesn't understand passion any more than a small child would, and Marco is so filled with tales of courtly love that he'd never try to teach her." He shook his head. "Incredible. So Lion stays away at Pisa and permits them to play like children here at Mandara."

"Perhaps they're all happy with the arrangement as it stands."

"I'm not happy with it, but I would have left it alone if Lady Caterina had not decided to alter the balance. She makes excuses to call Lion back to Mandara at every opportunity. She wants an heir for Mandara and she's clever enough to know Marco will never cuckold Lion to provide her with one nor will the besotted idiot marry anyone else. Which leaves only Lion to be lured back to Bianca's bed and his duty to Mandara." He straightened away from the door. "I agree with Lady Caterina that it's time the situation is resolved, but not in the fashion she's chosen. Lion deserves to be free of this yoke."

"Then in what fashion?"

"You," he said. "A permanent liaison that will discourage Lady Caterina's hopes and free Lion from the responsibility of Mandara. That's why you had to come here, Sanchia. Lion has been very careful not to bring any women to Mandara for fear it would shame Bianca. Lady Caterina must come to recognize that your presence here indicates a shifting in the balance of the situation."

"It means nothing." Sanchia gazed at him, stunned. "You're using me as a pawn."

"Yes," he said calmly. "But you'll be a beautifully cared for pawn and, if you give Lion a child, you'll never again want for anything."

"A child?"

"Had you not thought of that? There's a possibility you might be with child."

"No, I couldn't—" She had not yet had her flux but surely it was not yet her time. So much had happened it was difficult to remember.

"If you're not with child, I'm sure that happy circumstance will occur shortly." Lorenzo added, "And the child would belong to Lion just as you do, Sanchia."

"No! The child of a slave is free."

"Perhaps in Florence, but in almost every other city-state the child would also belong to the mother's master." He paused. "Unless you could convince him to free the child. I don't think you could bear to leave your babe and run away to this dream of freedom you're nurturing. Judging by the way you acquired your band of little friends in Florence, I believe you to have an extremely affectionate and maternal nature."

No, she'd never be able to leave her child, and how could she care for an infant by herself as a runaway slave? What if she became hurt or ill? She had seen the fate of children abandoned to the streets. She could feel the panic rising within her. "There is no child. There will never be a child." She blinked away the tears stinging behind her eyes. "I'm going away and—"

"I'd wait to determine that. It might be too late even now."

"You're very cruel," she whispered.

"No." For an instant his eyes held a distant sympa-

thy. "We can't all have what we want. We have to choose.
I choose Lion."

She drew a deep breath. "Well, I do not."

He smiled. "We shall see." He turned to go. "I'll
leave you now. I'm sure you'll need time to get over the
resentment you're feeling toward me and think about
what I've said. I'll return tomorrow to make sure all is
well with you." He opened the door. "Good day, Sanchia."

Sanchia gazed blankly at the door that had just shut
and then turned and moved slowly, heavily toward the
salon. A child? Why had she never considered a child? If
she carried his child, Lion would never give up searching for her to claim it. Surely God wouldn't be so cruel
as to give her a child. She had only to be patient and
Lorenzo's words would prove false.

She had only to wait and be patient.

As Lorenzo had predicted, Lady Caterina called on
Sanchia late that afternoon and was ushered into the
salon by an excited and awed Rosa.

Sanchia stood up, bracing herself as she closed the
book Lorenzo had given her. She smiled determinedly.
"You honor me, my lady."

"Yes, I do." Caterina Andreas gazed critically
around the room, evaluating the tapestry-cushioned
bench and matching hassock, the deeply recessed
leaded-glass windows, the polished oak cabinet. Her
gaze lingered longest on the huge amethyst on the lid of
the silver pitcher on the richly carved Venetian table.
"This is furnished quite pleasantly. You must be very
content here." She turned back to Sanchia. "Nevertheless, you must leave. I won't have you at Mandara."

Sanchia had been prepared for a dismissal but still
found herself startled at the bluntness of the statement.
"I have no intention of remaining here," she replied with
equal candor. "As soon as I'm permitted to leave, I will
do so. You've forgotten I'm not free to make that
choice."

Caterina's gaze narrowed on her face. "Yet you said

you considered yourself free even though my son does not."

"I do." She swallowed to ease the sudden tightness of her throat. "But there are certain considerations that may interfere with my attempting to leave at once."

"What considerations?" Caterina asked fiercely. "You like living in this fine house and having Lion pamper you with gowns and jewels? Well, it won't do. I won't permit—"

"No," Sanchia cut through the tirade. "I want nothing." She drew a deep breath. "That's not true. I'd be foolish not to want all of those things. Of course I want them. But not enough to—" She broke off and then said, "You don't have to worry about my staying here, Lady Caterina. Give me a little time and I promise you I'll leave Mandara."

"And what if I don't give you time?"

"Then I'll take it anyway."

A look of surprise crossed Lion's mother's face followed by grudging respect. "You're very bold for a slave."

"I'm not bold at all, but I am determined." Sanchia smiled sadly. "A slave isn't permitted the former and would not survive without the latter."

"Indeed." Caterina studied Sanchia. "The same could be said of a wife."

"I have no experience with which to judge the truth of what you say."

"I have." Caterina whirled toward the door in a flurry of violet silk skirts. "I'm not satisfied, but I'll obviously win no further agreement from you, and I'm not fool enough to waste my breath. I'll hold my peace for a time while you ponder your 'considerations.'" She shot a level look at Sanchia over her shoulder. "But if you're not gone by the end of the fortnight, you may expect me to take action. Be warned."

She didn't wait for a reply or issue a farewell but swept majestically from the room.

Sanchia sighed in relief. She felt as if she had been pummeled. It hadn't been easy to face Lion's noble mother as an equal when she was accustomed to behav-

ing with a show of servility even to shopkeepers. This
new life into which she had been tossed had a bewildering number of threats and challenges with which she
had to learn to contend, and today she had been
confronted with too many of them.

She didn't want to be thrust into the tortured
relations of the Andreas family. She didn't want to have
to face intimidating women like Caterina while she was
still so unsure of herself. She didn't want to be Lorenzo's
pawn or Lady Caterina's nemesis.

And dear lord, most of all, she didn't want to be
held captive to Lion Andreas by a child within her
womb.

"I like her." Caterina wrapped the quilt around her
nakedness and slipped out of bed. She padded barefoot
over to the table and poured wine into a goblet with one
hand while she clutched the quilt to her breasts with the
other. "She's no fool."

"She has strength." Lorenzo sat up and leaned back
against the carved mahogany headboard. "I thought
you'd appreciate Sanchia."

"It means nothing, of course. She still leaves Mandara." Caterina lifted the goblet to her lips and smiled at
him over the rim. "She told me she would leave as soon
as possible."

"Then I'm sure she'll make the attempt. I've always
found Sanchia to be truthful."

Caterina's smile faded. "She also said there were
considerations to ponder. Which smacks of your interference."

"Does it?"

She took another sip of wine and strolled back to
him. "You're a rogue, Lorenzo." She handed him the
goblet and sat down on the side of the bed. "If I were
wise, I'd put hemlock in this cup instead of good
Mandara wine."

"You are wise." Lorenzo sipped the wine. "Though
hemlock is far too obvious a poison for me not to

recognize. If you wish to murder me, you must be more subtle, Caterina. I am, after all, a master of the art."

Caterina tried to hide her start of surprise. In all the years she had known him, Lorenzo had never once mentioned his former profession to her. She took the goblet from him, drank a little and returned it to him. "Poison?"

He shrugged. "At times. It's cleaner than most methods and relatively safe. However, there are so many ignorant and bungling practitioners in Italy today that it's no wonder most noblemen and men of means have tasters."

"But you're no bungler."

He met her gaze with eyes as clear and cold as polished stone. "I'm the angel of death himself, my dear Caterina. I am superb."

She drew the blanket more closely around her to shut out the sudden chill. "You're no longer an assassin. You haven't been one for a long time."

"You're wrong. We always remain what we are no matter how our circumstances change. If you lost everything, you would still be a great lady. If I became the pope, I'd still be an assassin."

"Nonsense."

His long slender fingers caressed the raised design on the silver goblet. "Truth. Why are you so belligerent? Does it bother you that you've taken a murderer to your bed? A reformed assassin is acceptable, but a—"

"Why are we talking about this?" she interrupted abruptly. "What you were before you came to Mandara makes no difference to me. It's what you do in this bed that's important."

"What I am makes a difference to many women. It fills some with horror." He smiled. "And it fills others with lust. It's not every woman who's permitted to fornicate with the angel of death and live to boast of it. When you first came to my bed, I thought perhaps you might be one of those women. I admit I was disappointed, for I had great admiration for your strength and courage."

"Then why did you accept me?"

"I'm only a man and you are very beautiful."

"I'm not beautiful. My face is as long as a horse's and I'm as tall as a man."

"If strength and courage have beauty then there's no one more beautiful on this earth than you, Caterina."

She felt uncomfortable with his sudden gravity. "And I was not driven to you by some vile fascination. I came to you because you're clever and amuse me, and I lusted after you. No other reasons."

"One other reason."

She frowned in puzzlement. "What is that?"

"I offered no threat to you or to Mandara either through marriage or a wagging tongue. You were and are safe with me."

"Yes." She bent suddenly and put her lips to his forehead. "I do feel safe with you, Lorenzo. Safer than I have ever felt with any man. I wonder why?"

"No more than I wonder. The knowledge that you trust me fills me with incredulity. No one has felt safe with me since I was a young boy."

"Move over. I'm cold." She took the goblet from him and set it on the floor. "I'm coming back to bed."

She curled up spoon fashion with her back to him, her gaze on the embers glowing in the fireplace across the room. "How young a boy?"

"When I became the angel of death? Eleven. Though I didn't really reach that exalted status without years of practice in my trade. I was quite clumsy at first."

"I don't want to know about your rise in your 'profession,'" she said impatiently. "I want to know why."

"Greed."

"I don't believe that."

"It's the truth. Oh, perhaps not the first one."

"Who was the the first one?"

"Vito Martinado. But don't ask me the name of the last man I killed. I don't remember."

"Who was this Vito Martinado?"

"He was the captain of a merchant ship, a very unpleasant man. He had a fondness for young boys and he picked me up on the dock and took me to his room at the inn and used me for a week or so."

"Used you?"

"It wasn't the first time I had been so used. When you're alone on the streets of Naples, you expect to become prey. If you're lucky they feed and clothe you for a while before they find a new child with which to toy."

The matter-of-factness of his tone touched Caterina far more than any outburst of emotion would have. She felt a painful tightness in her throat.

"But the good captain had the same tastes as Damari. He liked to hurt me."

"Couldn't you run away?"

"He kept me locked in the room when he wasn't at the inn. He must have realized what a unique treasure I was." His hand moved to her throat and began to stroke gently. "You have a magnificent throat. Long and graceful—"

"And you had to kill him to get away?"

"He was hired to captain a galleon going to Bombay and decided to take me with him on the voyage, a decision with which I wasn't in agreement for obvious reasons. I objected. We struggled. I grabbed his knife and stabbed him in the heart." He kissed her behind the ear. "Your hair smells of flowers."

"I washed it today. You weren't punished for it?"

"In Naples? Murder is more common than not on the streets of that illustrious city." He sniffed again. "Lavender?"

"Yes." She swallowed hard. "What did you do then?"

"I had a most unfortunate aversion to being touched with intimacy for quite some time after that, and I had to eat. I decided since I'd committed a mortal sin and was damned to hell anyway I might as well reap the benefits of the trade. Murder was as profitable as it was common and I had great confidence in myself even then. I knew when I'd mastered my trade, no one would practice it with equal intelligence and ingenuity." His fingers moved up the long line of her jaw. "Lavender is delightful, but I think one of the scents from Arabia would suit you even better. They have something of the exotic about them, a maturity that—" He broke off and was silent a moment. "Tears?"

"The chimney must not be drawing well. The smoke . . ."

His fingertips brushed her cheek with a motion that was almost but not quite a caress. "Yes, that must be it. Smoke. For you're far too sensible to weep for a rogue like me."

"Far too sensible."

"And you're far too hardened to feel sympathy for the boy who died in that inn over thirty years ago."

"Far too hardened." She was silent a moment. "Did he die, Lorenzo?"

"Yes, there are some experiences that destroy what we are. Ask Sanchia. She went through that fire at Solinari, but she was born again. I was not. I was too earthbound to rise like the phoenix from the flames. The fire raged through and devoured me and left me empty. And each year that passed I grew more and more hollow until now I sometimes wonder why anyone who looks at me can't see through me as if I were clear water."

Two fingers gently touched her damp lash. "And you've suffered too much not to realize that though we must take what pleasure we can to alleviate the emptiness, we can never really fill it."

Was it a warning or a plea for understanding? She doubted if he would admit to either, and she didn't know if she would dare to answer if he did. "Yes, of course, I know that." Another tear brimmed and then slowly rolled down her cheek. "As I said, it's only the smoke . . ."

Thirteen

Lion returned to Mandara seven days later.

Sanchia was sitting on the balcony enjoying the afternoon sun when she saw Tabron picking his way down the twisting street toward her house. Her gaze rose from horse to master, and she felt a surge of emotion so strong she was dizzy with it. It couldn't be joy. Please God, it mustn't be joy. It had to be relief that Lion had suffered no harm from Caprino.

Lion raised his head and saw her. He reined in Tabron, his expression unreadable as he gazed at her for a long moment. "I've brought you a present." He jerked his head at someone riding behind him. "Though God knows why you would want him. He has the obstinacy of the mule he rides. He would scarcely let me stop to eat or rest in his eagerness to get to you."

Her gaze flew to the small figure

mounted on the mule Lion was leading. "Piero?" she whispered in disbelief. "Piero!" She jumped to her feet and ran toward the doors of the balcony, down the steps and out the front door. By the time she reached the gate Piero was squirming on the small mule's back, obviously trying to figure out how to dismount.

"Hold," Lion said as he slid to the ground. "I didn't bring you all this way to have you crack your stubborn head open on the flagstones." He reached up, plucked Piero from the saddle and set him down. "What good is a present if it's broken?"

Piero hurled himself into Sanchia's arms and held on with all his might. "Sanchia, I want to stay." He added with the fierce tenaciousness she knew so well, "I'm going to stay."

"I told you he was stubborn. He'll probably cling to you like a barnacle." Lion smiled faintly as he stood gazing at the two of them. "Just as he clung to that mule all the way from Florence."

"Piero . . ." Tears were running down Sanchia's cheeks as her palm caressed the little boy's fair hair. She hugged Piero's small, sturdy body closer as she looked over his head at Lion. "Why?"

"You care for him. Is that not reason enough?"

She started to speak, but he went on quickly. "Elizabet is now wed and seems content. Your Bartolomeo is fired with the desire to become the best printer in all of Florence and the *signor* appears well pleased with him."

"You went to see them?" she asked, surprise coloring her voice.

He scowled. "I knew you would want word of them. And after I finished my business I had time to spare to inquire."

"Caprino?"

"Lorenzo told you?" Lion shrugged. "He will no longer trouble you. As I said, the business is finished."

He meant that Caprino was dead. After years of fear Caprino's threat to her was now ended. Strangely, the knowledge brought no feeling of relief only an enormous weariness.

"He betrayed us." Lion's gaze was on her face. "He deserved to die. He was as guilty as Damari."

"What happened at Solinari is over. At first I was so angry I thought I wanted revenge, but now I wish only to forget about it."

"I'm not so gentle-natured. I told you I returned good for good and evil for evil. Solinari will be over when all who are responsible for what happened to you are punished." He swung onto Tabron's back. "I'll visit you this evening. There are things I wish to discuss." He glanced over his shoulder as he turned his horse and tightened his grip on the mule's lead rope. "You'd better feed the boy. He's eaten scarcely a morsel since we set out."

"I will." Her voice was still muffled with tears. "Lion?"

He reined in and looked back at her.

"Why?"

His gaze met hers, his expression impassive. "Solinari."

He turned and rode down the street in the direction of the castle.

"Sanchia." Piero was stepping back, wriggling out of her arms. "I'm staying, Sanchia. He said I could stay, but even if he hadn't, I'd stay anyway. I'm not going back to Elizabet."

"Shh, it's all right." Her palm cupped his cheek. She had forgotten how soft and warm a child's cheek could be. "You don't have to go back. But weren't you happy there? You look well." She grinned. "I can tell you've been living with a baker. You've grown plump as a pigeon since last I saw you."

He shrugged, his gaze fixed on her face. "I didn't belong there. I belong with you. I told him so when he asked me."

"Lion?"

"Lord Andreas asked if I'd be willing to come to you. He said that you'd been hurt and were lonely for me. Have you been lonely, Sanchia?"

"Yes." She hadn't realized how lonely until she had

seen Piero on that mule coming toward her. "I've missed you, too."

"It's because you belong to me and we should be together. That's what I told Lord Andreas," he said solemnly.

"And what did he say?" She lovingly smoothed Piero's hair back from his face.

"He said he understood and that I was going with him to Mandara."

Yes, Lion would understand about belonging and possessing, she thought without bitterness. As she gazed down at Piero, she was too filled with passionate gratitude to have any room for resentment. If Lion had taken much from her, he had also given back. "And you did come to Mandara." She hugged him quickly. "And didn't let Lord Andreas stop or rest until you got here. You're lucky he didn't smack that mule and send it running back to Florence."

Piero's jaw was set with determination. "I wanted to see you."

"And I'm glad you hurried." She rose from her knees and took his hand. "Now, come inside and I'll get you something to eat and a bath to cleanse you of the dust of the road."

He hung back, looking after Lion, who was disappearing into the distance.

"Piero."

"He understood, Sanchia. I didn't think he would, but he did."

She nodded, her gaze following Piero's with joy, bewilderment, and trepidation. She had been trying to develop more resistance to Lion since the day he had left Mandara but now found herself once more disarmed and uncertain. "I know, Piero." Then she turned and pulled him gently toward the door. "I think you'll like living here. It's even prettier than the baker's house."

"My Lord Andreas," Rosa announced and then scurried from the salon.

Lion frowned as he gazed after her. "What's the

matter with the wench? She looked at me as if I sported horns."

"She's only timid." Sanchia rose to her feet. "You should see the way she stares at Lorenzo."

"No doubt that's why he hired her for your service. It amuses him to prey upon the fear in which he's held."

"The fear is well deserved," Sanchia said, remembering how skillfully Lorenzo had kept her from attempting to leave Mandara with a few words a little over a week before. "He's a formidable man."

Lion studied her intently. "Did I detect a note of bitterness? What's Lorenzo been doing to you while I've been gone?"

"Nothing. He's been very kind to me for the most part. He calls on me every day to bring me a book from your library, and teaches me things he thinks I need to know."

"What things?"

"Oh, table manners and how to dance the pavane and the *moresca* and the difference between bad wine and good." She made a face. "Giovanni would have been delighted with that lesson." She met his gaze with bold directness. "He teaches me anything that he believes would prepare me to live in your house as your mistress."

"And you accepted the lessons?"

"Knowledge is never wasted." She paused. "Even though it may never be used in the way intended."

His lips tightened but he failed to rise to the challenge. "My mother tells me she called on you."

"Yes, to tell me she didn't want me here." She smiled. "And I told her I didn't want to be here either. Consequently, we agreed that I would leave as soon as possible."

"You think to annoy me with your defiance? I don't want you here either. We'll return to Pisa next week." He paused. "If you agree to my terms."

She stiffened. "Terms?"

"I've been thinking this last week and . . . I feel something for you that is out of the ordinary for me. There is not only lust, there is . . ." He paused again, searching for words. "Feeling. I don't believe I could be content now with just . . ." He halted again and then burst out with sudden fierceness, "Listen to me. I sound like a stupid, bumbling oaf." He took two steps closer. "Enough of this. I want you to live in my home and sleep in my bed, not only now but for the foreseeable future. I wish you to bear my children. In return I will give you your freedom, honor, and respect. What do you say to that?"

She stared at him, stunned. "I don't know what to say."

He suddenly smiled. "Then say yes. It's a good bargain; you'll never find a better. I have wealth enough to give you whatever you desire, and I won't ask you for more than I told you."

"What of Bianca?" she asked slowly.

His face became shuttered. "There's no need to hurt Bianca. She's content here at Mandara and we'll be equally content in Pisa."

"And will your mother also be content? Lorenzo said she is determined—"

"She will surrender her ambitions in time."

"Or perhaps you will surrender to her ambitions . . . in time."

"Sweet Mary, I have no desire to force Bianca back to my bed." He smiled cynically. "I was even relieved when I discovered Marco was besotted with her. It gave me an excuse to let her go her way and I to go mine."

"Unless you change your mind and decide your mother is right."

"I won't change my mind."

"How do you know? Everything changes. A month ago I was a slave in Giovanni's shop. Today I live in a fine house and Lord Andreas wishes to make me his mistress." Her voice was shaking. "Next month or next year you may decide you want a legitimate heir for Mandara and return to beget it. Then where would I be? Or you might grow bored with me and this 'feeling' would disappear. Would you take my children from me and let me go to another man?" She shivered. "I don't think I would like the life of your mistress any more than I did the life of a slave."

"I would not grow tired of you."

"How can you be certain? You have no knowledge of my mind, only my body, and you're still a stranger to me. I don't really know any more about you than I did when you first came to Giovanni's shop."

He stiffened. "Are you telling me you're refusing me? Perhaps you think to marry some other man who will give you the respectability you seem to crave."

"I have no thought of marriage. Who would marry me? I'm no longer a virgin and there are many women more comely." She moistened her lips. "But there's too much risk in what you offer me. I am to give everything and you may leave me tomorrow. I've been at risk all my life, but this would be different. This would put my children at risk also." She averted her gaze. "And I like Bianca. I would not want to hurt her."

"*Cristo*, not you, too? Everyone is trying to protect Bianca—Marco, my mother, you."

"And you. Why else would you want me to leave Mandara?"

He lifted his shoulders in a weary shrug. "Very well, I don't want to hurt her. God knows I've been careful these past thirteen years to bring no woman here to cause her shame. I saw my mother suffer enough over my father's adulteries." His voice suddenly vibrated with anger and exasperation as he continued, "But, by God, I want you and I *will* have you, Sanchia."

She dumbly shook her head.

Lion's eyes glittered with anger. "I will. You say you have no knowledge of me. Let me tell you of myself. I am not inconstant. I do not tire of things or people I value. But you don't believe me, and it seems I must demonstrate my ardor and steadfastness. How fortunate I have you here in my own house with time to persuade you to my way of thinking."

"Persuade?"

"Is that not how free women are tempted to couple with men?" He took a step closer. "You did not find me displeasing before. I believe we can assume that in future you will again find me pleasing." His hand reached out and gently cupped her breast.

She inhaled sharply and felt the color rush to her cheeks.

He smiled. "I'll tell Lorenzo to stay at the castle tomorrow and come to you myself. I also have lessons I'd like you to learn."

"You cannot change my mind." She tried to ignore Lion's hand fondling her through the fabric of her gown and hoped desperately he couldn't feel the response that caress was kindling. "I was going to take Piero for a walk around the city."

"In the morning. In the afternoon I'll send a groom to take him riding. We have a small pony in the stables that might do better for him than the mule." His gaze narrowed on her face. "Send Rosa away also. I want no one in the house when I come."

"No, I don't—"

"If she's still here, I'll send her away myself." He held her gaze with compelling force. "Don't argue with me, Sanchia. It's not easy for me to leave you tonight. I'll have no interference tomorrow. Not from Rosa." His clasp on her breast compressed gently and then released. "Not from Piero." His hand dropped slowly away from her body and he stepped back. "No one."

He turned and strode toward the door. Before reaching it he stopped abruptly and turned to face her, his gaze searching her face. "You said you wouldn't be here when I got back, but I questioned the captain of the guard, who tells me you made no attempt to leave. Why?"

"Perhaps I was waiting for an opportunity," she said evasively.

He shook his head. "Too tame. You may not think I know you well, but I realize you're not a person who waits for opportunities. You make them."

"I was waiting to find—" she stopped. "What difference does it make? I haven't changed my mind. I still intend to leave Mandara."

"Waiting for what?"

"Lorenzo suggested I might be with child. I was waiting to see if he was right."

His expression became arrested. "A child . . ." His gaze on her abdomen was a lingering caress. "And are you with child, Sanchia?"

"I still don't know."

"That would change things, would it not?" he asked thoughtfully. "A woman burdened with a child would have no easy time of it alone in the world." He suddenly smiled. "Lorenzo did well."

"I don't believe I'm with child." She added defiantly, "And even if I am, it would only mean I'll have to plan my departure carefully for the babe's sake."

He shook his head. "You're wrong, Sanchia. It would mean more than that if you carried my child." His smile widened. "A great deal more than that." He turned back to the door. "Until tomorrow."

When Sanchia opened the door the next afternoon it was to see Lion garbed in the same wine-colored velvet jerkin he had worn the first time she'd seen him in the piazza in Florence. She was immediately deluged with memories of that day: Lion's power and dominance, her own servitude and fear. She wondered resentfully if he had intended to remind her by wearing the garment today.

"Have you sent your servant away?" he asked briskly as he strode past her into the salon.

"Yes, but only because I knew you would—what do you have there?" She noticed for the first time that he was carrying two rolled-up parchment scrolls of about two feet in length under his arm.

He tossed one of the scrolls on the table and began to unroll the second scroll. "Sit down on the floor."

"What?"

"Sit down on the floor." He dropped down on the rug and smoothed out the parchment with careful hands. "How can I teach you, if you can't see what I'm talking about?"

She drew closer and looked warily down at the parchment.

Lion reached out, grasped her wrist and drew her down to her knees beside him. "This is the second Dancer. I call her *Caterina's Dancer*. You sailed to Genoa on the first Dancer I had built. This one will be much larger when it's finished."

She gazed in bewilderment at the sweeping lines and minute mathematical equations inscribed on the parchment. "This is a ship?"

"A design for a ship. The ship itself is only in the first stages at the yard in Pisa. Now." He pointed to one of the many slots in the side of the ship. "This is where the oars will be placed. You notice this is a trireme, which means that each bench on the galley is manned by three rowers, rowing with three separate oars."

"There weren't any oars on the ship that I was on."

"That's because it was a round ship with fully rigged sails, not a galley. I prefer the round ship, but many merchants will ship their goods only by galley because it's safer on the longer trips. The galley depends on the wind to carry it from one port to another, leaving the oars idle most of the time. But the moments when the oars are used are vital. Galleys don't have to sit off a dangerous shore and perhaps be blown onto the rocks or out to sea again. They can maneuver to land at many ports not possible for a round ship and—" He stopped as he glanced up and saw her expression. "What's wrong? Don't you understand?"

"I understand what you're saying, but I don't understand why you're telling me all this."

"You said you didn't know me." He met her gaze. "This is my life now. I thought it best to let you learn this part of me before any other. You must stop me if I go too fast. I fear I'll make an impatient tutor."

"Lessons. I thought you meant—"

"Oh, I did." Rueful humor twisted his lips. "But I decided this would be a better way to proceed. Not the most enjoyable but the least threatening to you. I hope you rid yourself of doubts soon as I don't promise how long my patience will last." He glanced down at the parchment. "There are three kinds of wood used in the building of every ship. Oak for the hull, ribs, stem, stemposts, beams, and planking; larch beams for the wide clamps and interior bracing; and fir for the masts and spars. I try to get my oak from Trevisana, but those forests are running low and I'll soon have to look farther afield. Perhaps the Po valley will yield—"

"I don't need a lesson in shipbuilding in order to learn your way of thinking," she interrupted. "My mind is awhirl with spars, masts, and triremes."

He looked up. "Then what do you need to know? Tell me, and I'll try to give you what you want."

For the first time he was completely open to her, and she suddenly found the temptation to explore his ideas and feelings irresistible. "Why shipbuilding? Why did you not go journeying like Messer Columbus?"

"Someone must build the ships for such enterprises. Safe ships, strong ships, ships that will last a journey around the world and back again." He added simply, "I wanted it to be me." He began to roll up the parchment. "I like the feeling of building something. From the time I was a small boy I knew only destruction. Perhaps I wanted to . . . I like the feel of it."

It was more than liking, Sanchia realized. There was an intensity, an excitement in his expression she had never seen there before. "But you talk of merchants and cargoes, not explorations."

"Commerce feeds discovery. Would Queen Isabella have given Columbus his ships if she hadn't believed there would be riches for her at the end of his journey? The clink of coins is a siren call and I'm not such a fool that I want to go begging myself. A balance can be struck that will give me both." He grinned. "As you can see, I'm an exceptionally greedy man."

He reached up and took the second scroll from the table and spread it out on the floor. "This is the plan for the round ship I'm building at the yard in Marseilles."

She vaguely remembered he had said he was away in France when the Wind Dancer was stolen. "Why did you purchase a shipyard so far away?"

"There's little interference from the local magistrates such as we suffer here, and the guilds are more concerned with the excellence of their members' workmanship and less with their contributions to charity. I've hired a fine shipwright there who will oversee the building of the ships. I expect better production there within the year than in the yard at Pisa."

She hid a smile as he went on in depth with the problems of dealing with the guilds and sailmakers and caulkers. He was so absorbed in describing his ships and the procedures for their construction that he seemed to overlook completely the fact she couldn't possibly comprehend half of what he was explaining to her.

"Then you have to consider the problem of battle engagements. The galley is better built to withstand attack, but the round ship is better in the attack itself. You must weigh the two and decide which is best for you."

"I shall do so," she said solemnly. "As soon as I have the ducats to commission the building of either."

He glanced up with a sheepish smile. "I think you're laughing at me. I'm accustomed to it. Lorenzo finds my enthusiasm very amusing."

It was not enthusiasm, it was a passion, and she was suddenly no longer amused but touched that he would share it with her. "I find it interesting but naturally a little confusing. You're trying to teach me in one afternoon everything you've learned in two years."

He nodded. "I told you I wasn't a patient man."

"I've noticed that lack in you."

He frowned and then suddenly smiled. "You're laughing at me again. I haven't seen you amused since before Solinari."

He was right, she realized with a start of surprise.

"You told me once that you wouldn't let the threat of Caprino rob you of joy," Lion said softly. "Don't let what Damari did to you rob you either, Sanchia. You don't want to give him such a victory."

She gazed at him for a moment and then smiled brilliantly. "No, I don't. I won't let that whoreson take one more thing from me than he already has." She looked down at the plan for the round ship. "Now tell me why this is shaped so differently from the galley."

Lion's gaze rested on her face for a thoughtful moment and then he too glanced down at the scroll and he began to answer her question.

Lion stayed for the rest of the afternoon, but not once did he touch her or betray any hint of intimacy in his speech or manner. When Piero returned to the house he conversed for a few minutes with the boy and then rose to leave.

"Your designs," Sanchia reminded him as she scrambled to her feet and reached for the scrolls.

"Put them in that cabinet." Lion nodded to the polished oak cabinet across the room. "I'll return tomorrow."

She smiled. "You wish to tutor me again in the craft of shipbuilding?"

"No, tomorrow I'll bring something else to show you."

She was lost in bemusement after he left. What an extraordinary afternoon it had been, and what revelations of himself Lion had permitted her. She felt more at ease with him than she ever had before and had been oddly reluctant to see him go.

"Shall I put them away for you, Sanchia?" Piero asked, his gaze on the scrolls in her hands.

"What?" She roused herself and smiled down at him. "No, I'll do it." She crossed the room, opened the cabinet, and placed the scrolls very carefully on the shelf inside. The scrolls were constructed not only of parchment and ink, but of Lion's dreams. Dreams should be well taken care of in a world where so few were realized. She closed the cabinet and, smiling, turned back to Piero. "Did you enjoy your ride? Where did you go?"

At first glance she recognized the mahogany chest Lion carried. How could she possibly forget it?

"The Wind Dancer?" she whispered.

He nodded as he kicked the door shut behind him and carried the chest into the salon. He set the chest on the table and opened the lid. "You suffered much for it. I thought you'd like to see it." He lifted the golden statue out of the box and carefully set it on the table. "The Wind Dancer."

She could see why Marco had thought the statue was alive when he had first seen it as a child. The muscles of the winged horse seemed to flex and flow with life beneath the burnished smoothness of the gold. It issued an irresistible invitation to be touched. Marco had forgotten to tell her the emerald eyes were faceted in such a way that they shimmered as if with an ever-changing expression.

She gazed at the Wind Dancer in silent absorption for several moments before moving slowly across the room to stand before it. She touched the base of the statue with a tentative finger. "It's . . . beautiful. What are these carvings?"

He shrugged. "Some sort of ancient script. It's said there was once a clay tablet that accompanied the Wind Dancer and that one of my ancestors carved the message from the tablet onto the base of the statue after the tablet was broken."

"What does the writing mean?"

"No one knows. Perhaps we'll never know." Lion affectionately touched one filigreed wing. "Perhaps he doesn't want us to know."

Lion was again speaking of the statue as if it were a living being and his touch had been a caress. She gazed with helpless fascination at the breathtakingly beautiful object on the table, and the emerald eyes of the Wind Dancer seemed to be gazing directly back at her.

Lion's gaze shifted to her face. "What's wrong?"

"I suppose it reminds me of Solinari. For some reason, I feel frightened when I look at it." She shrugged uneasily. "Will you put it back in the chest?"

Lion nodded slowly. "Certainly." He started to pick up the statue. "I never meant to—"

"What is that?" Piero stood in the doorway, his gaze fixed curiously on the Wind Dancer. "May I see it?"

Lion nodded and set the statue back on the table. "It's a statue of a horse called the Wind Dancer."

"Why is he called that?"

"Because he's a magical horse who dances on the wind and the clouds. Sanchia thinks he's a little more intimidating than your pony."

"Does that mean frightening?" Piero crossed the room and gazed gravely at the statue. The Wind Dancer and the small boy were almost on eye level, giving Sanchia the uncanny impression they were measuring each other. "He doesn't frighten me. Look, he's smiling."

Sanchia had thought the teeth of the Pegasus were bared, but now she could see how that parting of the lips might be interpreted as a smile. "Aren't you going for your ride this afternoon?"

Piero nodded, his gaze still on the statue. "I came to tell you good-bye. Donato is waiting outside." His index finger poked playfully at the Wind Dancer's muzzle. "I like him. Are we going to keep him?"

"No," she said quickly. "He belongs to Lord Andreas."

Piero looked at her in wonder. "He *does* frighten you. But why? He's beautiful, Sanchia, and he smiles . . ."

Sanchia nodded. "Yes, he's quite beautiful. Now why don't you hurry along? You're keeping Donato waiting, and it's very warm outside today."

Piero moved reluctantly toward the door. "We're going to ride out to the vineyard this afternoon. Good-bye, Lord Andreas." He paused as he opened the door for one last look at the Wind Dancer and then turned and was gone.

"Children always love the Wind Dancer. I did myself." Lion picked up the statue and carefully placed it back in its velvet lined container. "Time will dim the memory of Solinari, Sanchia."

She tried to smile as she avoided looking at the box on the table. "It's already dimming." She turned away. "Would you like a cup of malmsey? Rosa left a pitcher on—" She broke off as she felt his big hands fall on her shoulders.

"I want no malmsey." His voice was rough. "And I'm sorry I brought the Wind Dancer if it frightens you. It's always been a part of my life, and I thought it only fair I share it with you." He paused. "As I want you to share my life." One hand shifted the weight of her hair to one side, his lips lowered to touch the sensitive flesh at her nape with his tongue. "Your skin reminds me of the Wind Dancer. Golden, smooth, infinitely precious. The first time I saw you naked at Guilia's I thought of the Wind Dancer."

"Let's not speak of that time." She quickly stepped forward and away from his grasp. "I put away your designs as you bade me. Would you like me to get them?"

"No. Why are you running away from me?"

"I'm not running away. I only wondered—" A shudder ran through her as she felt his hands on her shoulders again. "Please, don't touch me."

"Why not? I like the feel . . ."

Her laugh held a hint of desperation. "You said that about building your ships."

"It's not the same." His hands moved up to her throat and his thumbs rubbed slowly, sensually, at her nape. "Turn around, Sanchia. I want to see your face so I can fathom your thoughts."

"I'm thinking that this is a mistake." Her voice was shaking. "I told you that you couldn't change my mind. I cannot come to Pisa—" She broke off as she felt his lips on the cord at the side of her neck. The caress felt far more arousing than it should have. The long, hard muscles of his body were pressed against her back and the heat of him enveloped her. She swayed back against him. "It's a mistake."

"No." He turned her around, his gaze on her flushed cheeks and trembling lips. "I'm closer than you believe to persuading you to my way of thinking." He reluctantly released her and stepped back. "And I will most certainly continue. Do you play chess?"

She didn't answer at once, surprised by his change of subject. "No, you forget I had no opportunity to learn such games."

He made a face. "Nor did I, until Lorenzo came into my life. He delights in chastising me regularly at the board. I think it only fair that I pass the punishment on to you. Tomorrow I'll teach you the rudiments of chess." He turned away and picked up the Wind Dancer. "Chess has very interesting tactics both of attack and defense. I believe you'll find it rewarding."

"Attack."

Lion's voice was soft as he moved his ebony knight forward, his gaze lifting to meet Sanchia's across the board.

She braced herself, staring blindly down at the chess board. "I don't believe I like this game. I seem to be always on the defensive."

"That's because you lack concentration." Lion sat back in his chair and smiled. "Why is that, I wonder?"

The smirking devil knew very well why she couldn't concentrate, she thought crossly. Lion worked very hard at making sure her thinking was blurred by her responses to him. Each time he had visited her in the last week it had been the same. He scarcely touched her, but the atmosphere between them was so charged with emotion and memories of what had gone before she had grown increasingly more tense with each passing day. Now, as she looked up and saw him watching her knowingly, she realized she must either surrender or put an end to it.

"Then I obviously should not play." She pushed back her chair and stood up. "And I will not play. You must go back to Lorenzo if you want another game."

He pulled a face. "But Lorenzo trounces me soundly. I'm the one who is on the defensive there." He smiled beguilingly. "Do you not feel pity for me? A man should triumph in at least one arena of endeavor."

She felt a melting within her and quickly averted her eyes from the roughhewn fascination of his face. When had she stopped thinking Lion's face hard and impassive? Of late she had found it was a game to try to catch the sparks of humor, the sudden alertness when something aroused his interest or curiosity, the intensity of his narrowed eyes when he was deep in thought. It was another dangerous sign of the growing disturbance he was capable of arousing in her. A sign she should have heeded long before.

"Not this arena." She turned and moved a few paces away from him, putting distance between them. He hadn't moved from his chair and yet she felt he was in relentless pursuit. "I've decided that you should not visit me any longer."

"Have you? I don't agree." He reached out and picked up her jade queen from the chessboard, his blunt, powerful fingers closing gently about it. "Why do you never wear green? I believe it would become you." His thumb rubbed slowly back and forth, exploring the intricately carved hollows, the smooth texture of the chess piece. "A gown the color of jade."

She gazed in helpless absorption at his fingers caressing the piece. His touch on the queen was light, skilled, infinitely sensual. She found to her surprised dismay that her breasts were suddenly swelling, the nipples peaking, pushing against the material of her undershift. She quickly looked away and crossed her arms over her chest. "Lorenzo chose a length of green velvet and ordered a gown made up of it, but it's far too fine to wear every day. I told him I'd have no use for such a gown, but he wouldn't listen to me."

"It's a fault of Lorenzo's." Lion looked down at the chess piece. "Do you know that some noblemen play chess with human pieces? They lay out their gardens as giant chessboards and choose the most attractive of their servants or loved ones to play the different pieces."

"I've heard tales of such a thing."

"You would make an exquisite queen."

Her gaze was drawn once more to the piece in his hand and her cheeks grew warm. "You're wrong. I'm not at all queenly. The lady Caterina should play that role."

His index finger rimmed the crown on the chess queen's head. "It's true the artist who sculpted these pieces used my mother as a model, but there's more than one kind of majesty." He set the jade queen down on the board.

Sanchia's breath of relief escaped in an audible rush and she immediately felt foolish.

"The idea of such a life-size game appeals to me." Lion smiled at her across the room. "I think we'll play it some day soon."

"I'll not be here to indulge in your fancies."

"No?"

"I told you I wouldn't stay. I told you I was only waiting until I was sure there was no child."

He went still. "And you're certain now?"

"Yes, my flux started three days ago."

"I must admit to disappointment. I was hoping for a child." He gazed at her thoughtfully. "Why did you not tell me before?"

"I did not wish . . . what difference does it make?"

"Could it be that you were enjoying our time together and didn't wish to mar it?"

"No." She ran her fingers nervously through her hair. "I mean, yes. It hasn't been unpleasant but—"

"And you have discovered you have a liking for me?"

She watched him without speaking as he stood up and circled the table to come toward her.

"We've shared laughter and thoughts these past days." Lion stopped before her, studying her expression. "I had hoped you would find something in me to like as well as fear."

"I do not fear you."

"Then why are you standing there barricading yourself against me?" He gently unclasped her arms that were still folded across her breasts and placed them at her sides. "I've never cared before whether any woman had a fondness for me, but I find it necessary that you do." He paused. "At least, you do not dislike me any longer?"

"We have had many pleasant hours together. I found you very . . . amiable."

His hands moved up to cup her shoulders. "Sanchia, tell me truly."

She felt helpless. If she told him the truth, he would be able to wound her and yet he had left himself open to hurt. Abruptly she knew she couldn't inflict pain on him. "I have found many qualities in you to like."

She was rewarded by a brilliant smile. He leaned forward and gave her a quick, hard, honey sweet kiss. Then his hands were gone from her shoulders and he stepped back.

"No more. You see how tame you have me? Soon I'll be caviling at your every frown and composing sonnets to your enchanting eyebrows like a true courtier."

Tame? She almost laughed aloud when she recalled how blatant had been his sensuality as he had toyed with the chess piece. He was tough, amorous, and lusty—and would always be so, no matter how hard he tried to cloak it.

"I haven't noticed you caviling of late."

"Oh, but that's because you haven't been frowning at me. Can't you see how delightfully we deal together? We would enjoy our hours out of bed as much as those in it." His eyes were suddenly twinkling. "Well, a slight exaggeration. Perhaps not *quite* as much."

She shook her head.

"*Dio*, what a stubborn wench you are. I should never have brought Piero here. He's obviously teaching you to be as obstinate as he is."

The words were spoken lightly but their very carelessness aroused her wariness. "You wouldn't take him away?"

He shook his head, his smile fading. "You do not know me as well as I hoped. I don't demand gifts back because none are given in return."

She had hurt him. She had an impulse to reach out in comfort, but she had already yielded too much. "I love him."

"Lucky boy. I have to plead for your admission of your liking for me and he's freely given your love." He shrugged. "Oh, well, I did not ask for love, did I? I suppose I should be grateful that you're teaching me the gentle art of patience." He turned and strode toward the door. "I'll leave you now. I can tell you're becoming nervous of me." He held up his hand as she started to protest. "Why else would you be talking about running away again? It appears I must return to my strategy of attack."

"Attack?"

"Attack and defense. The oldest game on earth. The game we've been playing all this week." He looked intently at her. "But the game is almost over, Sanchia. Why not give up now and save us both time and effort? If you don't do it today, you will tomorrow, or next week or next month." His voice lowered to compelling persuasiveness. "You like me. You lust after me. Why not live with me? There would be no shame in it. I would kill any man who offered you insult. You're a loving woman and, if you cannot love me, would you not like your own child to love?" His gaze swept down her body to her abdomen. "My mother says I'm unnatural not to want an heir of my own, but I have cared nothing for a child before this time." He paused. "Now I believe I'd like to have a child by you."

She swallowed to ease the tautness of her throat. "No."

"Yes," he said softly. "I can give you a babe to love and cherish. You want a child, Sanchia. Let me give you what you need."

His words were weaving velvet ribbons of emotion, binding her, luring her. She shook her head desperately. "There is too much risk to my feelings."

"But the risk seems less now, doesn't it? And, as time passes, coming to me will seem less and less fraught with danger. I have no intention of giving up when I'm so close." He smiled. "One night you'll let me come to your bed, and after that I'll never leave it." He bowed. "*Buona sera, cara.*"

Cara. That sweet, loving endearment he had used only once before to lure her helplessly into a storm of danger.

Now he was drawing her into danger again and she might be incapable of stopping him. Because that danger was gradually being transformed by Lion into a semblance of a welcoming beacon to guide her from the storm itself.

And she suddenly knew Lion was right: some night

soon she would be swept away by his determination and her own tumultuous feelings into welcoming him into her bed.

She turned abruptly from the door and gazed down at the chessboard, her heart pounding hard. She would be caught, held as closely as the jade queen in Lion's grasp.

It mustn't happen. But how to prevent it? She was his property, a captive in his house. He had only to reach out and she was there for the taking, and as long as that opportunity existed so did her danger of yielding.

Yielding. The thought brought a surge of disgust with herself in its wake. She was not a weak ninny who would submit either to her own temptation or to Lion's will. She took a step closer to the table and picked up the knight with which Lion had launched his game. It was time she stopped playing a defensive game and considered what she could do to save herself.

She set the knight back on the board, her brow wrinkling.

Attack?

Fourteen

Why have you come to see me?" Caterina Andreas leaned back in her thronelike chair before the fire. "You know you have no place at the castle. I don't want you here."

"Nor do I want to be here. We've discussed this all before." Sanchia gazed coolly at Lion's mother. "But I found it necessary to seek you out tonight for a reason I'm sure you'll approve. I want to leave Mandara at once. Will you help me?"

Caterina gazed at her silently for a moment. "Why do you need my help?"

Sanchia laughed. "Why would you think? I'm your son's slave and he will not permit me to leave him. Don't you think I could use help?"

Caterina's lips twisted. "Could you not whisper a plea for your freedom when he lies with you? I've heard a man is weak and pliable in his mistress's hands in that moment."

"I do not lie with him." Sanchia added, "Yet."

A flicker of interest crossed Caterina's features. "He goes there every afternoon and does not come home until after nightfall and you claim he does not lie with you?"

"Yet," Sanchia repeated. She moistened her lower lip. "But he . . . stirs me, and I won't deceive you. If I don't leave now, I do not know if I will be able to leave later."

"I see." Caterina studied Sanchia's face. "Then we must be certain Lion doesn't have the opportunity to 'stir' you again."

"You'll help me?"

Caterina nodded slowly. "I want you gone from here."

"Lion has given orders to all the guards not to permit me to leave through any gate. Can you countermand his orders?"

"He's gone that far?" Caterina looked surprised. "Indeed, you *must* be determined."

"Can you do it?"

"No," Caterina said. "Lion is lord of Mandara. If he were not in the city, I might be listened to by the captain of the guard, but not while he's in residence."

"Then can you find a way of helping me slip out of the city unbeknownst to him?"

"That's a possibility." Caterina frowned. "But it will take time to form a plan and make arrangements. A few days at least. Perhaps as long as a week."

"It has to be now. No later than tomorrow."

"I said it couldn't be done. You must be—" Caterina broke off as she noticed the desperation in Sanchia's expression. "Ah, he does stir you. Can you not withstand him for a few more days?"

"I don't know," Sanchia whispered.

"Let me think." Caterina rested her head against the high back of the chair. "Sit down. Together we should be able to find an answer to this problem."

Sanchia sat down on the stool Lion's mother had indicated and folded her hands in her lap. Her position was one of subservience and yet, curiously, she didn't feel at all servile at this moment. The silence between them was companionable and she felt a strong sense of kinship toward Caterina Andreas.

"Ah, I've thought of it." Caterina leaned forward, her dark eyes gleaming in the firelight. "A solution that will suit us both very well and turn the good Messer Vasaro's words back against himself."

Sanchia frowned in puzzlement at the reference to Lorenzo, but leaned forward to listen eagerly as Caterina started to speak.

"Lion!"

About to go out the door, Lion turned at the sound of his mother's voice. She was rushing down the stairs toward him.

"You mustn't leave now. I'll require your presence at supper tonight." Caterina had reached the last step and paused with her beringed fingers resting lightly on the bannister. "We have guests and it would be rude to ignore them."

"Guests?"

"Only a dozen or so. Messer Guido Ralzo and Fra di Bresgano, Lucretia Montagno and her daughter, Mona. Messer Della Rosa and his son who recently has returned from the university at Ferrara."

Lion's eyes narrowed suspiciously. "What are you at, mother? You take little pleasure in entertainments of this kind. I can't remember the last occasion when you invited anyone to sup with us."

"Then it's time I did, isn't it?" Caterina asked with a bland smile. "It's my duty to the citizens of Mandara. And your duty, too, Lion."

"I must go."

"Yes, I know. We've seen little of you since you've come home." Her tone sharpened. "Would it do you harm to sit at the table for one meal with your mother?"

Lion hesitated. "If you had let me know you had invited half the city of Mandara, I would have—"

"A dozen guests is not half the city." She smiled

faintly. "Though I'm planning a more festive entertainment in a week's time to which we'll invite five times the number. Naturally, since I've given you warning, you'll be happy to attend."

"We shall see."

"Yes, we shall see." Caterina moved forward and placed an affectionate hand on her son's arm. "But I think you'll be persuaded to play the host. I don't ask a great deal of you, Lion."

His expression softened as he looked down at her. "No, you ask very little. You rule Mandara much better than I."

"Nonsense. I merely devote time and effort where it's due. If you'd give up this playing at the building of boats and return where you belong, there is no telling what we could do with Mandara."

"But why would you wish to improve on perfection?" Lorenzo asked as he descended the steps. "Besides, what could you have here that you don't have now? If Mandara were larger and more powerful, you'd also have more poverty and corruption." He smiled as he stopped before Caterina and Lion. "No, Lion is right, Lady Caterina. Mandara is truly blossoming under your benevolent rule."

"There are times when I don't feel at all benevolent," she said turning to face Lorenzo. "And this is one of them, Messer Vasaro."

"But I'm sure you'll soon recover to become your usual gracious self." Lorenzo bowed mockingly. "Run along, Lion. With a hostess so exquisite at the table, your presence would be superfluous."

"No," Caterina said through gritted teeth. "At least stay for supper, Lion. I will make no argument if you wish to leave afterward."

Lorenzo looked at her with surprise. "Compromise? Now I wonder why you're willing—"

"I'll stay," Lion interrupted impatiently. "But I'll leave immediately after supper."

"If you like." Caterina's hand squeezed Lion's arm. "It will be delightful to have you with us for even a short time. Thank you, Lion."

"As Lorenzo said, no one will notice I'm at the table but if it pleases you I'll—"

Bianca's excited laughter trilled from the landing. Lion's gaze lifted to see Bianca rounding the curve of the stairwell. "Oh, Lion, is it not wonderful?" She called over her shoulder, "We're having such a superb time, aren't we?"

"A splendid time."

Lion froze as his gaze traveled past Bianca to the woman now coming around the curve of the stairwell.

Sanchia paused for a moment on the stairs to look down and meet Lion's stunned gaze. "My lord." She nodded and then turned to Bianca, who was now affectionately linking her arm with Sanchia's.

Lorenzo murmured an imprecation beneath his breath and then began to laugh softly.

"Is it not a lovely surprise, Lion?" Bianca pulled Sanchia swiftly down the stairs. "Your mother put Sanchia in my dressing room so that I can watch over her until she's completely healed and that sweet little Piero is in the chamber next to mine. Sanchia and I have been chattering and making plans all afternoon."

"Lovely." He stared intently at Sanchia's face. "And yes, a complete surprise."

Sanchia steadily returned his stare. "How could I refuse your mother's kind invitation?"

"Yes, how could you?" Lorenzo asked. "We've just been discussing how charming Lady Caterina can be."

"It's time for Sanchia to be among people who can care for her properly." Caterina stepped forward and gently took Sanchia's hurt hand in her own. "Solitude is all very well, but she'll be much better off here at the castle. Since, unfortunately, Sanchia appears to have no last name, I've chosen to give her one. I've informed my guests I have a young kinswoman here by the name of Sanchia Salmona. Do remember that, won't you, Lion? Now, come along, my dear, and I'll introduce you to our guests. I sent them to wander in my garden while it's still light enough to see how beautiful it is. I'm very proud of my rose garden."

"I'll escort Sanchia, mother." Lion's face was impassive as he stepped forward. "Like the dutiful host you propose to make me."

"I'll come too." Bianca smiled eagerly. "I'll show you the arbor where Marco painted my portrait, Sanchia."

"Yes, of course," Caterina said, "you must show Sanchia everything, Bianca. We want to make certain she knows how welcome she is here."

Lion darted his mother a cold glance. "Come along then, Bianca," he said.

A smile lingered on Caterina's face as she watched the three of them walk away from her.

"A bold move."

Her gaze shifted to Lorenzo. "It was your suggestion that I invite her to the castle, remember?"

"Because I thought it would annoy you." He grimaced. "And because I hadn't thought out the full ramifications."

"Neither had I until she came to see me."

"Sanchia came to you? Interesting. Am I to assume this is a concerted foray?"

"Yes."

"You know, of course, that this move has an element of risk? You're placing Sanchia constantly within Lion's reach."

"Extremely well chaperoned by Bianca, Marco, myself, and some dozen house guests."

"Ah, you didn't mention your guests would be staying at the castle."

"Perhaps I forgot." She looked innocently at him. "Why should I not rejoice in Lion's homecoming by celebrating with a few friends?"

"No reason whatever."

She made a face as she started to follow the others to the garden. "At least you could have the sensibility to behave as though you are properly dismayed and annoyed with me."

"I'm not annoyed. I revel in your cleverness and ingenuity." He fell into step with her. "I was wondering when you were going to make a move to correct the situation to your own satisfaction. You've been entirely too meek and retiring of late."

"You find me retiring? We must discuss that at a more convenient time."

"I'm always willing to be proved wrong by someone of your stature, Lady Caterina."

She paused as she reached the door leading to the garden and glanced at him with a frown. "Are you truly not angry with me?"

He smiled. "I detest disappointing you, but I couldn't be more pleased. This delay will make no difference in the long run, you know."

"It most certainly will."

He shook his head. "They want each other and lust overcomes all obstacles. You've merely made the consummation of that lust more difficult and therefore a thousand times more appealing. One of the foibles of human nature."

"I've made it impossible."

He chuckled. "At any rate, a magnificent challenge I look forward to meeting. Though I'm sure Lion will not be as pleased at your interference."

"Sanchia is pleased."

"She only thinks so, perhaps. Part of her may conspire to aid Lion in achieving his intentions. It's the nature of woman to want to propagate the species."

"You know nothing of a woman's nature. We do have needs besides that of birthing babies and providing a receptacle for a man's—"

"My dear lady, please spare me your lecture. I was speaking of the feminine gender as a whole, not of yourself. We all know how extraordinary a woman you are." He bowed politely. "And now I must mingle with your guests and leave you to play the grand lady. I've been by your side too long."

Without giving her a chance to reply he bowed again and strolled toward a group of ladies and gentlemen standing by the marble fountain in the center of the garden.

Caterina gazed after him a moment, feeling oddly flat. The garden seemed suddenly drained of the vibrancy of its glorious color. She also felt drained of color. When she was with Lorenzo she always felt clever and witty and wonderfully desirable. Perhaps because that was the way she saw herself mirrored in his eyes.

But this was foolishness. She *was* witty and clever and desirable. She certainly needed no man to mirror her qualities in order to pamper her feelings of her own consequences. She needed no man at all.

She deliberately looked away from Lorenzo and strolled down the path toward the arbor where Lion and Sanchia stood watching Marco push Bianca in the flower-garlanded swing hanging from the oak tree several yards away.

"What do you think you're doing here?" Lion asked in a fierce undertone, his stare fixed unseeingly on Marco and Bianca.

"Enjoying the sunshine," Sanchia answered, not looking at him.

"Enjoy it on the balcony of your house on the piazza."

"It has different hues here."

"Sanchia, I'm not—" He drew a deep breath, trying to control his temper. "I don't want you here."

"But I want to be here, your mother wants me here. Even Bianca wants me here."

He was silent a moment. When he spoke again, his voice was cold. "You think to avoid me?"

"It seems for the best. I told you—"

"I weary of what you tell me," he interrupted. "You had no need to run from me. I was giving you time." He turned to look at her. "But I'll give you no more. You've chosen your way. So be it." He turned on his heel and strode up the path, meeting his mother on her way to the arbor. He nodded tersely and would have marched past her had she not stopped him with a hand on his arm.

"It's for the best, Lion," she said quietly.

"Sanchia used those same words." Lion moved to the side so that her hand dropped from his sleeve. "Between the two of you I'm beginning to be convinced you must be correct. You chose for her to come here. Who am I to argue?"

"Lion, you don't want—"

"You don't know what I want. Your ambitions blind you. Yes, *blind* is an excellent word, for you will not see what you've done here today!" He paused. "I've tried for thirteen years to avoid hurting you and Bianca, but I'm done with it. I will not be coerced by you and Sanchia, Mother."

She glanced quickly at a couple who had stopped to admire the roses a few yards away. "Hush, someone will hear."

"Then let them hear. I no longer care."

"Bianca."

"You brought the threat to Bianca here when you took Sanchia from the house on the piazza and settled her so cozily next to my lovely wife. *You* try to keep the threat at bay now." He took a deep breath. "But, by God, you'll not succeed."

"Bianca is very happy you're here."

Sanchia turned from watching Lion stride away to see Marco walking toward her. Bianca was still sitting in the swing, looking dreamily at the boughs of the tree above her. Marco glanced over his shoulder and smiled. He turned to Sanchia. "It would be a kindness if you would not disappoint her."

"I wished to speak to you, Marco. I know I promised I would leave Mandara and that's still my intention. Let me explain why—"

"No explanation is necessary. The situation is more than clear. You came here to escape Lion, not to pursue him." He made a face. "Though my mother and Lion consider me a dreamer, I'm not a fool. As far as I'm concerned you're welcome here as long as you do nothing to hurt Bianca."

"I do not think you a fool." Her gaze went involuntarily to Bianca.

He shook his head. "No, there's nothing of the fool in the way I feel about Bianca." He smiled gently as he, too, looked at the child-woman on the swing. "She's the best part of what I am. She looks at me and sees me as I want to be. I'm not really a wonderful artist, you know. Compared even to the apprentices of Da Vinci and Botticelli I have no talent at all. But I work hard and I do grow better and perhaps someday . . ." He shrugged. "But, if I never develop more skill, if I never receive great inspiration, I'll be enough for Bianca. Just as she'll always be enough for me."

When Sanchia didn't speak, he glanced at her and then nodded slowly. "You find that a surprise? Yes, I know that she'll never be more than a child—though I didn't at first." He paused, searching for words. "When she first came to Mandara I thought she was the most loving, the sweetest maid in all of Italy. She touched my heart and made me feel as if it were always springtime when she was near."

"She is so very lovely."

"Yes." His gaze returned to Bianca. "When I realized she would never change, never become a woman who could be my—" He sighed. "You understand that I would never do anything to hurt my brother, but still there was the smallest hope. And then, suddenly, there was no hope. It wasn't an easy time for me."

Sanchia was unbearably moved. "You don't have to tell me this, Marco."

"Yes, I do. I like and admire you and want you to understand why I seem to be callous to your own needs." Marco shrugged. "We will say no more about it." He started to turn away. "She's becoming restless. I must return to her."

"Marco." Sanchia hesitated. "You said it wasn't easy for you. Why did you decide to stay here with her?"

"But you don't understand. It was too late for me." His smile held sadness as well as sweetness. "And though I know summer will never come, it's not every man who's privileged to live in eternal springtime."

Sanchia watched him walk away from her and heard Bianca's laughing greeting as he came near. A slanting beam of sunlight struck through the leafy branches of the oak tree and surrounded them in a pool of radiance as Marco pulled back the rose garlanded swing. Then, gently but strongly, he pushed Bianca forward so that she left the earth and soared toward the heavens.

"A message?" Borgia asked as he turned away from the window to look at Damari. "Why is it necessary for me to write to my father?"

"A mere precaution." Damari smiled ingratiatingly. "I believe I've found a way to obtain the Wind Dancer with absolutely no expense to you or His Holiness. But there's a certain risk that all of us might be less than adored by the populace should the method become known. Of course soldiers such as ourselves can dispense with the love of the masses, but a pope must be more careful."

"I'm sure your consideration for my father's position will be much appreciated." Borgia dropped onto a chair and looked up sardonically at Damari. "However, he can be persuaded to take a few chances if the rewards are great. What is to be the point of this message of mine?"

"Word has come to me that there are certain conditions prevailing in the small village of Fontana that would aid us in our purpose." Damari began to speak quickly and persuasively, outlining his plan with clear, stark phrases. It took only a few minutes and then he fell silent, waiting for Borgia's response.

Borgia was also silent, thinking. Finally, he nodded slowly. "It could accomplish our purpose. Though it offers a certain danger to you."

"I'm willing to take the chance. As I told you, my lord, I believe in my own destiny."

"You would have to believe very strongly to joust with fate in this fashion. However, as I said, it might possibly work."

"There's no question about it." Damari tried to keep the eagerness from his voice. "Naturally, if you consider the means too dangerous for you or His Holiness, I'll yield to your judgment. But I *can* do this, my lord."

"The sheer boldness of the plan endears it to me."
Borgia nodded. "I'll write to my father and put the
scheme before him."

"Immediately? Time is of the essence, as you can
see."

"At once." Borgia stood up and moved to the
bellrope across the room. "I'll send a messenger with
instructions to wait for an immediate reply. You'll stay
here at Cesena until word comes with my father's
approval."

"Do you think he'll give his approval?"

Borgia smiled. "I can be very persuasive, too, when
I wish."

Damari was reassured. Borgia wanted the statue
enough to take the risk, and everyone knew his influ-
ence over his father was growing stronger with every
passing day.

"Perhaps you could emphasize the legendary powers of the Wind Dancer?"

"No need to prod him. He's already mad to have it.
In his last communication to me he was babbling about
some equestrian statue at the Ponte Vecchio in Florence
where Buondelmonti was slain and supposedly started
the feud between Guelph and Ghibelline. He's sure our
fate rests with the Wind Dancer." Borgia sat down at the
desk and drew out a piece of fine parchment from
the middle drawer. "No, he's eager enough to possess
the statue, but he's an old man and grows cautious with
his years. I must stress that your plan can be accomplished without any real danger of discovery of his part
in it." He glanced over his shoulder. "And your plan is
not quite complete, Damari. I can add a few embellish-
ments that will better please my father and myself." He
picked up his quill pen and dipped it in the onyx
inkwell. "You're right. Were my father's part in the
scheme to overcome those at Mandara become known,
he could be forced from the Vatican." He began to write.
"Therefore there must be no knowledge of it."

A lackey came into the room in answer to Borgia's
summons and he said without glancing up, "I want a
messenger at once to take this to His Holiness."

Damari leaned back against the wall and crossed his arms over his chest, a smile of satisfaction on his face. It was truly a brilliant plan and one that would bring him immense enjoyment. What a pity he must wait for word back from that doddering old villain in Rome. He had been tempted to proceed with the venture without informing Borgia but had thought better of it. Both Borgias must be fully involved, fully committed.

"You're very pleased with yourself." Borgia had looked up and was gazing at him with a faint smile. "And well you should be. I could not have thought of a more effective stratagem myself."

"High praise, *Magnifico*."

"Truth." Borgia began writing again. "I had a young Florentine as my guest here this winter who would appreciate your ingenuity as much as I. Unfortunately, he's been recalled by the Signory. At the earliest opportunity, I must remember to introduce you to Messer Machiavelli."

Lion was watching her again.

After that first quick glance at him Sanchia averted her eyes and turned to smile at the younger Della Rosa. "I've never seen such a magnificent scene." She waved a sweeping hand around the great hall, indicating the chandeliers blazing with hundreds of candles, the richly garbed guests, the liveried lackeys rushing back and forth filling silver goblets. "So much color. And the music . . ."

"You speak as if you've never attended a festivity of this nature before," Bernardo Della Rosa said. "It's true that Lady Caterina presides splendidly over the table, but I've seen much more lavish food in Ferrara, and this music is merely tolerable."

"It seems wonderful to me." Sanchia added simply, "And it's true that I've never attended such a gathering before. This whole past week has been like a marvelous dream." She threw back her head and laughed joyously as she put her goblet to her lips and drank deeply. "And I think you lie when you say the music is not excellent.

Surely no musicians this side of heaven could make sweeter sounds, Bernardo."

He gazed in bemusement at her luminous face before admitting, "Perhaps I was overcritical. In Ferrara the musicans are—"

"I don't want to hear about Ferrara. I want to think only about Mandara and the music and—" She hurriedly set her empty goblet on the tray of a passing servant. "The pavane. Escort me to the floor, Bernardo. I should like to dance."

"You always want to dance." Nevertheless he set his own goblet down on the table next to him and took her hand. "I suppose you're going to tell me that you also never danced before you came to Mandara? You must have led a very sheltered life in Florence. Were you brought up in a convent?"

"Not exactly." She wondered what he would say if she told him the truth. She could imagine the distaste on his face and his instant withdrawal. Sanchia Salmano of good family, daughter of a kinswoman of the illustrious Lady Caterina's, was acceptable for flirtation and light-hearted dalliance but the slave-thief, Sanchia, would be instantly ostracized. Still, she refused to dwell on such thoughts now. After she left Mandara, she knew, there would be no more days of richness and splendor, so she must enjoy every moment.

They joined the ladies and gentlemen on the floor and began to tour the hall in the stately steps of the pavane. It was not Sanchia's favorite dance, but the music was lilting, the movements rhythmic, and Bernardo Della Rosa was staring at her as if he thought her beautiful.

Lorenzo was suddenly before her in the set. "You look enchanting tonight. A veritable Circe. You should always wear green."

"I've never seen you dance in public, Lorenzo." She glanced down at her jade green velvet gown with its cream satin undershift embroidered in shimmering gold thread. "And you should recognize this gown. You gave the seamstress every detail you wished to see in the execution of it. Do you not remember those first days at Mandara?"

"But the conception palls before the realization. You glow like a torch." He paused. "But I'd hood my flame when I smiled at young Della Rosa if I were you. I don't like the look on Lion's face."

"I like Bernardo. He makes me feel young. I've never had a chance to dance or play games before." She made a face. "Don't harp, Lorenzo. I'm happy tonight."

"I don't know why I'm bothering to try to save you. It would suit me very well to have Lion lose his patience with the game the two of you have been playing all week." He pointed his toe and led her forward with faultless grace. "But I find I'm reluctant to expose you to needless violence. Is that not peculiar?"

"Very peculiar." She cast a swift glance to the corner where Lion stood. Someone had approached him and he was no longer looking at her. Relief streamed through her, and she was immediately angry at herself. Lion could not hurt her by watching her, which was all he had done since that first evening in the garden. Caterina had kept her surrounded and occupied every waking moment of the last week and made sure she was escorted to Bianca's chamber each night. "But you need not be concerned. Lion has not—" She inhaled sharply as Lion glanced up and met her gaze across the room.

The color flamed in her cheeks and she looked away.

"You see?" Lorenzo asked softly. "Do not anger him more or he will snap, Sanchia." He smiled. "But perhaps that's your aim in dallying with Della Rosa. Perhaps you're weary of being without the sport Lion introduced to you."

"No!" She smiled determinedly. "I do not miss him. I do not want . . . Oh, go away, Lorenzo. Tonight I will be happy and pretend I have no more worries than those pretty girls sitting together near the hearth and giggling at everything one of them says."

"As you command." He shrugged. "But you're not like them. In a fortnight you'll be bored with this masquerade. You've dealt too long with reality to be tolerant of make-believe." The next moment the music signaled a change of set and Lorenzo was gone. Bernardo once more took her hand.

She would not think of Lorenzo's words. He was wrong. She had no wish for Lion to approach her and it certainly was not lust she was feeling toward him. She carefully squelched every thought that came to mind of their time together, and every day she was drawing farther and farther away from him. Soon she would not even notice whether he was staring at her or not.

The music stopped with a little flourish and she turned to Bernardo with a smile. "That was splendid. Now will you go ask them to play the *moresca*? That's so much more lively."

Bernardo nodded and started to move across the hall to where the musicians sat in the gallery.

"Hold." Lion was beside them. "You can dance later. It's time to sit down to supper." He smiled mockingly. "We mustn't spoil my mother's arrangements. I'm sure she's planned something spectacular."

Bernardo frowned. "But there's been no announcement."

"There will be." Lion signaled across the room to a servant and a gong was immediately struck. He turned to Sanchia. "Permit me to take you to your chair."

"She's promised me that honor, my lord," Bernardo said quickly.

Lion ignored him as he took Sanchia's hand and led her toward the table.

"But Lord Andreas, I was given—" Bernardo broke off as Lion turned and fixed him with a cold stare and then continued lamely, "I only thought not to deprive your lovely wife of your escort."

"My wife has an escort and, as you see, Madonna Sanchia has an injured hand." He turned and looked down at Sanchia before adding silkily, "As her host, I feel it my duty to share my trencher with the poor lady and help her in any way I can."

"I need no help." Sanchia moistened her lips as she tried to withdraw her hand. "I've learned to make allowances for my clumsiness."

"See how she protests?" Lion shrugged. "What a truly noble lady she is to struggle in silence with her infirmity. But I really can't allow her to sacrifice herself."

He seated Sanchia in a chair at the long table on the dais and then sat down beside her before motioning Bernardo away with a wave of his hand. "Enjoy your meal, Della Rosa."

Bernardo hesitated and then turned and stalked down to a chair at the far end of the table.

"You go too far," Sanchia said between her teeth. "Do you want to cause a scandal? What will everyone think?"

"Why, that I'm a gracious host aiding my guest. What else should they think? Bianca is clearly not missing my attentions."

Sanchia cast a glance down the table where Bianca and Marco were in animated conversation.

"And your mother?"

Lion glanced down the table at Caterina and met her glare with a bland smile.

"She will ignore us politely once she becomes accustomed to the idea, and her guests will follow her example. She has, after all, been expecting it for more than a week." He turned and dipped his hands in the basin of rosewater offered by a lackey and then dried them on the white linen towel offered by a second servant. "As you have, Sanchia."

"I haven't expect—" she trailed off as she met his gaze. She wouldn't lie. She had expected him to approach her at any time and, when he had not done so, the tension and anticipation had grown to an unbearable magnitude. "I had little time to think about you."

"Because you were playing with that fool Della Rosa." His lids veiled his eyes as the lackey set a silver server of soup before him and then moved to serve Sanchia. "Do you think him comely?"

"He's handsome enough." Sanchia added defiantly, "And he has a lovely voice. He's going to favor us with a song later."

"Intelligence, beauty, and talent." He picked up his

spoon. "And he seems to be enchanted by you. Tell me, do you seek a husband, Sanchia?"

"You know that he would never marry me."

"I'm not so sure. My mother would like to marry you off, and I'm sure she'd managed to scavenge a decent dowry for you even if it meant selling her jewels."

Sanchia laughed uncertainly. "You're jesting."

"No, but I'm glad the idea amuses you." He smiled as he lifted the spoon to his lips. "Because I doubt if your bridegroom would live to make it to the chapel."

She stiffened, her hand clenching the handle of the spoon.

"And if he did, he'd be a cuckold before nightfall. So I'd really not entertain the thought of marriage, if I were you." He paused. "You're not eating. At least try the soup. It's truly delicious."

She automatically lifted her spoon to her lips. She tasted nothing.

"You're not speaking. Why is that? You chattered unceasingly with that prancing coxcomb."

"Why are you doing this?" she whispered. "Why are you trying to hurt me?"

"Did it not occur to you that I, too, could be hurt?" His tone was low but savage. "You said you had a liking for me. I thought you might even—" He was silent for a moment. "Don't talk to me about hurt."

"You forced me to come to your mother."

"I used no force." His left hand had been resting on the table. Now it clenched into a fist. "It was no easy thing for me to show restraint and gentleness with you. All my life I've known only force and the prizes force brings. I wanted something different with you. I wanted your trust."

She didn't know what to say. Sympathy, guilt, fear, assaulted her in an overwhelming tide, deluging her thoughts, drowning her voice. She could only say, "It's dangerous to trust those who have power over you."

"It's more perilous to flaunt those who hold that power." His fist slowly relaxed and he glanced down at Sanchia's hand resting on her lap. "What a prettily decorated splint. That looks like Bianca's touch."

"It is. She used the ivory ribs of an old fan and sent Marco to the seamstress to get strips of the velvet with which my gown is made. Then Bianca fashioned these pretty little bows from those strips. It was very kind of them."

"Oh, yes, they're both exceptionally kind. Finish your soup. The second course is about to be brought in."

"I have finished." She watched numbly as the lackeys collected the soup tureens and with equal disinterest as a parade of lackeys entered the hall with a variety of meat dishes dressed to perfection. Under any other circumstances she would have been as enthralled as the other guests at the sight of roast boar garnished with apples and roses, mouth-watering peacock and, finally, a towering pastry likeness of the castle of Mandara itself, complete with battlements and a miniature garden. The display was met with exclamations and applause as the lackeys proudly toured the hall before repairing to the long carving table on the far side of the room to strip the dishes of their culinary magnificence and carve them to be served. Meanwhile other lackeys were bustling around the table with fresh basins of rosewater and pouring more wine until the trenchers of carved meat and gravy were brought to the dais.

As was the custom, there was one trencher for every two people, and Sanchia found herself staring down at the trencher placed between Lion and herself with dismay. In spite of her claim, it was going to be very difficult to manage knife, spoon, and bread with any measure of dexterity. She started to reach for her knife but Lion stopped her.

"It will be quicker if I feed you," Lion said as he held up the small piece of bread. "Open your mouth."

She found herself opening her lips and taking the bread and then a bit of meat and then bread again. His feeding her was excruciatingly intimate. She wished desperately to have the meal over and done with.

"Again."

His thumb caressed her lower lip as he placed a morsel of meat on her tongue. Her lip began to throb and she instinctively jerked her head away from his hand. "Enough. I want no more."

"I think you do." He smiled at her. "And I certainly want more." He reached for a cluster of grapes, took one, and pressed it to her lips. "Something sweet and full." His gaze moved over the low-cut bodice of her gown. "And firm."

She took the grape, and tart sweetness flooded her tongue. She should look away. The heat tingling between them was thickening in intensity. She realized with desperation that the soft linen of her undershift was abrasive against the sudden sensitivity of her nipples.

She looked down at the table. That was a mistake, too. His big hand still held the cluster of grapes, and memories suddenly assaulted her of those broad, powerful fingers toying with the jade queen, outstretched before the fire encased in heavy leather gauntlets, jerking the neckline of her gown with frantic haste to bare her breasts. . . .

"Your cheeks are flushed," Lion said softly. "Are you warm, *cara?*"

Not warm. Hot, melting. She felt as if the blood was running molten just beneath the surface of her flesh. She quickly picked up her goblet and drank deeply.

"It's a warm evening and will grow warmer. Another grape?"

"No. Nothing." She sat her goblet down and it was immediately refilled by the lackey. "Is it not time for the dancing to start again? It seems we've been at the table a long time."

"It seems a long time to me, too." His hand released the cluster of grapes and dropped casually to his knee. "If we don't leave the table soon I'll have to find something to amuse me. Do you know what I have in mind, Sanchia?" His hand disappeared beneath the heavy damask cloth covering the table and pressed against her upper thigh.

She went rigid, her gaze flying to his face. He was looking straight ahead, his expression bland, only the leaping pulse in his temple betraying his arousal.

The warmth of his palm burned through the layers of velvet and satin, and her limbs began to tremble. Her hand was also trembling as she hurriedly reached for the wine goblet again. "Take . . . your hand off my skirt," she hissed.

"Why? It gives you pleasure. You're quivering like a little bird. Shall I push the skirt of your gown up and touch your flesh, rub those soft, tight curls? No one could see. The table and the linen hides my hand. I could fondle you and bring you even more pleasure." His palm was rubbing slowly back and forth. "Would you like that?"

"No." She could barely force the word past the tightness of her throat.

"I think you would. Of course, you'd have to be careful not to cry out when your pleasure peaked." His nostrils flared and a flush mantled his cheeks. "Why don't we see if you enjoy it? Part your thighs, *cara*, and I'll—"

"The *moresca*!" Lady Caterina was on her feet, motioning to the musicians and guests. "Let us see if we can still manage to move after we've eaten and drunk so heartily."

The announcement was met with laughter and groans by the guests and the wild, spirited strains of the *moresca* from the musicians in the gallery.

Bernardo was suddenly by Sanchia's side. "May I escort you to the floor, Madonna Sanchia?"

Lion's hand on her thigh suddenly tightened. Warmth, strength, demand.

A demand she must not answer. "Yes." Her hand was still trembling as she set her goblet down on the table. Would Lion move his hand and release her? "I love the *moresca*. Did I not tell you?"

Lion's hand dropped from her thigh and he leaned back in his chair.

Sanchia rose hastily to her feet and fled down the long table and the three steps leading from the dais to the floor. She had escaped. Or had she been permitted to escape? A hasty glance over her shoulder revealed Lion still lolling at the table, looking dark, sensual, and slightly sinister in his black velvet slashed jerkin. His expression was lazy, arrogant, as if about to command a performance expressly for his pleasure.

Bernardo snatched four bracelets of bells from the overflowing tray the lackey was extending toward them and slipped one over each of her wrists and then his own. The hall resounded, shimmered, with the merry sound of bells and tambourines, music, and laughter.

Bernardo ran to the other side of the room to join the men, and Sanchia took her place with the women. Bianca was laughing excitedly and even Caterina's dark eyes were glowing with exhilaration as she slipped the bracelets over her wrists, straightened her scarlet velvet skirts and signaled the musicians to start again.

Sanchia lifted her arms over her head, the bells on her wrists jingling. She found herself laughing aloud with the same excitement as Bianca. No, it was not the same. Her excitement was not only with the dance but with the way Lion was looking at her, the way the blood was pounding in her veins, the feel of fabric touching her flesh as she twisted and turned and stamped and whirled. The torches on the walls blurred into blue-orange flame before her eyes, and the bells and the tambourines rang and echoed not only in her ears but in her heart and her body.

The excitement was growing as they all joined hands and circled faster and faster and then broke and whirled by themselves again. The laughter bubbled up in her throat, and she felt almost too breathless to release it. The men and women in the hall were only streaks of violet, crimson, blue, and gold.

A hand grabbed her wrist, pulling her out of the whirling throng and behind a stone pillar.

"What. . . ." She gazed up dizzily to see Lion's face above her. "No, I want—"

His lips were on hers, parting them with his tongue, plunging deep inside with a low groan. His powerful body pressed her back against the pillar and she could feel the tension of his muscles, his arousal rampant. He lifted his head. "This is what you want." He rubbed yearningly against her. "Isn't it, Sanchia?"

She clutched desperately at his shoulders as a wave of heat surged through her. She couldn't think. The bells, the tambourines, the music, the blood singing through her veins were all too loud. "No, someone will see . . ."

"They're all dancing." His lips pressed quick, hard kisses on her temples and cheeks. "No one can see us here. Open your mouth." She didn't realize she had obeyed him until his tongue filled her mouth, toying wildly with her tongue. "I wanted to do this at the table," he muttered. "*This* is how I wanted to feed you."

She tried to stifle the moan trembling in her throat but he heard and lifted his head. "Come with me. You need me. I'll give you what we need." He was already pulling her toward the door.

She shouldn't go. But she found herself stumbling after him and could think of only one protest. "They'll miss us."

"The *moresca* goes on forever, you know that." They were out in the corridor and he was urging her up the stairs. "And what if they do miss us? They've suspected Marco of being Bianca's lover for years. They'll think it only natural that I take my pleasure." He lifted her in his arms as he started up the steps. "It *is* natural, Sanchia. Natural and beautiful and right. Don't you know that?"

She didn't know anything anymore. Her mind was whirling as if she were still dancing, and her heart was slamming against her ribs until she thought it would burst. She should resist Lion and this lust cascading through her. It was madness to lie pliant and helpless in his arms.

But she wasn't helpless. She could fight him if she chose.

Yet she knew with a sudden despair that she wouldn't fight him. Not tonight.

She murmured his name and closed her eyes as she buried her face against the black velvet of his jerkin.

Fifteen

You appear to be looking for someone, my lady. May I be of some small service?"

Caterina whirled to face Lorenzo. "You know very well who I'm looking for, you demon from hell. Where are they?"

"Lion and Sanchia? I have no idea. How many hundreds of chambers does this huge castle contain? However, wherever they are I'm sure they're in no danger of being disturbed. Lion is your son and would have provided against that possibility."

Caterina's hands clenched into fists at her sides. "You saw them leave the hall?"

Lorenzo nodded. "I spared a glance or two for them when I wasn't looking at you. By the way, you do dance the *moresca* splendidly. Your vigor gave the steps a certain glorious—"

"I should not have danced at all. I should have been more watchful. I saw what was going on between them earlier this evening."

"Do you really think you could have stopped Lion? You were fortunate he didn't act sooner. We both know it was only a question of time until he broke free of the chains you wound around him." He smiled faintly. "No, you should have done exactly what you did do tonight: smiled and danced and made us all happy to see your joy."

She gazed at him, startled. "Happy?"

He looked surprised himself. "Did I say that? How very common of me." He thought about it. "But perhaps it comes closest to what I was feeling as I watched you."

She frowned suspiciously. "Do you seek to distract me?"

"Have I ever lied to you?"

"No," she said slowly. "Never."

"Nor shall I ever." He turned. "And now I'm going for a walk in your lovely garden. Would you like to follow me or do you intend to tear through the castle, searching chamber to chamber for your missing offspring? It would do no good and make you look exceedingly undignified."

She hesitated, glancing around the crowded room.

"They will not miss you as long as the wine is flowing and the musicians play." He added softly, "And I will miss you if you don't join me, Caterina."

He turned, walked away from her and was soon lost to view in the throng.

Caterina stood very still. The hall was suddenly too hot, the music too loud, the company far too boring to tolerate.

He would miss her if she did not come to him. Lorenzo had never before indicated her company was important enough to him to miss.

She started slowly across the hall, nodding and smiling as she skirted the dancers on her way to the garden where Lorenzo waited.

Lion set Sanchia down before turning and slamming the chamber door. He was breathing heavily, his chest rising and falling as he leaned back against the door. "*Dio*, I think my heart may burst. You're heavier than you look."

She gazed at him in astonishment and then burst into laughter. Those blunt, unvarnished words were so typical of Lion. "You didn't have to carry me up those thousands of stairs. We must be at the very top of the castle."

"We are." He turned and shot the bolt. "This is the tower where we keep the Wind Dancer." He turned to face her. "And I was afraid if I made you walk up all those stairs you might change your mind." He crossed to the stone fireplace and knelt to light the logs laid in readiness. "You're already having second thoughts, aren't you?"

The wood caught, flared, revealing the broad, strong planes of his cheekbones, the glittering darkness of his eyes as he turned to look at her. She drew a deep breath. "I don't think I had a first thought. I wasn't thinking at all."

"That was my intention." He stood up and came toward her. "And I shall endeavor to make sure you remain in that state."

She took a hurried step back. "Lion, this is not—"

"It is." His hands cupped her cheeks and he tilted her face up to look into her eyes. "Trust me, *cara*."

She could see in his eyes twin flames reflected from the fire. She felt helpless in her fascination.

"Is it so difficult to trust me?"

"Yes. I . . . I think I've had too much wine."

"You're not drunk." His lips feathered her temple. "*In vino veritas*."

But was that the truth? There was only chaos in what she was feeling. She was hot, tingling, as dizzy as when she was dancing the *moresca*.

"I like your gown. I knew you'd look wonderful in that color." He pushed her away from him and took a step back. "Jade queen, shall we start our play?"

"But you always win."

"Not this time." He took off his black velvet jerkin and threw it aside. "This time we both win. Do you remember when I had you undress for me in the barn?"

She felt a tightening in her chest. "Yes."

"You were frightened." He took off his fine white linen shirt and dropped it on top of the jerkin. He stood before her in only steel gray hose and calf-length black boots whose soft leather molded his legs with the same delineation as the hose. "I wanted you to be frightened. I wanted you to be so afraid that you'd never forget you belonged to me."

The dark hair thatching his chest looked soft and springy and she felt a tingling in her hands. She wanted to touch him, run her fingers through that curly mat, explore the powerful muscles cording his chest and shoulders.

He took off his boots and began to untie the points of his hose. "You don't look frightened now."

But she was frightened. More frightened than she had been in the barn when she had acted on his command. Because she suddenly knew he wouldn't command her now. What she did would be by her own will.

The steel gray hose were gone now and he was naked. "Come to me, *cara*."

She couldn't move. Her gaze traveled down his chest to the tightness of his muscular belly. Then down . . .

"You can't be shy." Lion stood with his legs apart, blatantly aroused, the essence of bold masculinity. "Attack, Sanchia, I stand defenseless."

"But not weaponless," she murmured, her gaze fixed on him in total absorption.

"Then let me sheath my weapon." His eyes were suddenly glinting with humor. "You have the means. Do I have to come to you?" He held out his hand. "*Cara*?"

She took one step forward, then another, and suddenly she was directly in front of him.

He took her right hand and raised it slowly to his lips. He kissed her palm lingeringly, his gaze never leaving hers. "Square one, jade queen. Not so hard, was it?" He moved her hand to his chest and she felt the pounding of his heart beneath her palm.

"I belong to you." He said softly. "Say it."

Her eyes widened. "What?"

"It's true, you know. I belong to you, just as you belong to me. Say it."

"You . . . belong to me."

"Forever."

Stunned, she gazed speechlessly at him.

He pressed her palm harder against his chest. The beating of his heart seemed in some mysterious fashion to beat within her. "Forever, Sanchia."

"It cannot be."

"We will talk of it later." He slid her hand slowly down his body to clasp it around his manhood. He held it there as a shudder racked through him. "Dear God, I can't wait any longer. Will you take me into you?"

His face was drawn as if in pain, and she felt a sudden surge of tenderness that swept away her last reservations. Why was she hesitating when she had known when she left the hall she would not be able to stop herself from yielding? "I think I . . . must."

"Thank the saints." He took her hand from him and stepped forward, his hands on her gown. He stopped. "Remove it quickly or I swear I'll have to push up your skirts and take you as I did on that pile of hay in the barn. *Cristo*, what I'd give for a bed at this moment."

There was no furniture at all in the chamber, she realized as she glanced around dazedly, only a rug thrown down before the hearth.

"Hurry, I cannot wait long and my hands are shaking so that I can do nothing but fumble."

Her hands were trembling, too, but she managed to strip off the gown and undershift. She was reaching down to take off her slippers when she felt his hands on her waist lifting her. "Clasp me," he muttered. "Your legs . . ."

Her limbs encircled his hips and he was pressing against her, into her, with frantic urgency. He sank home.

Her neck arched back as she gave a low cry. Ridged fullness. Deep. So deep.

His palms cupped her buttocks and held her to him,

forcing her to take all of him. She heard him mutter something beneath his breath. A curse, a prayer . . . She could not tell which it was.

"Hold on." His palms kneaded the rounded flesh of her buttocks as he stood still, his eyes shut, his nostrils flaring with each breath. "Tighter."

"I cannot . . ." Still, she tried, and heard him groan deep in his throat as if he were in agony.

Then he was sinking to his knees on the floor, lowering her so that her naked back rested on the rug as he plunged in and out of her body in a rhythm both primitive and forceful.

Completion. Joining. Sanchia bit her lower lip to keep from screaming as jolt after jolt of sensation rocked through her. His hands were petting her, his fingers pressing, rotating. "Sanchia, it must . . ." His hips moved back and forth in a flurry of short, hard thrusts. "May I give to you? Please let . . ."

He was entreating her. The knowledge filled her with wonder. He moved with raw, blind sensuality, taking, giving and yet he was pleading with her for acceptance.

"Give . . . to me." Her words were little more than a whisper as her limbs tightened strongly around his hips. "Give!" She arched up helplessly as the pleasure burst through her, spasming, exploding.

He pulled her upright on him again, crushing her close as his own pleasure peaked and then soared.

He rocked her back and forth, breathing low, whispering love words into her ear. His lips moved yearningly across her cheek to the corner of her lips. "Sanchia, did I not tell you? We must have this. How can we live without it?"

At the moment she didn't think she could live without it. She was part of him. He was part of her. Pleasure . . . possession . . . passion . . . Nothing had ever seemed more natural than having Lion within her, having his hands caressing her naked back, having his lips on her lips.

He raised his head. "Thank you, *cara*." His voice was grave.

She buried her cheek on the soft wiry mat on his chest and his fingers reached up to tangle in her hair. "Why do you not speak?"

"I don't know what to say. I'm too full—" She broke off as she felt the reverberation of his laughter beneath her ear and she realized her unintentional play on words. "Well, that too."

He flexed lazily within her. "If you think I'm going to leave you yet, you are very much mistaken. I've waited too long to reach this haven to withdraw until I've sated both of us." He pushed her away from him to smile down at her with surprising sweetness. "I think you'll like this game far better than chess. Shall we move to another square? There are many strategies left to test."

"Not yet. I'm not sure how I even came to this point."

"I am sure." His hands cupped her breasts. "And it was not the *vino*. I seduced you. I think I did it very well considering I've never attempted to lure a woman to my bed before. My nature is usually too rough and blunt for seduction. I would never have succeeded if you hadn't already wanted me as much as I wanted you." His hand moved down and began to stroke her belly. "Do you believe it possible I've given you a child?" He laughed softly. "Do you feel me stir? I grow ready just thinking about my child moving in you and—" He broke off as he felt her stiffening against him. "Sanchia?"

"I didn't consider a child. I didn't . . ." Panic was rising within her. "How could I be so stupid?" She began to struggle but he held her immovable against him. "Let me go, Lion."

"No." His voice was fierce. "You want to be here." His hand lay heavy on her belly and he began to rub slowly back and forth. "And you want my child in your womb. I used no force. You took my seed willingly."

"The child would be a bastard and I a whore. I've lived only a shadow life since the moment I was born, and now you want me to live in those shadows for the rest of my life." Her hands pushed at his shoulders. "I should not have done this. I should not have let you—"

"Do you think I would not give you marriage if I

could?" His hands grasped her shoulders with bruising force. "Do you want me to murder Bianca so that I can take you as my wife?"

Her eyes widened in horror. "No, I didn't mean—"

"I cannot undo my marriage. As God is my witness, I wish I could." His eyes were fierce in his set face. "I cannot make you my wife. I can only make you my love."

"Love?" she whispered.

"It must be love. I told you I had feeling for you. What else could it be?"

"You did not say you loved me."

"The word is hard for me." His hands opened and closed on her shoulders. "I've never said it before." He burst out, "I've never felt it before. I can't say I like it. It twists my gut and makes me want to smash something."

"It doesn't sound like love."

The fierceness faded from his expression as he looked down at her. "It also makes me wish to . . . treasure you. To care for your needs and protect and defend you." He slowly lifted her off him. "And to have you feel something besides lust for me. I know I can rouse you to want to lie with me but—Why do you sit there and say nothing?"

"I'm confused. I never expected you to say these words."

"And I never expected to say them." He gazed at her directly. "You have no love for me?"

"I don't know." She shivered. "*Dio*, I hope not."

A flicker of pain crossed his face. "You are honest, at least." He shrugged. "So I must depend on lust to draw you to me. It was no more than I anticipated. Lust and perhaps my child in your body." He turned toward the fire.

She began dressing quickly, in a fever to be gone.

He glanced over his shoulder. "You're in a great hurry. Do you think I mean to keep you locked here in my tower room to use for my pleasure?"

"Of course not." Her trembling fingers made a futile attempt to tidy her hair. "I've already been in one prison for your sake. You would not cast me into another." She moved toward the door.

"Unless I cast myself into it with you."

She undid the bolt and threw open the door. "And you would not do such a foolish thing. You love your freedom too much."

"Sanchia."

She stopped, not looking at him.

"Do you believe me when I say I love you?"

"I don't know." She turned to face him. "I have a question for you. Was it your intention to lure me here only to get me with child?"

"What do you think?"

"I think you capable of it."

"You're quite right." His smile was bittersweet. "I'm capable of most acts of ruthlessness, but I thought you knew I had no liking for deception."

She was again aware of pain beneath the toughness he wore like armor, and that perception awoke an answering hurt within herself so sharp she instinctively took a half step toward him. "I do know you're an honest man. I did not mean . . ." She shook her head wearily. "I spoke without thinking. I didn't believe I would be so weak as to let you couple with me again. It frightens me to realize I'm not as strong as I thought I was." She straightened and gazed intently at him. "But it will not happen again. I am on guard now."

"It will happen again," he said quietly. "And again and again. I'll waylay you in the garden, I'll pull you into any vacant chamber that has a bed, a quilt, or a cushion on the floor. It will keep on happening until you admit you want what we're doing more than food or drink or sleep. Until you let me take you away from here to live with me."

He meant it. Once again Sanchia felt panic rising within her. She muttered an exclamation that was half despair, half protest, turned and fled from the chamber and down the spiral steps.

She stopped at the bottom of the first flight of stairs and leaned her cheek against the cold stone of the wall. She could not go back to the hall and face Caterina and Bianca. She had betrayed both of them. She had betrayed herself. She could feel the tears sting her eyes as she ran down two more flights of stairs and along the corridor toward Bianca's chamber. She would go to bed. She would go to sleep and not think of Lion or the way his face had looked when he had said he loved her or her own agonizing response to his words. It couldn't be love between them. Wouldn't love bring joy? Marco and Bianca loved each other and the joy shone from their faces. Surely if she loved Lion, it would be the same?

The tears were running down Sanchia's cheeks as she paused outside Bianca's chamber. She had forgotten Bianca's maid, Anna, would be waiting up for her mistress. Sanchia could not arouse Anna's curiosity with these stupid tears or she would doubtless mention it to Bianca.

She turned and ran down the hall to the chamber which Piero occupied next door, quietly opened the door, and slipped into the room. The fire in the fireplace had burned low and only the orange-red embers sparked up the chimney. The faint glow revealed Piero's fair hair gleaming on the pillow on the big bed across the room, and Sanchia immediately felt as if a cool, soothing hand had been laid upon her heart. Here was a love with no pain, a love that would leave her with honor *and* independence. Whole. She moved closer to the bed and looked down at Piero. His long lashes curved on his round cheek, and he appeared even younger than his six years now that she could no longer see the wariness in those bright blue eyes.

Even as the thought occurred to her, his eyes opened to gaze up at her. He was instantly awake. "Sanchia."

"Shh, all is well. I wanted to make sure you were sleeping." She tucked the coverlet more closely around him. "It was a fine, splendid party. I'll tell you all about it in the morning."

He raised himself on one elbow. "Why are you crying?"

She wiped her eyes swiftly with the back of her hand. "No reason. I'm merely tired."

"You don't cry when you're tired. Is your hand hurting?"

"No, next week I'll take off the splints and it will be

quite well." She reached out and smoothed his hair. "Go back to sleep. I'll sit here awhile."

His gaze searched her face and then he shook his head. "Lie down. I want you to hold me until I go to sleep. Will you do that, Sanchia?"

She hesitated and then lay down on the bed beside him. "Why do you want me to hold you? Are you afraid of the dark?"

"Of course not. I'm not afraid of anything." The denial came fiercely. "I just thought it would be . . . nice." His arms came around her and he held her tightly. "Good night, Sanchia."

"Good night, Piero," she whispered. Her throat was so tight she could scarcely speak. She was obviously not lying here to comfort, but to be comforted. Piero, with that instinctive wisdom he had learned so young, had comprehended her pain and bewilderment and was trying to soothe it in the only way he knew how. Her heart swelled with poignant tenderness as she nestled closer to the warmth of Piero's small body.

Yes, this was the only love she wanted in her life. This was the best kind of love.

"You've made this garden into an Elysian field." Lorenzo's gaze ran admiringly over the rows and rows of brilliant blooms as they walked slowly toward the arbor. "I've always liked to stroll among your roses."

"You've phrased it well. For over thirty years I've wrested peace and forgetfulness from this earth." Caterina's proud gaze followed Lorenzo's. "The castle grounds were overgrown, a tangle of thorn bushes when I came here as a bride." She paused to touch the petals of one full-blown damask rose before strolling on. "And the castle was in little better condition than the grounds. Carlo's father had been without a wife for over ten years and the servants had grown lazy without a mistress. It was foul as a pigsty. But I set to work and soon had it in order."

"I'm sure you did." Lorenzo smiled at her. "I can see

you tearing through the castle with a broom in one hand and a whip in the other."

She shook her head. "I was not then as I am now. I had just reached my thirteenth year when I was given to Carlo in marriage and my home was very different from Mandara."

"How different?"

"Serene, well ordered. My mother would never have permitted conditions such as I found at Mandara, and she would have swooned if she had seen the kitchen."

Lorenzo chuckled. "Do you think to make me pity that thirteen-year-old bride? You are not your mother. If you had not had a challenge to overcome, you would have ridden out and found one."

"What a hardhearted rogue you are." She suddenly laughed. "But you're right. In those early days I would have gone mad if I hadn't had a great deal to do. I can remember kneeling in the dirt and digging and stabbing my spade into the earth. I spilled out all my rage and sorrow and loneliness to feed and water this garden. It's a wonder anything at all grew."

"But you brought forth beauty."

"Yes, it's strange how indifferent nature is to why we nurture it. It simply keeps on blossoming and giving as if we had lavished it with love instead of hate or despair." She was thoughtful for a moment. "And then one day we look around and see all this beauty we've helped to create and suddenly the love is there. Is that not queer, Lorenzo?"

"It's the way nature tricks us into slaving to do her bidding. Children are the same. Nature makes infants winsome and amusing so that they won't be strangled when they bring so much trouble to their unfortunate parents."

"Lion was a terrible baby, but Marco was as even-tempered as an angel."

"But you preferred Lion."

"I did not say that," she said quickly. They walked in silence for a moment. "Lion was so like me. Impatient, wild, curious. It was natural I should feel close to him."

"Very natural. You're still very much alike."

She shook her head. "But we grew away from each other when Carlo spirited him off." She dropped down on the marble bench beneath the arch of the arbor. "Lion was only seven when Carlo insisted on taking him on his first campaign. Scarcely more than a baby. He said Lion must learn the ways of war early as Carlo had done from his father. I screamed and ranted but it did no good."

"And what did you do?"

"I cleared another tract of land for an increase of my garden." She indicated a place to the left of the arbor in which roses of a deep red flourished. "And I dug in the earth from dawn until sunset every day for two months and every time I tore into the earth I pretended it was Carlo's heart. When he came back in the spring he told me how glad he was I had found such a gentle, womanly occupation to keep me from meddling in men's affairs."

Lorenzo laughed and sat down on the bench beside her. "*Cristo*, what a dullard the man must have been."

She pointed to the graceful marble fountain in the center of the garden. "Marco designed that fountain when he was only fifteen. He was . . ." She stopped and her hand dropped to her lap. "Why am I out here chatting about flowers and fountains? I should be doing something. Lion is somewhere inside—"

"My dear Caterina, as inflamed as Lion was when he dragged Sanchia away, you can be sure the act has already been done. He's every bit as passionate as his mother. What is that pleasant little jingle I've been hearing?"

Her gaze lowered to her left wrist. "I've forgotten to take off one of my bell bracelets." As she slipped the slender circlet from her wrist it gave off a silvery tinkle. She held the circlet between her slim, nervous fingers and turned it around and around, gazing down at it unseeingly. "Did I give up too easily?"

"You've not given up at all. Tomorrow you'll be planning and plotting how to separate them again."

"Yes, but perhaps I should have done something

before this. I don't know why I was so lacking in determination. Am I getting old, Lorenzo?"

"No, Caterina, no one is younger than you."

"I have gray in my hair."

"You have steel in your soul."

"I think I saw a line beside my mouth this morning when I looked in the mirror."

"Impossible. It was a crack in the mirror."

She was silent a moment, and then burst out laughing. "What sweet lies you tell me, and you say you always speak the truth."

"I am telling the truth. Is your garden any less beautiful now than in its first flowering thirty years ago?" He shook his head. "It has only changed, grown, matured. It's been disciplined by harsh winters and your own hand, but each spring it renews itself. You're like your garden, Caterina." He looked out over the acres of flowers. "Perhaps you *are* this garden."

She glanced at him in surprise before her gaze shifted back to the bells in her hands. "Trust you to be extravagant. You compare me not to a single rose but to an entire garden."

"And the rich earth that nourishes it and the sharp thorns that protect it."

"Lorenzo, I . . ." She stopped and shook her head. "I value our friendship."

"Friendship is a fine thing."

"It is so pleasant sitting here in my garden with you."

"You don't have to make polite conversation with me. I am only Lorenzo. Sit and be at peace."

She nodded and tilted her head to look up at the night sky. So many stars, remote and uncaring, as they shone down on a turbulent world. But no turbulence existed tonight in this garden. There was only Lorenzo, moonlight, the scent of roses, and the silvery music of the bracelet of bells she turned slowly in her fingers.

"You must send me away," Sanchia said as soon as she entered Caterina's chamber the next morning. "Now. Today."

Caterina looked coolly at her as she put her quill pen back onto the ivory inkstand. "I wasn't sure you hadn't changed your mind. You didn't appear overeager to leave Lion last night."

A flush stained Sanchia's cheeks. "I made a mistake. I told you he makes me . . . That's why I must leave now before it happens again. You said you could find a way to smuggle me out of the city. It's been over a week since I came to the castle. Surely you've discovered some way for me and Piero to leave."

Caterina nodded slowly. "The day after tomorrow, Messer Kalando's merchant caravan goes to Venice to sell wine from our vineyard. I'll send for the man and see if I can slip you out of the city with his train. However, they'll be moving too slowly for Lion not to overtake them, so you and Piero must branch off and hide until Lion has stopped searching the immediate area. Then you can rejoin the caravan before it reaches Venice." She paused. "You're welcome to leave Piero here. I've grown very fond of him in the last week."

"He wouldn't stay. He says we belong together," Sanchia said. "But, if I find I cannot give him a good life, I'll send him back to you in spite of his protests. It's kind of you to offer him shelter."

"I am not kind." Caterina rose to her feet and closed the account book. "Piero is welcome here because I like and admire the child." She met Sanchia's gaze. "As you would have been welcome under other circumstances."

Sanchia's eyes widened in surprise, but she was given no chance to reply. Caterina was reaching into a drawer and taking out a soft leather pouch. "There are a hundred ducats here together with a ruby pendant worth ten times that amount. It should keep you very well until you find gainful employment." She held out the pouch. "Well, take it. Did you think I meant to send you out in the world to beg or steal?"

Sanchia reached out mechanically to take the purse. "Thank you. I'll return the money as soon as I—"

"It's a gift, not a loan." Caterina frowned. "Have the courtesy to accept it as such and say no more about it."

She came around the desk and strode toward the door. "Now set to packing. I'll try to send your baggage to Messer Kalando this evening." She opened the door and stood waiting for Sanchia to depart. "This is the wisest thing for you to do, Sanchia."

"I know it is." Sanchia crossed the room and would have left the chamber if Caterina hadn't stopped her by placing a hand on her arm.

"If you have need of anything, you must send word to me. I will know no guilt over sending you away."

Sanchia smiled with genuine warmth. "It's my choice. There is no guilt, Lady Caterina."

Caterina gazed at her with a fierceness that suddenly reminded Sanchia of Piero's challenging glare. Was Lion's mother's ferocity used as the same armor? "I thank you for your help and I'm sorry if I brought you worry and pain. Good-bye, Lady Caterina."

"It's not good-bye yet. You cannot leave until tomorrow night." Caterina hesitated. "I visit the sick today. Perhaps you'd like to delay your packing and accompany me." She added quickly, "It would keep you out of Lion's way."

"I think I'd like to go with you." Sanchia was again conscious of that sense of companionship that was close to kinship blossoming between them. "If I'd be no trouble."

"If I thought you'd be trouble, I would not have suggested you come," Caterina said gruffly. "I'll meet you in the courtyard when the chapel bell tolls the half hour." She released Sanchia's arm and almost pushed her from the room. "See that you don't keep me waiting."

The door slammed in her face, and Sanchia turned and moved quickly down the hall. She understood Lion's mother even less than she understood Lion himself, but both of them fascinated her. It would do no harm to try to get to know Caterina a little better on this last day before she left Mandara. After tomorrow, it was unlikely that she would see either of them ever again.

Not see Lion again? She was wrenched with agony

and drew a deep breath to try to stifle her betraying response. Lion would never give up, and she would not have the strength to withstand him if she stayed here at Mandara.

Yes, she and Piero must leave the city—and Lion as soon as possible.

Sixteen

In the afternoon Piero disappeared.

Sanchia, Caterina, and Bianca did not return to the castle until almost dusk, and Rosa was waiting when they rode into the courtyard.

"It wasn't my fault," Rosa said as soon as she saw Sanchia. "It was that stupid groom's duty to watch over the boy. I couldn't be expected to trot after him into the town, could I?"

Sanchia felt her heart leap and then began to pound wildly. "Piero?" She got down from the mare and ran over to where Rosa stood on the steps. "What are you talking about? What's happened to Piero?"

"It wasn't my fault. I always watch him like a hawk. You know that, Madonna Sanchia." Tears were streaming down Rosa's cheeks. "It was that stupid Donato who—"

Sanchia grabbed Rosa's shoulders and

shook her. "Stop babbling and tell me what's happened to Piero."

"I don't know." Rosa gulped and her face twisted in an ugly grimace as she tried to suppress her sobbing. "He was out riding with Donato and the oaf lost him. He should have kept better watch over the boy. If I had been there, I would have—"

"How could he lose him?" Sanchia shook her again. "Piero's not foolish. He wouldn't just wander away. How long has he been gone?"

"All afternoon," Rosa said. "Donato told me they were in the *mercato* and he turned his back for an instant and Piero was gone."

"All afternoon? Why did no one send for me?"

"A good question," Caterina said grimly. "And has anyone told Lord Andreas the boy's disappeared?"

Rosa shook her head miserably. "Donato rode into the courtyard only five minutes before you came. He's been scouring the city for the child. He thought to find him before dark and had to return without him. I sent him to find Lord Andreas and confess he had lost Piero."

"Surely nothing could have happened to Piero," Bianca said comfortingly. "After all, he's only a child. Perhaps he wandered away. I've often become intrigued watching all the tradesmen working at their crafts in their windows and found myself going farther than I intended."

"Piero wouldn't have done that." Sanchia's hands dropped from Rosa's shoulders. "He would never—"

"We'll find him, Sanchia." Lion was coming down the steps, pulling on his leather gauntlets. He gave a crisp order over his shoulder and Donato started on the double across the courtyard. Lion turned to Bianca. "Find Marco and have him meet me at the stable. I last saw him painting in the garden."

Bianca nodded and ran to the castle.

"Piero is a sensible child," Caterina said sharply. "Sanchia is right. Why couldn't that dimwitted groom find him?"

"We'll soon know," Lorenzo said as he joined Lion.

"The people in the city know Piero is under the protection of this family, so no harm should come to him."

"How do you know? So many things can happen to a child alone in the streets," Sanchia said fiercely. "You know that, Lorenzo."

"Yes," Lorenzo said gently. "Evil things can happen anywhere, but Mandara is safer than the streets of Naples or Florence, Sanchia. Trust me. It is true."

Sanchia turned to Lion. "I'm going back with you. Perhaps something frightened Piero and he's afraid to answer when called. He'll know my voice and come to me."

Lion nodded. "Come then." He came a step closer, lifted her onto her horse and handed her the reins. He gazed steadily at her. "We'll find him, Sanchia. I promise you. We'll search until we do."

"He's so little." Sanchia blinked back the tears. "We've got to find him, Lion. I love him so."

"I know you do." For the briefest instant Lion's hand covered Sanchia's and then he was gone, striding across the courtyard in the direction of the stable.

They found no sign of Piero that evening, though Lion ordered the search to go on far into the night. The next morning they returned to the city and searched the houses and shops from cellars to roofs.

Piero was not found.

In the late afternoon Lion rode at the head of a troop of men out the city gates to look for him in the countryside surrounding Mandara. It was to no avail.

Piero was not found.

Four more days passed while Lion searched neighboring villages and then in desperation traveled to a Franciscan monastery some eight hours distant.

"You must get some sleep," Caterina said briskly as she strode out on the battlement toward Sanchia. "You've scarcely rested since the boy disappeared. Getting ill won't bring Piero back."

Sanchia's gaze remained fixed on the vineyards to

the north of the city. She lifted her hand to rub her temple. "I can't remember if they tried the winery."

"The second day." Caterina paused. "Even the vats."

Sanchia shuddered. "He's dead, isn't he? He must be dead or we would have found him."

"Nonsense. We should have found him even if he was dead. So not finding him proves nothing."

Caterina's abrasiveness was oddly comforting. "That's right. They would have found his bo—" She couldn't say the word. Her hands clenched on the stone ledge, trying to fight down the sickness the thought brought. "Bianca told me she's praying for him. I tried to pray, but I'm not sure God listens to me anymore. I've broken so many of his laws. I've stolen and lied." Her voice lowered to a whisper, "I've committed adultery."

"I've never been sure God hears me either. I have an idea He leaves alone the people capable of solving their own problems and concentrates on those who can't. It may not seem just to us, but we should not argue with Him." Caterina drew her crimson cloak more closely about her. "It's growing cooler now that the sun has gone down. Come in and sup with me. You can do no good out here. Lion will return when he returns and not before."

"I'll join you shortly." Sanchia turned and once more gazed out over the countryside. She suddenly stiffened. "Is that someone coming?"

Caterina squinted at the puff of dust barely discernible as horses and riders at a distance. "Possibly. Yes, I think those are horsemen."

"Lion!" Sanchia turned and ran toward the door leading to the stairs.

"He's still far away," Caterina called after her. "Be careful. You'll hear nothing if you fall down those stairs and crack your head."

"I'll be careful but I must . . ." Sanchia's words trailed behind her as she left the battlements and started down the first curving flight of stairs.

It was almost an hour later when Lion rode into the courtyard. Sanchia ran forward, her gaze searching Lion's face. "Piero?"

Lion smiled. "We found him. He's well, Sanchia."

Sanchia swayed and reached out to clutch at Tabron's saddle. "Where?"

"He'll be here soon. I rode on ahead to tell you." Lion swung down from the saddle and put his arm around Sanchia's waist to steady her. "Marco's bringing him. Piero wouldn't ride any longer in the wagon in which we found him, so Marco took him up behind him."

"You found him at the monastery?"

Lion shook his head. "Not three miles from here. We were returning from the monastery when we saw a wagon pulled over on the shoulder of the road. Piero was in the bed of the wagon lying on a pile of blankets. He was bound hand and foot and blindfolded."

"Bound." She was stunned. "But why would anyone do that to Piero?"

Lion shook his head. "God knows." His lips tightened. "But I intend to find out."

For the first time Sanchia noticed the deep lines of exhaustion graven on either side of Lion's mouth and the dark circles beneath his eyes. Lion had been searching unceasingly for five days with even less sleep than she had gotten. She took a step nearer and laid a hesitant hand on his cheek. "You must rest. You look so weary."

"Now I can rest. The boy—"

"Sanchia!"

Sanchia's gaze flew to the mounted men who had just galloped into the courtyard. Lorenzo and Marco, and behind Marco clutching at his waist a small, beloved figure.

"Piero!" She dashed across the courtyard.

Piero released his grip on Marco and swiftly slid off the horse into Sanchia's arms. "I'm back." His arms were so tight around her she could scarcely breathe. "They took me away but I'm back, Sanchia."

"Where have you been?" Her hands moved over him anxiously. "Are you all right?" She wrinkled her nose, half laughing, half crying. "You smell *terrible*, and where did you get those horrible rags?"

"I don't know." Piero's hands were moving over her hair caressingly. "I don't know anything. I was walking in the market . . . and then my head hurt—" He took a step back and looked at her gravely. "I couldn't see anything when I woke up. I thought I was blind. Then I heard them talking about the blindfold and then I knew—"

"*Gran Dio*, the boy is filthy." Caterina came down the steps to the courtyard. "Ask him questions after he's had a bath and a meal."

"A good idea." Marco said, making a face. "And a bath for me too. I must smell as bad as Piero after having him cling to me all this way." He looked around the courtyard. "Where's Bianca?"

"In the chapel praying." Sanchia took Piero's hand and gripped it tightly. "Why don't you go tell her Piero's back safely?"

"Well, perhaps I shall just stop by." He dismounted and tossed the reins of his horse to a hovering groom. "She'll want to know her prayers have borne fruit."

Lorenzo sniffed. "Rather overripe fruit. Be sure not to get too close or you'll overpower her."

Marco grinned and started toward the chapel.

A small wagon pulled by a shaggy horse was being driven into the courtyard; it was followed by the eight riders Lion had taken with him that morning. Sanchia looked hard at the wagon as her hand tightened on Piero's. Why had he been tied up and left in the wagon? More, why had he been taken in the first place?

"The bath," Caterina said firmly. She knelt and gave Piero a vigorous hug, then rose and took his other hand. "Rosa will be very glad to see you. She's been weeping and wailing ever since you disappeared, young Messer Piero. Come along now."

Sanchia hesitated as she passed Lion, her gaze on his strained, weary face. "Thank you," she whispered. "I'll always remember—" Her voice broke and she turned and hurried up the steps with Piero and Caterina.

There would be time later to tell Lion how much Piero's return meant.

"I must see you."

Lion stood in the doorway to Piero's chamber. He was fully dressed, even to his cloak and gauntlets and Sanchia hurriedly stood up from her chair beside the child's bed and moved toward him. "What is it?" she whispered.

"I'm leaving for Pisa with a company of men." He drew her from the room and shut the door softly. "A messenger arrived only minutes ago from Basala, my shipwright at the yard."

"What message?"

"Damari has set a torch to all the ships in the yard."

"Oh no!" She grasped his arm, her eyes misting with tears. No wonder Lion's face was set in lines of suffering. Damari might just as well have attacked Lion's family as those ships. "All of them?"

"All four," he said hoarsely.

"Is Basala sure that Damari is responsible for the fire?"

"Damari made certain Basala *knew* who was responsible. He boasted he was going to come back and burn the yard itself." He grimaced. "He may have done it by now."

"And if he has?"

"I'll follow him and set a torch to the bastard." He paused. "Will you be here when I return?"

Sanchia hesitated, realizing he wasn't asking for an answer to a question, but a promise. Her heart went out to him. He had spent five days in exhaustive search for Piero and now must leave to face still another catastrophe. At this moment she would promise him anything. "I'll be here."

"Good." He started to turn away, but stopped abruptly and asked, "How is the boy?"

"He is very tired. However, children have great recuperative powers and I'm sure he'll be better after a night's rest." She frowned. "I don't understand any of this, Lion. Who took Piero? None of it makes sense."

"What did he tell you?"

"Only that he was blindfolded the entire time he was gone. He heard nothing to indicate where he was or who did this to him. He was evidently kept in a room by himself most of the time and only taken out among people once or twice."

"That's all he knows?"

"He said he heard heavy breathing, moans . . ." She sighed in disappointment. "Maybe he'll remember more in the morning."

"Perhaps. Go to bed now. You can accomplish nothing by sitting and watching him sleep."

"I don't want to leave him yet. I just got him back and I don't want to let him out of my sight."

"I'm leaving Marco and a full company of men here in Mandara with orders to watch over all of you. They won't let anything happen to him." His hand touched her cheek gently. "I should be back within a fortnight even if I have to chase Damari back to Solinari."

"First the Wind Dancer and now the shipyard. Why does Damari hate you so much?"

His lips twisted. "Because of who I am—my father's son and therefore the master of Mandara. And because of who he is. His mother once lived in the pretty house you occupy on the piazza."

Her eyes widened in astonishment. "He's your brother?"

"*Dio*, no! His mother was the widow of a shopkeeper and he was two years old when she became my father's mistress. She was a coarse, earthy woman but she held my father longer than most." His expression darkened. "She flaunted the association and those years were very difficult for my mother. Damari was seven when my father finally gave in to my mother's pleas and sent him and his mother away from Mandara, but he came back when he was twelve years old and asked to be taken into my father's service."

"And he wants whatever is yours."

"But he'll not get it." Lion turned away. "Good-bye, Sanchia."

"Lion." She didn't want him to leave. She had a

sudden vision of Damari's face as he stood over her in the dungeon. Malevolence. Evil. Death.

He looked at her inquiringly. No matter what she said, he would still go after Damari, she realized. "Go with God," she whispered.

A brilliant smile lit his face, then he was striding away from her down the corridor.

"How is Piero?" Caterina asked as Sanchia entered the hall the next morning.

"Still sleeping. I thought I'd pamper him and bring breakfast to him in his chamber."

"A little pampering can do no harm." Caterina paused. "You know that Lion left for Pisa last night?"

Sanchia nodded. "Damari."

"I would not have had this happen." Caterina frowned. "The shipyard was troublesome to me, but I would not have had Lion lose it at the hand of that bastard."

"I know you would not," Sanchia answered. "And Lion knows it as well. He's too much your son not to realize your thinking on the matter."

Caterina's brow cleared. "You're right, Lion is not fool enough to think I mean him harm." She took an apple from the bowl and put it on the trencher with a piece of melon. "Go feed the boy. I'll be along soon to see how he does and put a few questions to him. We have to get to the end of this coil."

True to her word Caterina arrived in Piero's chamber only a quarter of an hour later.

"Still in bed?" She swept into the room with a smile and strode toward the bed.

"No!" Sanchia said sharply. "Don't come any closer." Her gaze never left Piero's face.

Caterina stopped short. "What's wrong?" Her gaze raked Piero's flushed face and glittering eyes. "The boy is sick."

Sanchia nodded jerkily. "The blankets in the wagon where Lion found him. What did you do with them?"

Caterina frowned. "Why, I sent a lackey last evening

to distribute them among the poor. They were well-woven wool and—Why do you ask?"

"Piero said his left arm is sore." Sanchia's voice was low, the words barely audible. She took the child's arm and raised it carefully over his head.

"Mother of God!"

A red and pus-filled boil as large as a hen's egg lay in the curve of Piero's armpit.

"Thirsty." Piero jerked his arm away and turned on his side. "Drink, Sanchia."

"Right away, *carino*." Sanchia moved toward the door. "I'll be back in a moment."

Caterina followed her out into the hall and closed the door.

Sanchia whirled to face her. "Is it what I think?"

"I'm not sure," Caterina said slowly. "I've never seen anyone who actually had it. I was only a child when it came to Florence in 1470 and it never spread to Mandara, thank God."

"But I've heard stories." Sanchia pressed her palms back against the panels of the door. "That's how it starts."

"Sometimes. Sometimes there are no boils at all." Caterina turned away, her movement sluggish for someone who was usually so brisk and forceful. "I have to . . . to do something."

"What?" asked Sanchia. "What can you do?"

"I'll send someone to collect those blankets. No, I'll do it myself. Perhaps it's not too late."

"I've heard anything spreads it. The wind . . . the touch of befouled clothing . . ." Sanchia's eyes widened in horror. "The rags we took off Piero. I sent Rosa to burn them. She'll be in danger too."

"Rosa, Marco, Bianca, and you and me," Caterina enumerated. "We all touched Piero. Perhaps even Lion . . . Who knows who's safe from it?"

Sanchia closed her eyes and sank back against the door. "Pray God we're wrong."

"Well, we'll soon know. The plague isn't shy about making its presence felt."

Rosa fell ill that night and died at dawn the next day. No one else in the castle appeared to be ill, nor was there any sign of illness in the city.

Caterina came into Piero's chamber to give Sanchia the news that no one besides Rosa was ill. She lingered to stand looking down at Piero. "How does he?"

"I don't know." Sanchia shook her head wearily. "He's in great pain. He wakes and sleeps and wakes again."

"He's fighting hard. It is said the plague has two heads and the one that produces the boils is not so deadly as the other."

Two heads. It brought to mind a picture of a monster Medusa lying in wait to pounce on the unwary.

"I'll prepare another poultice for the boils." Caterina turned away. "And then return to sit with him while you rest."

"No." Sanchia sat down in the chair by the bed. "He knows when I'm not here and grows more restless."

"You should—" Caterina shrugged. "Send word to me, if you change your mind."

As she left the room, Sanchia leaned her head against the high back of the chair. Who would she send? Sanchia wondered dully. No servants would come near this chamber.

"Sanchia."

Her gaze flew to Piero's face. His lids had opened and he was looking at her with those brightly burning blue eyes.

"More water, love?"

He shook his head. "I'm sick, aren't I?" he asked hoarsely. "Very sick."

She nodded.

His jaw set stubbornly. "I won't die. You'll see, I won't die."

"Of course you won't." She smiled shakily. "You're much too willful to allow any sickness to best you."

"But it would help if you'd lie down and hold me. Would you do that?"

"Of course, *carino*." She got up from the chair and lay down beside him on the bed. Her throat ached as she felt his arms go around her with the same loving protection he had shown the night before he had been taken away from her.

"I won't leave you," he muttered as his eyes closed. "I know you need me."

"Yes, stay, love." Her voice broke. "I do need you so much."

"I won't die . . ."

Piero died six hours later, after experiencing so much pain Sanchia was almost glad to let him go.

Caterina was there at the end, and it was she who closed the fierce blue eyes for the last time and led a numbed Sanchia from the room. "Can you weep? Sometimes it's better if you can."

Sanchia shook her head.

"Then keep busy. Wash him and prepare him and take him to the chapel. I've had several men building coffins for the last few hours. I thought we might have need of them." She paused. "After you've finished come to Marco's chamber. That's what I came to tell you."

"Marco," Sanchia repeated numbly.

Caterina nodded. "Marco has fallen ill. He needs you. He needs us both."

"Plague?"

"Yes. We aren't as fortunate as I had hoped. There doesn't seem to be any pattern about the length of time it takes to strike someone down." She turned and her voice was slightly uneven. "I must go to my son. Come when you can. You're needed there now and will probably be needed even more later."

Bianca was in Marco's chamber when Sanchia returned from taking Piero's body to the chapel. In her yellow silk gown she looked as incongruously lovely as a buttercup. She insisted on staying in the chair beside Marco's bed in spite of their protests.

At one point Marco begged Caterina to send Bianca away. "She won't understand," he whispered. "She's not meant to. . . ." Once more he lapsed into unconsciousness.

"Bianca, do go sit in the garden," Caterina suggested gently. "Sanchia and I will tend to Marco's needs."

Bianca shook her head, her hand tightening around Marco's.

"We'll take wonderful care of him." Sanchia's hand clasped Bianca's shoulder. "I promise you, *cara*."

"But why should I go to the garden?" Bianca glanced up at Sanchia in wonder. "Marco won't be there. I can't go there without Marco."

Sanchia had a sudden poignant memory of Bianca and Marco laughing and playing on the flower-garlanded swing.

"Marco is sick," Bianca said with dignity. "I'll stay with him until he's better."

"But he may not—" Sanchia's eyes widened. Bianca *knew*. The knowledge that Marco might not live was there in the serenity of Bianca's face. Marco had been wrong about how much of the true world Bianca could understand. She not only had understood but had accepted.

Marco opened his eyes at that moment and Bianca turned swiftly back to him. "They wanted me to go to the garden. Isn't that silly?" She smiled down at him. "We can always go to the garden another time when you're well enough to paint me. You said you wanted to paint me in the swing, remember?"

"Yes." His gaze caressed her face. "Beautiful. So beautiful . . ."

"But right now we can sit here and think about all the flowers and your lovely fountain, can't we?" Her palm caressed his feverish forehead. "It's so hot today. Why don't you try to think of the water flowing and the smell of the roses?"

"I will."

"And we'll be sitting there on the bench together beside the fountain and you'll be teasing me."

"Together . . ."

"Oh, yes, we'll always be together. God is good. He'd never make us part."

His eyes closed. "Together."

They were together four hours later when Marco died.

Caterina stepped forward and gently unclasped Marco's hand from Bianca's. "Take her to her chamber, Sanchia." She closed her eyes tightly for an instant before opening them to say huskily, "I must stay here and prepare my son."

Bianca nodded obediently. "Yes, I'll go now." She stood up and looked down at Marco's face. "*Arrivederci*, Marco."

Not good-bye. Just till we meet again. Sanchia was barely able to suppress her tears as she gently took Bianca's arm and propelled her toward the door. Bianca's step was unsteady and Sanchia glanced up, expecting to see her face contorted with sorrow. Bianca's expression was serene. "Sanchia, I'd like to see the priest."

"We sent to the cathedral for him several hours ago, but he didn't come." Sanchia added gently, "Marco was a good man, Bianca. God will accept him without the last rites."

"God has already accepted him," Bianca said. "The priest is for me. I'd like to take confession before I die."

Sanchia gazed at her in shock. "Bianca, what—"

"I do not feel well. I told Marco the truth: God *is* good." She smiled radiantly at Sanchia. "Together."

Sanchia's hand tightened on Bianca's arm. "As soon as I put you to bed I myself will get the priest."

Bianca collapsed on reaching her chamber and lingered for another two days before she was devoured by the monster ravaging Mandara.

It was proving to be a virulent, insatiable, indiscriminate monster, bringing down servants, soldiers, women, children. Fully half of those in the castle had been struck down by the third day and Caterina told Sanchia the townfolk had been as tragically affected. Sanchia was left with the nursing of Bianca while Caterina tried to ease the suffering of her people beyond the walls of the castle.

Sanchia was forced to send for Caterina at the hour of Bianca's death.

"Dear God," Caterina said softly as she opened the door and the foul stench assaulted her. "Dear God in heaven."

"I need more water. The servants were bringing me a pitcher of water every few hours and setting it outside the door, but they haven't come back since last night." Sanchia was dabbing futilely with a towel at the black suppurations on Bianca's body. "I've got to make her beautiful again. How can I make her beautiful, if I have no water to wash her?"

"Her boils burst." Caterina swallowed hard and then came forward to stand beside Sanchia. "Most of them die before that happens."

"I need water."

"There is no water. The well in the city is fouled. I am permitting everyone to come to the castle and use the cistern in the courtyard for their needs. The cistern is dry now, too." Caterina gently closed Bianca's lips which were stretched wide in a silent scream. "We'll have to take a wagon to the vineyard and bring back water from the well there."

"I must get her clean. She was so beautiful . . ."

"Shh, I'll help you." Caterina took the towel away from Sanchia. "But this little cloth won't do. I'll try to find a sheet and perhaps some water in a ewer in one of the bedchambers." She turned and left Bianca's chamber to return in only minutes.

"She kept asking for the priest," Sanchia said numbly as they washed Bianca's pitifully boil-covered body. "I couldn't tell her the priest was either gone or hiding, so I lied to her. When she was in such pain that she couldn't tell the difference, I pretended the priest was here and took her confession myself. Was I wrong, Lady Caterina?"

"Caterina." Lion's mother shook her head. "I would have done the same. God is too busy striking us down to bother with confessions at the moment." She turned to Sanchia. "You'll have to help me build a coffin for her. The men who were building them in the courtyard appear to have run away, and there's no one to do my bidding. Do you know anything of carpentry, Sanchia?"

Sanchia shook her head.

"Neither do I, but it can't be so difficult if those cowardly louts were able to do it." Caterina shrugged. "There must be some dignity in death. We're not savages to pile our dead on the door stoops or leave them in the gutters as those beleaguered souls in the city are doing."

"Is that what's happening?"

Caterina nodded. "There is no sanity. There's weeping and wailing from some and drunkenness and rape from others." She straightened. "I'll get my needle and thread and we'll sew a shroud from this sheet. Then we'll try our hands at fashioning a coffin. Where's Anna? She can help us with the sewing."

Sanchia tried to focus her mind on something besides the last harrowing hours with Bianca. She hadn't seen Bianca's maid, Anna, since a short while after Bianca collapsed. "I think she may have run away too. She was frightened."

"We're all frightened." Caterina went to the door. "We'll probably have to carry Bianca down to the chapel ourselves. Perhaps we'd better build the coffin in the chapel." She opened the door and left the chamber.

Sanchia sat in the chair beside the bed and closed her eyes. *Please, God, you've taken the innocent, the shining, the beautiful. Please, no more.*

"Are you ill?" It was Caterina's sharp voice behind her.

"No." Sanchia opened her eyes to see Caterina in the doorway carrying her sewing basket. She straightened in the chair. "I was only resting a moment."

"There will be time for rest later." Caterina strode forward and set the basket on the bed. "Help me wrap the sheet around her."

It was well after dark when Bianca lay secure in her clumsily crafted coffin in the chapel.

"Come, do not linger here. They're no longer with us. Do you not feel it?" Caterina pulled Sanchia from the chapel and down the steps to the courtyard.

No torches lit the darkness.

No footsteps of grooms or guards sounded on the cobblestones.

Sanchia ran her hand wearily through her hair. "Perhaps I'm too tired to feel anything."

Caterina nodded. "We must rest." Her hand dropped from Sanchia's arm. "But first come with me."

Sanchia followed Caterina into the castle and up the stairs, but instead of going toward the bedchambers Caterina went to the door at the end of the hall leading to the tower.

"Caterina?"

"Come."

Sanchia followed her up the steps, past the chamber where Lion had carried her the evening that seemed so long ago. They stopped at a door at the very top of the tower.

Caterina opened it and preceded Sanchia into the room.

It was the chamber of the Wind Dancer.

The statue was not in its chest but sitting atop a pedestal. Across the moonlit chamber the eyes of the Pegasus appeared to shimmer with life as it stared blindly at them.

Sanchia took an instinctive step back. "I don't want to stay here."

"Please, if you would be so kind. I need someone here with me. I'll try not to be long." Caterina's voice was unsteady. "I have to say good-bye to my son. There's been no time before this. Marco liked this room."

Sanchia felt a rush of sympathy. Both she and Caterina had been forced to submerge their grief for the dead to help the living. She, too, had need to say good-bye. "Of course." She shut the door. "We'll stay as long as you like."

"Sit down and rest." Caterina indicated a chair across the room. She dropped down on the rug and leaned her head back against the stone wall. "And I'll sit here. Have you ever noticed children will never sit on chairs when they can sit on the floor? I used to bring Marco here when he was a small child to see the Wind

Dancer and we would sit here on the floor together for hours and talk and play games."

Sanchia sat down beside Caterina. "I know. Piero used to sit on the floor beside my chair at the scribe table when I was copying and I would reach down and stroke his hair." She had to stop for a moment to steady her voice. "His hair was as soft as spring air beneath my fingers."

"Marco's skin felt like rose petals to the touch."

"Piero's voice was hoarse as a frog's when he first got up in the morning."

"Marco's fingers were always stained with paint when he came to meals."

"Piero was so terribly stubborn."

"Marco was so very gentle."

There was a long silence in the room.

Caterina said, "I can remember how Marco used to stare at the statue and make me tell him all the stories about the Wind Dancer that Carlo's father had told me. There were so many stories. . . . I was afraid I'd forget them, so I had a scribe set them down on parchment and had them bound in a book."

"And you gave it to Marco?"

Caterina shook her head. "Lion has them somewhere among his papers at the shipyard. By that time, Marco was no longer coming here. He had begun to paint and the Wind Dancer no longer gave him pleasure, only pain."

"Why?"

"I asked him that question once. He said he knew he'd never be able to fashion anything one tenth as beautiful and the knowledge of his own inadequacy filled him with sadness." Caterina paused, gazing at the statue. "It filled me with sadness too. For I knew I'd lost those hours with him and he'd grow away from me just as Lion was doing. Marco was never again as much mine as he was during those hours in this room."

Sanchia's gaze shifted from the Wind Dancer to see Caterina's eyes glistening in the dimness of the chamber. She did not know what to say. "Marco loved you. He seemed to love everyone."

"Yes, but Bianca most of all. I should not have tried to take Bianca from him. I thought it was for the best." Caterina's eyes closed. "Now I don't know what is for the best. Nothing is clear."

"No, nothing is clear." Sanchia reached out tentatively and covered Caterina's hand with her own.

Caterina stiffened and for a moment Sanchia thought she'd pull away. Then Caterina sank back against the stone wall, her fingers clinging to Sanchia's. "Is it selfish of me to want to mourn my son when so many others are dying? Surely a son's death deserves a private grief." She paused and when she spoke again her voice vibrated with pain. "*Marco!*"

Sanchia could feel the tears running down her cheeks as the grief of her own loss welled up within her in an overwhelming tide. Her shoulders began to shake as great sobs racked her body and she wept for all of them. Piero and Bianca and Marco . . . and all those whose names she did not even know.

And the emerald eyes of the Wind Dancer gazed serenely at Caterina and Sanchia as they huddled together, silently sharing their grief, until neither had more tears to shed.

The next morning after waking from an exhausted sleep Caterina and Sanchia left the tower room and the Wind Dancer and went out again to face the Medusa.

The first order of the day was the fetching of the water from the well in the vineyards. They hitched a horse to a wagon and Caterina drove into the city.

Mandara was silent, the hooves of the horse clattering noisily on the cobblestones as the wagon wound through the twisting streets leading to the outer gates.

Rats and birds swarmed in the streets. Occasionally Sanchia would see a corpse left lying in the gutter or on a stoep as Caterina had described. She hastily looked away, especially when she caught sight of scurrying motion near the bodies.

The city gates were unguarded, thrown wide. They passed through, immediately bearing north to traverse the few miles to the vineyard at as fast a clip as the lone horse could manage.

"It appears deserted," Sanchia said as they approached the large fieldstone winery. "How many men work in the vineyard?"

"Only one or two at this time of year. Of course, at picking time there are many more." Caterina reined in the horse and wagon before the well. She raised her voice and called loudly, "Ho! Is anyone here? Leonardo!"

No answer.

Caterina shrugged. "It seems we'll have no help." She leapt down from the wagon. "I had hoped for better luck. We'll be able to manage only the small casks by ourselves." She strode toward the winery. "Start drawing water from the well. I'll roll the casks out and you fill them."

The task of drawing buckets of water from the well and pouring them into the casks was not so difficult after Sanchia developed a rhythm for the work. However, it was when the casks were sealed that the real labor began. Even the small casks weighed well over a hundred pounds when filled. Lifting the casks onto the bed of the wagon was an unbearable strain on Sanchia's and Caterina's muscles. The sweat was running down their faces and soaking through their gowns in dark patches when the last cask was stowed.

Caterina leaned against the wagon, her breath coming in gasps. "*Cristo*, I'm glad that's over. I never realized water could be so—What's wrong with your hand? It's bleeding."

Sanchia glanced down. A small cut bled freely on her right palm. "I don't know. I must have cut it on one of the casks. Perhaps it's a splinter. It's not important."

Caterina frowned. "What do you mean it's not important? It could fester." She lifted her skirt and began tearing at her undershift. "I've seen splinters that have laid low strong men. Do you want to go to your deathbed, you foolish—" She gazed at Sanchia in bafflement.

Sanchia laughed. She laughed so hard she was

forced to cling to the side of the wagon to keep from falling to the ground. "Caterina, you can't . . ." Laughter continued to overwhelm her.

"I see nothing the least bit amusing."

"Caterina, *madre di Dio*, if I go to my deathbed in Mandara it won't be due to a splinter. There's *plague*."

Caterina's eyes widened and then she began to chuckle. "I believe I've heard rumors to that effect." In another moment she too was laughing helplessly, tears running down her cheeks. "I didn't think." She shook her head. "A splinter. Sweet Mary, a tiny splinter . . ."

"We shouldn't be laughing," Sanchia gasped. "There's nothing at all funny." She started to laugh again. "Why can't I stop?"

"Lorenzo once said something about how nature protects." Caterina wiped her cheeks with the back of her hand. "Perhaps laughter is the way nature keeps us sane when there's too much sorrow to be borne." She shook her head. "Anyway, I feel the better for it. Now give me your hand and let me bind it. If the plague doesn't kill you, I won't have this idiotic splinter doing so."

Sanchia offered her hand and stood patiently while Caterina cleaned and bandaged the tiny cut.

"You could stay here, you know," Caterina said in a low voice as she tied the knot in the makeshift bandage. "You might be safe here away from the city."

"And I might not."

"It's not your home. No duty holds you at Mandara."

"You need me."

"Yes, I need you," Caterina said wearily. "And God knows I don't want you to leave. You . . . comfort me."

Sanchia nodded, feeling great affection for Caterina as she looked at her. The woman before her was no longer the elegant, queenly lady of Mandara. Caterina's amber silk gown was stained and her face carved with deep lines of weariness and suffering. Yet Caterina had never looked more the *illustrissima* than she did at this moment. "And you comfort me. Therefore it only makes sense that we stay together." She gently took

Caterina's arm. "We'd better go. They need the water in the city. Where shall we unload it?"

"On the steps of the cathedral. We'll keep two of the casks for the castle and leave the others."

"Should it not be rationed?"

"Who is to ration it? The priest is gone and we'll be too busy nursing the sick." Caterina turned and strode to the wagon. "We'll make a trip every day and draw fresh water." She climbed into the driver's seat. "Unless this well also runs dry or becomes polluted. It wouldn't surprise me. Good fortune seems to have forgotten Mandara."

Sanchia found her life in the days to follow a despairing round of fetching water, nursing the sick, preparing the dead, and building their coffins. Only one young scullery maid recovered from the disease, and Sanchia had no faith her cure was permanent. Death was everywhere. Why should anyone be spared? She knew it was only a matter of time until the Medusa touched her as well. When children as innocent as Piero and Bianca were taken there was no doubt a sinner such as she would be taken, too.

And poor, shining Marco . . .

"I went to the piazza to fetch the physician for young Donato. To no avail, I see," Caterina said as she knelt beside Sanchia on the cobblestones of the courtyard. "Here let me help you with that." She began to bathe the body of the groom, who had died only minutes ago. "It's strange how we no longer notice the stench," she said absently. She looked up. "The physician has fled the city."

"He could not help anyway." Sanchia shrugged. "But fleeing will do him no good." She looked up at Caterina. "We're all going to die, aren't we?"

"Probably. But I resent the whoreson giving up the battle before it's lost. I didn't. You didn't." She tossed the cleaning cloth back into the water in the basin. "The city is almost deserted. Those who aren't dying or cowering in their houses have fled like the physician."

Sanchia spread a clean linen sheet over the body of Donato. She supposed she should say a prayer over him, but she couldn't seem to think of any words.

"Some of the sick have crawled to the steps of the cathedral and lie there begging God and the saints for aid. I doubt if God will answer. Perhaps you'd better go and see if you can substitute."

"Me? Alone?"

Caterina nodded. "I'll soon be of no help to you."

Sanchia stiffened, her gaze flying to Caterina's face. She had thought she had become numb to all sorrow but she found she was wrong. "When?"

"When did I notice this pesky boil beneath my armpit? Last night."

But Caterina had kept on working unceasingly, probably on strength of will alone. Sanchia studied Caterina's face and for the first time noticed the flush mantling her cheeks and the lines of pain drawn around her lips. "I won't leave you."

"I didn't think you would." Caterina's smile lit her strained face with sudden brilliance. "I suppose I should try to persuade you to do so and go to those who have more need, but I think I'll indulge myself by dying with a friend nearby. I have no desire to die alone and smothered by four walls." Her smile faded and she held out her hand to Sanchia. "Will you come with me to my garden . . . friend?"

Sanchia slowly stood up and took Caterina's hand. She held it very tightly as they walked to where the Medusa waited in the sunlight, among the roses for Caterina.

"Why didn't he come back?" Lion murmured, his gaze on the charred skeleton of the *Dancer* at the dock. "He said he was returning to burn the shipyard. Why didn't he do it?"

Lorenzo shrugged. "Perhaps Borgia snapped his fingers and he had to come running. Damari is clever enough to put aside his own personal vengeance where his ambitions are concerned."

"Or perhaps he wanted to draw me to Solinari where he had set his trap."

"Basala said he had only a small troop of men when he raided the shipyard. Do you think he had a larger force at—"

"I don't like it," Lion cut in with sudden violence. "Any of it. It doesn't feel right."

Lorenzo's gaze went back to the wreckage of the ship and then to the other blackened hulls sitting in the shipyard. "This has hurt you. Consider that you may not be thinking clearly."

Lion's hand tightened on the reins. "Damari meant to hurt me," he said hoarsely. "And he's depending on me to rush wildly to Solinari after him. Why?"

Lorenzo merely gazed at him.

"And why didn't he burn the ships and shipyard when he came here and discovered we'd taken the *Dancer* and sailed for Genoa? It would have been a better opportunity. Why did he hold his hand then and strike now?"

"He could have wanted to destroy the *Dancer* as well."

Lion shook his head. "I don't think so."

"Then do we go to Solinari and reconnoiter?"

Lion was silent, his gaze on the *Dancer*. "What if Damari meant to draw us not to Solinari but away from Mandara?"

Lorenzo stiffened, his gaze whipping to Lion's face. "You think he might have persuaded Borgia to give him reinforcements to attack the city?"

"I don't know what he's done, but all this has an odd feel to me." Lion suddenly called over his shoulder at the men milling around the shipyard, "Mount up! We're going back to Mandara."

Seventeen

Sanchia was sitting on the steps of the chapel, her head resting back against the stone wall, when Damari rode into the courtyard.

The setting sun was behind him, and at first he appeared only as a squat, dark figure against the blood-red orb. Then, as he drew closer, she recognized him, but oddly felt not the least surprised. It seemed fitting that he should be here in this place of death and sorrow.

"Ah, Sanchia, how pleasant it is to see you." Damari swung down from his horse. "You'll forgive me if I don't come any closer. It's only wise to take certain precautions. Tell me, do you have the disease as yet?"

"Probably." Sanchia shook her head wearily. "I don't know."

"And the Lady Caterina?"

"Dead. Yesterday." She paused. "I think

it was yesterday. They're all dead. Marco, Bianca . . . Piero."

He nodded. "Excellent. I was hoping the lady had been taken. Now, if you'll excuse me, I have business inside the castle, I'll rejoin you shortly."

He crossed the courtyard and went briskly up the stone steps and into the castle.

Sanchia leaned her head back against the wall and closed her eyes. She should probably go back down to the piazza and see if any more victims had been brought to the cathedral. She would go soon, but it was comforting to sit there next to the chapel. She didn't feel so alone when she was this close to Caterina and Piero.

"Wake up and bid me good-bye, Sanchia."

She opened her eyes to see Damari tying a familiar mahogany chest on the hindquarters of his stallion. The Wind Dancer.

"You see I have it again. I told you I'd get it back."

He seemed absurdly pleased, she thought with vague surprise. Did he think the loss of the statue mattered now?

"You didn't believe me, did you?" He glanced up as he tightened the rope. "I'm truly glad you're here to see my triumph. I was afraid there would be no one left alive to appreciate my cleverness."

"No one is alive."

"Well, you're half alive. That will do." He smiled. "Tell me, did the boy die at once? I thought he was ill when my men put him in the wagon."

Piero. He was talking about Piero. "Not right away." She managed to focus on what he was saying. "It was you who took Piero?"

"One of my men, actually. It was truly a brilliant plan. It had come to my ears that the plague had attacked a tiny coastal village not far from Solinari and it was only necessary that we spread the disease here. Now who would make a better carrier than the child you had taken to your bosom? My informant had already told me that both you and the child were here at the castle. We had only to steal the child, smuggle him out of the city, and transport him to Fontana. We kept him in the charnel house there for two days, making sure he was properly exposed to the disease."

It was Damari who was the monster of death. The horror of his words pierced her apathy and exhaustion. She gasped. "How could anyone do such an evil thing?"

"Of course, it was necessary to conduct the plan with the most exquisite precision and timing," Damari went on calmly. "I returned to Pisa to raid Andreas's shipyard and draw him and a goodly portion of his men from Mandara. Then I sent two of my men with the wagon and orders to abandon it a few miles from the city gates. After the raid I had to bring my men back here to stop those who were fleeing the city."

"Fleeing . . ."

"But of course. The disease couldn't be allowed to spread. Borgia and His Holiness were afraid there would be an outcry if the disease were carried into another city." He smiled. "I assured them that wouldn't happen, so I waited in the hills and when the scared rabbits came streaming out of the city we eliminated them with a barrage of arrows. I had to be careful to keep my men at a distance. Those who I find it necessary to bring close to the plague will also have to be eliminated."

"But you're here now."

"Ah, but I'm not afraid of the disease." He rubbed his pitted cheek. "If I was meant to die of any disease, the pox would have gotten me when I was a child and that Lady bitch persuaded her husband to send my mother and me away from Mandara to a pox-ridden village. No, I was spared to do great things, to lead armies, to create kingdoms."

Sanchia shook her head. "You'll die here, like all the rest. Everyone dies here."

For a moment an expression of uneasiness crossed Damari's face because of the certainty in her tone. "Not me. I have another fate awaiting me." He gave a final tug to the rope and swung onto the saddle. "Do you smell the smoke yet?"

"No."

"I do." He lifted his head and sniffed. "I set fire to

the castle and to the gardens. My men are torching the city now. Another precaution His Holiness insisted on my taking. Naturally, we torched the village of Fontana after we took the boy from the charnel house."

"Lion . . ."

"You're wondering why I let Andreas leave when he too might have become infected?" He shrugged. "I had to accept the risk. I had to draw his forces away so I could be sure of walking into the castle unopposed. If he does carry the plague elsewhere, we'll merely put out a story that he fled in terror from the disease and it was his fault the sickness was brought to more innocents." He smiled. "I will, of course, now proceed back to Solinari and dispose of him at my leisure."

As he gazed down at her a flicker of regret passed over his face. "I'd really like to take you with me. I quite enjoyed our time together in the dungeon. It's not often that one runs across a woman with the courage and endurance you possess. I had promised myself another such experience after Andreas took you from me." He shook his head. "Too bad. But Borgia would be most irate if he learned I'd let anyone live who knew of his and his father's involvement."

"You're going to kill me?"

"I've already killed you," Damari said. "I was merely considering resurrecting you for a few day's amusement. Good-bye, Sanchia. If you're fortunate, the fire may end your life before the plague does. I hear the plague gives a very painful death."

"Yes." She closed her eyes again, trying not to see the pictures his words brought to mind. "Yes, it's very painful."

She heard the clatter of Damari's horse's hooves on the flagstones as he left the courtyard. A moment later the first acrid wisp of smoke drifted to her nostrils.

They came upon the first dead seven miles from Mandara.

Lion looked down at the body of a child of perhaps eight years crumpled in the road beside a wagon. An arrow had pierced her narrow chest, pinning her to the wood of the wagon wheel.

Lorenzo reined in beside him. "A man, a woman, and two more children are lying farther down the road."

"Arrows?"

Lorenzo nodded. "The wagon is piled high with furniture and household goods. It looks as though everything was tossed into the wagon with great speed. They obviously left the city in a hurry with no intention of returning."

"And were waylaid and murdered." Lion looked away from the child lying against the wagon wheel. "Women and children too. Nothing appears to have been stolen. Why would they have been murdered?"

"Shall I order them buried?"

"No." Lion turned his horse. "Later. We have to find out why they were running from Mandara. Hurry."

They came upon two more bodies a mile down the road and then an entire family butchered a quarter of a mile farther. After that, Lion stopped counting the dead that littered the road and gullies and spurred on toward Mandara.

They first saw the glow lighting the night sky as they left the foothills.

Lion heard Lorenzo's harsh imprecation but couldn't tear his gaze from the macabre, obscene beauty of the sight before him.

"Mandara." Lorenzo gazed stonily at the burning city in the distance.

Lion heard the shocked murmur of the men riding behind him. They had wives, friends, families in that inferno just as he did, he thought dully. Sanchia, his mother, Marco, Bianca . . .

"Caterina," Lorenzo said hoarsely. "There have to be prisoners."

Lion felt a spring of hope. Lorenzo was right. None of them had to be in the burning city. He spurred forward and put Tabron into a dead run.

"Lion," Lorenzo shouted above the thunder of the horse's hooves. "If it was Damari, where's the condotti?"

The same thing was bothering Lion. On this level

plain the torches and movement of an attacking army should clearly be visible. There was nothing. No army. No horses. No catapults or other war machines. Nothing.

Nothing but Mandara being devoured by flames.

Lion saw Sanchia when they were within three miles of the city.

She was plodding slowly, blindly down the road and, if the illumination from the burning Mandara had not lit the countryside with unusual clarity, the troop would have ridden her into the ground.

"Sanchia!" Lion held up his hand to halt the troop and reined in Tabron. "*Dio*, what's happened here?"

She didn't seem to hear him. She kept walking, her gaze fixed on something he couldn't see. Her brown velvet gown was torn, filthy, her hair a wild tangle of grease and soot.

"Sanchia." Lion dismounted and strode toward her. "Are you hurt?"

She kept plodding forward.

Lion stopped before her and grasped her shoulders. "*Santa Maria*, answer me. Are you hurt?"

Her blank gaze finally focused on his face. "Lion?" she whispered. "I thought you were dead. I thought everyone was dead but Damari. It's not right that he should live, you know. He shouldn't be allowed to live when everyone else in the world is dead."

"Everyone isn't dead, Sanchia. You're alive."

She looked at him in wonder. "No, I'm not. Damari killed me just as he did everyone else. Caterina, Marco, Piero, Bianca."

Agony tore through him as his gaze went over her head to Mandara. "All dead?"

"Of course," she said, surprised that he should ask. "Everyone is dead."

He felt the tears sting his eyes even as he shook her. "You're *not* dead, Sanchia. We're both alive."

"That's right, you're alive. You told me." She suddenly stiffened, her eyes going wide with horror. "No!"

She tore out of his grasp and backed away. "Don't touch me. Are you mad? The plague . . ."

Lion went icy cold. "Plague? You said Damari, Sanchia."

But she had turned and was running wildly back toward Mandara, the skirts of her tattered gown flying behind her.

Lion pounded after her. "*Cristo*, Sanchia. Stop. No one is going to hurt you." He drew even with her and grabbed her in his arms. "Sanchia *cara*—"

"You don't understand." She was struggling desperately to free herself. "I'll kill you. I don't want to kill you. Only Damari. Let me go!"

The tears were now running unashamedly down Lion's cheeks. "*Cara*, no . . ." He drew her closer, his hands feverishly stroking her sooty hair. "Shh . . ."

She abruptly gave up, slumping against him. "It's too late anyway. You've touched me. Even Damari was afraid to touch me. Medusa . . ."

He caught her as she swayed, collapsing into unconsciousness.

The bitter odor of smoke was gone. Now the air was pervaded with the odor of wood and something fruity, yet musty.

Sanchia opened her eyes to see Lion bending over her, bathing her forehead. Dusk enveloped them. The only light piercing the dimness was the sunlight pouring through two small windows high above her. Dust motes danced in the dual brilliant streams of sunlight and she gazed at them in dreamy fascination.

Two dancing sunbeams . . .

Lorenzo had said that about Bianca and Marco, hadn't he? But those sunbeams were no longer dancing; they lay still and quiet in the chapel.

But was there a chapel? Would the stone have withstood the heat of the flames that engulfed Mandara?

"Fire . . ." Her throat was raw, and it hurt to speak. Had she been screaming? She had felt the screams welling up inside her, but she believed she had kept them from coming out.

"No more fire, Sanchia," Lion said gently. "You're not in Mandara any longer."

"Where?"

"The winery." He smoothed the damp cloth on her temples. "You remember the winery?"

"Yes." She looked around and could discern the shadowy outline of a huge wooden vat and oak casks in the dimness.

"Keep covered. It's cool here." He pulled the blanket over her and she suddenly became aware she was nude beneath it.

Lion was without clothes, too, she realized in bewilderment. Strange.

"Do you know who I am?" Lion asked.

"Lion."

Relief lightened his expression. "And what happened at Mandara?"

How could she forget? How could anyone forget. "Plague." She was suddenly jarred into full wakefulness. "Get away from me!" She sat upright and tried to slide farther from him. "Plague!"

"Be easy. I've been with you here for over a week." Lion said gently. "If I'm fated to fall to the disease then I'm already infected."

She looked at him, stricken. "A week?" She closed her eyes. "Dear God, why?"

"Why did you stay in Mandara to care for those I loved?"

"I was there."

"And I am here. Open your eyes and look at me, Sanchia. Do I appear ill or racked with the disease?"

She opened her eyes. He looked strong and vigorous in spite of the lines of weariness and sorrow she saw in his face. "Sometimes it doesn't happen right away."

"And sometimes it doesn't happen at all. Was everyone stricken in Mandara?"

"It seemed as if they were." She shook her head in confusion. "There were a few that were not ill but, as I said, sometimes it takes more time for one or the other. I don't know if any lived or not."

"I think it likely some survived, if the fire didn't kill them."

The fire. "Damari and his men set the fire. I watched him do it but I couldn't seem to move. Then it came to me that if Damari lived, he could do this again. I couldn't let him repeat such a monstrous act. So many died . . . Did I tell you about Piero?"

"Yes, you told me everything." Lion's eyes glittered brightly in the dimness of the room. "You raved and ranted until I thought I could not bear to hear any more. I believed you would very likely go mad."

"Perhaps I did. I keep seeing—"

"No," he said fiercely. "You will heal in mind and you will heal in body. I will not lose you, too. Do you hear me? You will heal!"

The passionate force of his voice almost convinced her he could hold both death and madness at bay. Poor Lion. He had lost so much. His family. His ships. His home.

She had thought she was incapable of feeling ever again, but to her surprise she felt a faint stirring within her. She looked away from him. "Why do we have no clothing?"

"I burned the clothes you were wearing and the ones I had on when I found you."

When she looked at him inquiringly, he shrugged. "It seemed a good idea at the time. I know nothing about plague." He paused. "I bathed us both in hot water every day and clothing would have just gotten in the way. It seemed a sensible precaution to take. When you swooned I told Lorenzo and the men not to come near us and brought you here to the winery. They're encamped beyond the vineyard. Lorenzo comes every day with fresh food and water and sets it outside the door." He nodded at a pile of blankets against the wall. "I've boiled those blankets and dried them in the sun. If you like, I suppose I could fashion you something to wear from one of them."

"Soon." She felt no discomfort in either Lion's nudity or her own. More than her clothing had been stripped from her in the past weeks. "How long are we to remain here?"

"Another week. Then, if neither of us falls ill, it will be reasonable to assume you did not carry the plague."

"Reasonable." She looked at him and found herself suddenly shaking. "There's no reason or justice connected with that monster. It strikes the good, the innocent, the strong. Caterina—" She choked back a sob. "Forgive me. I know it must hurt to have me speak of her. She was your mother, and she—"

"Hush." He was suddenly holding her in his arms, his fingers tangled in her hair as he rocked her back and forth in an agony of sympathy. "I know she was not kind to you. She meant well—"

"No, you don't understand," Sanchia whispered. "I loved her, too. We became so close those last days that when she died it was almost like losing Piero again. I loved her."

"I wish I had said good-bye to them," Lion said hoarsely. "I should have taken the time to say good-bye. If I had known—"

Sanchia felt something warm and wet on her temple. *If.* The eternal word of regret. Sanchia's arms slowly went around his shoulders to comfort as well as take comfort. Caterina had said something about regrets that she must think about and then share with Lion and Lorenzo. But not now. The pain was too fresh and new. Later there would be time enough.

Why, she was thinking about the future, she realized with astonishment. Perhaps she was beginning to believe that Lion could in some magical way keep the Medusa from taking them both.

But she must not let her hopes rise, for that was another way the Medusa tricked and deceived, giving a little only to take away all. Sanchia would not allow herself to hope until she was sure the monster had passed them by and would not look over its shoulder to smite them down.

Later that night, they sat before the small fire Lion had lit in the center of the winery. Lion had draped her in one of the blankets to protect her from the cold, and his arm around her formed another comforting barrier.

She did not look away from the fire as she said haltingly, "I do love you, you know."

He stiffened and then his arm tightened around her. "No, I didn't know."

"I knew I loved you in that first moment when I thought you might also get the plague. I believe I didn't realize it before because love was different from what I had thought it would be." She gazed pensively into the flames. "It's not sweet and gentle like the emotion Dante felt for his Beatrice, is it?"

"No."

"It twists and turns and makes you ache with lust and then with tenderness, but still the love remains. Somehow I thought there would be . . ." She stopped, thinking about it. "A splendor."

"Perhaps there is splendor for people who have an easier path to tread than we."

"Perhaps."

They were silent.

"I thought it important that you know I love you before we die," she said. "I think we should—"

"We aren't going to die."

"Oh. Well, if we do." She leaned her head back against his chest and closed her eyes. "No, it's not at all like Dante said. I didn't even think of you very often once Caterina and I set to nurse the dying in Mandara. Only now and then when there was time." She paused. "But when I did think of you, it was with love. I want you to know."

"I do know." Lion's voice was thick as his arms clasped her closer still. "I know, Sanchia."

"Good." She opened her eyes to gaze wistfully once again into the heart of the fire. "Still, it would have been quite wonderful if there had been splendor . . ."

A week later Sanchia and Lion walked out of the half dusk of the winery into the full sunlight.

Lorenzo was waiting with the reins of two horses in one hand, a pile of clothing for Lion in the other, and a smile on his lips for Sanchia. "Ah, how . . . interesting you look." His gaze flicked to Sanchia's hair before shifting to the coarse gray blanket Lion had slit in the middle and then slipped over her head to form a loose robe. "That garment has a kind of barbaric charm when combined with her wild red hair, don't you think, Lion? Yes, she'd definitely be a fit mate for Attila the Hun."

She gazed at Lorenzo in wonder. He was behaving exactly as he had before. Everything in the world had changed since that time . . . except Lorenzo.

"Why are you looking at me like that?" he asked mockingly. "Are your wits so dazed you cannot give me my proper set-down? I suppose I must make allowances for your recent ordeal. However, I hope you will not be long about it, or I'll be forced to deprive you of my company. You know how I detest being bored."

He turned to Lion, who had discarded his blanket and was quickly dressing in the clothes he'd brought. "I've taken the liberty of sending the troop to Pisa with instructions for your steward to give them each a small sum to start a new life somewhere else." His gaze went to the blackened stone of the walls of Mandara. "They obviously have no future here, and you have no immediate use for them."

Lion nodded. "You did well." He pulled on boots. "Have you found other survivors of the fire?"

"Only a handful. We quartered them in a field a few miles from here and as yet there's been no sign of the plague among them." He grimaced. "And we spent most of the week burying the bodies in the foothills we chanced upon when coming here. There were eighty-seven of them."

"The population of Mandara numbered well over a thousand," Lion said. "Damari has claimed a high toll."

"What do we do now?" Lorenzo asked. "I admit I'm abysmally weary of sitting around and waiting for you two to rise like Lazarus from the tomb. Damari?"

"Not yet. We go to Pisa. But first, I have to visit the survivors and see how all goes with them." Lion swung onto Tabron's back.

Lion's sense of responsibility again, Sanchia thought.

There was no longer a Mandara, but as long as his people needed him he was ready to give. "Should I go with you?"

Lion shook his head. "Sit in the sun and rest. Lorenzo and I will be back shortly."

"I've done little but rest for the past two weeks."

"Tarry here. It will do you no harm and will save me worry. Lorenzo said these people 'appeared' to be free of the plague. I'll not go close, but I don't want you within miles of them."

Sanchia nodded in acceptance. Lion would go no matter what she said or did, and she had no desire to see the refugees from Mandara. The sight would stir too many memories of those last days. "I'll stay here."

"*Santa Maria*, such meekness." Lorenzo mounted his horse. "Where is your spirit, your tartness? What a disappointment you're proving, Sanchia. And you, too, Lion. You have the settled air of a couple married a decade or so."

Sanchia's gaze met Lion's and the faintest smile touched her lips. In a strange way she felt Lorenzo was right. During their week of isolation together they had known only sorrow and fear and the need to comfort each other. The bond between them had toughened and yet become more supple, like fine leather after years of use.

As if he had read her mind, Lion nodded imperceptively. "We'll return soon," he said as he and Lorenzo set off.

Sanchia sat down on the bench beside the door of the winery and closed her eyes as she lifted her face to let the rays of the sun bathe her cheeks. The air was clean and sweet, and a feeling of peace gradually settled over her. With it came the strange certainty that the plague was gone.

The Medusa had moved on.

Lion returned alone two hours later. When she inquired into Lorenzo's whereabouts, Lion shrugged as he reined up before her. "He's gone to Mandara. God knows why. There's nothing there but ashes and ruins. He said he had a whim to see it one more time before we left."

"A whim." Sanchia turned to look thoughtfully at Mandara. She could not imagine anyone wanting to go back to that charred wasteland. Then, suddenly, she knew why Lorenzo had returned. "I have to go back too. Will you take me?"

"No!" Lion turned to look at her in amazement. "Why, by all the saints, would you be mad enough to do that?"

"Not madness. And not a whim," she said soberly. "But I have to go back. There's no danger there now. Not even the plague could have lived through the inferno."

"You can't be certain."

"No, but I feel it so strongly." She smiled. "It has passed us by, Lion."

"If you have to go, then I'll go with you."

"No." She held up her arms and he muttered a curse as he swung her up before him on the saddle. "You can take me to where the city gates once were." She settled herself back against him. "And wait for me there, as I waited for you here."

Lorenzo was sitting on his horse looking at the blackened ruins of the rose garden when Sanchia guided Tabron through the rubble to draw even with him.

She flinched as she looked around the garden. The devastation of the town had moved her terribly when she was riding through it, but this ruin had much more emotional meaning for her. Where there had been flowering beauty there was now only charred bushes, blackened fountains, cracked benches. The wooden arch over the arbor had crashed down to bury the marble bench beneath, and there was no sign of the pretty garlanded swing where she had watched Bianca and Marco at play that first afternoon.

Lorenzo didn't look at her. "I don't want you here."

"She did," Sanchia said quietly. "She called me friend and held out her hand to me and said, 'Come with me to my garden, for I don't want to die alone.'

And I took her hand and we stayed here together and talked of many things until she could no longer speak sensibly. But even then she held my hand tightly and would not let it go until she was taken. I wrapped her in a sheet and dragged her to the chapel to lie with the others. I had to make her coffin with my own hands. She—"

"Be quiet. I don't want to hear this," Lorenzo said hoarsely. "Leave me."

"I cannot leave you. What she said in this garden has worth and meaning for all of us. She said she had no regrets about anything she had done. She only wished that she had taken more time to nurture and appreciate the people around her as she had this garden."

"Is that all she said?"

"No, but it was all much the same. Live in the rose gardens of life, live fully and well, and do not fear the thorns." She paused. "She did say one more thing. But that was much later, when the pain had nearly crazed her and she no longer knew of what she spoke. She said, 'I love you, Lorenzo.'"

He stiffened as if she had struck him. "She was . . . an extraordinary woman and my very good friend." His voice was uneven. "Naturally, you will not repeat her words, as they could be misunderstood."

"You don't have to protect her any longer, Lorenzo," Sanchia said softly. "And certainly not me. I would not even tell Lion this, but you have the right to know. Because I think you are one of the gardens Caterina didn't get a chance to nurture and bring into full bloom."

He was silent, gazing out over the charred garden. "It was not an easy death?"

"No, none of them died easily."

Lorenzo's hands suddenly clenched on the reins. "She was—" When he spoke again his voice was so low she had to strain to hear. "I thought I was . . . empty inside, but she was there all the time."

"She'll still be there as long as we remember her."

"Yes." Lorenzo turned his horse and Sanchia felt a thrill of pity as she saw the stark desolation in his usually expressionless face. "But she's not here in this garden any more. I thought perhaps she might be."

Sanchia turned Tabron to follow him, but he suddenly reined in and glanced sharply over his shoulder at the blackened wreckage of the marble bench in the arbor. He tilted his head to one side as if he were listening.

"What is it?" Sanchia asked, puzzled.

"Nothing." His gaze was still on the arbor. "I thought I heard something."

"What?"

"Bells." He turned and rode slowly out of the garden. "It must have been the wind rustling through those burned bushes, though I could have sworn I heard the jingle of bells. . . ."

Eighteen

I'm sorry, Lion," Sanchia said softly as her gaze first wandered over the blackened remains of the *Dancer* at the dock and then to the wreckage of the three ships in the yard. Seeing this senseless devastation filled her with the same sadness she had felt when riding through the streets of Mandara. "Is there nothing you can salvage?"

"As you can see, the shipyard is still intact. But what is a shipyard with no ships? It takes a good two years to build just one and nothing to show for it until it's sold. I'd have to start over." He got off Tabron and lifted Sanchia down. "And I'm not sure I have the heart for it."

"You have the heart for it," Lorenzo said as he dismounted. "Wounds may leave scars, but they don't change what we are." He grimaced. "And what I am now is stiff, odorous, bad-tempered and likely to become more so if my needs are not met quickly. Where is your shipwright? No wonder Damari wreaked such havoc when we're able to ride into the yard in bright daylight unchallenged."

"I hired Basala because he was an excellent shipwright, not a soldier, Lorenzo. It's just a little past dawn, and he's probably still asleep." Lion nodded toward the small brick house a short distance away. "Why don't you go see if you can rouse him?"

"I shall." Lorenzo strode toward the house. "Which service will certainly entitle me to the first bath."

Lion turned to look back at the *Dancer* and said haltingly, "I cannot offer you a great deal now. Everything I owned at Mandara was destroyed. My only wealth lies in the shipyard in Marseilles, and it may bear no fruit for many years. I can give you no more than a plain roof over your head and plain food on the table."

Sanchia gazed at him in disbelief. "*Dio*, Lion, I have never had anything of my own. A roof over my head is all I'd ever ask. I knew the life I tasted in Mandara could never be mine."

"It *will* be yours," Lion said as he whirled and faced her. "Someday I'll build you a castle more beautiful than Mandara and you'll reign there like a queen."

"Like Caterina?" Sanchia shook her head. "It's not the life I want and it wasn't the life she wanted either. Not at the end."

A spasm of pain crossed Lion's face at the thought of his mother's death. "What do you want then?"

"Work. Peace. Children." Sanchia found the tears stinging her eyes. "Yes, children. I think I should like a son like Piero."

Lion touched her cheek with gentle fingers. "Lorenzo is right. Wounds heal, *cara*."

"I'm already healing." Her lips trembled as she tried to smile. "It will take time and there will be scars, but I will heal. Thank you for being so very kind to me."

"Kind?" He frowned. "Did you think I'd use you ill after all you've been through?"

"No, I only wanted to—"

He cut through her words. "You'll have work

aplenty during our first years and, if God is willing, you'll have your children, but I can't promise you peace. I'm not a peaceable man." He put his fingers on her lips as she started to speak. "And there's no reason you shouldn't have the castle, too. If you have no inclination to rule it yourself, then raise one of our children to watch over it."

She studied his face. He was healing also, but it was perhaps even more difficult for him than for her. He had suffered not only the loss of his loved ones but all that he had built these last years. She remembered the expression on his face when he told her of the joy he took in building after a life filled with destruction. Now in order for his wounds to heal he must build again and with a lavish hand. "That seems a sensible plan. I will take your castle." She pretended to think. "And a stable full of fine horses, and a palazzo in the country and—"

"Stop." He was smiling faintly. "You'll have to give me many sons to work in my shipyard to make it flourish enough to provide you with all those riches."

She smiled back at him. "That was my intention. One to be master of the castle, one to send exploring to distant lands, one to help you in the family business. I think we should have at least five children if that would be of no bother to you. Shall we—"

"Lord Andreas, you honor me with your presence." Basala was hurrying toward them, a warm smile on his thin, intelligent face as he struggled into his leather jerkin. "May I express my regret at your loss? God has not been kind to you of late. When your man arrived here with the news of the burning of Mandara"—he shook his head—"what a blow to you, my lord."

Lion nodded. "You issued them the sum Lorenzo requested?"

Basala nodded. "But there is not much left in the coffers." He hesitated. "Have you decided what you'll do here? I do not wish to hurry you, but the guilds have been most insistent I either release their members or put them to work again."

"We will talk of that later." Lion gestured to Sanchia. "You remember Madonna Sanchia. As you can see, she's once more in dire need of clothing. Can your good wife find something for her to wear?"

"If she has nothing herself, I'm sure she can persuade the master carpenter's wife to accommodate the madonna."

"That would be most generous of her," Sanchia said. "I understand your wife furnished me with two gowns when we left for Genoa. I'm sorry I was too ill to thank her at that time."

"She was glad to be of help and my lord was most generous. He gave her thrice their value." Basala studied Sanchia. "May I say you look considerably more robust than you did then? You were so pale and wan I thought you'd surely die before you reached Genoa. Is your hand healed?"

"Entirely, except for a slight stiffness in one of the fingers."

"But it must have been a long and terrible illness to turn that pretty hair white. The same thing happened to my second cousin who underwent—"

"White?"

"Madonna Sanchia needs to bathe and rest, then break her fast," Lion said quickly as his hand grasped Sanchia's arm and urged her forward. "If you please, Messer Basala."

"Of course, of course. This way. I believe my wife is already heating water for a bath for Messer Vasaro." The shipwright hurriedly led them toward the house.

"White?" Sanchia asked in bewilderment. "What did he mean?"

"It doesn't matter, *cara*. It only makes you more beautiful."

Then they were in the house and Sanchia was meeting the shipwright's cheerful, vigorous wife, Lisa. It was not until Lisa Basala led Sanchia to a small antechamber for her bath and left to go to the kitchen to heat more water that Sanchia's question was fully answered.

She stood before a highly polished oval of brass and gazed at her reflection with wondering eyes. The face in the mirror was the same face she had always known, smooth, unlined, the face of a woman still in her sixteenth year. It was the hair framing her face that was changed. A single lock of startling white shone against the dark auburn of the hair brushed back from her left temple.

So the Medusa had not left her untouched after all.

"I told you it only made you more beautiful." Lion stood in the doorway behind her.

"Why didn't you tell me?"

"Women are sometimes strange about such things. I didn't want to disturb you. It wasn't important."

She reached up to touch the shining white streak. "Another scar."

"No." He moved behind her and pressed his lips to her left temple with the same infinite gentleness he had displayed toward her since she had awakened in the winery. "A medallion of courage." Then he was gone, leaving her to gaze at the familiar stranger.

Lion and Lorenzo were deep in conversation when she entered the salon two hours later but broke off immediately when they saw her.

"That shade of blue is entrancing on you, but I admit I do miss your barbaric blanket," Lorenzo said as he rose to his feet. "Gowns are rather ordinary, are they not?"

"Basala and his wife will return shortly and we will have dinner," Lion said. "I sent him to make a few arrangements, and his wife went to the *mercato* to see about having shoes made for you."

Sanchia came forward and stood before them. "Those 'arrangements' wouldn't be concerned with purchasing passage for me on the first ship to Marseilles?"

Lion stiffened. "And if they are?"

"I would not go." She held up her hand to stop his protests. "Do you think me so simple I wouldn't guess your plan? You intend to whisk me off to a place where you think I'll be safe while you both go after Damari. I would have had to be blind and deaf not to notice the two of you whispering and plotting on the way here from Mandara."

"We didn't want to disturb you," Lion said. "You said yourself you wanted peace."

"But not until I've earned it."

"*Santa Maria*, who could have earned it more than you? What you went through at Mandara should have earned you a lifetime of peace."

"Not while Damari's alive."

"Lorenzo and I will attend to—"

"No." Sanchia met his gaze. "After Solinari I just wanted to forget what Damari had done to me, but for what happened at Mandara there can be neither forgiveness nor forgetfulness."

"*Cristo*, Sanchia. I will not involve you again with that bastard."

"Then I'll involve myself," she said fiercely. "You forget I was *there*. I have memories that will be with me all my life and there must be justice. I will not be able to bear to remember what he did unless I can remember he was justly punished and I had a part in seeing to his punishment. Do you realize what he did to Piero? He was only six years old and—"

"Shh, we know, *cara*. We know."

"And Caterina. She didn't deserve to die. None of them deserved to die."

"She's right," Lorenzo said abruptly. "She's entitled to her part in this, Lion."

"And is she entitled to the danger? You saw what happened to her at Solinari and then we had ducats aplenty to pave our way. Now we only have our wits against Damari and his condotti."

"Then they'd better be exceedingly sharp wits." Lorenzo moved over to the window to stand looking out at the ruined hulls in the shipyard. "And we obviously need all the help we can muster. If you won't take her, then I will."

Lion made a violent motion with his hand. "Damn you, Lorenzo, what if I—" He broke off as if afraid to speak the thought gripping his mind.

"What if you lose her, too? Don't worry. You're so

besotted with Sanchia that you'd probably die gloriously defending her and therefore have no time for foolish regrets."

Sanchia gazed at Lorenzo blankly and then began to laugh. The laughter was tentative, rusty, but still it was laughter and she felt the knot of anger and sorrow within her miraculously loosen. "That has all the macabre logic I would expect of you, Lorenzo."

"I am always logical."

"I don't like it." Lion shook his head wearily. "But I obviously can't move either of you."

"It's very wise of you to surrender, for you may well need Sanchia." Lorenzo turned away from the window. "Because I won't be able to help you with Damari."

Lion's gaze narrowed on his face. "That is your choice, of course."

"You think I back away from the task?" Lorenzo shook his head. "But you speak only of Damari. You've forgotten that he wouldn't have been able to do what he did if he hadn't had the approval and support of Borgia and the pope. Damari was the sword, but the Borgias were the ones who wielded it. In my eyes it's Cesare and Alexander who bear the brunt of the blame."

"Certainly a good portion of the blame."

"And consider this, throughout his entire career Cesare Borgia has adopted whatever methods he found at hand to conquer the cities in his path. The ploy Damari used to defeat Mandara had the advantages of economy and complete devastation. Who is to say Borgia will not choose to use the plague again if the need arises?"

"Dear God," Sanchia whispered.

"Exactly. If justice is to be done, it must be done to all three." Lorenzo smiled. "And, as I'm the most qualified for the task, I'll volunteer to be the dispenser of justice to the noble house of Borgia."

Sanchia and Lion gazed at him in astonishment.

"You would kill the pope?" Sanchia whispered.

"Do you not believe he deserves it? He's totally corrupt, a man who has lusted for power his whole life long. Did he not buy the papacy with blood and ducats?

Does he not have the blood of any number of people on his hands?"

"No one is saying the world would not be better off without him." Lion hesitated. "But, *Dio*, it would be hazardous, if not impossible. Both Borgias are surrounded by guards at all times. How would you manage it?"

"I have no idea. Something will come to me. I'm most ingenious when offered a challenge of this magnitude." Lorenzo paused. "But you may be sure their deaths will not be easy."

He had asked if Caterina's death had been easy, Sanchia remembered, and she had told him that none of the deaths at Mandara had been easy.

"So Damari is mine," Lion said.

"And Sanchia's. Don't be selfish, Lion." Lorenzo turned toward the door. "I'm going to Cesena to make a few inquiries regarding the whereabouts of Duke Valentino. I should be back in a few days. Will you still be here?"

Lion nodded. "I've decided to sell the shipyard to Basala and keep only the one in Marseilles. It will take that long to complete the transaction."

Sanchia looked at him in surprise. "You're leaving Italy?"

"*We're* leaving Italy. There's nothing here for us now. I told you once that Mandara was my country." He shrugged. "And now there is no more Mandara."

Lorenzo nodded. "It's best to put Mandara behind you." He opened the door. "We'll talk more when I return."

Lorenzo returned on the evening of the third day as he had promised.

"Borgia has left for Rome," he announced. "He departed almost immediately after he was paid a visit by Damari. The good duke was said to be in excellent spirits, so it's safe to assume that he journeyed to his father with the Wind Dancer."

"And Damari?" Lion asked.

"He was planning on returning to Solinari 'to dispose of Andreas at leisure,'" Sanchia quoted bitterly.

"But he won't stay there long. It will worry him that I haven't launched an attack on Solinari, and he'll need to know if I've spread the disease so he can take steps to protect the Borgias. He'll probably come here to Pisa first." Lion frowned. "And bring enough men to make sure we have no chance to resist him."

"Then I believe it's time to complete our plans," Lorenzo said with a faint smile.

Lion nodded. "And to put them into motion."

The next morning Lorenzo left Pisa for Rome.

The following day Lion and Sanchia departed for Florence.

It felt very strange to Sanchia to be riding through the same Porto San Friano from which she had departed those many months ago. Yet it had not actually been so long, she realized with a slight sense of shock. They had left Florence through this gate in early March and it was now only late July. It seemed a lifetime since Lion had come to Giovanni's shop for that frightened, nervous child.

She was thinking of that other Sanchia as if she were some other person entirely, she thought sadly. Well, and so she was.

"You're very quiet." Lion asked, "Are you weary?"

Anxiety threaded his voice and Sanchia tried to smother the impatience it aroused in her. His cosseting at first had brought her a sense of security and comfort she had badly needed, but now that she was stronger it was unbearable. "I was thinking about how many things have happened since I left Florence. I'm no longer the same person."

He flinched. "Who would not change after the punishment I've dealt you?"

"You meant me no harm."

"That didn't stop harm from coming to you. I am to blame."

Sanchia sucked in her breath. Lion's pampering,

the way he avoided touching her as if she were one of the holy saints instead of a woman he wanted, all stemmed from his sense of blame. "Who knows what would have happened to me if I had stayed here?" she asked softly. "It could have been as bad. No place is entirely safe."

"If I hadn't taken you away, you would never have known Damari."

"But there was already a Caprino in my life."

"It's not the same."

Dio, the man was stubborn. It would obviously take more than words to change his mind. "Do you think Giulia will help us?"

"We'll find out shortly. Her *casa* is—" He broke off with the sharp intake of breath of a man struck an unexpected blow.

Sanchia looked at him in alarm. "What is it?"

"Nothing. I just forgot about the doors." Lion reined in and sat looking at the magnificent bronze doors of the baptistery of the cathedral of Florence, his eyes glittering with sudden moisture. "Ghiberti's Gates of Paradise. When Marco and I were boys my father brought us to Florence whenever he visited Lorenzo de' Medici. My father insisted I go with him to the palace to learn the ways of dealing with princes, but he permitted Marco to run free. Marco was giddy with joy. He was drunk with the art of Michelozzi and the ideas of Alberti, the beautiful statues and the paintings." He stopped, unable to go on for a moment. "And most of all he loved those bronze doors. He'd get up before daybreak so he could see the first light of dawn strike them, he'd go four streets out of his way to catch a glimpse of them. Once he said to me, 'Lion, if I could sculpt something as beautiful as those doors I'd never ask for heaven. I'd stand outside all day long and ask everyone who passed, Did you see them? Did you really look at them?'"

Sanchia swallowed to ease the sudden tightness of her throat. "I grew so accustomed to walking by the cathedral that I scarcely noticed the doors."

"Not Marco. Beautiful things were always new to

him." He shook his head. "But most of us do forget to take notice of what is familiar to us. It's only when they're lost that we realize how we valued them."

"That's true." Sanchia wanted desperately to comfort but knew there was nothing she could say to ease the depth of suffering she sensed in him at this moment. "But perhaps if we remember that, we can learn to—"

"It's not *enough*. It's too late." His hand tightened with sudden violence on the reins. "I want him back! I want all of them back, Sanchia."

She was silent, gazing at him in an agony of tenderness.

Then he straightened his shoulders and deliberately loosened his grip on the reins. "I'm behaving foolishly," he said gruffly. "I'm not a boy to cry for what's beyond my reach." His gaze shifted to her face. "I've distressed you."

"Distressed *me*?" She was exasperated. She could feel the tension and sorrow coiled within him, but he allowed her only an occasional fleeting glimpse before he walled it up inside himself again. "It's you who are in distress."

"Nonsense. All goes well with me." He nudged Tabron forward. "Come along. Giulia's *casa* is on the next street."

Giulia Marzo looked up warily from her account book as the maid showed Lion and Sanchia into her chamber. "What a surprise to see you, Lion. I believe you stated the intention of never visiting me again." She looked from Sanchia to Lion. "I see you still have your little slave. Has she brought you pleasure?"

"More than I've brought her." He gently pushed Sanchia down on a chair by the door. "Sit down, *cara*. Since Giulia is failing in courtesy, we must take our comfort where we may."

"When did you do otherwise?" Giulia asked dryly. "As I remember, you always did exactly as you pleased." She paused. "As it pleased you to kill Caprino."

"Did his death disturb you?"

She shook her head. "In truth, you did me a favor. I moved quickly and took over a number of Caprino's enterprises. Being a woman, I was not able to assume fully Caprino's place, but let us say I now possess considerably more power than when last you saw me."

"I rejoice in both your success and my small part in it." Lion's tone was mocking. "Though I must confess I was tempted to slice your pretty throat as I did Caprino's."

She stiffened, and her gaze darted to the bellrope across the room. She forced a smile. "Why would you want to do that?"

"Caprino had only one way of learning that our destination was Solinari. Naturally, I put a few questions to him about the name of his informant." Lion smiled. "The only reason I didn't come after you, Giulia, was that I blamed myself for mentioning it within your hearing, and Caprino said he suspected you withheld the information until you thought it would do him no good. His venom was so great that I was forced to believe him."

Giulia let her breath out in a rush of relief. "I meant no harm. It was only business."

"And you're an excellent businesswoman, are you not?" Lion took a step closer. "That's why I'm here. I have a proposition to make."

Giulia's eyes glinted with sudden interest as she leaned back in her chair. "I'm always ready to listen to a proposition as long as there's profit in it."

"There's profit. I wish you to draw Damari to Florence. Sanchia said you had dealings with the man at one time."

"Once." Giulia made a face. "However, I acted through Caprino."

"But he knows your name?"

"Of course, everyone knows of my casa. He asked Caprino specifically for one of my women."

"Do you know what he did to her?" Sanchia asked fiercely.

"It was not my concern," Giulia said quickly. "The girl made no objection to going. In truth, she was filled with happy anticipation."

"She could not have known—" Sanchia shook her head. "He is a monster."

"It was not my concern," Giulia repeated, adding in a lower tone, "he was not supposed to kill her. He cheated me."

Sanchia gazed at her in disbelief and opened her mouth to speak, but Lion cut in quickly, "We wish you to send a message to Damari telling him you have Lionello Andreas and his slave, Sanchia, under your roof. Say we fled to Florence and begged you to take us in, and that you hear he will pay dearly to get both into his hands."

"Why would you come to me instead of Mandara?"

"There is no longer a Mandara."

"Indeed?" Giulia was clearly astonished. "It seems you have more reason to want vengeance against Damari than I believed. What is your purpose in drawing him here?"

"What do you suppose?"

Giulia nodded. "And he wants you enough to come here to capture you?"

"More than enough."

"And how much are you willing to pay for my help?"

"Five hundred ducats."

"It's not enough. There is risk aplenty."

"It will have to do. I have no more to give you."

"I will think on it." Giulia stood up. "Come back tomorrow."

"I want your answer now," Lion said bluntly. "And I'll have it now."

Giulia smiled faintly. "You were not always so impatient." She hesitated, a frown furrowing her wide brow. "Very well, the bargain is struck."

"Good. We'll speak more on this later." Lion helped Sanchia to her feet. "We have no place to stay until Damari arrives. Will you give us two chambers?"

"Two?" Giulia's smile became malicious. "If you require two chambers, she must not be giving you as much pleasure as you claim. I warned you it would be so."

"Sanchia has been ill." Lion turned to the door.

"And she is not well yet. Will you give us accommodation or not?"

"Certainly. It will be my pleasure." Giulia moved gracefully to the door. "Perhaps it's best that I have you under my eye. I don't think it would be safe to tease Damari with a prize he wants and then not be able to produce it."

"You have only to offer, not produce." A sudden sharpness had edged Lion's tone.

Giulia smiled sweetly over her shoulder. "A mere slip of the tongue, *caro*. Come this way. You'll naturally occupy the chamber that pleased you in the past, and we'll find something suitable for the girl."

"I am *not* ill," Sanchia hissed at Lion as they followed Giulia down the hall. "I'm quite well now. Why did you tell her—"

Giulia had stopped before a door and abruptly turned to face them. "This will do for you, Sanchia." She opened the door. "I'll send up a tub and hot water for a bath." She sniffed delicately. "That horse odor is quite reminiscent of the way you smelled when first you came here. I do hope you've gotten over your aversion to soap and water."

Sanchia bit her lip to keep back the stinging reply that trembled on her tongue. She must not let the woman anger her. Lion had said they needed Giulia. "Thank you, I would like a bath."

"Will you need me?" Lion asked, the familiar frown of concern on his face.

"No, I will *not* need you. I'm perfectly well." Sanchia entered the room and slammed the door behind her, immediately resenting the sound of Giulia's low laugh.

Why was she so angry? She should have ignored Giulia, not let the woman's manners prick her. Yet there was no doubt Giulia's spite had disturbed her composure. It was stupid to let Giulia trouble her when she had not done so in the past.

But then she had not known she loved Lion.

And she had not known how it felt to have him inside her body, the hot, dizzy pleasure as he plunged and lifted her to his every stroke.

Santa Maria, her body was coming alive, stirring with lust and anticipation at the thought of the next time Lion would come into her.

Not only her body, but her emotions were being reborn. She was experiencing lust, anger, jealousy. Yes, jealousy of the hours Lion had spent in Giulia's bed. Jealousy of her beauty and her knowledge of how to please him. It was clear the woman wanted him still; she had made no overtures, but the invitation had definitely been implied. Would that invitation be accepted?

Lion had possessed no woman since he had taken Sanchia that night in the tower room, and no one knew better than Sanchia that he was a man of strong desires. Sorrow had emptied them both of everything but tenderness and the desire to comfort and receive comfort, but, if she was coming alive, who was to say that Lion's desires were not also awakening?

Cristo, and what a damnably inconvenient time for that to happen with Giulia Marzo at hand not only to stoke but to appease his lust.

Sanchia took herself to task—she had been through so much she had thought she was done with petty emotions.

She knew suddenly she wanted desperately to live fully . . . to feel, to nurture her rose gardens as Caterina had told her to do. She wanted to bear children and know love as it was meant to be.

The Medusa had left her alive and by all that was holy she would *live* that life.

Nineteen

"Forgive me, Messer, but I understand you have a room to let."

"Then your understanding is at fault." Luigi Sarponi had a deeply creased, heavily jowled face, and the scowl now twisting it was obviously meant to discourage and intimidate. "I have no room to let and, if I did, it would not please you. My house is not for such as you. Find somewhere else to stay. There are plenty of lodgings going begging since summer is here. Rome in summer isn't a healthy place to be."

"Are you not Luigi Sarponi?"

"I am."

"And did you not work in the kitchens of His Holiness until the month of April three years ago?"

Luigi nodded warily. "I did."

"Then you're exactly the man to whom I wish to speak. Allow me to present myself.

am Lorenzo Vasaro." Lorenzo took a step forward and, as the light from the candle on the table fell fully on Lorenzo's face, Luigi instinctively took a step back.

"We have many matters to discuss." Lorenzo smiled. "And I think after we have had that discussion you will find you do have a room to let."

"You speak in riddles." Luigi Sarponi poured wine in Lorenzo's wooden goblet and then his own before sitting down at the scarred table across from him. "What do you want of me?"

"Only what you want for yourself." Lorenzo leaned forward across the table. The light from the tallow candle cast shadows beneath his high cheekbones and lit the crystal coldness of his eyes. "What you've wanted for over three years."

"And what is that?"

"The death of the Borgias."

Sarponi went rigid. His gaze searched Lorenzo's impassive face. "You are misinformed."

"Because you've not shouted your hatred of them to the four winds? If you had done so, I would have no use for you." Lorenzo smiled. "But if I should be wrong and you have no interest in the subject, I've no wish to bore you. Should I leave your house?"

Sarponi lowered his gaze to his goblet. "Why did you come to me?"

"I've been asking questions, very discreet questions, but I find my inquiries are usually answered."

"I can see how they would be," Sarponi said sourly. "And after you leave, they cross themselves and pray to the saints you'll never come back."

"Exactly." Lorenzo chuckled. "But you do not fear me, do you, Luigi? I did not think you would. I've heard you're a surly, bad-tempered rascal who fears neither God nor the devil."

Sarponi lifted his goblet to his lips. "Neither God nor the devil can do any more to me than they've done already."

"Which of them took your son, Luigi?" Lorenzo asked softly.

Sarponi paused for an instant and then drank deeply and set his empty goblet down on the table. "The devil." He looked up to meet Lorenzo's eyes. "What do you know of my Mario?"

"I know he was murdered one night by a masked band roving the streets of Rome. They killed and mutilated for the pleasure of it, and I know that shortly after his death you resigned your position as second cook in the kitchens of His Holiness to take a far less lucrative position in the kitchens of Messer Obano. You gave no reason for leaving the Vatican, and it was assumed Messer Obano paid you a fat bonus to come to him."

"But you do not believe it?"

Lorenzo shook his head. "Rumor has it that Cesare Borgia led the band that murdered your son. Indeed, there are stories he and his bodyguards still find it amusing to indulge their tastes in that fashion, but now they tend to go abroad to do so."

"They are not stories," Sarponi said hoarsely. "It is the truth. What is the blinding of an artist or the murder of a boy to the great Il Valentino? The duke and his father are in league. Alexander sits on the papal throne and we kiss his feet and he lets his beloved son indulge in any act of cruelty and—" He halted the rush of words and drew a deep breath. "Mario was not like me. He possessed a sweet nature and always had a smile for everyone. He was apprenticed to become a cobbler. I told him he should become a cook like me, but he said as long as people had to walk he would not go hungry."

"You're sure it was Borgia who killed him?"

"He was attacked only a short distance from here and was not dead when he was brought home to me. He had eight sword thrusts through his body but he was not dead." Luigi gazed blindly at the flickering flame of the candle. "They toyed with him. They felt safe because of their masks, you see."

"But he still recognized Borgia?"

"No, it was the medal. Borgia's cloak fell open and

Mario saw the order of St. Michael that the French king had given the duke. Il Valentino takes great pride in the gift and wears it always."

"But you said nothing to anyone?"

Luigi's lips twisted. "Who would I tell? His Holiness? Or perhaps Michelotto Corella, the duke's favorite assassin? No, I would only have ended up in the Tiber. But I will no longer serve either that serpent in the Vatican or his vile offspring." His gaze shifted from the candle to Lorenzo. "Are you going to kill me now?"

"Why should I do that?"

Luigi shrugged. "It occurred to me you might be one of Borgia's assassins tying up loose ends."

"But still you spoke to me."

"I have no great fondness for life anymore. I have no wife and my son is dead." He rubbed his neck. "I work, I come home, I sleep. There's little reason to fight to hold on to such a life."

"I have no intention of killing you."

A spark of interest flickered in Luigi's dark eyes at Lorenzo's slight emphasis on the last word. "Borgia? Truly?"

"Both Borgias." Lorenzo smiled. "With your help. Do you not think this project could stir a bit of interest in you?"

"Possibly," Luigi said cautiously. "But how can they be murdered? Both go about with guards."

"I wasn't thinking about a knife between the ribs."

"Poison? There's no taster at the Vatican, but that's because none is needed. One of the guards is in the kitchen the entire time the meal is prepared and accompanies the servants to the dining hall."

"Hmm, I didn't know that. It's a circumstance that may present difficulties."

"Difficulties?" Luigi laughed shortly. "The guard never takes his eyes off us. It will be impossible."

"The Borgias will be dead within a month's time."

Luigi started to argue, then stopped and studied Lorenzo's face. "I . . . I believe you."

"But will you help me?"

Luigi hesitated. "You want me to go back to work at the kitchen of His Holiness?"

Lorenzo nodded. "And help me to get work as a cook's helper there also. I understand the duke has been dining with his Holiness at almost every meal since his return from the Romagna."

"They say his pox has flared up again and he won't be seen abroad." Luigi shook his head. "You don't look the part of a kitchen lackey."

"Then you must help me to change my appearance so that I do."

Luigi regarded him critically. "Perhaps if you don't gaze at anyone directly. Your eyes—"

"I'll be as shifty-eyed as you could want me to be."

"And you're too clean. You must have clean hands, but a bit of grease and dirt on your face and hair would help." He smiled maliciously. "And no more baths for you. You smell too sweet."

Lorenzo flinched as he glanced at Luigi's unkempt gray hair. "I'm sure no one is a greater authority on the subject of dirt. I place myself entirely at your disposal." Lorenzo paused. "Agreed?"

Luigi nodded slowly. "Agreed."

"*Bellissima*," Lion said as Sanchia opened the door at his knock.

Sanchia made a face. "At least I no longer smell of horse."

"I thought you would like to visit Elizabet and Bartolomeo this evening. Then we could sup at the tavern on the piazza. It will be more pleasant than eating here."

Sanchia brightened. "Could we? I was going to visit them tomorrow, but I would like to see them right away."

"And they will want to see you."

Her smile faded. "I'll have to tell them about Piero."

"I've already paid them a short visit to advise them you were coming. I informed them of Piero's death."

Sanchia felt a surge of warmth at his thoughtful-

ness. Then Lion gently took her arm in a protective
clasp and escorted her down the hall. "You've suffered
enough. Now it's time to lean on me and let me take the
burdens."

He was doing it again, she thought worriedly,
treating her as if she were the helpless child Bianca had
been. She must do something to put a stop to it.

Yet after they had paid their visit to Elizabet and
Bartolomeo she was passionately grateful to have his
strength to lean on again.

"What's wrong?" Lion's gaze was fixed anxiously on
her face as he led her toward the piazza. "You seemed
happy enough when you were with the newlyweds, but
now you look . . ." He seemed to search for a word.
"Melancholy."

"It's nothing." She felt the foolish tears brimming
and determinedly blinked them back. "It's stupid of me,
but I suddenly feel . . . alone. Elizabet and Bartolomeo are so happy and busy with their own lives. They
don't need me anymore, do they?"

"Didn't you want it so?"

"Oh, yes. I told you I was being foolish." She walked
faster, not looking at him. "I suppose it's because I feel
they're now as lost to me as Piero."

"Sanchia." Lion's hand grasped her arm. "You're
not alone while you have me."

She swallowed. He was showing her that exquisite
gentleness and sweetness again, as if she were a frail
invalid who needed great care or she would slip away
from him. Perhaps that was the way he did view her, she
thought with sudden panic. What if he felt no passion
for her, only guilt and responsibility?

Suddenly, she saw where she must lead them.

"You're right. I'm not alone. I have you and
Lorenzo." She walked faster. "No, I don't really have
Lorenzo. No one has Lorenzo now. Except perhaps you.
Do you think he does well in Rome? I did not like—"

"It's not only Elizabet and Bartolomeo, you've been
acting strangely since we arrived at Giulia's *casa*. If you

wish to withdraw from the plan, only tell me and I will go another way."

"I don't wish to withdraw. Why do you persist in thinking I'm afraid? I'm not afraid of Damari."

"Then what do you fear?"

"Nothing." She broke away from him and hurried on ahead. "And I'm not hungry. I think I'll go back to the *casa* and go to bed. You go to the tavern without me."

"You should eat. You've had nothing since—"

"I'm not hungry." She was running, dodging through the crowds of people as she had when she was a thief in these very same streets.

"Sanchia!"

She ignored Lion's shout and kept on running. She heard his steps pounding behind her on the flagstones but he did not overtake her until she was running up the stairs to the second floor of Giulia's *casa*.

His hand was rough on her shoulder as he spun her around. "What in God's name is wrong with you? Are you ill?"

"No, I'm not ill." She pulled away from him and finished climbing the stairs. "I'm not weak or afraid." She hurried down the corridor toward her chamber. "And I'm not going to shatter if you say a harsh word to me."

He had caught up with her again and his hand on her arm brought her to a halt. "That's fortunate, for I'm about to say a number of harsh words." His eyes were glittering with anger as he dragged her down the hall, threw open the door to his own chamber, and pulled her inside. "I do not deserve this, Sanchia." He slammed the door. "I know your state is delicate but—"

"My state is not delicate," she said through her teeth. "How many times must I tell you? But perhaps you wish to think me delicate so you have the excuse not to touch me. Then you will feel free to summon Giulia Marzo here and—"

"I don't want Giulia in my bed," he shouted.

"Why not? You told me once that you would not touch me if she was near."

"I lied. I was angry that you stirred me so."

"But now I do not stir you with anything but pity. So why should you not take Giulia to your bed?"

His hands hovered around her throat as if he'd like to strangle her. "*Cristo*, is this my reward for patience? You do not stir me? *Madre di Dio*, I even wanted to take you in the winery when you were helpless and grieving and balanced on the edge of madness. I, too, was grieving but my body did not recognize or respect that grief." He dragged her into his arms, and her hands slid to his tight, muscular buttocks. "I'm so angry with you I want to beat you, but still I want you." He pulled her into the hollow of his hips and she felt the hardness of his arousal against her. "Tell me, am I stirred, Sanchia?" He did not wait for her answer but lifted her in his arms and carried her to the bed. "I do not want Giulia. I want you!"

He tossed her on the bed and flipped up the skirt of her gown and undershift. He untied his points and his manhood sprang boldly free. He moved quickly between her thighs. "Does this feel as if I'm stirred, Sanchia?"

He plunged deep, wildly grinding his hips to reach the quick of her.

She cried out, her hands reaching out blindly to clutch at his shoulders.

He froze. "Did I hurt you?" His fingers moved between them, petting her, arousing her. "It's your own fault. Did I hurt you, dammit?"

"No," she whispered. "It's only—"

"Then *take* me."

The rhythm was wild, hard, almost brutal in its hunger and passion. Her head thrashed back and forth on the pillow as she attempted to keep from screaming with the intensity of the lust shuddering through every muscle and nerve in her body. She tried to help him but she was shaking too badly to do anything but hold him. He was trembling, too, she realized dimly, his breathing harsh, his chest moving in and out as if he were running.

He cried out and threw his head back, his strong

neck arching, his body going rigid as if he had been struck by an arrow. "Sanchia, I can't hold—"

"Don't!" Her own pleasure exploded in a fiery release that left her stunned and weak.

Minutes later she felt him leave her and carefully pull down her skirts but she was still too dazed to open her eyes. Something cold and metallic pressed against her lips. "Drink this; it will restore you."

She opened her eyes to see his set face above her. He was still angry with her, she realized dazedly. She raised herself on one elbow and took the silver goblet. "I have need of restoration."

He flinched. "You made me angry."

"I believe it. You weren't gentle."

"It was your own fault," he said fiercely. "What manner of man do you think I am? You could expect nothing else."

She took another sip of wine. "I remember you told me I must take you into me whenever you had need. At least, you didn't push me up against a tree this time."

He scowled. "I suppose you're going to try to leave me again. Well, I won't permit it. If you want me to tear up your bondage papers, you must wed me." He glanced away from her. "It will not be a bad life. If you do not anger me, I'll try to be gentle with you."

"Wed you?"

"Why are you surprised? I told you I would give you marriage if I could. *Dio*, we even spoke of children."

She shook her head. "I never thought of marriage for me. It seems strange . . ."

"Then think on it now. For I will not let you go."

She nodded solemnly, her lashes lowering to veil her eyes. "I shall think of it."

He frowned. "You've thought long enough. What say you? I'm no longer as wealthy as—"

"Yes."

"You agree?" He gazed at her uncertainly. "You're not angry with me?"

She tried to smother a smile. "What would be the use? You would not change." She paused. "Thank the saints."

His gaze narrowed on her face. "You do not mind my roughness?"

She shook her head. "It is a part of you. I cannot separate the roughness from the gentleness. I cannot say 'Yes, I will love this side of Lion Andreas, but no, I will not love the other side.' I love the entire man."

A slow smile lit his face. "Truly?"

"Truly," she said softly. "I love the lust and the gentleness and the stubbornness and the—What are you doing?"

"Undressing you." His laughter was joyous. "I wish to give you more lust to love. We will deal with the rest later." He met her gaze and said softly, "But this time we will take our time and I will also show you gentleness." He grimaced. "If I can."

And Sanchia's laughter joined Lion's as she fell back on the bed and welcomed him once more into her arms and into her body.

"Why did you do it?" Lion's fingers were gently stroking the shining white lock at her temple. "I'm not a fool. I know you deliberately forced me to anger when I only wanted to show you I could give you honor and sweet words."

"I wanted to bring you back to me and it was the only way I could think to do it. I realized I was coming back to life and I wished you to travel the same road with me." She paused. "And perhaps I was a little afraid. You were so different . . ."

"Most women would have applauded the difference. Why would you be fearful of it?"

She laughed shakily, and brushed her lips against his bare shoulder. "I am a slave. Slaves are not treated with gentleness and sweet words. It made me uneasy." She paused. "For a while I even wondered if perhaps you felt it your duty to care for me because of the service I did at Mandara."

"Not duty—love. I honor you for what you did at Mandara, but I loved you long before." He was silent a moment. "Will you wed me?"

She raised her head to look at him in surprise. "Of course. I told you I—"

"Now. We have time before Damari comes. We will go to the priest tomorrow and make the arrangements."

She gazed searchingly at him. His expression was taut, strained. "Why do you feel the need for such haste?"

"I want you to be mine. Is that not reason enough?"

And he wanted her to be protected by his name if by chance they were not successful in killing Damari, she realized, chilled. He wanted her safe, if death took him from her. Her cheek lowered to nestle in the hollow of his shoulder. "It is reason enough. I would like to feel you are mine also," she whispered. "Yes, let us go to see the priest tomorrow."

"What do we do here?" Luigi asked testily. "The sun is too hot for strolling in the woods. I have no liking for all this greenery and fresh air."

"You have no liking for anything that you cannot brew in a pot or cauldron." Lorenzo's reply was absent as his gaze searched the trees and shrubbery on either side of the path. "I wonder how you ever came to beget a son. You like neither man, woman, nor beast."

"I concocted a fine mulled cider one night and imbibed so much the scullery maid appeared as appetizing to me as a glazed piglet with an apple in its mouth. She birthed Mario nine months later and left him in a basket in the kitchen when she ran away with a sailor. A father at my age!" Luigi mournfully shook his head. "I was so angry when I saw the babe that I burned the goose I was roasting."

"What a charming love story. It arouses not only pathos but also the palate. I'm sure you were a splendid father."

"I got used to it," Luigi said in a growl. "After a time I even . . . liked it."

Lorenzo darted him a glance. "How old was the boy when he was killed?"

"Seventeen." Luigi walked in silence for awhile. "I talked to Simonedo about you yesterday."

"Ah, the illustrious master of the kitchen. What does he think of my work?"

"He thinks your wits are addled. He says you sidle around the kitchen like a scared snake and never say a word."

"Well, you told me not to look at anyone. I thought it best not to speak either."

Luigi grunted.

"You do not agree?"

"Maybe. It's true your tongue has the sting of a scorpion. Simonedo says you work hard enough, and he thanked me for my recommendation. What think you of the guard who watches the food preparation?"

"An extremely sharp-eyed individual."

Luigi nodded. "Laraba has the eyes of a falcon. The Borgias have used poison often enough themselves not to be careful in choosing a good man, and with Laraba, we'll have to be magicians in order to slip poison into the food."

"I agree." Lorenzo had stopped, his gaze on a tall shrub abounding with clusters of delicate pale rose blossoms. "Is that not a pretty sight, Luigi? I wasn't sure I could find this beauty here on the outskirts of Rome. In my own birthplace of Naples you see these bushes frequently, indeed they grew in my garden. Ah, how lovely it was to see the first flowering in spring. Hand me the hatchet."

Luigi scowled as he handed the hatchet to Lorenzo. "I don't know why I had to carry the hatchet anyway."

"It was only sensible. You're built like a bull and have a comparable strength. Why should I be the beast of burden when you're far more suited to it?"

"And now you're taking the cuttings of silly bushes? I warn you, I'll not let you plant them in my little patch of a garden. That's only for my herbs."

"Luigi, I'm truly hurt you won't share your plot of earth with me." Lorenzo was quickly chopping several large branches from the bush. "Now what is better? A spot of blossoming beauty for the eyes or herbs and vegetables for the stomach?"

"The stomach. You'll not plant your stupid flowers in my garden."

Lorenzo sighed as he handed Luigi back the hatchet. "Oh, very well." He gathered the branches up in his arms. "I guess I'll have to find something else to do with them."

"I've sent the message to Damari," Giulia said as soon as Lion opened the door in answer to her knock. "Santini is to deliver my letter. Caprino used him once before, so Damari will recognize him and perhaps feel safer." She smiled. "Santini is one of the assets I acquired from Caprino's demise. He's a reliable man and trustworthy as long as an opponent's bribe is not too great."

"We cannot ask more than that, can we?" Lion asked. "A bribe or a threat can be equally effective to control a wavering loyalty."

Giulia's smile faded. "What is your meaning? Do you think to threaten me?"

"Only if it's needed."

Giulia's gaze went past his shoulder to Sanchia, who still occupied the big bed across the chamber. Her lips tightened. "I see you will no longer have need of the other chamber."

"No." Lion paused. "We go to the priest today. We plan to wed before the week ends."

"Wed?" Her eyes widened. "You'll wed her? But why should you—" She quickly schooled her angry expression. "I suppose you must do as you think best." She turned away. "I will tell you when I receive word from Damari."

"You're getting twigs and branches all over my floor," Luigi complained. "I won't pick them up, you know."

"My dear Luigi, I'm well aware you keep nothing clean in this hovel but your pots and trenchers." Lorenzo chopped another outcrop of lance-shaped leaves from the branch between his knees. "And I'm sure you'll suffer no profound distress from the mess I'm adding to this disaster of a room."

"I didn't ask you to move in here." Luigi added, "Mario kept the house clean. I tried to tell him it was unhealthy but he would laugh and say, 'Papa, your fine food will have a foul taste if seasoned with dust. Come, we will spend the evening sweeping and polishing.'"

"And you've obviously done neither since he died." Lorenzo tore off a delicate pink blossom from the branch and tossed it at Luigi, striking him on his cheek. "Admit that you like having me here. I give you someone on whom to vent your bilious spleen."

"I do not like you here. Why should I?" Luigi picked up the blossom and sniffed at it. "You're not good company as was my Mario. You only waste my hard-earned money by burning my candles to read your fine books and speak only to make mock of me."

"But I also eat your delicious cooking with an appreciation you don't encounter every day."

"That is true," Luigi said grudgingly. "You're no fool when it comes to the important things of life. Perhaps that's why I tolerate you."

"Perhaps." Lorenzo put the now denuded branch aside. "Hand me that other branch, will you?"

Luigi pushed the branch toward him across the table. "But I will go for no more walks with you in the woods. I could have spent the morning in far more important occupations."

"I realize it was a great sacrifice for you."

"And for what?" Luigi stood up and began to gather the discarded twigs and branches from the floor. "To give you something to whittle." He carried the bundle of branches to the hearth and dumped them on the stones.

"What are you doing?" Lorenzo asked mildly.

"I'm certainly not tidying up after you," Luigi said quickly. "You can clean up your own mess. I only thought to save myself from carrying in fresh wood for the evening fire."

"A very practical thought." Lorenzo lowered his

gaze to the branch between his knees as he sliced off another twig. "But I really wouldn't do that if I were you."

"Why not?"

"Because, if you strike flint to those branches," Lorenzo cut off another blossoming twig, "within a very short time we will both be conspicuously dead."

"You're trembling." Lion's hand tightened on Sanchia's as they walked up the steps to the cathedral. "There's no reason to be frightened." He smiled. "After you've braved the plague, marriage to me cannot be so bad."

"It's not fear." Sanchia moistened her lips with her tongue. "I don't know why I feel so uneasy."

"Are you not content with this marriage?"

She nodded. "More. I am happy with this marriage. I love you. I will always love you, *caro*."

He leaned forward and brushed his lips to her temple. "As I will always love you." He stopped as they entered the dimness of the cathedral. "Wait here. I will talk to the priest." He genuflected and moved swiftly down the aisle.

She watched him walk down the marble aisle toward the priest, who had turned away from the altar and was gazing curiously at them. Lion was all that was strong, forceful, and beloved. She had never dreamed she would possess a love so powerful and passionate as this. Why then was she feeling this sudden anxiety at the thought of linking her life to Lion's?

Perhaps it was because she had read too many stories of noble courtly love and her own love was so very much of the earth and the living.

A ray of sunlight struck the stained-glass windows, and as it passed through, it turned into a rainbow, effulgently bathing Lion and the robed priest. The scent of flowers, incense, and candles drifted to Sanchia, enfolding her in their heady fragrance.

Lion turned away from the priest and held out his hand to her.

She genuflected and started down the aisle, her gaze fixed on Lion's face.

Then he smiled at her and she was suddenly filled with a sense of wonder and a joy as radiant as the light streaming through the windows. The radiance swept through her, lifting her up, until she felt as if she was sparkling with the same jewellike brilliance as the light surrounding Lion and the priest.

Dear God, it was so simple. Why hadn't she understood before what was so clear now?

Love, like life, was composed of plateaus and valleys, of serene silences as well as the clarion peal of trumpets. Pain and turmoil were necessary. . . . How else would they learn to appreciate moments such as this?

Splendor.

Twenty

Why have you chosen to meet me here?"
Damari gazed at Giulia with suspicion. "Why
not at your own *casa*?"

"This is a pleasant enough inn, a safe
distance from Florence." Giulia turned away
from the window overlooking the stable yard.
"I see you've brought a sizeable detachment
of your men. I assumed it would be so."

"I will not lose Andreas or the woman
again."

"But you cannot lose what you do not
have." Giulia paused. "Yet."

"I *will* have them."

"If the price is high enough." She motioned to the men in the courtyard. "And
you'll not take them away from me with those
numbers. I have the money to muster thrice
this force to guard what is mine."

"You? A whore?"

"Did you not recognize Santini? He's only

a sample of what I've taken from Caprino. I shall soon be the most powerful woman in Florence. Caprino was a clever man and I learned much from observing him over the years."

"I do not deal with women."

"I know. You prefer to abuse them." She shrugged. "I've not forgiven you for Laurette. It will drive my price higher."

Damari hesitated. "You have them? Truly?"

"In the palm of my hand. They came to me to ask me to help them lure you into their net. They offered me five hundred ducats. I warned them it was not enough to satisfy me, but Lion was foolish enough to believe me when I finally agreed."

"And how much would satisfy you?"

"Fifteen hundred ducats."

"Ridiculous. You'll take far less."

She shook her head. "If you want Andreas and his whore, you will pay my price."

Damari seethed with fury. The greedy slut meant what she said. "Where are they?"

"Safe from you." She smiled. "But not from me."

Damari's hands closed into fists at his sides. "I will pay a thousand ducats, you filthy strumpet."

"I don't like being insulted. The price will now be sixteen hundred ducats."

"You daughter of filth, you cannot—" Damari, seeing her expression, tried to smother his rage. "I will pay your price."

"Excellent."

"But I do not have that large an amount with me. You'll have to wait for payment. When I return to Solinari I'll send you the fee."

She laughed in genuine amusement. "I am to trust you?" She shook her head. "By all means go back to Solinari, but without what you came for."

"I tell you, I do not have the ducats here."

"Then we will have to think of something else." She was silent a moment. "I will bring them to you at Solinari. We will exchange the merchandise for the ducats on the spot."

"How will you get them there? Andreas is no fool."

"But he trusts me." She added, "With reservations. It's difficult for a man to believe a woman who has given him pleasure would betray him."

"I want his woman too. For such a price I'll not be cheated of her."

"The woman also," Giulia agreed. "God knows I have no fondness for her."

"How will you do it?"

"As you so delicately pointed out, I am a whore and therefore familiar with many powders and potions to make the women in my house more compliant. A little bigger dosage and Lion and his little slave will sleep all the way to Solinari." She lifted a brow. "Unless you want me to kill them? It's all the same to me."

"No," Damari said. "I want them alive."

"I thought that would be your wish. Well, you'll soon have them both at Solinari to do with as you please."

Damari felt a sweet surge of pleasure that almost submerged his anger and frustration at the arrogance of the bitch. Well, perhaps the whore would have a surprise waiting for her when she rode through the gates of Solinari. She had a streak of iron within her that might be very exciting to break. "When?"

"Give me a day or two to ease their suspicions and then I'll slip the powders in their wine." She moved toward the door. "It can be no longer, as they're expecting me to receive a message from you any day."

"Then in a week's time?"

She nodded as she opened the door. "If all goes well, you can expect them to be delivered to you one day next week."

"Why not slip the branches into the pile meant for the fires in their bedchambers?" Luigi asked. "You said the smoke would kill."

"It's not a certain enough method," Lorenzo said. "It is August and a fire is not needed often. We might wait weeks for a fire to be lit and even then, if the chimney is clean and draws well or if they do not come too close, the fumes might only make them ill. No, it's best to use the branch as a spit to roast the meat for the table. The wood of the branch will poison the food as it cooks."

Luigi stooped and picked up one of the long branches, gazing at it in fascination. "What bush is it that bears death as well as pretty flowers?"

"The oleander." Lorenzo smiled at him. "A very useful plant. There's not one part of it that's not deadly. One leaf will kill a man. Even the nectar of those 'pretty' flowers will send a man to his grave."

"You're sure they'll get enough poison in the meat to do the task?"

"No, but it's our best chance." Lorenzo lifted his goblet to his lips and gazed at Luigi over the rim. "Now you remember what you're to do?"

"I'm not stupid. You've told me enough times," Luigi said sourly. "I slip the branches into the kitchen woodpile tomorrow morning."

"But today you make sure the chimney in the kitchen is drawing strongly." Lorenzo added grimly, "Even if you have to sweep it yourself. If you don't, I may find myself as dead as His Holiness since I'll be tending the spit."

"You know the scullery maid usually tends the spit."

"Tomorrow I will tend the spit. Create a new sauce with which to baste the meat and insist to Simonedo that you cannot trust the maid with the task. That will give you a reason to keep others away from the hearth. We don't want anyone breathing the smoke and becoming ill before the meat is done. Immediately after the meat goes on the spit you claim illness and leave the kitchen. I'll slip away as soon as the meat leaves the kitchen and join you here. Be ready to depart Rome at once."

"A new sauce is not created overnight," Luigi said, outraged and ignoring all the details except the one most important to him. "It takes time and many efforts before the right mixture is blended in the right proportions. Anyone who knows anything about fine cooking knows you cannot create a sauce—"

"Perhaps for common, ordinary cooks, but you tell me you're extraordinary."

"You know I'm extraordinary."

"Then prove it. A new sauce by tomorrow morning."

Luigi scowled. "You believe you are very clever. Well, I refuse to commit the sin of desecrating one of my dishes. We will murder the Borgias next week."

Lorenzo shook his head. "Everyone knows Cesare is importuning his father for fresh funds for a new campaign. He may not be in Rome next week."

"But I cannot concoct . . ." Luigi frowned fiercely. "Honey. Perhaps I can use honey with just a sprinkle of cinnamon . . ."

Lorenzo smiled with satisfaction as he leaned lazily back in his chair and stretched his legs out before him.

"Why is Giulia being so kind to me?" Sanchia asked as she turned in a circle before Lion. "Look at this gown. It must be one of the finest in her wardrobe, yet she not only gifted me with it but also sent a servant to alter it. Do you not think that's strange?"

"It's a very pretty gown. I like those blue ribbons on the bodice. Perhaps white does not become her as it does you."

"She looks beautiful in anything." Sanchia made a face. "And don't tell me you haven't noticed."

"I notice only the beauty of my own wife, as is proper in a virtuous married man." A glint of mischief appeared in his dark eyes. "Though I admit I prefer you without the gown. It could be that Giulia is not being kind to you, but cruel to me." He tilted his head and looked at her critically. "Yes, you're entirely too fully clothed. Send the gown back to her and we'll—"

A knock interrupted and they both turned as the door opened to Giulia's touch. She carried a silver tray which held three silver goblets and smiled as she moved gracefully toward them. "That gown looks enchanting on you, Sanchia. It never suited me." She set the tray on the polished table and picked up two of the goblets, handing one to Sanchia and one to Lion. "I found this Mandara wine you brought the last time you came to see me, Lion. You always liked it better than any wine Florence could boast." She picked up her own goblet. "Drink," she said softly, her smile lighting the luminous beauty of her face. "And then I'll tell you of the good news that's come to my ears regarding our friend Damari."

The whoreson chimney was not drawing well!

Dio, only minutes ago the flames had been drawing perfectly, and now it was casting thin billows of smoke into the kitchen!

Lorenzo turned his face away from the spit on which the honey-basted lamb was roasting and took a deep breath. Then, holding that breath, he turned back and leaned closer to the flames to peer up the chimney and try to see where the blockage occurred.

"How goes the lamb?"

Lorenzo turned to see the head cook, Simonedo, frowning impatiently at him.

Lorenzo hurriedly averted his gaze and muttered, "It's almost done, only a few more minutes, but the chimney . . ."

"What? Speak up, dolt."

"The chimney does not draw well."

"It's probably only another pigeon." Simonedo turned away. "There's a crook in the chimney and every now and then a pigeon flies down and becomes caught. We'll send a sweep up tomorrow to remove it. Douse the fire after the lamb is done."

A pigeon. Mother of God, a pigeon!

Lorenzo smiled grimly as he settled before the fire, carefully blocking the fumes from the rest of the kitchen with his body and trying to avert his face and take shallow breaths.

Cristo, if this smoke continued to billow, it was not only the lamb that would be done this night.

The pounding on the door was oddly erratic.

When Luigi threw open the door he saw Lorenzo on his doorstep.

"*Santa Maria,* why are you knocking? You've never showed me such courtesy since that first night you barged into my life. Where have you been? You should have been here hours ago. Did all go well?" Luigi grinned. "My sauce was superb. It's too bad the duke and His Holiness won't appreciate it. I was tempted to stay and hear the outcry." He paused. "Why are you just standing there? Come in and I'll give you a glass of spiced wine and you can tell me how Cesare choked on his own bile. You told me not to stay, but you couldn't resist lingering yourself, could you? It's just like you to deny me the pleasure but take it yourself."

"I did not stay."

"Then where have you been?"

"I became . . . lost."

"Lost? How could you become—" Luigi broke off and suddenly reached out a hand and pulled Lorenzo into the room and into the circle of light from the candle. He inhaled sharply. Greasy sweat coated Lorenzo's face and blank, dilated pupils dominated the gray of his eyes. "What happened?"

"A pigeon. Is that not amusing? A pigeon . . . in the chimney. I thought of everything but—"

"Why did you not leave or make some excuse to douse the fire?"

"We were too close."

"*Stupido. Idiotto.*" Luigi's dark eyes glittered in the candlelight. "You tell me to stop and get out if anything goes wrong and then you do this. You have the brains of an ox and no more sense than a beheaded chicken."

"I truly wish you would stop . . . calling me vile names." Lorenzo swayed, his eyes glazing. "I'm sure it's not proper behavior"—his knees buckled—"toward . . . a dying man."

"Madonna Giulia Marzo is at the gates with a wagon, my lord."

Damari felt a rush of excitement. "I've been expecting her." He stood up and motioned for the lackey to leave. "Let her in."

"She has a company of men with her."

"What!"

"She says she will not enter your gates without protection."

"How many men?"

"Fifteen."

The bitch was craftier than he had thought. Fifteen men were no threat to the palazzo, but there was a possibility he would have to let her return safely to her *casa* in Florence.

Damari cursed steadily beneath his breath as he strode out of the palazzo and across the grounds, his gaze fixed on the multitude of torches held by the soldiers beyond the gates.

He stood just inside the gates and shouted. "You have brought me what you promised?"

Giulia Marzo rode her horse forward from her position beside the wagon and smiled at him in the torchlight. "In the bed of the wagon. See for yourself."

"I will. Draw your soldiers away from the wagon." He turned to the guard. "Open the gate. Four of you come out and surround me while I'm beyond the gates."

A moment later he was kneeling on the hay in the wagon and peering down at Lionello Andreas and Sanchia. They appeared to be in a deep sleep, but he had to make quite sure.

He raised his hand and then brought it cracking down with vicious force onto Sanchia's left cheek.

She did not stir.

"Satisfied?" Giulia edged her horse closer. "My powders do not fail me. Now, my money."

"Come in and get it." He smiled. "But naturally I can't permit your hired soldiers to accompany you."

"Then I cannot permit you to take my merchandise." Her lips tightened. "I've gone to much trouble to bring them here, and you're beginning to make me angry. Perhaps I should forget our bargain and return them to Florence. I'm sure Lion is desperate enough to take your life to reinstate his offer of five hundred ducats."

"No!" He jumped down from the wagon. "Open the

gates," he called out as he strode through the soldiers toward the gate. "Someday, Madonna Giulia, I'll take great pleasure in introducing you to my friend, Fra Luis. As a matter of fact, he's at the palazzo now awaiting the arrival of Andreas and Sanchia. A pity you cannot stay and join us."

He stood aside and watched as the wagon and the riders rode through the gates.

He took a step nearer to the wagon, his gaze searching Andreas's face. "They're lying very still. You haven't killed them, have you? I want them ali—"

A sword was pointed only inches from his throat!

Lion's dark eyes glared fiercely at him as his blade jabbed at Damari's throat. How had that whoreson Andreas snatched a sword from beneath the hay and moved so swiftly? Damari's hand dropped instinctively to the hilt of his own sword.

"Do not draw it," Andreas said coldly. "I'd like nothing better than to slit your gullet."

"To me!" Damari screamed. "You fools! To me!"

"They're occupied at the moment," Lion said as he again pricked Damari's throat with the sword. "That was my first instruction to Giulia's men. As soon as we were through the gates, a sword point at the back of every guard."

Andreas's words were confirmed by the glance Damari darted them out of the corner of his eye. "You fool, there are more guards in the palazzo. You cannot fight all of them. We outnumber you."

"You won't for long." Andreas motioned to one of the soldiers, who immediately rode to the open gates and waved a torch in a wide arc three times. "There are some seventy-seven men waiting in the woods who will be here shortly. That should be a sufficient number since your men are hired men just as are these soldiers of Giulia's. They owe no loyalty to you, and I imagine the first thing they'll do once you're dead is strike a bargain so they can have their share of the sacking of the palazzo. They certainly won't waste time trying to vanquish a dead man's foes."

Sanchia was wriggling out of the wagon to stand

beside Lion. A livid bruise marked her left cheek, but her expression was as cold as Andreas's. "*Buona sera,* Damari. You said you wanted to spend more time with me, and I could think of no better place than Solinari."

"You seem very pleased with yourself," Damari snarled. "I must commend you on your endurance. You didn't flutter an eyelash when I struck you."

"I was expecting it." Sanchia gazed at him steadily. "And I should thank you. It was you who taught me endurance, Damari."

"And will teach you more. Fra Luis waits for you in the dungeon. You remember Fra Luis?"

"I remember." Sanchia shook her head in wonder. "Do you not realize that it's over? You're going to die, Damari."

He shook his head. "It's not my fate to die by the hand of such as you. I have a great destiny. I'll follow the Borgias to power no one could dream exists. My men will soon rush out of the palazzo and rescue me."

"They don't seem in any great hurry."

"Let's get it over." Giulia rode forward and reined in beside them. "I have no liking for violence."

"You betrayed me, you whore." Damari's face twisted with anger as he looked at her. "We had a bargain and you betrayed me."

"As you would have betrayed me," Giulia said. "In truth, I was close to aligning myself with you, but suddenly I asked myself why I should receive only sixteen hundred ducats when your palazzo must have so much more?" She motioned and a half dozen of the soldiers dismounted. "The maze. Beware, it's guarded."

She watched as the men drew their swords and started at a trot toward the south entrance of the labyrinth. "Sanchia obligingly drew a map for them to follow and Lion still had the key to the storehouse. We even have a wagon to carry away your treasures. The only question was whether I could obtain the services of this company of soldiers in time for our departure. Fortunately, that was resolved four days ago when they were unexpectedly released from the service of Lord

Gondolfo." She smiled mockingly. "Destiny, my lord Damari."

"You should have taken my ducats. This way you'll get nothing but a short sojourn in my dungeon."

"I'll get half of the treasure." Giulia paused. "But even if the reward were not great, I still might have sided with them against you."

"Then you're a fool as well as a whore."

She shook her head. "Laurette. Caprino told me once it was bad business to let any defeat go unpunished." She lifted her head and smiled again as she saw the rest of the company of soldiers thundering down the road toward the open gates. "You cheated me, but no one will ever try to cheat me again after they learn what happens here."

"Enough of this chatter," Lion said impatiently. He called to the captain at the head of the column, "Bind those guards and secure the palazzo." He turned to Damari. "And you will accompany us to the maze to wait for the treasure to be brought out of the storehouse."

An hour later the palazzo had been secured and the wagon loaded with paintings, large coffers of ducats, jewels, and golden plates.

Damari watched, agape, as treasure after treasure was carried past him. "It will do you no good. I'll get it all back. Just as I got the Wind Dancer back." He smiled maliciously. "Your Wind Dancer is gone forever, Andreas. It rests in the pope's private treasury and will stay there."

"I wouldn't be too certain. Forever is a long time, and it's said the Wind Dancer always returns to my family . . . eventually."

"Bah! It's gone forever. You will see."

"Perhaps, but you will not," Sanchia said. "Take off your clothes."

Damari whirled on her. "What?"

She motioned with the torch in her hand. "Your clothing. Take it off. Everything."

"I will not!"

She took a step closer. "Then let us see if your

destiny will guard your skin from a scorching." She shoved the flaming torch perilously close to his face.

He took a hurried step back and felt the point of Andreas's sword in his back.

"Bitch." Andreas's sword bit through Damari's jerkin and shirt and pain lanced through him. He began to undress, tearing off his clothing piece by piece in rhythm with his muttered curses. Finally he stood naked between the two of them.

"Light the north entrance of the maze," Lion called over his shoulder.

Damari watched as one of the soldiers loading the wagon seized a torch from a companion and ran toward the corner of the labyrinth.

"Now," Lion said softly. "Into the maze, Damari. You shouldn't object to dying there. As I remember, it's a place for which you have a great fondness."

"You're going to chase me through the maze?"

"Oh, no." Lion shook his head. "We're going to let the flames chase you. There's been little rain this last month. The hedges should take the flames easily . . . and spread rapidly, Damari. The north entrance will be blocked by flames in a few minutes." He nodded toward the opening in front of them. "We'll fire this entrance as soon as you pass through."

"If I pass through."

"Your choice. The sword or the maze. Does that not sound familiar? I admit I would prefer you to choose the maze. There's a certain justice in it." Lion's expression hardened. "I'll enjoy seeing you burn as Mandara burned."

"Perhaps the flames will spare you for your great destiny," Sanchia said softly. "As you spared the people of Mandara, as you spared that poor Laurette."

"They *will* spare me. You think you've bested me?" Damari shook his head as he turned and strode toward the entrance. "I'll live to see you all dead."

He smelled the smoke, heard the crackle of flames in the shrubbery behind him as soon as he entered the maze. The bitch and Andreas were wasting no time.

He could see a flare lighting the night sky ahead of

him. The north entrance was burning. He instinctively started to run, thorns tearing at his naked flesh as he brushed against the hedges. He would escape. He had to escape. His destiny must be fulfilled.

Those fools had forgotten there was a way out other than the entrances they had set afire. The west hedge through which Andreas and his brother had escaped had not been replanted. He could wriggle through the hedge and then hide in the shrubbery until they were gone.

His breathing grew painful as he ran. The damned smoke was growing thicker, causing his eyes to tear and sting.

Ah, just ahead was the hole in the hedge!

He sprinted forward and started wriggling frantically through the opening. He cried out as the thorns pierced his legs and buttocks and stabbed into his genitals. He would kill them for this outrage! He would kill them all!

"No, Damari."

He looked up and froze, no longer feeling the bite of the thorns and sharp twigs.

Sanchia was standing outside the circular opening in the hedge, a torch in her hand. Her expression was stern as she slowly shook her head. "There has to be justice." She lit the branches at the top of the opening. "Piero." She lit the left side. "Bianca." She touched the torch to the right side. "Marco." Finally she touched the flames to the bottom of the circle. "Caterina."

"No!" Damari heard himself screaming as he backed out of the opening as the flames licked at him.

The bitch stood there beyond the flaming circle looking as delicate and fragile in her white gown as the figure on a cameo.

"One more," she said quietly. She tossed the torch into the center of the opening. "Mandara."

The hedge blazed high, a solid sheet of flame.

He was going to die, Damari thought dazedly. No, it could not be true. He scrambled away from the flaming hedge and onto the path. He began to run down the path, trying to see through the ever-thickening smoke.

There had to be a way out. He was screaming the words, he realized.

The burning hedges were all around him now, the fire coming closer, still closer.

He turned the corner.

Another wall of flame!

No matter how swiftly he ran, he could not get away from it. The flame touched the naked flesh of his back, and in agony he threw back his head and howled. The rest of his flesh was catching fire as easily as had the hedges.

No, it could not be. He had a destiny. . . .

Lorenzo opened his eyes to see Luigi's scowling face above him. He swallowed and moistened his dry lips. "I take it I've yet to depart this earth, as you bear not the slightest resemblance to an angel."

"Why would you think you deserve heaven?"

"For killing two arch demons?"

Luigi shook his head.

Lorenzo made a face. "They didn't die?"

"Well, you didn't totally fail. The pope will probably die at any moment. They say he was administered extreme unction at vespers today." Luigi lifted a goblet of wine to Lorenzo's lips and fed him a sip. "And Cesare may yet succumb. The servants say he didn't eat as much of the lamb as his father, but he lies gravely ill in a sickroom above the Borgia apartments."

"How long has it been?"

"You've been ill for five days."

"And we're still in your house?" Lorenzo's gaze searched Luigi's face. "I told you to leave Rome at once."

"And why should I obey a man who's stupid enough to poison himself?"

"You stayed to care for me?"

"I stayed because I had no need to go. The fools think both His Holiness and his son fell victim to the same bad-air illness that's struck down nearly everyone in Rome." He grinned. "I told you that Rome in summer wasn't a healthy place to be."

Lorenzo began to laugh weakly. "No one is thinking it peculiar that they both fell ill on the same day?"

Luigi shrugged. "There are those few who murmur of poison, but they speak of the banquet that Alexander and the duke enjoyed at the vineyards of Cardinal Adriano Corneto on August fifth. They say the Borgias wished to poison Corneto but the goblets became switched. Corneto also—conveniently—has fallen ill."

"*Jesú*, that thought is as foolish as the other. Even I couldn't brew a poison that would delay the effect for almost two weeks." Lorenzo hesitated, considering the advantages of such a potion. "Though it would be a challenge to develop one. Since Cesare is still alive, perhaps I should think about it."

"Think about going back to sleep and getting well."

"Ah, you worry about me."

"I care nothing if you live or die." Luigi gave him another sip of wine and then gently wiped Lorenzo's lips with a surprisingly clean cloth. "Why should I? I just grow tired of cleaning up your vomit and hearing you moan. Who is Caterina?"

Lorenzo was silent.

"Don't answer me then. It's not really as if I want to know anything about you." Luigi set down the goblet on the floor and stood up. "Go back to sleep, and if you vomit again you can wipe it up yourself."

"Luigi."

Luigi turned to face him.

"I . . . thank you."

Luigi looked quickly away. "It will be much easier to get rid of you when you're on your feet than to drag your stinking carcass out the door."

"Have I ever mentioned the sweet eloquence of your discourse?" Lorenzo closed his eyes and rolled over on his side. "I'll sleep for a while, but awaken me in a few hours. There's something I must do."

"You can do nothing. You're as weak as a starving kitten mewling for its mother's teat."

"What a truly denigrating comparison." Lorenzo didn't open his eyes. "If I cannot do the task myself, then you must help me. Wake me . . ."

—————

"Hold the lantern higher. It's black as a chimney in this alley. Do you want me to stumble into the Tiber and drown?" Luigi tightened his grip around Lorenzo's slender form. "I know you have no fear for yourself. You'd probably float. They say the devil guards his own."

"My dear Luigi, it's humiliating enough having to submit to being carried like an infant without being insulted as well. Are we nearing the Vatican?"

"Just ahead," Luigi panted. "And you're heavier than an infant. About the weight of a boar dressed for serving or a side of beef before it's spitted and—"

"Stop." Lorenzo's tone was pained. "I realize you're enjoying my plight, but please refrain from comparing me to one of your dishes." He peered into the darkness ahead but could see nothing beyond the circle of the lantern light except the warm mist rising from the river. "If you continue in this vein, I'll be forced to walk and deprive you of this purely temporary feeling of superiority."

Luigi grunted. "And fall into a heap on the floor as you did when you tried to get out of bed?"

"I can walk—" He halted as Luigi snorted and then conceded, "A little. I just have to become accustomed to the idea that my limbs have only the consistency of pasta dough. I'm sure you appreciate that compand—Ah, there it is."

Luigi stopped short. "This is stupidity. We have no business here at this time of the evening, and those Swiss guards will cleave our heads like melons with their halberds. Let me take you back to the house."

"After I've patiently suffered all the insults and vilification you've heaped upon my hapless head? We will definitely go on." Lorenzo paused. "Or I'll go on. I don't think the situation will be as perilous as you believe, but, if you prefer, you can put me down and I'll go on alone."

Luigi muttered curses as he started toward the gates. "You have the brains of a peahen. The pope may lie dying but he's still the pope. The Vatican is guarded more closely than any palace in all of Italy, and Cesare's guards have formed a cordon around him while he lies helpless. There's no way you can kill him now."

"I know I cannot kill him. I must wait for another opportunity. That's not why we came."

"Then, by all the saints, what are we doing here?"

"The pope has something I want, and this is the best time to pluck it from his treasury."

"And now you think of robbing the papal treasury?" Luigi shook his head. "*Cristo*, do you know how difficult that will be?"

"Not difficult at all, if our timing is correct." Lorenzo's gaze searched the darkness of the courtyard. "And I believe it very well may be. Where are the Swiss guards, Luigi? Where are the mighty forces that guard His Holiness?"

Luigi frowned as his gaze wandered over the empty courtyard. "Why, I don't know . . ."

"It's as I thought: Confusion, turmoil, and disorder. When a great house falls it leaves terror and chaos behind. Take me to the Torre Borgia."

"The private apartments?"

"We must determine whether the pope is dead. Cesare wouldn't act while there was even a chance his father would live."

"Cesare is ill in his bed and almost as weak as you."

"But I'm here. Do you think Cesare is less determined than I? If he isn't there himself, his lieutenants will be hovering around the pope's chamber like vultures."

Luigi continued to mutter obscenities while he made for the Torre Borgia.

A loud crashing and excited laughter could be heard as soon as they entered the apartments.

"Judging by all this merriment, it's safe to assume Alexander is dead," Lorenzo said. "Put me down in that chair and go to the bedchamber and see what information you can gather from those poor souls attending His Holiness. No doubt they've become crazed with grief or they'd never see mirth in this sad occasion."

Luigi set him in the highback cushioned chair Lorenzo had indicated. "You will be all right?"

"Certainly. I shall sit here and enjoy studying Pinturicchio's magnificent murals. I'd heard they're truly the best things he's ever done."

"Murals! You study pretty pictures when the Swiss guards could rush in at any minute and cut off our heads?"

"Well, what else is there to do?" Lorenzo leaned back in the chair. "And I imagine you might find a Swiss guard or two in the bed chamber of the pope, but I seriously doubt if they'll be guarding him." He set the lantern on the table beside him and tilted his head to look critically at the mural. "I hear Alexander posed for that figure in the *Resurrection*. Do you think Pinturicchio caught his likeness?"

Lorenzo smiled as Luigi threw up his arms, turned and strode from the room.

Luigi returned only five minutes later. "The pope is dead and his valets are sacking his chambers. Burchard, the master of ceremony, is the only official on hand and he cannot stop it. He says the entire Vatican has gone mad. They're all trying to salvage what wealth they can before Alexander's death becomes widely known." He paused. "Michelotto Corella demanded the key to the papal treasury on behalf of Cesare not thirty minutes ago."

"Ah, then we're in time." Lorenzo straightened in the chair. "By all means let's proceed to the treasury."

"I was afraid you were going to say that. You're insane, you know. Corella is Borgia's assassin, his bravo, and obeys Cesare's orders without question. Rumor has it he even garrotted Madonna Lucretia's second husband when the man lay helpless in his bed."

"I've never admired stranglers. They lack subtlety and imagination and rely only on physical strength. I'm sure we can overcome such a dullard." Lorenzo struggled to his feet and stood, swaying. "Shall we go?"

"You expect to overcome Corella when you stand there weaving as drunkenly as a thieving butler of the wines?" Luigi sighed and picked Lorenzo up again in his arms. "Madness."

The doors of the treasury were thrown wide, and a stream of men wearing the scarlet-and-yellow colors of the house of Borgia were hurrying from the chamber carrying plates of silver and gold and large coffers.

"I told you this was madness," Luigi whispered as he set Lorenzo down in the shadows beyond a turn in the long hall. "There are too many of them."

"I only need one," Lorenzo said absently as he gazed surreptitiously around the corner. "That guard appears to be of my height and weight and there's no one coming down the hall behind him." He nodded at the man striding toward them down the hall before leaning down and reaching into his boot. "Be prepared to grab the coffer he's carrying. It's probably filled with ducats and we don't want them spilling out and scattering all over the floor."

"Why should he—"

The soldier came even with them and Lorenzo stepped swiftly forward, encircling the guard's neck from behind and jerking him the two paces around the turn of the hall. His poniard moved with lethal accuracy and his victim made no sound other than a soft expulsion of breath as the dagger entered his heart.

Luigi caught the coffer as it fell from the dead guard's hands. "*Maraviglioso*. What an artist you are. What a splendid butcher you would have made!"

"Drag him into that chamber and strip him." Lorenzo leaned weakly back against the wall. "Quickly."

Ten minutes later, with Luigi's help, Lorenzo had struggled into the guard's uniform and Luigi had hidden the naked corpse in a window embrasure.

"Now what?" Luigi whispered.

"Now I go to the treasury and get the prize for which I came." Lorenzo smiled. "And you stay here, my friend."

"You cannot even walk without staggering."

"Corella was obviously in a hurry and did not bother

lighting many torches. The hall is so dimly lit no one will notice whether I stagger or not."

"When you enter that chamber Corella will see you're not one of his men and throttle you."

"Then you'll not have to worry about carrying me back." Lorenzo started down the hall. "Stay here. If I don't return in ten minutes, leave the Vatican without me."

"I'll do it," Luigi vowed. "Why should I endanger my life for a madman? The minute you go into the treasury, I'll be gone."

The treasury seemed as far distant as hell from heaven to Lorenzo. Another Borgia guard strode out of the treasury staggering under the weight of the enormous pile of gold plates he was bearing. Lorenzo hastily averted his face but the soldier hurried by him without giving him so much as a glance.

Dio, the floor was quaking beneath his boots. Each step drained a little more of Lorenzo's strength, and by the time he reached the treasury door his limbs were shaking uncontrollably.

"It has to be here somewhere. His Grace said we were to be sure to bring it to him." A powerfully built man across the huge room was pushing aside heavy trunks filled with jewels and plates. "Search harder. It's a plain mahogany chest."

Corella, Lorenzo thought, as he stared at the bravo's grim expression. Relief flooded him as he realized he could not make out the features of either Corella or the other two soldiers in the chamber. There were only a few candles scattered about the enormous room and, if Lorenzo couldn't see Corella and his men clearly, then he must be equally cloaked by the gloom.

He stepped deeper into the shadow to the left of the door and bent over as if searching among the trunks and coffers as the other two guards were doing. His head started to swim and he clutched desperately at a large trunk until his vision cleared.

"There it is!" Corella pointed to the mahogany chest half hidden behind a five-foot golden vase on which a depiction of the Last Supper had been sculpted. "Take it."

As Lorenzo straightened and moved quickly forward, a short, stocky soldier also headed for the chest from the opposite corner of the room.

Mother of God, Lorenzo thought. He could scarcely walk and now he was being forced to run races!

Lorenzo reached the chest first, snatched it up, whirled, and started toward the door.

"Wait!"

Lorenzo froze, keeping his back toward Corella.

"Perhaps we can pour some of these ducats into the chest. We must make every trip count. Open it and see if there's room."

Lorenzo set the chest on the floor, unfastened the latch, and opened the lid. The emerald eyes of the Wind Dancer twinkled up at him as if in amusement at his predicament.

"No room," he said hoarsely. He slammed the lid shut, his fingers fumbling as he fastened it.

He picked up the chest and staggered toward the door.

"Is it so heavy? If you drop it, I'll lop off your *coglios, stupido.*"

"Heavy," Lorenzo muttered as he weaved out of the room. Perspiration beaded his forehead and he could feel the bile rising in his throat. The few steps remaining to the turn in the hall might just as well have been a mile.

He wasn't going to make it.

He couldn't make it.

He made it!

He felt himself jerked around the turn in the corridor and the chest plucked from his hands.

"*Santa Maria,* you're stubborn." Luigi tucked the chest beneath his right arm as his left arm encircled Lorenzo's waist. "Why couldn't you give up?" He walked Lorenzo down the hall. "Is it because you wish to make my life even more miserable than it is already?"

"You said you were going to leave."

"I decided I was in no hurry. I needed to rest after hauling your scrawny carcass across Rome."

"I see." Lorenzo smiled. "How fortunate for me. Could you loose your grip around my middle? You're cracking my ribs. I haven't been held so tightly by a man since my childhood in Naples. Are you sure you have no romantic inclinations toward the male sex?"

"For that insult I should loose you and let you sprawl at my feet." Luigi added quickly, "And I'd do it, but then I'd have to go to the bother of picking you up again. If I left you here, someone would remember that I recommended you for the pope's kitchen and I'd end up in the dungeons of Sant' Angelo too. It's certainly not that I care what happens to you."

"Certainly not." The moist night air felt good on Lorenzo's face, and he breathed deeply as they left the confines of the palace behind them. "I'd never make that mistake in judgment."

"That is good." Luigi's powerful arm tightened around Lorenzo's waist to support more of his weight. "A man would have to be a dunce to care what happens to a madman who'd risk having his neck twisted off by Corella just to steal from the papal treasury. What's in this chest to make you take such a chance?"

Lorenzo saw the dull, gleaming waters of the Tiber directly ahead and exultation surged through him as he realized there was no sound of pursuit behind.

Per Dio, they had done it!

"There's a gift in the chest. A special gift for a very good friend."

Twenty-One

Do you think he will come?" Sanchia leaned over the rail, her gaze anxiously searching the crowd milling on the dock below. "I don't see him and it's almost time to sail."

Lion gently pulled the hood of the laurel green cloak over Sanchia's shining auburn tresses. "Lorenzo always keeps his promises. He'll be here."

"But what if—there he is!" She pointed to the familiar elegant figure moving lithely through the crowd. "He looks well. I was afraid the illness might have lingered."

"You worry about everything these days," Lion said indulgently. "He wrote months ago that he had recovered his health."

"Then why did he stay in Rome? Alexander was dead and he could not touch Borgia after the duke doubled his guards. I thought he might be ill and not wishing to worry—he's carrying something." Sanchia's eyes widened as she recognized the familiar mahogany chest. "Dear lord, it's—"

"The Wind Dancer." Lion's expression lit with excitement. "*Santa Maria*, he has the Wind Dancer!"

Pain knifed through Sanchia as memories swelled. The dungeon at Solinari, Piero's solemn, wondering eyes as he had gazed at the statue in the salon, the Pegasus staring sightlessly at Caterina and herself as they wept for their dead, Damari tying the Wind Dancer on his saddle as he unfolded horror after horror to Sanchia. Her hands clutched at the wooden rail with white-knuckled force.

"How in Hades did he manage this?" Lion turned and saw her face. "What's wrong? Are you ill again?"

"No." She tried to smile. "It brings back so many memories. Mandara . . ."

Lion's hand covered her own on the rail. "Mandara's gone. We're starting a new life, *cara*. The memories will fade."

"*Dio*, married over four months and still holding hands and cooing like turtledoves."

They turned to see Lorenzo striding up the gangplank. "It's enough to make me shudder." He came toward them, a smile on his face. "Or, as my friend Luigi would say more crudely, vomit."

"You are well?" Sanchia asked.

Lorenzo put the chest containing the Wind Dancer down on the deck. "Very well." His gaze searched her face. "And you, my dear Sanchia, are blooming."

"I'm with child," she said simply.

"Ah, that is good. Renewal." He turned to Lion. "I've brought you a present."

"I see you have." Lion clapped him on the shoulder. "*Madre di Dio*, how on earth did you get it?"

"On the night Alexander died I went back to the Vatican." Lorenzo grimaced. "Or rather Luigi carried me to the palace, for I was not yet myself. Michelotto Corella demanded the keys to the pope's private treasury the moment Alexander breathed his last and made off with a hundred thousand ducats, together with a fortune in plates and gems, and took them to his master, who was too ill to accompany him. I managed to appropriate the Wind Dancer while Corella was stealing whatever else his men could carry." A pleased smile touched Lorenzo's lips. "I understand Borgia was most irate with Corella for failing to bring him the statue with the other treasures."

"I imagine he *was* a trifle upset," Lion said dryly. "Borgia needs every asset he has since the papal monies have been cut off. I've heard he scrambled desperately to save his power even to striking a bargain with the new Pope Julius."

Lorenzo nodded. "I've been watching with great interest as he starts his slide to hell. You know that Julius has now imprisoned Borgia until he agrees to give the passwords that will cause his commanders to yield Borgia's strongholds in the Romagna?"

"You think he will do it?"

"Eventually. But that doesn't mean Borgia will be defeated. He's a brilliant man with a will of iron. It takes a great deal to rend iron, but I now have the time to make his destruction complete." He paused. "I've come to say farewell."

Lion stiffened. "It was planned that you come with us. You've changed your mind?"

"Borgia still lives."

"But you said yourself he's losing power."

"His destruction is not certain. I must make sure." Lorenzo met Lion's gaze. "Damari's death was too easy."

"I assure you he didn't find it so."

"He didn't have time to see everything he had built falling away from him. I'll make sure Borgia will be aware of every step of his downfall."

"Where do you go? Rome?"

"Perhaps." Lorenzo gazed down at the crowds on the dock. "Though I've been thinking about returning to Mandara."

"Mandara!" Sanchia gazed at him in bewilderment. "But there's nothing there."

"The vineyard is still there, and the winery. I could build a small cottage."

Lion shook his head. "You? In the country?"

"There's an order and symmetry to the growing of the grapes that has a certain appeal for me. The process is much like the bringing to harvest of any bold endeavor." Lorenzo started to turn away. "The vineyard's as good a place as any to watch and wait for opportunity to ripen."

"Wait." Lion gestured to the chest on the deck. "Take this with you."

Shock jarred Sanchia. "Lion . . ."

Lorenzo swung back to face him. "You don't want it?"

"Of course he wants it." Sanchia tried to steady her voice. "He loves the Wind Dancer."

"But I also love my wife."

"It's part of your family," Sanchia said. "You told me—" She drew a deep breath. "I would not deprive you of it."

A tender smile lit his face. "It's my choice, Sanchia. It would please me if you could feel toward the Wind Dancer as I do, but you cannot." He paused. "And I will not have it always near to remind you of what you suffered. You told me once that what I felt for you didn't compare with what I felt for the Wind Dancer. Perhaps you might have been right then, but you'd be wrong in saying it now."

"No, it will be fine. I can—"

"Hush, *cara mia*." His left hand reached up to gently smooth the silver lock at her temple. "It's settled. There's a legend that says the Wind Dancer always returns to my family. Its return now won't be by my will." He turned back to Lorenzo. "The Wind Dancer is yours, if you will accept it."

"I will accept it."

"I wasn't sure you'd want it." Lion smiled crookedly. "I seem to remember your saying you believed it was a siren luring men to destruction. After Mandara, I thought your belief would be doubly reinforced."

"I've changed my mind." Lorenzo gazed thoughtfully down at the chest. "It wasn't really the Wind Dancer that caused the destruction of Mandara. It was the ambition and greed of men. Damari and Cesare's ambition and Alexander's greed. Together the three of them might have conquered all of Europe. But in a convoluted fashion, it was the Wind Dancer that put a halt to all their plans." He stooped and picked up the chest. "I promise I'll find a good use for it."

"Lorenzo." Lion took an impulsive step forward. "Come with us."

Lorenzo shook his head. "You don't need me. Perhaps I'll come to visit you someday so that I may learn how fortunate I am to be free of the chains of domestic bliss."

"You will be welcome." Lion's voice was husky. "Always."

"Lion, you grow maudlin," Lorenzo said mockingly. "I must leave before you burst into tears and—"

"I would do so, if it would make you come with us," Lion said simply.

The smile faded from Lorenzo's face. "That was a foul blow. You . . . unman me."

"I love you well."

"Another blow." A sudden warm smile lit Lorenzo's face. "Farewell, my friend." He turned and strode away from them.

"Stop him." Sanchia clutched at Lion's arm. "Don't let him leave like this."

"I cannot stop him." Lion's eyes glittered moistly as he watched Lorenzo stride down the deck. "He's made his choice."

"And you're too honorable to try to make him waver in it." Sanchia's tone was exasperated. "You love him. He belongs to you. Have you not lost enough people who belong to you?"

"This is different. It's his right to decide."

"It's different only because you have the chance to claim him again." She saw the stubbornness in his expression and grew impatient. "If you'll not do it, then I will. I will not lose him too." She took a step forward. "Lorenzo!"

He looked over his shoulder.

"If you will not come now, promise you'll come when you finish what you have to do."

"Perhaps." He turned away again.

"Not perhaps. We *do* have need of you. Lion has a fancy to build me a fine castle. You know I have no training to run such an establishment. You must teach me."

"You will learn by yourself." He continued to walk away from them.

"It's going to have the finest rose garden in all of France. I'll need your help in planting it."

His stride faltered for an instant and then he continued walking.

"If our child is a boy, we'll call him Lorenzo."

"God help him."

"No, *you* must help him."

Lorenzo started down the gangplank.

"And if the child is a girl, we'll call her Caterina."

He stopped on the gangplank, the line of his spine suddenly rigid. It was a moment before he turned to face them. "Ah, Sanchia, I always did say you were a clever urchin."

His gaze was a warm caress, embracing them both. Then he turned and strode down the gangplank to be lost from sight a moment later in the crowd on the dock.

"Oh, Lion," Sanchia whispered. "Will we ever see him again?"

Lion's arms went around her from behind and drew her back against him. "I don't know." His lips gently brushed her temple. "You did your best."

"Because I love him, too."

They stood watching, still hoping he would return or that they might have a last glimpse of him. They watched even after the gangplank had been raised . . . even as the ship put out to sea.

"The breeze is cold," Lion said. "You should go to the cabin."

It was cold, she thought. The sky was as leaden gray as the sea, and the wind had a sharp bite to it. Not a promising day to start a journey.

"Soon. I want to stand here until I can no longer see the land. It seems strange to realize I may never return."

"Does that thought make you sad?"

"No." She hesitated. "Yes. I don't know." She nestled back against him. "My feelings change from moment to moment. Only one thing is certain. I want to be with you. All the rest will fall into place."

The coastline was barely visible now and she had to strain her eyes to see it. Soon it would be gone and they would sail into the unknown.

Dragons waited in the unknown, Lion had said on that night they had sailed toward Genoa.

Well, she and Lion were strong enough to defeat any dragon who dared hurl his flames at them. There might be struggles ahead in that unknown, but there would also be great rewards.

"You're very quiet," Lion said. "What are you thinking, *cara*?"

"Of dragons." She straightened and squared her shoulders as she turned to smile into his eyes. "And of splendor."

Epilogue

THE BUDDING

On April 12, 1504, the major strongholds of Borgia's forces in the Romagna were yielded to Pope Julius, and Borgia was released from his imprisonment. People expected Duke Valentino to flee immediately to his old friend and comrade in arms, King Louis XII of France, but for some mysterious reason, instead he sailed south to Naples, then in the hands of Spain.

On May 26, 1504, the Spanish forces in Naples arrested Borgia. They sent him by galley to be imprisoned at the Castle of Seville and later at the fortress of Medina del Campo.

October 23, 1504
The Vineyard, Mandara

"There's a messenger waiting for you in the stable yard," Luigi said sourly. "I suppose this means you'll let my dinner get cold."

"Not necessarily." Lorenzo pushed his chair back from the desk and strode across the room.

"I'll not keep it hot for you," Luigi called after him. "I'll throw it to the pigs."

"We have no pigs," Lorenzo shouted back at him.

"And whose fault is that? I've told you that we should have pigs. If you will buy no pigs, how can I make pork dishes? Thanks to your miserliness I'll soon forget all my skills."

Lorenzo stepped onto the stoop of the cottage and accepted a folded and sealed piece of parchment from a freckle-faced messenger who was little more than a boy.

"Dismount and come inside and refresh yourself."

The young man quickly shook his head. "I have orders to wait for an immediate reply, Messer."

Lorenzo broke the seal and opened out the fine leaf. Unsigned, the message consisted of only one line of script.

Is it enough?

"I'll return in a moment." Lorenzo wheeled and went inside the house to his desk. On the bottom of the letter he scrawled in bold, decisive script.

It is not enough.

He returned to hand the parchment to the messenger.

He did not bother to watch the young man's departure as he closed the door of the cottage.

THE FLOWERING

After Queen Isabella's death, King Ferdinand of Spain decided it would be a brilliant move to release Borgia and take advantage of his military acumen to make him his generalissimo in Italy. However, fate once again intervened to strike down Borgia's ambitions. The Castle Medina del Campo in which he was imprisoned was in Castile, and under the control of Ferdinand's daughter, Juana. There appeared to be no reason for her to turn on Borgia with such venom, but she did. On the day Ferdinand asked for the prisoner to be released, she had Cesare indicted on charges that he had conspired in the deaths of his brother, The Duke of Gandia, and Alfonso of Bisceglie, his brother-in-law. On September 4, 1506, Ferdinand finally abandoned his efforts to obtain Cesare's freedom and set sail for Naples without him.

October 15, 1506
The Vineyard, Mandara

The messenger from whom Lorenzo took the letter this time was not a boy, but a man in his prime who accepted a cup of mulled wine from a grudging Luigi while Lorenzo broke the seal and scanned the contents of the dispatch.

"Wait here." Lorenzo went into the cottage and straight to his desk. The terse message he had received was exactly what he had expected.

Enough?

The answer Lorenzo scrawled on the bottom of the letter was almost as brief.

Not enough.

He strode back out into the stable yard, gave the letter to the liveried messenger, and sent him on his way.

THE VINTAGE

Six weeks after Ferdinand sailed for Naples, Cesare Borgia escaped from the Medina del Campo and fled to Pampeluna, the capital city of his wife's brother Jean D'Albret, the king of Navarre. His brother-in-law welcomed him with wild enthusiasm, seeing the chance of using Borgia's military genius to further his own ambitions. The king spoke of supplying Borgia with new armies to start him once more on the road to conquest. However, Navarre was very poor, and in desperation Borgia sent an envoy to his sister Lucretia in Italy asking her to speed to him enough of the family art treasures to yield three hundred thousand ducats from their sale. The messenger was arrested on Pope Julius's orders.

Borgia also sent a message to King Louis of France begging him to pay the one hundred thousand ducats owed him as part of his bride Charlotte's dowry and also the sizeable revenues of his dukedom of Valentinois so that he might regain his former power and affluence. King Louis not only refused to pay either sum, he revoked Borgia's title, taking away his dukedom of Valentinois and stripping him of royal arms.

By March 1507 Cesare Borgia at the age of thirty-one was ravaged by the swiftly progressing and debilitating French pox and was without power, money, or land. Shortly after he received word from his steward, Don Jaime de Requesnez, of his loss of Valentinois, Borgia was ordered by the king of Navarre to subdue the rebel lord, Don Juan, count of Beaumont at Viana. Borgia was heading a garrison at Viana when an alarm was sounded that the garrison was being attacked. He jumped out of bed, dressed, and giving no orders to his men, flung himself on a horse and rode alone through the city gates. It was said later that Borgia was screaming and cursing and appeared completely mad. He rode alone into the enemy camp in a ravine nearby and attacked them, still shouting wildly and uttering oaths.

At dawn Borgia's soldiers rode out of the city and soon found Cesare Borgia's naked corpse hacked and pierced with twenty-three bloody, hideous wounds.

April 7, 1507
The Vineyard, Mandara

I grow impatient. What more could you desire? Enough?
Lorenzo's gaze lifted from the letter to the window across from his desk through which the scarred and blackened city walls of Mandara could be seen.

Then, with a faint smile on his lips, he picked up his

pen and scrawled a single word at the bottom of the parchment.

Enough.

May 21, 1507
Bourges, France

Lorenzo strolled down the long, gleaming corridor, his gaze lingering in admiration on the splendid paintings on the wall of the gallery.

The liveried page stopped and looked reproachfully back at him over his shoulder. "Please, Monsieur Vasaro, His Majesty is most anxious."

Lorenzo nodded, but his pace failed to quicken. "His Majesty has many fine paintings. Is that a da Vinci?"

The page nodded. "His Majesty admires Monsieur da Vinci very much indeed. However, there are many more beautiful objects in His Majesty's private apartments."

The page threw open the tall, beautifully paneled doors at the end of the corridor. "Monsieur Vasaro, Your Majesty."

King Louis hurried forward. "*Mon Dieu*, Vasaro, you took your time about it." He stared eagerly at the chest Lorenzo carried. "Is that it?"

Lorenzo nodded as he crossed to a Carrara marble table and set the chest on it. "Yes." He unfastened the chest and opened the lid. "As I promised."

He started to lift the Wind Dancer out, but Louis forestalled him. "No, let me." With reverent care Louis took the Wind Dancer from its velvet nest. "Ah, it's as exquisite as I remembered. I thought perhaps anticipation might be playing tricks with my memory." He cast Lorenzo a resentful glance. "Your obstinacy in this matter did not please me. Three years is a long time to wait."

"For me, also, Your Majesty." Lorenzo smiled. "But a bargain is a bargain."

"You could have relented. You didn't have to have everything to your exact specifications," Louis said peevishly. "I did what you asked. I told Borgia he would not be welcome here and forced him into Spanish hands. That should have been enough for you."

Lorenzo was silent.

"And do you know how difficult it was for my envoy in Juana's court to manipulate her into turning against Borgia? The woman is now tottering on the verge of madness."

"But he managed the task."

"Because I told him I would have his head if he didn't." Louis carried the Wind Dancer across the room and set it on a black marble pedestal. He took a step back, looking at the statue appraisingly. "I had this pedestal carved two years ago for the Wind Dancer. How do you think it looks?"

"Superb. You have exquisite taste, Your Majesty."

Louis was silent for a long time, staring at the statue. "Do you know that the soldiers at Viana who saw Borgia ride out that night think he meant to end his own life?"

"Then he's effectively barred his way to heaven, if he had not done so before."

"You would condemn his soul to hell as you did his body to the grave?"

Lorenzo did not answer.

"When he first came to my court I thought him the most charming, the most brilliant man I had ever met." Louis's gaze remained on the Wind Dancer. "He would have been destroyed even if I hadn't aided you, wouldn't he?"

"Perhaps, but it's not likely."

"You're a hard man." Louis grimaced. "And as sharp and cutting as a Toledo blade. I have use for you in my retinue. What say you to a post at my court?"

Lorenzo shook his head. "I have a fancy to go to Marseilles to visit friends who have recently been blessed with a child."

"A boy?"

Lorenzo shook his head. "A girl. They've named

her Caterina after the child's grandmother and say she resembles her in many ways."

"A pity it was not a boy. They must be disappointed."

Lorenzo smiled. "They don't appear to be."

"You are tired of your vineyard?"

"Let us say, it's time I nurtured something other than grapes. Perhaps I will plant a rose garden."

"You'll be disappointed. There is little profit in flowers."

"We shall see."

Louis took a few more paces back, frowning with dissatisfaction at the statue. "It does not look as well on the pedestal as I thought it would. The pedestal is not worthy of it. The Wind Dancer overshadows everything around it."

"So it does."

Louis fell silent again before bursting out with sudden defensiveness, "I did only what was for the best in destroying Borgia. It's only right and proper the Wind Dancer should be here at the royal court of France. All of the Italian city-states are fading in power, but France is beginning to shine like the sun. The Wind Dancer should belong to such a nation. Do you not agree, Vasaro?"

Lorenzo gazed at the statue and a curious smile touched his lips. "Yes, Your Majesty, I believe that France is now exactly the right place for the Wind Dancer."

An errant beam of sunlight streaming through the long windows surrounded the Wind Dancer in an aura of radiance, kindling the emerald eyes to brilliant life and striking the parted lips of the Pegasus at an angle.

And, for the briefest instant, the Wind Dancer seemed to smile.

AN AFTERWORD
FROM THE AUTHOR

I have interwoven fiction and fact so closely in *The Wind Dancer* that I believe clarification may be in order.

The historical customs, costumes, and political events of the day are as accurate as my research could make them.

Actually the black death devastated Europe's population during the fourteenth century, but there were still isolated outbreaks of plague during the fifteenth and sixteenth centuries.

As for the Borgias, the brilliance, greed, brutality, and ruthlessness of Pope Alexander and his son, Cesare, are well documented. Although there is no record of their sanctioning such an atrocity as occurred at Mandara, it's certainly not beyond the realm of possibility they would have done so. Both father and son did fall ill on that fateful day in August, and it was indeed assumed they had been poisoned. Many historians still cling stubbornly to the theory of attempted assassination, while others believe the Borgias succumbed to malaria after being bitten by mosquitoes while dining al fresco with Cardinal Adriano Corneto at his vineyards. Medical knowledge and records were so scanty at the time that neither claim can be substantiated.

Cesare Borgia's bravo, Michelotto Corella, did raid the treasury on the night of the pope's death. Alexander's apartments in the Torre Borgia were ransacked by his valets, and his body lay unattended all through the night. It's entirely possible that someone could have infiltrated the Vatican during that chaotic period.

The oleander is as deadly as I've indicated, and it did grow in Italy during the period of the Renaissance. Though, as Lorenzo says, the poisoners of the day were principally bunglers and lacking in skill, a master assassin such as Lorenzo Vasaro might well have discovered and used the plant to his advantage.

So much for fact.

Could the fictional portions of *The Wind Dancer* really have happened?

The Renaissance was an age of velvet and armor, of abject poverty and untold wealth, of plague and assassination, of saints and sinners, of Michelangelo and Machiavelli. It was a time when the world was being reborn and boldly shaped to fit the needs of the men and women strong enough to conquer and hold it.

Of course this story could have happened.

The spellbinding stories of those who are drawn
into the world of the legendary WIND DANCER
continue in Iris Johansen's . . .

STORM WINDS

A June 1991 Bantam Book
on sale in early May

REAP THE WIND

A November 1991 Bantam Book
on sale in early October

*Coming next in Iris Johansen's trilogy of
romances about characters whose lives
have been touched by the legendary
WIND DANCER*

STORM WINDS

ON SALE IN MAY 1991

STORM WINDS is set against the turbulence and promise of the French Revolution. Clever and daring banker Jean Marc must retrieve the Wind Dancer from Marie Antoinette for his ill and aging father. Jean Marc's schemes lead him from the danger of Paris to the tranquil gardens of southern France, to the perilous mountains of Spain. But soon his passion for the quest is overshadowed by his growing love for the one woman who can fulfill his dreams, the fiery artist Juliette.

In the following excerpt from STORM WINDS, we enter a scene in which Jean Marc, attacked and wounded, is being nursed by Juliette to whom he is wildly attracted, though feeling guilty, for she is quite young.

*J*ean Marc's temperature began to rise.

The fever lasted two hours during which time Juliette bathed Jean Marc with cool water and tried desperately to keep him from tossing and spilling out of the bed onto the floor.

During the middle of the night the fever receded and severe chills took its place. The chills racked him in great convulsive shudders and worried Juliette more than the fever had.

"I . . . have . . . no liking . . . for this." Jean Marc's teeth were clenched to keep them from chattering. "It should teach me well the foolishness of—" He broke off as another shudder ran through him. "Give me another blanket."

"You have three already." Juliette abruptly made a decision. She stood up. "Move over."

He gazed at her blankly. "What?"

She drew back the covers, lay down beside Jean Marc, and drew him into her arms. "Be at ease," she said impatiently as she felt him stiffen against her. "I'm not going to hurt you. I only seek to warm you. I often held Louis Charles like this when he had the night chills."

"I'm not a child of two."

"You're as weak as a puling infant. What difference does it make?"

"I believe a great many people would be happy to enumerate the . . . differences."

"Then we shall not tell them. Are you not warmer with me here?"

"Yes, much warmer."

"Good." His shivering had almost stopped, she noticed with relief. "I'll hold you until you go to sleep." She reached up and gently stroked his hair. A few minutes later she said impatiently, "You're not at ease. I can feel you hard as a stone against me."

"How extraordinary. Perhaps I'm not accustomed to females slipping into my bed in order to 'ease' me."

"As you say, the situation is extraordinary." Juliette levered herself up on one elbow and gazed sternly down at him. "You must not think of me as a female. It's not good for you."

His lips twitched. "I'll endeavor to dismiss your gender from my mind. I'll think of you as a thick, woolen blanket or a hot warming brick."

She nodded and again lay down beside him. "That's right."

"Or a smelly sheepskin rug."

"I do not think I smell." She frowned. "Do I?"

"Or a horse lathered from a long run."

"Do you have the fever again?"

"No, I was merely carrying the image to greater lengths. I feel much more comfortable with you now."

"You laugh at the most peculiar things."

"You're a most peculiar fem—sheepskin rug."

"You *are* feverish."

"Perhaps."

But his brow felt only slightly warm to the touch and the shaking of his body had almost stopped.

"Go to sleep," she whispered. "All is well."

A few moments later she felt his muscles relax and his breathing deepen.

At last, he had fallen into a deep slumber.

* * *

"You've painted long enough. Come here and play a hand of faro with me."

Juliette didn't look at Jean Marc as she added more yellow to the green of the trees in the painting on the easel before her. "What?"

"Play cards with me."

She cast an abstracted glance over her shoulder at him lying on the bed across the room. "I'm busy."

"You've been busy for four hours," Jean Marc said dryly. "And will probably be at that easel for another four if I don't assert my rights."

"What rights?"

"The rights of a bored, irritable patient who is being neglected in favor of your precious paints and canvas."

"In a moment."

She was conscious of his gaze on her back as she resumed painting.

"Tell me what it's like," he said suddenly.

"What?"

"Painting. I watched your face as you worked. Your expression was extraordinary."

Juliette was jarred out of her absorbtion into uneasiness. He had been in that bed watching her for hours every day and never before made comment. Her art was a private, intensely personal passion, and realizing he had been observing her so closely as she worked made her feel naked. "Painting is . . . pleasant."

He laughed softly. "I hardly think that's the correct term. You looked as exultant as a saint ascending the steps to heaven."

She didn't look at him. "That's blasphemy. I'm sure you know nothing of how a saint would feel."

"But you do?" He coaxed, "Tell me."

She was silent a moment. She had never tried to put her feelings about painting into words, but suddenly she realized she *wanted* him to know. "It's as if I were swathed in moonlight and sunlight . . . drinking a rainbow and becoming intoxicated on all the hues in the world. Sometimes it goes well and the feeling is so exquisite it hurts me." She kept her gaze on the painting so she wouldn't know if he laughed at her. "And sometimes I can do nothing right and that hurts me too."

"It sounds like an exceedingly painful pastime. But it's worth it to you?"

She nodded jerkily. "Oh, yes, it's worth it."

"Something beautiful?" he asked softly.

She finally glanced at him and found no sign of amusement in his intent regard. She nodded again. "Something beautiful."

A brilliant smile lit his lean, dark face and she found herself gazing at him in fascination. Jean Marc's thick black hair was rumpled and his linen shirt opened nearly to the waist, revealing the white bandage and a glimpse of the triangle of dark hair on his chest, but he still managed to exude an air of graceful elegance. Dear Heaven, how she wanted to paint the man. She had persistently asked him to permit her to sketch him ever since he had started to mend—and he had just as persistently refused her.

"Well, I feel it my duty to rescue you from this painful pleasure," he said. "Come and play faro with me."

"Shortly, I wish to finish this lit—"

"Now."

"You're fortunate that I play with you at all. You've grown very spoiled this last week. But I believe you were spoiled before you became ill."

"Spoiled?" Jean Marc levered himself upright against the headboard. "*I'm* not the queen's favorite. How could a poor bourgeois man of business become spoiled?"

"I'm not the queen's favorite either. It's my mother

who has her affection," Juliette said. "And Monsieur Guilleme says there are few noblemen in France who are as rich as you are."

"You shouldn't listen to gossip."

"Why not? You will tell me nothing of yourself. You're like one of the mirrors in the Hall of Mirrors at Versailles. You reflect only. You've revealed nothing of yourself to me."

"And it's your duty as an artist to uncover my hidden soul?"

"You're laughing at me again." She turned back to the painting. "But it's quite true. I've already learned some things on my own about you."

"Indeed?" His smile faded. "I'd be curious as to the nature of your discoveries."

"You're spoiled."

"I beg to differ."

"You hate for anyone to see you weak and helpless."

"Is that extraordinary?"

"No, I feel much the same. And you're not so cold as you appear."

"You said that once before." His lips twisted. "I assure you it's not a safe assumption to make about me."

She shook her head. "You asked Monsieur Guilleme yesterday about the plight of the peasants nearby and gave him a purse of gold to distribute among those in need."

He shrugged. "Some of those poor clods attacking the carriage were walking skeletons. It was little wonder they let themselves be whipped into a frenzy and try to steal."

She continued to enumerate. "And you bear pain much better than boredom."

"That truth I will own. Most certainly. Come and play cards with me."

His smile was coaxing, banishing all hardness and lighting his face with rare beauty. Juliette dragged her gaze from his face back to her canvas. "Why should I play with you when I could be painting?"

"Because I wish it and you're all that's gentle and obliging."

"I'm not oblig—" She stopped as she saw the wicked arch of his black brows. "The physician said you could get up for a little while tomorrow. Soon you'll be able to do without me entirely."

"And you'll go back to Versailles?"

She nodded vigorously. "I shall be very glad to see the last of you. You laugh at me. You take me away from my work. You make me amuse you as if I were—"

"It was your decision to stay," he reminded her. "I told you I'd be a bad patient."

"And you told God's truth."

"I regret you've suffered so grievously at my hands. I'm sure every minute has been an interminable strain."

That devil, Jean Marc. He knew very well it had been no such thing, she thought with exasperation. It was not fair he should be able to understand her with such ease when she was able only to see a little beyond the hard and glittering surface he displayed to the world. He knew she enjoyed both their sharp-edged banter and their comforting silences. Being with him stimulated and excited her in some strange fashion. She never knew how he would treat her. He would tease her as if she were a small child; at other times he seemed to forget the age difference between them and talk to her as if she were a woman grown. She looked forward to his company in the same way she looked forward to immersing herself in her painting, knowing she would be swept away but still eager to yield to the force. Now he was treating her with indulgent amusement and she had a sudden desire to shock him. "I haven't finished telling all

I know of you. I believe you've fornicated with that tavern maid who serves our meals."

His smile vanished. "Germaine?"

"Is that her name? The one with breasts like Juno."

Jean Marc was silent for a moment. "Women of quality don't speak of fornication, Juliette, and certainly not to gentlemen."

"I know." Her hand was shaking a little as she added a little more white to her brush. "But I do speak of it. Have you?"

"Why do you think I have?"

"She stares at you as if she'd like to eat you."

"Look at me, Juliette."

"I'm too busy."

"Look at me."

Juliette glanced over her shoulder and inhaled sharply as she saw the expression on his face.

"No." He enunciated every word softly and with great precision. "You don't want to wander down that path. Not unless you wish to learn exactly what I did with Germaine."

A hot flush stained Juliette's cheeks. "I only wondered. I need no description."

"Description? I wasn't speaking of words."

Juliette pulled her gaze away. "You're teasing me again."

"Am I?"

"Yes." She added white to the blue of the sky in the painting, while she tried desperately to think of another subject of conversation. "If my presence is so boring, perhaps I should let Marguerite tend to your needs."

"You would not be so cruel. How can you stand having that gloomy-faced harridan about? She stalks around the inn like a crow scratching for worms. Does the woman never smile?"

His tone was teasing again and Juliette breathed a sigh of relief. "She smiles at my mother. She was my mother's nurse since the day she was born and loves her very much. Most of the time I see very little of her when we're at the palace. She serves my mother now." Juliette kept her gaze carefully averted. "Marguerite doesn't like being here, but the queen thought I should have a woman in attendance while I saw to your needs, so she sent Marguerite back to the inn to serve as my chaperone."

"Quite proper. However, totally unnecessary. You're scarce more than a child."

Juliette didn't argue with him though she really couldn't remember a time when she thought of herself as a child—and it was not as child that he had looked at her a few moments before. "The queen believes in being discreet."

Jean Marc raised his eyebrows.

"She does," Juliette insisted. "You mustn't believe what those horrible pamphlets say about her. She's kind and a good mother and—"

"Foolishly extravagant and self-indulgent."

"She doesn't understand about money."

"Then she had better learn. The country's on the edge of bankruptcy and she still plays at being a shepherdess in her fairy-tale garden at Versailles."

"She gave to the relief of the hungry from her own allowance." Juliette put her brush down and turned to face him. "You don't know her. She gave me paints and a painting tutor. She's *kind*, I tell you."

"We'll not argue about it." Jean Marc's gaze narrowed on her flushed face. "I have a feeling if I say anything more about her sublime Majesty, you may take a dagger to my other shoulder."

"You'll see when you go to Versailles," Juliette said earnestly. "She's not what they say of her."

"Perhaps not to you." Jean Marc raised his hand as she opened her lips to protest. "As you say, I'll judge when I'm admitted to the queen's august presence."

Juliette stood frowning at him, not satisfied. "She doesn't understand. She's like a butterfly that has always lived in a garden filled with flowers. You wouldn't expect a butterfly to understand why—"

"I wouldn't expect a butterfly to be queen of the greatest country in Europe," Jean Marc said mildly.

"Yet you have no hesitation about asking a boon of that butterfly just as all the rest of the world does. What do you wish from her? A patent of nobility? A great estate?"

"The Wind Dancer."

She gazed at him in astonishment. "She will never give it to you. Not the Wind Dancer."

"We shall see." He changed the subject. "But your threat to inflict your Marguerite on me will not come to pass. I've sent word to Paris for my cousin, Catherine Vasaro, to be brought here tomorrow. Perhaps she'll be more sympathetic to the ennui of a poor, wounded man."

Juliette became still. "Your cousin?"

He nodded. "A distant cousin and my father's ward. My nephew, Philippe, escorted her from my home in Marseilles to Paris, and I received word yesterday they had arrived." He smiled teasingly. "Catherine's everything that's gentle and kind. Not at all like you."

Juliette suddenly had a vision of a woman as tall and voluptuous as the tavern maid with a radiant halo suspended above her lovely head. The thought ignited a bewildering pain somewhere deep within her. Why should it matter to her if this Catherine was as virtuous as a saint?

We rejoin Jean Marc and Juliette some months later. His young and innocent cousin Catherine has been

*attacked by men under the leadership of a ruthless villain.
Juliette has stayed with Catherine and, though worried
about her physical condition, is more desperately worried
about the young woman's state of mind. . . .*

The flame of the candle burned above her bed, hanging
like a shimmering topaz teardrop on the velvet of the
darkness. She should really concentrate on learning to
paint fire, Juliette thought drowsily. She had tried once or
twice, but the elements were terribly difficult to master.
Fire kept changing from gold to emerald, to amber, to
ruby-red. People were much easier to paint . . .

"Are you well?"

A deep masculine voice, taut with tension, issued
from somewhere beyond the flame.

Juliette's gaze searched through the flame for the face
behind the candle. High, intriguing planes, bold black
eyes, and that beautifully cynical mouth.

Jean Marc!

He was here. After all the years of waiting, he was
here. Wild joy soared through her as instinctive as it was
bewildering.

"Answer me."

She sat bolt upright in bed, jarred wide awake and
into anger by the sharpness of his tone. "Why did you
not come for Catherine? She's your responsibility and it
was so wrong of you to—"

"Hush." Jean Marc's fingers were shaking as they
pressed her lips, silencing her. "For God's sake, don't
rail at me. I've just come from the *abbaye* and I thought
you both dead. I rushed here and—Philippe came in
time then?"

"Philippe?"

"I sent Philippe to—" He broke off as he saw her
bewildered expression. "My God, he *didn't* come for you."

"I told you no one came for Catherine." She gazed at him fiercely. "You let those *canaille* rape her. And if they had killed her, too, it would have been your fault. For weeks the carriages came and took the students away, but none came for Catherine."

Jean Marc went rigid with shock. "Raped?" His rich olive complexion looked suddenly muddy in the candle-light. "My God, that . . . child."

"They raped old women and children much younger than Catherine."

"And you? Are you hurt? Did the swine attack you?"

"After seeing—"

"*Merde!* Juliette, did they hurt you?"

"Catherine was attacked by two men and she's—"

"You told me about Catherine. I asked about you." He grabbed her shoulders and made her look into his eyes. "*Tell me, were you raped?*"

"No."

His breath escaped in an explosive rush and his grip on her shoulders loosened. "One blessing. I have enough guilt to bear without your being hurt added to it."

"More than enough guilt. Why didn't you come?"

"I had urgent business in Toulon. When the rever-end mother's message reached me, I sent Philippe to fetch you and Catherine from the *abbaye*. He should have been there days ago."

"Perhaps he had 'business,' too, and didn't think Catherine's welfare important enough to waste his time."

"I don't know why he isn't here." Jean Marc's lips tightened grimly. "But I intend to find out."

"It's too late. Two days too late." Juliette could feel her eyes filling with tears and determinedly blinked them back. "They *hurt* her, Jean Marc."

"I know they did." Jean Marc stood there, looking at her. "There's no use saying I'll regret what's happened for the rest of my life. All I can do is try to heal the harm that's been done. You're sure nothing happened to you?"

"Nothing important." She frowned. "Oh, I did have to kill a man."

The faintest smile broke the somberness of Jean Marc's expression. "You don't consider killing a man of importance?"

"He was a *canaille*. He was raping Catherine."

Jean Marc's smile vanished. "A *canaille*, indeed. I regret you deprived me of the pleasure."

"There was another man. If you can find out who he is, you can kill him."

He bowed. "Many thanks. Your generosity over-whelms me. Now, tell me how you escaped being butchered at the *abbaye*."

She briefly related François Etchelet's and Dantor's roles in their flight.

François Etchelet," he murmured thoughtfully. "I owe him a debt."

"I assure you his rescue was most reluctant."

"Reluctant or not, he saved you."

"True." She threw back the covers and jumped out of bed. "We must talk. Come down to the scullery and I'll find you something to eat."

"I'm going to be allowed to break my fast? I thought my laggardliness had put me beyond redemption in your eyes."

Profound weariness and sadness lay beneath the mockery in Jean Marc's voice, and for the first time, Juliette noticed the deep shadows imprinted beneath his eyes, the layer of dust mantling his elegant dark blue cloak. She suddenly felt a rush of protectiveness that banished both anger and resentment. "You care for Catherine. I know you would not hurt her deliberately. Perhaps they were only stupid."

A faint smile played on his lips. "I'd forgotten that sharp tongue of yours. I only remebered . . ." He trailed off and fell silent for a moment, looking at her. "How kind of you to acquit me of malice, if not witlessness."

"You *should* have come for her. What business could be so important that you—"

"The assembly has confiscated eight of my ships for their navy in the past year," Jean Marc interrupted. "I was hoping to salvage some of my cargoes stored in the warehouses at Toulon before those greedy bastards managed to steal them too." He shook his head wearily. "It seemed very important at the time."

"*Eight* ships? That's a great many."

"They would have taken the lot if I hadn't seen this coming and sent most of the Andreas fleet to Charleston harbor two years ago."

"You knew they would steal your ships?"

He nodded grimly. "Oh, yes, at the first opportunity or excuse. The majority of the illustrious members of the assembly are as corrupt as the nobles of the court they supplanted. The only way to deal with them is by bribery and evasion."

She shivered. "The world seems filled with thieves and murderers. François tried to tell me why the *abbaye* had been attacked, but I couldn't understand it. I'll never understand it."

"It was madness. How can anyone understand madness?" His gaze met hers. "As God is my witness, I never suspected the *abbaye* would be attacked, Juliette. I sent Philippe to fetch you both to Vasaro merely as a precaution because of the unrest in Paris. If I'd thought there was any real danger, I would have come myself." His lips twisted. "You're right, I was stupid."

The pain and the bitter denunciation in his tone hurt her in some odd way, and she said quickly, "Perhaps you weren't completely at fault."

"Are you softening?" He shook his head. "The blame was mine and you had the right to condemn me." He reached out and wound his forefinger in one of the tight curls at her left temple. "You have much too tender a heart beneath all those thorns, you know."

The tip of his finger was resting lightly against her cheek bone while he lazily tested the silky texture of the curl between his thumb and forefinger. The action was almost unbearably intimate. She swallowed. "Nonsense."

"But you must never show that softness. Not to me." His gaze was mesmerizingly intent. "It's dangerous for you. Never let me see a weakness, Juliette."

"I don't . . . I don't understand."

"I know you don't." He smiled cynically. He released the curl and it instantly sprang back into its former tight ringlet. "And only God knows why I'm saying it. It must be a combination of guilt and shock that has me behaving with such uncharacteristic gallantry. I guarantee after I've slept awhile that I'll be fully myself again and you'll find me a fit antagonist."

"Antagonist?" Juliette frowned at him. "I don't wish to fight you."

"Yes, you do," he said softly. "You've fought me from the beginning. It's all part of the game."

STORM WINDS
by Iris Johansen

a Bantam Fanfare book
on sale in May 1991

"One of the most versatile and talented authors of the last decade." -- *Romantic Times*

Enter the irresistible world of

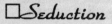

Bestselling romance writer Amanda Quick takes us back to the days of Regency England in these stirring novels of love and adventure.

☐ *Seduction*   28354-5 $4.50

☐ *Surrender*   28594-7 $4.50

☐ *Scandal*   28932-2 $4.95

Available wherever Bantam Fanfare Books are sold or use this page for ordering:

A fiercely independant woman, a proud and stubborn man -- bound by passion, torn apart by injustice.

THE BELOVED WOMAN
by Deborah Smith

The Trail of Tears: The forced exodus of the Cherokee people from their homeland in Georgia to make way for the white gold miners and settlers. Katherine Blue Song's family never lived to see the Trail of Tears -- they were massacred just as she returned from Philadelphia, where she'd been one of the country's first women trained as a doctor.

Justis Gallatin, a white man, a rough and ready man, was Jesse Blue Song's friend and partner. Before he buried the victims of the massacre, he made a solemn promise to protect Katherine. But the lovely and head-strong Cherokee healer would not be protected or owned by any man -- her destiny was with her own people, to use her skills on the long arduous journey westward.

The Beloved Woman is a novel which traces the lives of two people caught up in the tide of history, who are hurtled together a passion as vast as the lands they loved, lost, and fought to regain.

On sale in March wherever Bantam Fanfare Books are sold.

AN209 -- 2/91

THE LATEST IN BOOKS
AND AUDIO CASSETTES

Paperbacks